Wh
Angels
Sleep

(The Rob Blackstock series – Book 2)

By Bill Yeates

****

Where Angels Sleep

A global increase in the number of drug overdose deaths is of little concern to millionaire Rob Blackstock until three of his employees die and he learns that the police are treating it as murder, made to look like an overdose.

When his own wife is the obvious target of a failed murder attempt it becomes personal. Rob decides he has skills that can help end these crimes and joins the British faction of an international task force fighting against drugs.

He teams up with an ex-girlfriend and together they travel to South America to check out the organisation strongly thought to be plotting these murders. Their investigations lead to proof that stories of vast sums of Hitler's Nazi gold are true and it is being used to fund a new Nazi empire controlled by drugs. By infiltrating the organisation they learn that the new self-appointed Fuhrer's plans include the removal of the British Prime Minister and the American President then on mid-summers day announce to the world the dawning of a new Nazi era and the creation of the United States of Britain and America with him as its president.

Rob has little time to uncover the details of the plot codenamed OPERATION BIRDBATH and the identity of the London agent known as Gabriel.

To my daughter Karen Elizabeth

Chapter 1

"Good morning Prime Minister, this is Bernard Howe. I trust you have read my report on the Russian incident. I must say a most satisfying result and my team all back home safely. Mr. Blackstock and Mrs. Williams both did exceptionally well, so much so that I've asked them to join MI-6. They would both be a considerable asset.

Ma'am, have you seen the news this morning. Another High Court Judge was found after taking a drug overdose last night. He is in a critical state but should live. That takes the total to eleven senior members of the legal sector in five weeks. I have a meeting with Pippa Johnston MI-5 at 12:30, to discuss a joint investigation."

****

A noise disturbed her and Sue woke from a deep sleep. It took a moment for her to gather herself. The green glow of the numbers on the clock sitting on the bedside table told her it was a few minutes past six. She rolled over onto her back and lay thinking. Yesterday she had woken as Susan Williams today she was Mrs. Susan Blackstock. Married to millionaire Robert Blackstock, who she met less than three weeks ago but from the moment they met she knew what was coming. They had both lost their previous partners in tragic circumstances and knew they wanted no time lost.

She was not only married to this man lying naked next to her, but now also a mother of two teenage children, Lucinda fifteen and Justin thirteen. They would be starting a new school year next week, after a summer break neither of them will forget. Justin, or JB as he preferred to be called, will be returning to Edinburgh as a boarder and Luci will be starting her first term at a sixth form college in York.

Light was coming in through a gap in the curtains and she was able spend time looking around the room. It was certainly a man's room. No feminine touches at all. It was the room Rob always used when he stayed with his parents. Eric and Rose had a large house, there were at least six other bedrooms. Luci and JB had one each because they had lived here with their grandparents, since their

5

mother had been killed. Rob's business took him all over the world and he tried to spend as much time as he could with his children. This was his room. Now it's our room!

The noise that had woken her was getting louder and she could now hear voices. Then she realised what it was. This was a racehorse stable; the noise was coming from the yard where the horses were being got ready for exercising. It had been a hot night and the window had been left wide opened. On previous nights the window had been closed.

Sue's thinking drifted from thought to thought, she began to wonder how her life was going to change now, that she was married. Would she keep her job as task force leader with her brother-in-law's security company, which would mean she would have to be based in London? She didn't find the job overly demanding but she liked how it enabled her to meet some interesting and important people. Earlier this year she had been involved with the security at Harry and Megan's wedding. Then three weeks ago it was the job that introduced her to Rob.

Perhaps she could start her own detective agency. She was well qualified, having been a Captain in the Military Police, before her husband had been blown up in Afghanistan.

Of course there might be a place for her in Rob's business. He supplied horses to the movie industry, trained stuntmen and coordinated stunts for movies and TV. After all, she was good with horses and she was an outstanding marksman with both rifle and hand gun. There should be something she could offer.

There was also a vacancy as manager of Eric's horse racing stables. The current manager, Phil Parsons, was going out to India to setup a new stuntman training academy in Bollywood for Rob, on the same lines as those he had in UK and USA. She had some managerial skill and she knew how racing stables worked, because she had worked in one before joining the army.

Then there was the offer that Sir Bernard Howe had made to both her and Rob, for them to join MI-6, which they had not yet had chance to discuss.

Everything had happened so quickly. She hadn't had time to think ahead, to plan her future, their future. But she did know that she wanted her future to be with her new husband.

Sue walked across the room to the window and pulled back the curtain. Then with the curtain held in front of her, she looked out of the window at the string of horses walking down to the exercise track.

Rob was beginning to stir. Sue stood watching him then slowly walked around the bed and sat on the bed next to him. She leant over and gently rubbed his nose with hers and then lightly kissed his lips.

"I'm very sorry Mrs. Williams. I got married yesterday and I really want to save myself for my bride," Rob joked.

Sue reacted by swiftly pulling the duvet off his naked body and climbing on top of him. With a knee on the bed either side of Rob she lowered herself down onto him, gasping as he entered her. There was a knock at the bedroom door.

"Just a moment!" Sue called in panic, as she climbed off Rob, slipped on his t-shirt to cover herself and opened the door to see Rose standing there.

"Sorry dear. I heard you walking across the floor, so knew you were awake. Only Rob said he had two large suitcases we could borrow. I'm starting to pack for the cruise. We're being picked up at 8:30 tomorrow."

"They're over there in the corner, mum," Rob said pointing.

"Thanks. I'm planning breakfast for 8:00. Come down as soon as you're ready." She smiled at Sue as she left and Sue closed the door behind her.

Rob held out his hand to draw Sue back to him.

"Forget it sunshine. We need to shower and get dressed. Are you coming?" she said over her shoulder, as she walked into the en-suite.

They were sitting at the kitchen table, drinking a coffee, when Eric came in from the yard.

"Hi dad, everything okay out there this morning?" Rob asked. "You look deep in thought!"

"No there's nothing wrong," he replied," in fact it's quite the opposite. All the lads are quite buzzing and they're all talking about the same thing, those two Russian lasses of yours. It seems they all saw Eva and Ana leave to go to your wedding yesterday and they made quite an impression. Even Sally and Lizzy were making approving comments."

"The two girls were dressed to turn heads deliberately. Rob had got wind that the press were going to be outside the registry office. He was worried that Luci would attract the attention of the photographers and images of her would be all over the tabloids and the social magazines. She's far too young for that sort of publicity," Sue explained. "I invited the girls to the wedding and asked them to distract the photographers."

"And it worked," Rose added. "They are very pretty young ladies and so kind to look after Luci when she was so desperate and in need of help. Luci told me how they got dragged into the sex industry, to earn money to pay the man who brought them to London."

"Luci told me that they had been forced into the sex industry as exotic dancers. They had shown her videos of their act." Sue said. "She said it was extremely erotic, very professionally performed and they were extremely sought after, earning big money, but they were desperate to pay their debt and get away."

"I certainly admire their work ethic. They are so focused on achieving their objectives that they will do what it takes without a second thought. I've offered them a job," Rob added.

"Luci was telling me about that yesterday morning," Eric said, "something about running a stall."

"It's a little more than that dad," Rob replied. "I've still got to finish scoping the role with Pete Doyal. But basically it's about making sure good quality food and drink is available whenever anyone needs anything on location. At the moment, we're wasting a lot of time and a lot of food, trying to feed the team and not getting it right."

At that moment the back door opened.

8

"Good morning Phil," said Rose, greeting the tall black man who managed the racing stables. "Breakfast is nearly ready, pour yourself a coffee and grab a chair at the table."

"I'm going to have to have a word with those Peterson twins Eric. They haven't shown up again this morning. That's three times this month. I'm going to give them a final warning that if it happens again, they'll be out."

"The Peterson twins! Not Alex and Brian they must be forty by now. I thought you got rid of those two layabouts ten years or more ago, dad?" Rob questioned.

"I did and they went off to Australia working at a racing stable near Melbourne. They returned home last Christmas time. Although they are getting a bit old to be stable lads, they are very experienced and I was a little shorthanded at that time, so offered them both jobs."

"Does the family still live at the Old Vicarage? I could ride over and see them this morning, tell them what's what. Fancy a ride out Sue? It's about an eight mile round trip," Rob said as he took a hot plate of bacon and eggs from Rose.

"Yes I'd like that, so long as no one will be shooting at me this time." Sue pulled a face remembering riding with Rob in Hyde Park and being shot at by a Russian mafia boss.

Rob drove Sue to his own stables at his training academy, just a mile down the road. He selected a couple of horses, got them saddled and they set off.

As they rode down quiet country lanes Sue said," Rob we need to talk about our future."

"Do you mean about that MI-6 thing that Sir Bernard offered us?"

"No I mean everything. It's alright for you; nothing really has to change, other than you have a wife to consider. But for me it's harder. You'll be spending time in Yorkshire running and working your academy plus time with your family, especially during holidays. The rest of the time you could be anywhere in the world, wherever the next movie contract takes you."

"A lot of that time will be in London," he interrupted.

"Maybe it is, but I'm there almost all the time. London is where Williams Security is based and where all our work is. That's what I do; I keep people safe when they are in London. I can't just get up here to be with you when you are here, especially during holidays, they are my busiest times. So I would only be with you when you're in town. What's that, twenty five per cent of your year?"

"Probably about that, yes."

"Well that's not good enough Rob. I married you, all of you not just a quarter. I want to be with you all the time and be part of your family as often as I can. If I stay in London, that cannot be! When I was married to Tony we weren't together much because of us getting deployed to different countries. I don't want that life again."

"We're nearly at the Peterson place now; it's just over the next crest. So why not leave this until we get back and we'll study the options this afternoon and discuss it properly before you decide. CHRIST! That's the Peterson place, swarming with police. I see four cars. And they're putting up yellow tape around the place. What the hell has happened?"

They rode down the bridle path from the crest of the hill and came out onto the lane leading to the Old Vicarage, where the Petersons had lived forever. They were a bit isolated out here, beyond the outskirts of the village, but they were always involved in village life and well liked. So why were there so many police here?

"Good morning, Constable." Rob said as he climbed down from his horse. "What's happened here then?"

"I can't say sir. It's not my job to speculate."

"Then who can? Who's in charge?"

"That will be D.S. Tracy Longhorn, York C.I.D. sir."

"Go and tell her I'd like a word."

"Can't do that sir, Can't interrupt her, she's busy."

"Is she in the house? When she comes out tell her Robert Blackstock would like a word."

Rob walked back to Sue and the horses. "This looks serious Sue. You don't get all this for a break in."

"I agree. It looks to me like a murder scene."

"I've asked to speak with the officer in charge as soon as possible."

"Look behind you Rob. Someone has just coming out. Your constable has said something. They have looked over here, smiled and now walking this way."

Rob turned and immediately recognised the officer and she him. They threw their arms around one another in greeting.

"Sue, this is Tracy Mills. Tracy this is my wife, Sue."

"Pleased to meet, you Sue. You're a lucky girl, I could never pin him down. It's Tracy Longhorn now Rob, I'm married with two kids at home."

"Tracy and I were at high school together. We spent a lot of time in the bike shed, I seem to recall," Rob said to Sue.

"That's right. Experimenting as we used to call it. It was in that shed that I lost my... Well you know. It was a long time ago."

"What's going on here then, Tracy?"

"Well, Patrick and Jill came back from an evening at the Dog and Gun. Got here around mid-night and found their two sons lying unconscious on the floor. They rang 999 for an ambulance. But when it got here they found both of the gentlemen dead. They called the local police to say there was evidence that they had both taken a heroin overdose. The local police came out and a very bright constable spotted a few things that didn't look right and the York team was called in. We have initially confirmed that both died from a drug overdose. A P.M. will confirm that. But the evidence around the place suggests that the drugs had been tampered with so this was possibly a double murder made to look like your standard overdose."

"Why I wonder? Those two might have been a little roughish at times but they'd never hurt anyone. So why would someone want them dead."

"You knew them well, did you Rob?"

"Up until about ten years ago they worked for my dad. In those days I knew them well enough. Then they started drinking and became unreliable, so dad let them go. I understand they went to Australia, returning recently. Dad was shorthanded at the stables so took them back."

"Yes, they did go to Australia but only for a couple of years. They then came back to London and five years ago we picked them up for drug dealing. They served four years and came out last December," Tracy said.

"So you think this might be something related to the drug dealing then?" Sue enquired.

"That is our thinking at the moment, Sue. But it's early days. Nice to see you again, Rob. We must get together sometime, have a drink and catch up. 'Bye to you both for now." With that she walked back to re-join her colleagues.

"So that was your first love, was it Mr. Blackstock?" Sue joked.

"I wouldn't say that. But Tracy was my first physical love," he replied.

They took a different route back to the academy, which took them across open uncultivated rolling countryside, where they could really give their horses their heads and gallop. Only when it came to the last mile, where they were on country lanes again, did they walk.

On reaching the stable block they spent a long time cleaning and rubbing down the horses, which gave them time to cool down after their hard run across the rolling fields. It was lunchtime when they got back to the racing stables and when they walked into the kitchen, they were surprised by the return of a familiar face.

"Madge, good to see you're back. Is your daughter better? You remember Sue, don't you?" Rob said putting his arm around his bride.

"Yes! Congratulations to you both. I was disappointed to have missed the wedding when Rose told me the news. My daughter is fit again, thank you. So I'm back here to pick up my housekeeper duties, starting with lunch for you. I've baked a quiche. Will that be okay with a little salad?"

"More than okay Madge, something smells wonderful. Do you need any help?" Sue enquired.

"I'm fine thanks; just sit yourselves down with a cold drink. I've called the others, they will be through in a minute. There's beer in the fridge or I've made some fresh lemonade. Help yourselves."

Rose and Eric came through carrying empty glasses.

"Phil won't be joining us, Madge. He's had a call from York police. They've asked him to go in and see them."

"That might be to do with the Peterson twins. They were murdered last night. Police were all over the Old Rectory when we got there earlier."

"Good heavens what had they done to deserve that?" Rose asked.

"The police are thinking it's drug dealer related. The twins were released from prison last December, after serving four years for dealing and whoever did this, made a good attempt to make it look like they took an overdose."

When lunch was over Rose and Eric went upstairs to finish their packing. Tomorrow they will fly from Manchester to Malta, where they will join their cruise ship for a three week tour of the Mediterranean.

Sue and Rob moved into the lounge and sat together on the sofa.

"Now, what were you saying about wanting to decide what your role will be in future." Rob asked.

"I was saying," Sue replied," that in my job, I'm more or less tied to London which will mean we'll see little of one another and I'll see even less of your family. So I think at the very least, I need to be Yorkshire based."

"But I assumed you would be travelling with me and we'd always be together."

"Oh you did, did you? And how would you expect me to spend my time when I wasn't being paraded in front of your film people. I need a job that taxes me, allows me to use my skills. Williams Security is barely stretching me most of the time. It's only getting involved in planning events like Harry and Megan's wedding that spur me on."

"Well I need a P.A."

"To do what, keep your diary up to date and answer your phone? No thanks."

"So what are you thinking?"

"Well, I was once a pretty good detective, so I could open an agency in York or Leeds but there again they are not specifically centres of crime, so my guess is I'd be doing divorce work and that's not appealing. I know Phil will be leaving soon. As a Captain in the army I have management experience. I also know how racing stables operate from my year spent working in one. So I could apply for the job. Alternatively, I have skills I could teach to others and may be of use to you in the academy."

"Okay I get your drift. No need to decide today but I think you should at least do the tour of the academy, that we give all of our applicants, so you get a feeling of what we do and still see whether you're interested. What about the MI-6 offer? You've not mentioned that."

"For the good reason that the offer was made to both of us. We haven't discussed it yet. It affects us both and would change everything. So the next thing is to sort out my tour of the academy and while dad's away, why don't I shadow Phil and see what his role is all about?"

"Sounds like a good idea. But can we also discuss the MI-6 offer in those three weeks and at the end make a decision."

"Sure."

Rose rushed into the lounge. "Sorry, I didn't know you two were in here. But I've just seen Phil come back and I've waved at him to come inside and tell us what's going on."

Eric came in dragging a suitcase behind him. "That's going to cost me an arm and a leg in excess luggage duty," he said pushing the case into the corner of the room out of the way.

Phil followed Eric into the lounge and sat himself down.

"You look white, if I dare say that Phil," Rose said. "What did the police want?"

"Well, you remember Charlie Riches taking a fall at Doncaster last week and breaking his collarbone."

"I certainly do," Eric interrupted. "He was due to ride in the big race on the last day, I had to get that kid to ride it and we only got a second. We should have won that one."

"He had to have blood tests at hospital which showed a high level of heroin in his system. Possibly the reason for his fall. Last night his wife found him dead on the bedroom floor, apparently from an overdose. However, the police are suspicious that it is not as simple as that. They are saying he may have been murdered. He had Blackstock Racing as his employer and me named as contact. I was called in just to answer a few questions and whether I knew he was a user."

"Who did you meet with?"

"D.S. Longhorn. A very attractive lady. Very thorough, but gave nothing away."

"So Tracy is looking at a bigger picture than just the Peterson twins murder. She didn't let on to us that there had been another murder locally," Rob said.

"We're on the edge of something big here, Rob. Let me make a few calls and see what I can uncover. Why don't you follow up with Tracy, take her up on having a drink somewhere."

"You know this D.S. Longhorn, Rob?" Eric asked.

"So do you dad. But you know her as Tracy Mills. Remember when I was about Justin's age, there was a girl hanging around here all summer?"

"I remember. She worked here during her holidays all through the time she was at uni."

"That's the one. Sue and I spoke with her up at the Peterson's place. I'll give her a ring after lunch and see if she's really interested in a drink and a chat over old times."

"I'll tag along if you don't mind," Sue said. "She might give something away about the murders which may help me or at least give me a lead. Besides I might learn something I don't know about my husband's past."

"That was a strange conversation," Rob said as he re-entered the lounge and placed his phone on the coffee table and sat down next to Sue.

"Is she still keen to meet you for a drink?" Sue asked.

"Oh Yeah. But it will have to be early evening Thursday because on Friday she is off down to London. Apparently, she has been temporarily seconded into a task force being set up to deal with a major new terrorist threat."

"Does that mean she's off the murder case?" Sue asked.

"I assume it must do. We'll find out on Thursday."

Chapter 2

"Good morning Mr Luggard. Things are going well here in London. My contact in the Met is telling me that the British police are totally confused by what is happening and don't have a clue as to who is behind it all. They think it is coming from one of the Middle Eastern extremist organisations. We now have hooks into sixteen of the thirty names on your list, including the two politicians, the judge, the army general and six of the businessmen, including the two bankers." This Blackstock is going to be more difficult. Never been a user, so it won't be as easy to get them hooked on your stuff. We'll need another approach. Apart from that one, the list will be complete by the end of the month and you can start using some of these people."

****

Rose was up early the following morning. She couldn't remember the last time she and Eric had been on holiday. It just didn't seem to happen, but here she was about to go on a three week cruise and getting a bit worked up about it. She didn't actually like travelling, especially flying, plus having never been on a cruise she was even more worried in case she didn't like it. It was not the sort of holiday you can easily cut short.

Eric struggled downstairs with the second heavy suitcase and stood it on its end by the door. "I'm glad I don't have to carry that too far," he said looking up at Rob and Sue, who were following him down the stairs.

Their taxi was already a few minutes late and this didn't help Rose's anxiety. Eric noticed Sue looking at his wife who had a very worried expression on her face. "Don't worry Sue, Rose will be fine once I get a couple of vodkas into her at the airport."

"I'm sure you'll be alright, Rose," Sue said trying to comfort her. "If you need a drink or two to keep you calm, then have one. I know several people who don't like flying. You're on holiday so simply relax."

The taxi finally arrived ten minutes late. After lifting the two cases into the boot and helping them into the back of the taxi, Rob leant in and said," Now, have a good time the pair of you.....'Bye..." Then he shut the door.

Rob and Sue stood and watched the taxi until it was out of sight, then turned and went back indoors.

"We need to go and speak to Phil and see if he's happy for you to shadow him for a couple of weeks," Rob said. "He should be in his office at this time of day."

Rob was right. They could see him through the office window as they approached, so knocked on the door and walked in.

Phil was on the phone, talking with an owner who wanted to be with his horse. He ended the call and looked up to see Rob and Sue standing in the open doorway.

"Why do some owners think that just because they are stabling a horse with you that they also get a hundred percent of your time and resources?" Phil complained. "Sorry you two, I'm sure you're not interested in my issues. What can I do for you?"

"Who was that giving you grief so early in the morning?" Rob asked.

"That brainless tub of lard was Ross Jenkins. Welsh twit!"

"Not Ross Jenkins the coal miner, who had that big lottery win. Seven million wasn't it?"

"The very same, but let's change the subject."

"Actually that's part of the subject we want to ask you about. Do you see owner management as a big part of your role here?"

"I do," Phil replied," and it takes up far more of my time than I am happy with. It can get a bit messy sometimes, like with our Mr. Jenkins today. Eric does his bit when he is around. That helps quite a bit."

Rob continued," In six to eight weeks time you'll be off to India, to begin setting up the new company. Has anything been done to find a replacement for you here?"

"I've given it some thought but not got anywhere yet, other than thinking about possibly promoting our head lad, but that would be a big step up for him. Probably too big a step up."

"I think you're right. What about dad? has he said anything at all about anyone he has in mind?"

"He's not said anything to me. I don't even know if he's given it any thought at all. You know Eric, not one to think too far into the future."

"Quite! Well we may have a solution standing right here." He turned and nodded towards Sue. "Sue spent a year working in stables a few years back, so she knows how things work, she also has management experience. Perhaps if she could work alongside you for a couple of weeks, she could pick up everything she needs to know. She's a quick learner and she's looking for a new job in this area, something that will challenge her and get the grey matter bouncing a bit."

"That's a great idea! Certainly she can shadow me for a couple of weeks or so. Whatever it takes."

"Thanks Phil," Sue said giving him a broad smile.

"This is not a good week," he said. "I'm in Doncaster tomorrow and Ayr on Saturday. But I think next week I'm here every day, so why don't we begin your training 7:15 Monday morning."

"That suits me. 7:15 Monday morning it is then. We'll leave you now, so that you can get on with whatever you need to be doing. Thanks again Phil. Come on Rob let Phil get on." Sue dragged Rob out of the office.

As they walked back to the house Rob asked, "now we've set the ball rolling with Phil, have you given any more thought to any of your other options? What about the detective agency idea?"

"I'm thinking that to be a non-starter. I did some research yesterday and the crime rate in York and the surrounding area is not great at all. It's criminal investigations I'd want to be doing. Divorce work doesn't appeal at all. If I do get a full time job somewhere, I can still do a little investigation work in my spare time, just like I'm thinking of doing with these local murders."

"I've given some thought to what you could do at the Stuntman Academy. The way we normally operate, is to call in specialists in certain subjects as and when they are needed. For instance, I do two days driving cars with them, someone else teaches

19

them how to roll and crash vehicles. I also do three days horse riding, so in total I'm doing just five days out of a twelve week course, so you see nothing like a full time role. You said you could teach them how to use hand guns, but to be quite frank no one cares whether or not they can hit a target, just so long as it looks as if they can and that they'll learn at acting school. There are some topics which take longer but there is only a handful of full time staff on the payroll and they are all on the admin and facilities side of things. I'll set up a session for you to see how things work."

"Being your P.A. is of no interest at all," Sue continued. "That leaves the places at MI6 that Sir Bernard Howe offered the two of us. I don't know about you but I'm not a hundred percent sure what he was offering. If he wants us as full time field agents, running around the world like James Bond then I don't think it's for us. The Russian caper was one thing, but doing similar missions week in week out does not appeal. I've only just got you, I do not want to risk losing you so soon and we've got the kids to consider, it wouldn't be fair on them."

"I agree," Rob replied. "I sort of enjoyed the experience of the Russian mission; I got quite a buzz out of it. But when I look back at the danger we were in and what might have happened. We were incredibly lucky to come home in one piece."

"If he's looking to use us in some sort of consultancy role, supporting field agents then that would be different. Have you given any thought to him asking you to setup a training unit?"

"No, is the short answer. I've given it some thought but not anything I can discuss with Sir Bernard. I really need to sit down with the team and see what we can offer... How about riding out again after lunch?"

"Love to!"

While Sue and Rob were tucking into a late breakfast the next day, Rob received a text message from an unrecognised number.

"It's from Tracy," he said. "She's got to see a few people in the village this afternoon so will leave her car at her sister's place and walk down to the Dog and Gun for seven o'clock. She says how about a meal together?"

20

Sue looked across the table at him reading the message again. "Are you sure you're happy for me to tag along? I won't be cramping your style or playing gooseberry?"

"Don't be daft. I admit that I had a thing for her once, but that was a long, long time ago. I'll ring the pub and book a table for three and text her back."

"She's leaving her car with her sister. Is she from a local family?"

"Born and lived in the house her sister now owns. It's that big white house across the other side of the valley. Look, you can see it quite clearly," he said pointing out of the window. "It's only about half a mile as the crow flies. As kids we used to flash torches at one another. Eventually we learnt Morse code and sent some rather crude messages to one another. Quite crazy when you think about it. Anyone could have seen and read those messages. But no one ever said anything. I see Ruth quite often out and about in the village, but it's a lot of years since I last saw Tracy. I didn't even know she was married and had kids. We've got a lot to catch up on; I hope you won't be too bored."

As Rob opened the door of The Dog and Gun to allow Sue to walk in ahead of him, he heard a voice behind him call out," hold that door!" He turned to see Tracy rushing across in front of the post office next door to the pub. When she reached him in the open doorway still holding the door open she moved close and kissed him on the cheek. Sue had reached the bar and had turned in time to see the kiss. As Rob and Tracy walked towards the bar Sue moved forward to meet them half way, linked her arm through Rob's and said," hands off! This one's mine." Tracy responded by linking arms on his other side and saying," But I found him first." They both laughed and Tracy said. "Just look at him, he thought for one horrible moment that he was going to see a real cat fight. Pleased to meet you Sue. I saw the picture of your wedding in the paper the other day. I must say you looked gorgeous in that dress. Who were the other three good looking girls?"

"Well, the smallest one was Rob's daughter Lucinda and the other two are Russian friends, but that's a story for another time. Rob's booked us a table haven't you dear? I'm ready for some food; I've not had anything to eat since lunch time."

21

"Me too!" Tracy replied. "In my job you learn to take meals when you get the chance. But for the next few weeks it looks like I'll be on regular hours, so maybe things will be better."

"Yes, Rob said something about you joining a task force in London. Does this mean you're off the local murder investigations?" Sue asked.

Rob interrupted," We're on table six over in the alcove. Can I get you two sexy things a drink?"

"I'll have a large Merlot please, darling," Sue answered.

"That sounds good, I'm staying with Ruth tonight. I'll have the same please Twiki."

"You two go and sit down, I'll bring the drinks over."

"As they walked to their table Sue leaned in close to Tracy to ask," why did you call Rob Twiki?"

"Well when I first got to know him everyone called him Robot instead of Robert. At that time there was a TV series called Buck Rogers and I had a massive crush on Gil Gerard who played Buck. The robot in that series was called Twiki, the name just stuck. God knows why I still remember that."

"Twiki! Yes I like that. Do you mind if I use it?"

"Please do. As you said, he's yours now."

Rob arrived with three glasses and a bottle of Australian Merlot. He sat down filled the glasses and passed them to the two women. "So what's hubby doing this evening? You said you have kids, is he babysitting? Does he know you're seeing an old boyfriend?"

"I don't know and I don't care what he thinks," Tracy replied. "Sorry, that wasn't called for. The thing is we're going through a messy divorce at the moment. The kids, Sarah seven and Luke five, are out of the war zone staying with James's parents in York for a while. James is in our house and I'm back here in the old house with Ruth, her husband John and their five kids. Thank God it's a big house. Anyway James is fighting for custody of the kids saying that it is my career that has caused our marriage to fail and would prevent me caring properly for the kids. In a way he's right. Work is a huge part of my life and also I'm not really the maternal sort. Don't get me wrong, I love my kids and would do anything for them; I'm just not a good mother. Can we change the subject now please? What are we all eating?"

"Sorry to hear your sad tale, Tracy," Sue said. "I'd recommend the steak. They do a fantastic fillet here. Not too big and comes with a few curly fries and a simple salad."

The waitress appeared at Rob's shoulder. "Are we all ready to order or shall I give you a few more minutes?" she asked.

"I'm ready," Sue said. "I'll have the fillet please, medium rare."

"The same for me, please," Tracy added

"And another for me, but can you make mine a rare one please?"

The waitress finished writing in her note book and said," So that's three fillet steaks, one rare and two medium rare." Rob smiled at her and nodded. She smiled back and walked off towards the kitchen.

Tracy continued," You asked earlier if I was off the local murder investigation team. Well I am and I'm not. We've now had three murders with the same or at least very similar M.O.'s. Funnily enough there's a connection with Blackstock stables with each of them. That's just on my patch this week. But in the UK there have been nineteen in the last month. That's not all. We can account for twelve in Western Europe and twenty two in the States."

"Christ that's over fifty!" Sue gasped. "Are they all the same? Murders made to look like overdoses?"

"Almost all of them, yes. There are a couple in the States that might be genuine overdoses."

"Is there any connection between the victims? Anything at all that links them?" Sue asked.

"Doesn't appear to be. We've got sportsmen, councillors, a doctor, shop keepers and just ordinary people. I got a call from MI-5 Homeland Security midday Tuesday, just after I'd seen you two in fact. My boss had been on the ball and had registered the death of the twins with central command. Wheels must have turned very quickly after that, because it was Pippa Johnston who rang me, she's some big cheese at MI-5."

"She's actually the acting head of MI-5," Sue interrupted. "I've known her for some time. I've worked with her a couple of times. She appears to be a very nice lady, but keeps herself to herself."

"I didn't know you were in security, Sue!" Tracy said in a surprised tone.

"Yes she's a task force leader at Williams Security," Rob said. "That's how we met. Sue helped me out with a few issues."

"Williams Security and your name was Williams," Tracy looked at Sue. "Any connection?"

"My father-in-law started the company and it's now run by my brother-in-law but I'm leaving the firm shortly," Sue replied.

"Father-in-law? Does that mean you've been married before?" Tracy probed.

"My first husband was blown up in Afghanistan."

"Oh, I'm sorry. Anyway Pippa Johnston told me that this was being treated as a terrorist attack and an international coordinated task force is being set up. She asked me to join the UK element of that task force. Well, with my personal life on the rocks, I've got nothing to lose, so I jumped at it and I go down to London tomorrow to meet the rest of the team. Apparently my boss recommended me to her."

"That sounds incredibly interesting. I'm a little envious, but I'm looking at new opportunities up here," Sue said. "I've had too many years without anywhere I could really call home and now I just want a simple family life, if that's possible with this lump," she gently punched Rob on the arm as she said it.

They left the pub at 9:45 because Tracy still had to pack. For the first half mile they walked together sharing torch light and still talking about the old days when Tracy and Rob had spent so much time together. Sue just listened and made mental notes.

Eventually they came to the road where Tracy turned off towards her sister's house. It was no more than three hundred yards for her to go and they could see lights on in the house. They said goodnight and Tracy gave Rob a kiss.

"Don't let it be so long until we see you again. Come up to the stables some time. Mum and dad would love to see you again and Sue and I intend spending quite a bit of time there," Rob said as they parted.

As Rob and Sue walked home with his arm around her shoulders, they discussed their evening.

"These murders are dreadful," Sue said.

"It doesn't bear thinking about," Rob replied. "Where do you start to look for the ones who are doing it?"

"When it was just three murders that all had a connection to the Blackstock stable, I thought I would be able to do some investigation and help out, but this is so big that I'd be better staying out of it."

Even in the dim light Sue could see that Rob was deep in thought. "You've still got a thing for her haven't you, Twiki?" she said.

Rob stopped, turned Sue towards him and kissed her long and hard. "I'll be truthful," he said. "I don't really know. But I've got a thing for Keira Knightly and Emilia Fox, but that doesn't mean if I ever met them that I'd want to sleep with them. Now, if I were to meet Sue Blackstock things would be different."

"Come on then, what you waiting for?" she said running off.

Chapter 3

"Sir Bernard, Pippa Johnston here. I had a good interview with Tracy Longhorn and her commander was right, a very bright lady well able to think outside of the box, so I've added her to my team. I've also got Doug Green, one of my best investigators, to agree to join the team. That completes my team of six and you said you'll have six names for me and that you would ask Michele Blunt to lead. I've made available a command room at Brent House and I am getting it set up and kitted out for the whole team to make it easier to communicate with each other. I have booked you into a meeting for next Monday morning to be briefed on the plan, then we'll get the team to share all they know about these murders and we'll get this investigation moving forward."

****

Rob's alarm woke them at 6:00 Monday morning. He had to leave early to get to London for a meeting with the head of a new film company, wanting to negotiate terms for Rob's company to supply stunt men and horses for a new film about Dick Turpin. Sue was up early too, so that she would be ready at 7:15 when Phil would arrive and her training would begin.

After a strong coffee and a dish of cereal, Rob was ready to leave. He had no need for luggage because he was going to stay in his London flat. Two weeks ago it had been broken into and ransacked and he had asked his cleaner, Mrs. Parfitt and her husband, to clean the place up and get it habitable again. On Saturday they had sent him photos of what they had done which amazed Rob, it all looked as good as new. They must have worked incredibly hard.

"I've got to meet this guy at 2:00 at the Dorchester. By the end of the day I will have a better idea of how much work is needed to finalise a contract, but I don't expect to get away until Friday afternoon," he told Sue as he kissed her good bye.

"Rob," Sue called after him as he went to the door. He turned and she said. "Rather than struggle with the Friday afternoon traffic why not stay over the extra night and drive home fresh on Saturday morning? You won't miss out on time with Luci; she's going to a disco Friday night and staying in York with her mate Lisa. Then Saturday morning she's got an interview for a Saturday morning job. It might be an idea to take Mr. and Mrs. Parfitt out for a meal Friday night, as a thank you for what they've done at the flat. Somewhere nice, somewhere they wouldn't normally go to. Treat them to a bit of luxury."

"That's a very good idea," he responded. "I'll do that, if you don't mind me being away the extra night?"

"I'd rather that than worry about you in that mad Friday get-away traffic when you're tired. Now get a move on and text me when you get to the flat." She heard a faint call of "Will do," as he closed the door behind him.

A quick glance at the kitchen clock told her she had just ten minutes before Phil would be arriving and expecting her to start work. Quickly she drained the last half cup of coffee and cleared cups and dishes off the table, leaving them on the counter next to the sink and went off into the gun room to find a pair of boots that might fit. Thankfully she found some which were most likely Luci's. Sue couldn't imagine Rose wearing boots with a face painted on them. Hanging on a hook behind the door she found a quilted jacket with the Blackstock name and logo embroidered on the left breast pockets. It was a size too large but she would manage. As she walked back into the kitchen the back door opened and Phil poked his head through the opening.

"Good morning Sue. You look ready, so let's get started. First job is to check that everyone has arrived and the lads are getting the horses out on the gallops. We'll introduce you to each member of staff as we come to them. We'll tell them that you are learning how the stable works. It's close to being the truth and should be enough to avoid too much speculation."

"Sounds good," Sue said." I've been really looking forward to this. Let's get started."

They barely stopped for lunch just grabbing a chocolate bar and a piece of fruit. Working through lunch allowed Phil to get away by 5:00, which enabled him to spend a little time each day planning and preparing for his new role. Rob had asked him to set up a new stuntman academy in India on the same lines as the British and US ones. He was researching differences between Indian and British company law. He was also trying to learn some of the basics of the language, at least enough to greet people and order food and a drink. Most importantly he was building a list of tasks that needed to be done and identifying who he needed to contact to get it done. A good plan would be essential when he got to India.

It was actually 5:20 when their day ended. Sue felt it had gone well, but she was both mentally and physically exhausted. She was desperate for a shower and a good drink. As she walked through the back door into the kitchen, she was greeted by Madge with a cup of tea in her hand.

"Saw you coming across the yard and thought you would need this," she said holding out the cup of steaming liquid.

"I was thinking of something a little stronger, but a tea will be nice. Thank you!"

"Your meal will be ready in about half an hour," Madge said. "I've done a steak and ale pie with new potatoes and broccoli for you and Luci."

"It smells wonderful. Thank you Madge! I'll jump in the shower and get cleaned up ready," Sue said as she put her empty cup down on the table.

Luci came into the kitchen as Sue was pouring herself a glass of red wine and Madge was dishing up the meal. "Can I have a glass please, Sue?" she asked.

"I don't see why not," Sue replied.

Madge put plates of food in front of them. "I'll just wash the pans and then be off for the day. When you've finished just leave your plates by the sink, I'll wash them up in the morning. There's a fruit cake in the cake tin for your afters."

"You're too good to us, Madge," Luci said.

Madge just smiled back at her as she removed her apron, hung it on the back of the door, wished them a pleasant evening and left.

"You look tired, Sue," Luci said.

"Absolutely knackered." Sue replied "It's a long time since I did physical work."

"Why don't we take the rest of that bottle into the lounge and find a girly movie to watch."

"That would be nice," Sue said as the phone started to ring. "That will be your father." She lifted the handset and pressed the green button without looking at the number. "Hello".

The voice on the other end said," Good evening Mrs. Blackstock, Bernard Howe. Hope you are well?"

"Very well thank you, Sir Bernard."

"Very good. Is Rob about I'd like to speak to you both?"

"He's in London until Saturday. Is this about the offer you made?"

"No, no, this is something completely different, but I can't go into any detail over the phone. I wonder if you could pop into my office sometime soon."

"Rob's supposed to be ringing me this evening; in fact, I thought you were him calling. I'll discuss with him what we can do and get him to call you and set something up."

"That would be good. Can I stress that the matter is quite urgent. I'll leave it with you and wish you good evening."

Sue pressed the red button to end the call and the handset started ringing again. This time she checked the screen and saw it was Rob calling," Hello darling, have you had a good day? Thanks for the text earlier."

"Excellent day thanks. Who have you just been on the phone to? I've been trying to get through for ages."

"Sir Bernard Howe."

"Is he chasing for an answer to his offer?"

"No! He wants to talk to us both A.S.A.P. about something he can't talk about on the phone. He wants you to ring and book a meeting with him."

"Well, I was going to say to you that Mrs. Parfitt and her husband have said yes to your suggestion for Friday and I was wondering if you could get down here to join us? But if you were to come down early we could meet with Sir Bernard."

"I'd need to check with Phil, but I could catch an early train and be down there by 10:30."

"I'll have to have a meeting early to sign the contract with this new client that we've been working on today. It's going to take the next three days to finalise, but sure to be ready for then, so 10:30 should allow me time to get to the station to meet you. When you've spoken to Phil tomorrow text me and I'll ring Sir Bernard and get something set up."

"I'll ask him first thing."

"Good girl. Now, how was your day with Phil?"

As soon as she saw Phil the following morning, Sue asked him whether it would be okay for her to miss Friday. "Actually Sue, Friday was going to give me a bit of a problem. We've got five horses racing at Haydock and I need to be there to organise things and be on hand if there are problems. I wouldn't have time to spend time with you. Not that you'd be in the way, but you wouldn't be learning much either. It would be better for you to come to Sandown on Tuesday when we only have two runners. So I'm happy for you to go off on Friday and we'll pick up again next week."

Sue sent Rob a text," Friday okay with Phil."

When Rob rang Sue that evening he said, "I've arranged to see Sir Bernard at 1:30. He sounded very keen to get us into his office. It must be something very big. So ring me when you get on the train then I'll know exactly what time to be at the station to meet you. We'll have a bite to eat then go and see what he wants."

Tuesday had not been as demanding for Sue as Monday had been. Much of what they did was the same every day, so wasn't new to her. At the end of the day Phil told her how impressed he was at the speed she had picked things up and as he had a mountain of work to get through, he was going to let her run things for the morning. Wednesday afternoon was always the vet's weekly visit, so he'd take the lead again for that.

Sue managed quite comfortably on Wednesday morning. She even handled an incident when two of the lads started a fight in the yard. In the afternoon she spent time with the vet and Phil stepped back as much as he could. Thursday started the same with Sue in charge. She had to call the vet in when one of the horses returned lame from the gallops. In the afternoon, she worked with Phil in the office preparing paperwork needed to go with the horses running at Haydock the next day.

Madge's husband drove Sue into York Friday morning to catch the 08:05 fast train to London. Luci scrounged a lift to save her carrying her disco clothes and overnight things on the school bus. They dropped her off at her friend Lisa's house on route to the station.

Due to maintenance work on the line, the train was running twenty minutes late which Rob was thankful for because he was also running late and walked up to the platform gate just as the train pulled in. As Sue dragged her overnight bag towards the gate, she saw Rob waiting. She waved her free hand and lengthened her stride. When she reached Rob she stood her bag on end, threw her arms around his neck and kissed him, as if they'd been parted for months.

"Wow! That was worth waiting for. I should go away more often," Rob said. "How was your journey?"

"Awful!" she replied. "Too many smelly people in a small space. There was no first class so I had no alternative."

"And the government are always telling us to use public transport," Rob said "They should try it themselves sometime. Do you want a coffee or go straight back to the flat? I've got food in, I thought an omelette for lunch, as we're eating later."

"One of your omelettes would be great, but can we go to my house first. I've only brought a few overnight things; I thought we could pick up something from my house for me to wear this evening and also fill a bag with more of my clothes to take with us back to Yorkshire tomorrow."

Rob took her bag and they left the station, hailed a taxi and headed for Sue's house in Twickenham, just a couple of hundred yards from the rugby stadium. "Have you booked somewhere nice for us this evening?" She asked.

"A table for four 7:30 at Petrus. The Parfitt's are going to meet us there."

"That's Gordon Ramsey's French restaurant, the place you took me on our first evening. Very suitable! The sort of food that they will enjoy but not the sort of place they would take themselves to."

When they arrived at the house, Sue went straight upstairs to pack her clothes. Rob called up the stairs after her. "I'm making coffee. Do you want one?"

"Yes please darling, I'll only be a few minutes."

Rob was at the breakfast bar in the kitchen when Sue came down to join him. She was carrying a small flight bag. "I've packed things in here for this evening and filled a big case to take back to Yorkshire, we can pick that up later. The case is a bit heavy; can you bring it down for me?" she asked. "What are we going to do with this house Rob? I don't really want to get rid of it, but your flat is better located for our future needs."

It's a good little investment. You'd be best off getting in touch with an agency to rent it out as furnished accommodation. Should earn you twelve to fifteen thousand a year, maybe more."

"That sounds sensible. I need to finish getting my personal bits removed, then get someone in to look the place over."

"We need to get moving and get your stuff back to the flat. There's no time for me to cook lunch now, so we'll grab a sandwich on the way."

At 1:30 they were standing in the reception of the S.I.S. Building, Vauxhall Cross waiting for someone to collect them and take them to meet with Sir Bernard. The lift doors opened and an Asian featured girl smiled and walked towards them. "Mr. and Mrs. Blackstock, welcome to MI-6. Sir Bernard is expecting you but is on the phone with the P.M.. at the moment. If you come with me you can wait in his side room."

They waited fifteen minutes drinking a coffee brought in by the young Asian girl. Sir Bernard joined them in the room with a bundle of folders under his arm. "Susan, Robert, thank you for coming in, sorry to have kept you waiting. I see Lillian got you a coffee. I'll try not to keep you too long."

"Good afternoon, Sir Bernard. What's so urgent and can't be discussed over the phone?" Rob asked.

"First I need to give you a bit of background, so that you can understand why we have a problem," Sir Bernard began. "Have either of you heard of Luggard Shipping?"

They both nodded. "One of the world's biggest shipping lines," Rob responded. "Based in Venezuela I believe and profits coming from shipping Venezuelan oil around the world."

"You're right Rob. The line is actually not the largest in number of ships but in tonnage. Only the U.S. navy has more ships. The line is solely owned by Ernst Luggard, listed as one of the top twenty richest men in the world, much of that wealth has come from decades of drug running to North America and Europe. But bear with me, I need to tell you a bit about how the empire got started."

Rob interrupted," This is all very interesting, Sir Bernard but I can't see how this impacts us."

"Just give me a few minutes more and I assure you the connection will be clear. Much of what I'm about to tell you has come from official sources but some has come from personal accounts. It has all been pieced together by a team of analysts here at MI-6. The story begins with Ernst's father Emil, born January 1st 1900 . The fifth son of a Prussian farmer. The family name at that time was von Luggard. As a sixteen year old he lied about his age to join the army. There is no record of him ever fighting in any battle of the First World War. He next appears as a junior officer in Hitler's reformed army in 1933. He saw action with German forces during the Spanish Civil War, gaining valuable experience which, in the early months of 1940, he put to good use as the German troops pushed the French and British towards the coast. He was awarded the Iron Cross in 1944 for his efforts in defeating allied airborne troops that landed at Arnhem. Medical records from that battle have him as having lost his left leg and being sent to Berlin for further treatment. Ten months later his name appears on a staff list for the Wolf's Lair along with an S.S. officer Eva von Luggard who we assume to be his wife."

"Wolf's Lair. That was Hitler's command centre wasn't it?" Sue enquired.

"It was," Sir Bernard continued. "Notes found in a notebook in the desk drawers of one of Hitler's secretaries report that on April 21st, Hitler called three of his most trusted officers to him. He gave each of them one third of the German gold with instructions to take it somewhere new and use it to rebuild the Third Reich. We believe von Luggard to be one of the three because of an entry in the log of the commander of the troops defending Berlin airport. The entry says that at 3:50 in the morning on the 22nd April, a man with an artificial left leg, a woman and four other men loaded eight heavy crates onto a plane and took off flying south. Are you following this?" Sir Bernard said as he opened a second folder to continue his story.

An Emil Luggard is next reported in a Kavanayen village elder's diary for May 10th. Kavanayen is a village near the bottom of Angel Falls in Venezuela. The diary entry says that five men and a woman had walked into town, claiming to be Germans escaping the Nazis, who were hunting them because they had been supplying the allies with information about troop movements. Their plane had developed a fault causing them to crash on Auyantepui Mountain approximately two miles from the head of Angel Falls. It had taken them twenty one days to find a route down and were in poor health, having survived on what little food they had in the plane, plus fruit and berries on route.

Snippets of information then tell us that over the next two years, Emil builds a ranch at the site of his plane crash. He also advertised back in Germany for young men wanting a fresh start to come and join him. There was a great response and he selected twenty with naval experience and paid for their transportation across the Atlantic. In 1947 he buys his first ships, six of them and installs his own men as captains. During the Prohibition years in America, there were many ships smuggling liquor from South America into the Southern states. This trade continued after the end of Prohibition because demand greatly exceeded what home sources could produce. But now production was fully restored, with war over, shipments from Europe were on the increase and new airline routes were being established. Eventually profits totally dried up and Emil bought boats at extremely low prices. The following year he bought six more. His ships also continued trading with US states and, using old smuggling contacts, got large quantities of drugs onto the American market for the post war drug boom. This is where you should be taking interest because I'll now start making links to current events. Are you following me?"

"I think we're following you so far, please continue," Sue said checking the time on her watch.

Sir Bernard continued," At this time, the Caribbean islands were opening up for tourism and with his growing fleet Emil made vast profits by shipping goods to the islands. Emil had also purchased land and planted vineyards which were now producing some quality wines. There are no records to support this, but it is reasonable to suppose everything was funded by the Nazi gold.

During the 1950's Venezuela's oil reserves became a significant resource and Emil again was one of the first to grasp an opportunity. He bought the first of his tanker fleet and began shipping oil all over the world. New destinations widened his market for drugs. He was now a major shipper of Columbian produced drugs to America and Europe.

Emit had one child, Ernst. He was born December 1st 1948, his education until he was sixteen, was at home where his mother tutored him in a strict Hitler Youth style. In 1962 Emil moved his family to Caracas where he was able to use his growing fortune to influence political direction. Ernst was sent to Germany to complete his education. In early 1964 Emit was elected Mayor of Caracas and appointed Eva as Deputy Mayor. Photographs of him accepting the appointment appeared in several international newspapers and were seen by the War Crimes investigators. In October 1966 Emit von Luggard was brought to trial facing charges that he had ordered the execution of every man, woman and child in a Belgian village after the bodies of two German soldiers had been discovered in a shallow grave behind the village meeting hall. He was found guilty and sentenced to life in solitary, with limited visiting rights.

Once he was eighteen, Ernst visited his father for one hour once a month for almost three years, until Emit died of heart disease. Ernst completed his degree courses and returned to Venezuela later that year. In the meantime Eva had promoted herself to Mayor and taken over the running of all Emit's businesses.

Ernst made Angels' Rest his home, the two mountain paths from the valley were closed off, making helicopter the only means of access. He lived there with several friends he had made at university and a number of locals brought in to perform the manual tasks about the ranch. There were three or four young ladies brought in to do laundry and cooking, one in particular Ernst took a shine to and later married. In 1973 Ernst's twin boys were born, but his wife died in childbirth. Ernst moved to Caracas asking Eva to bring up and educate the twins which she did in a Hitler Youth style, while he took control of the businesses." Sir Bernard closed the file in front of him and looked across the table at Rob and Sue. "That brings us more or less to the current status. Like Ernst, the twins completed their education in Europe. Now in their forties, Ralph is an accountant with a large firm in New York and Josef is a senior solicitor with Crane's in London. Eva died in 1987 and Ernst moved his base of operations to Angels Rest from where he oversees his growing fortune. The locals call it 'Lugar Donde Duermen Los Angeles' '*The Place Where Angels Sleep*'. You'd like to think that with satellite imagery and all the other stuff like that, we'd be able to watch what he's up to. But that's not enough; we can't listen to what he's planning or see what he does indoors. We need eyes and ears in that fortress"

"I'm sorry Sir Bernard but I still don't see any connection to us," Rob said.

"Well, you've heard how Ernst has become rich and powerful. I believe that somehow he is connected to all these murders."

"I'm with Rob on this one. I don't see any connection," Sue said.

"Eric has an Achilles heel. In 1991 he married again and a son was born. He was educated in England and is a complete opposite to his elder brothers. His father idolises him. Kurt has no interest in the family business's he is only interested in fast cars and the Miami party scene. Ernst pays for everything without question. He is gay, but likes to have a pretty girl with him to appear to be like others at the parties. Six weeks ago, his girlfriend was found dead in a hotel room lying next to his lover. Both shot in the head. Everyone thinks Kurt did it, but there is no evidence to gain a conviction. Last month the C.I.A. put three female agents at a party that Kurt attended. They were all told to flirt with him. The trap worked and he left with Sandra Brown. They have been seen together several times since then."

"That's a very risky position to put a young girl in," Sue said.

"It is, but we need to get someone inside Angels' Rest and when Kurt goes home for a weekend, which he does regularly he will take Sandra with him. Now this is where you come in Rob, if you are willing to help out."

"Depends on what you're asking me to do."

"Well," Sir Bernard responded. "Kurt is a very enthusiastic young man, desperate for some public recognition. He is as very keen rally driver, just not a very good one. Raw talent but no control, you know the sort. He has entered the Dakar rally the last three years and never lasted more than three days. You know about the Dakar rally Rob?"

"Sure," Rob answered. "It's an annual event that began in the late seventies. Originally running from Paris to Dakar, Senegal. But due to the unstable political situation in West Africa it moved to South America in 2009. It's an off-road endurance race for modified vehicles in many categories. Never the same course twice. Competitors die every year. It's not for me."

" I'm not asking you to enter the race Rob, but to help someone else to. We know that your American company has a contract to work on a film shortly to be made and that some scenes will be shot on location in Florida.

"That's right! A new Tom Cruise film. It's about three months ' work, starting in two weeks 'time."

"Quite so. Our plan, if you are agreeable, is that you will join your team in Miami and our Miss Brown will pose as your niece and introduce Kurt to you. Kurt spends most of his time in Miami, so there should be no problem meeting with him. You then must get to know him, get him to talk about the Dakar rally. I know you entered in 2006. We need him to trust you and to take you on as his coach for next January's event. He regularly takes people back to Angels' Rest for weekends and we need him to take you there, which would give you an opportunity to learn something of Ernst's plans. As a man you'll have access to places Sandra can't get to, perhaps even into his communications centre. We need to identify any weakness in the defences up there; we may need to send troops in sometime in the future. Maybe there is an option to do some practice with Kurt close to Angels' Rest so you can get a close-up look at the perimeter." Sir Bernard then turned to Sue. "Susan, we'd also like you to travel with Rob. Your observation and detective skills would be of great value to the mission. Think of this as a honeymoon paid for by Her Majesty."

Sue gave Rob a look of horror and Rob nodded in response and turned back to Sir Bernard. "We appreciate your confidence in us, Sir Bernard, but must decline. I'm not the James Bond type. It's a long time since I last did any rally driving and I don't think I would make a convincing coach. Also Sue and I were only married a few days ago, we've only known one another a few weeks, we've got a lot to get sorted. I'm sure Sue will agree that we're not prepared to put our lives on hold for three months or so, on the off chance of obtaining some information about someone whom you THINK is behind these murders. I'm sure you've got alternative plans you can use."

"I completely understand, although I'm a little disappointed that you are reluctant to get involved. You are correct, we do have a plan 'B' but it's not as easy to set up. Thank you for your time this afternoon and if you change your mind, when you've had time to think things through, please give me a call. You have my number I believe?"

Sir Bernard stood, shook hands with Sue then Rob, turned and left the room with his bundle of folders under his arm. Within a couple of minutes the Asian girl entered the room and escorted them down to reception. They handed in their visitors' passes to the desk clerk and left the building.

Chapter 4

"This woman is going to prove difficult to get three doses of the drug into, boss. The first should be quite straight forward, her husband is away at the moment so she's sleeping alone. We just creep into her room one night and stick her with it. She'll wake with a head ache but otherwise not be aware of anything out of the ordinary. We might get away with something similar for the second dose but getting the third dose into her and setting the trigger phrase in her subconscious won't be easy and we'll need to give some thought to how best we can do it."

****

"Wow! That was quite a story," Rob said to Sue as they walked away from the building.

"It did go on a bit, but I guess Sir Bernard felt it all relevant to give us a full picture of what's happening. We are right not to get involved, aren't we Rob?"

"We'd be well out of our depth. We're not trained for this sort of thing. The risk would be tremendous," he replied.

Sue checked the time on her phone. "We'd better get a move on. It's already gone five. We don't want to be late for Mr. and Mrs. Parfitt."

It was late Friday afternoon and it took ages to get a taxi. So they went first to Sue's house, where Rob quickly grabbed Sue's bag of things for the evening, while Sue stayed in the taxi chatting to the driver. Then they headed back towards Rob's flat. As they sat looking out onto the busy slow moving streets Sue's phone buzzed indicating an incoming message.

"It's from Phil," she announced. "He says the stable has one horse running at Epsom on Monday and it would be the perfect opportunity for him to show me what he does at race meetings. He says that he could divert and pick me up at the flat on route."

"That makes a lot of sense. With just one horse running he'll have lots of time to show me all the ins and outs of race day. But we were going back to Yorkshire tomorrow. I've got stuff to do on Sunday."

"Well, why don't you go and leave me here. I can spend the week-end at my house sorting out what I want to take back to Yorkshire and what I want to get rid of."

"If you're happy to do that, it suits me."

They arrived early at the restaurant and as their table was ready, they were shown straight to it. Rob ordered them a gin and tonic each while they waited for the others to arrive. The Parfitts were ten minutes late and Sue immediately noticed that Mrs. Parfitt had obviously been crying.

"Please take a seat," Rob said as he stood to greet them, shaking hands with Mr. Parfitt. "Mr. and Mrs. Parfitt sounds so formal, would it be okay if we call you Emily and Paul." They both nodded in response but Emily kept her eyes towards the table.

"What's wrong, Mrs. Parfitt?" Sue asked." Has something happened? Can we help?"

"Oh madam," Emily responded. "We had the most terrible news this afternoon. Our landlord has given us notice that we are to lose our flat in two weeks. We've been there twenty eight years. Never missed a rent day. It's our home, the place our son grew up in. How are we going to find somewhere new in just two weeks?"

"Why only two weeks? Surely he has to give you longer than that. What he's doing isn't legal," Sue said.

"He says he told us three months ago and again six weeks ago. Even showed us copies of letters he says we had. But neither of us recalls seeing them."

Sue looked at Rob and immediately he knew what she was thinking so smiled at her and nodded.

"We've got a solution for you, which if you are both happy with, will solve a big problem which we have and were only discussing a little while ago. Our problem is what to do with my house, now that we live together. It's only a small little two bed house in Twickenham but it has got a garden and a garage. We don't need that as well as the flat, but I don't want to sell it either, so we were planning to rent it out part furnished. I'd be very pleased for you to rent it from me. You could move in next week! No need for you to give me references and I'm sure Rob will agree that the work you and Paul did to get his flat cleaned up will be as good as a deposit. What do you say?"

"That's very kind of you Miss, but we can't afford the rent on a house."

"I'm sure we can come to some sort of agreement. Let's say that for now you pay me the same as you pay for your flat now, plus you do all the maintenance on the house and garage and keep the garden in good order."

Tears appeared in Emily's eyes as she reached across the table and squeezed Sue's hands. "We can't thank you enough, miss and you as well sir. We'll be forever in your debt."

Paul stood and walked round the table to shake Rob's hand. "Thank you sir."

"Okay. Let's look and see what's on the menu," Sue suggested.

Next morning Rob took Sue to her house and left her there and drove back to Yorkshire. He rang ahead and told Madge about the change of plan. When he arrived home, he found a note from Madge on the kitchen table saying she had gone shopping in York but would call in mid-afternoon. His evening meal would be ready at 7:00 but if he was hungry there was cold meat and salad in the fridge.

After walking through to the living room he spent a few minutes going quickly through his post, and seeing that nothing needed urgent attention, he returned to the kitchen. He carved two thick slices of bread off the loaf that he found in the bread bin, then stuffed as much meat and salad as he could between the two slices of bread and set out to walk the mile or so down the lane to the Stuntman Academy.

Having been away all week there was a mountain of paperwork waiting for him in his office and the afternoon slipped by quicker than he wanted. At 6 o'clock his phone rang, interrupting him and forcing him to break, from what he was doing to answer the call. "Hi Sue, how's the house clearing going?"

"Very well," Sue replied. "The Parfitt's arrived at 8:30. They really are a hard working couple, they've only just left. We sorted out what I want to keep and will bring with me up to Yorkshire. We've also agreed what would be good to leave behind and the garage is now full of the stuff to get rid of. Some is only good enough for the bin but a lot of it is worth giving to a charity shop. Mr. Parfitt said he will deal with all that. They are coming back early tomorrow so that we can give the whole place a thorough deep clean, whilst it is so close to being empty. Well that's my day, what have you been up to?"

"I've been stuck in the office all afternoon, catching up on some paperwork. Just about all done now, so I'm going to call it a day. I could do with a drink. Have you got much stuff to bring back to Yorkshire?"

"Four bin bags full of clothes and a couple of boxes full of odds and ends. So no, not too much."

Sounds like quite a bit to me. Certainly a car load. I need to deliver a contract to Warner's Studio sometime early this week. What if I drove down on Monday and you get Phil to drop you off after the race meeting. We can then load my car and anything that won't fit can go into Phil's. Then we can all drive back Monday evening."

"Honestly Rob, there's not that much. We could get it all into Phil's car. No need for you to come and get me."

"I've got to come down anyway with this contract," Rob argued.

"Well, if you're okay with all that driving," Sue responded. "It would mean the Parfitt's can have the keys and start moving their stuff in. They've got a nephew with a van who's offered to help and do a bit each evening."

"Right then, I'll aim to get to the house 5:00 or there abouts, you and Phil should be there around that time. Now I'm going back to the house to get that well-earned drink. Madge said she would be getting a meal ready for 7:00, so I've got time for a nice long shower and maybe a second drink before then."

"It's alright for some, getting a home cooked meal and sitting down with a drink. I've just got one egg left in the fridge, a tin of beans and a can of coke. My little TV is in one of the boxes. So it's an evening with a couple of magazines and an early night. Enjoy your evening. Good night darling."

As Rob walked in through the back door of the main house he was hit by the strong aromatic smell of whatever Madge was cooking and he was drawn towards the kitchen.

"That smells wonderful Madge, I can't wait to taste some."

"I've made you one of your favourites Mr. Robert, beef curry. There will be plenty so it will do tomorrow as well. It will be ready in about 45 minutes."

"That's perfect, just time for me to have a beer then take a shower before I sit down."

He poured a beer and was about to take it through to the lounge when there was a knock on the back door. He opened it to see Tracy Longhorn stood smiling on the lowest step.

Surprised to see her he said," Tracy you're looking good! Have you come to arrest me?"

"You said I should call round for a drink with you two sometime soon, so here I am," she said holding out a bottle of red wine.

"I did, didn't I? Come on in. Sue's not here. She's in London sorting out her house, deciding what to leave behind and what to bring up here."

"Oh, I'll come back another time when you've both at home. I should have rung you before coming over."

"Don't be silly, you're here now, I'm on my own and some company would be nice."

"Okay then, if you're sure. That curry smells good. Does Madge still work for you?"

"Hello Miss Mills, long time since you last came calling on Mr. Robert," Madge said as she saw Tracy appear round the door.

"Hello Madge. Yes a very long time and I'm Tracy Longhorn now married, with two kids," Tracy replied.

"And she's a senior police officer in the local force Madge, so don't mention the drugs in the kitchen drawers," Rob added with a smile.

"It's all right sir, I tipped the last of them into the curry so there will be no trace," Madge added to the jest.

"Talking of curry, will you join me for a bite to eat? Madge says there's plenty." Rob asked.

"If you're sure? It does smell rather good," Tracy answered looking from Rob then to Madge who seemed to be happy about her staying.

"I'll lay a second place at the table then shall I? You two go on into the lounge and have a drink and I'll call you when it's ready. About thirty minutes."

Rob led Tracy through to the lounge." Can I get you a drink?"

"Just a tonic please, Rob. I'm driving."

"So what brings you back to Yorkshire so soon? Last time we saw you, you were heading for London, to join a special task force or something."

"That's right. I'm being loaned out, so to speak, to MI-5 for a team investigating this drugs thing that's getting so many people killed. It was only supposed to be for six weeks, but now looks like being indefinite. So I'm back here for the weekend to garage my car and fill a couple of suitcases with clothes. Then it's back to London on Monday on the early train."

"I'm driving down to London on Monday. Why don't you let me take you and save you struggling with heavy cases on the train?"

"That would be fantastic Rob! Thank you."

"Not a problem. Now I think that was Madge calling us through. Time to eat."

The table was set for two with glasses and the bottle of wine Tracy had brought with her, which Rob picked up, twisted the top off and filled the glasses. "Will you join us for a glass of wine, Madge?" he asked.

"No thank you, Mr. Robert. I shall be going soon. My husband is taking me out. It doesn't happen too often, so I want to stay sober to make the most of it. When you've finished, just leave your dishes on the side and the leftovers in the fridge, I'll deal with it all in the morning. Enjoy your meal both of you. Good evening."

"Thanks Madge, enjoy your evening out," Rob called as Madge left the house.

"This is a very nice wine," Rob said as he topped up both glasses.

"So, how is the investigation going?" Rob enquired.

"It's still very early days, but we do have several very good leads and a very strong case building against Ernst Luggard, a rich business man and known to be a major player in the South American drugs world. But so far the evidence is all circumstantial and we need some real hard evidence before we can go after him. But as yet we have no idea what his end game is and what he is trying to achieve."

"Why is he top of your list?"

"Heroin found at one of the scenes was analysed and can only have come from South America. These days very little comes out of South America without passing through the hands of the Luggard Empire. He has such a tight control over his business that he has to be aware of what is going on at the very least. But why? What does he hope to gain?"

"I guess, as you are part of the task force, you'll have heard of Sir Bernard Howe?" Tracy nodded and looked curious. "Well yesterday, Sue and I were called to a meeting with Sir Bernard at MI-6. He was trying to recruit us into what I can only assume to be your task force."

"Are you in?"

"No. We didn't see what we can do to help. It's a bit James Bond like for us." He filled the glasses again emptying the bottle then cleared the table. "Let's go through to the lounge where we can relax."

"I really shouldn't stay too long, Rob," Tracy said.

"And leave me on my own? You've had half a bottle of wine so you can't drive, anyway."

"You're right of course; I'd better call a cab."

"Don't be silly. You can stay the night here and chat some more. Take your car back in the morning."

"What are you suggesting, Robert Blackstock?"

"Nothing at all. Just offering you a bed for the night to save you getting a taxi. Then having to get back here again tomorrow, to recover your car. You can have my room and I'll take the couch. Now let's see if I can find another bottle of wine."

"Wake up Tracy, it's morning," Rob said as he lightly shook his guest's shoulder. She didn't stir. Rob shook a little harder. Still no response. "Come on girl, we didn't have that much wine last night."

Still she didn't stir and Rob was beginning to get worried. She was breathing but it seemed very laboured. Something was obviously not right and he needed to do something quickly. He ran to the top of the stairs and shouted down to the kitchen. "Madge, quickly call an ambulance! Tracy is up here and I think there is something seriously wrong with her. I can't wake her."

Chapter 5

"Gabriel your man is an idiot! He injected the wrong woman. Your target is in London. Why did you not know? The family and the police now know she is our target and we won't get another chance to get anywhere near her. Getting someone inside Williams Security is critical to our plan we must hook into another member of their management team and when we do don't mess it up."

****

The ambulance was twenty minutes getting to the house and Rob could see that Tracy was deteriorating, her breathing was getting worse. The paramedic carried out a few basic tests then turned to Rob and asked. "Is she a long term heroin user?"

"What?" Rob was totally shocked at what he was being asked.

"I'm pretty certain she has overdosed on heroin. I've seen it several times. I'll give her something to start to counter the effects, but we need to get her back to hospital quickly for a full treatment, before organ failure becomes an issue. I'm going to have to report this to the police, they'll want to talk to you I'd imagine. It would be good if you can find any drugs she may still have, so they can be analysed."

Still in shock Rob just nodded. The previous evening she appeared so normal, he would never have guessed she was a drug addict.

The ambulance left, it's blue light flashing, as it hurried out of the gate. Rob returned to the bedroom to search as the paramedic had suggested. Her clothes were lay across a chair, he found nothing in them. She only had a small handbag that also contained nothing that he wouldn't have expected to be there. Apart from her watch, a couple of rings and a necklace on the bedside table she had no other possessions in the room. There was no reason to suspect she had hidden anything amongst his things in the room.

An unmarked police car pulled into the drive a few minutes later and two plain clothed officers showed their warrant cards to Madge who had opened the door to them. She showed them through to the lounge and Rob came downstairs ready to be questioned. The paramedic must have contacted them as soon as they were on their way to hospital and because of who Tracy is, detectives were here, rather than uniformed officers.

They questioned Rob for more than twenty minutes until they were totally convinced he knew nothing about it.

"Can you show us the room she was in please, sir?" The taller of the two detectives asked.

Rob showed them to his room, then stood back just outside the door and watched them systematically search the room. The shorter one bent down by the window.

"Over here Len. This looks a bit odd. I'd say someone has recently climbed through this window from the outside. Look on the ledge out there, the algae has been disturbed and there are traces of it on the window sill and on the carpet in front of the window."

The taller detective, obviously the senior of the two, took pictures with his phone then use it to make a call. Rob could only hear a few words of what he said but he clearly heard the words S.O.C.O. and murder. The detective ended his call and walked towards Rob who stepped back onto the landing.

"I must ask you to stay out of this room, Mr. Blackstock and make sure that no one enters it until I say they can." The detective said. "I'm sealing this off as a probable crime scene."

"What crime officer?" Rob asked.

"The attempted murder of D.S. Longhorn."

"But no one knew she was going to be here. She only decided at 9:30 yesterday evening. It was a last minute thing because we had been talking and she'd had more to drink than was safe for her to drive." Rob explained.

"Who normally occupies that room, sir?" the detective asked.

"I do, with my wife but she is un-expectedly in London this weekend."

The detective wrote something in his notebook and looked thoughtfully out of the landing window, then turned to Rob.

"I think that whoever came through that window expected to find your wife alone in that room and mistook D.S. Longhorn for her. I believe that your wife was the real target and that D.S. Longhorn was just unlucky to be in the wrong place. My inspector is on his way here, sir. He will want to ask you more questions when he arrives but in the meantime can you think of anyone who may want to harm your wife?"

While he was waiting for the inspector, Rob rang Sue. He told her everything that had happened and asked if she knew of anyone who wanted her out of the way.

"Williams Securities is not that sort of firm, Rob," she said. "They don't deal with individuals. They are more about keeping people safe at events. Like ensuring no one attacked the Queen at Harry and Megan's wedding or foreign dignitaries don't get assassinated when on state visits. I can't think of anyone who would know who I am, let alone want to do me any harm."

"What about when you were in the army?" Rob pressed.

"Sure, loads of squaddies I picked up and had locked up. A few officers, too. But never for anything serious and never for more than a few months. No Rob, I can't think of anyone, sorry."

"Well if you do think of anyone, let me know straight away. I'm going to have to go, the inspector has just arrived. Have a good day at the races tomorrow, I'll see you at around 5:00, bye."

"Mr. Blackstock, this is Inspector Harris. He'd like a few words with you."

"Thank you D.S. Peters. Can you perhaps stay and take notes for me, if you will?"

"Mr. Blackstock, terrible thing to have happened. My sergeant tells me that it was you who found her and possibly saved her life. May I start by asking how long you have known D.S. Longhorn and why was she sleeping in your bed last night? Are you having an affair with Mrs Longhorn?" the inspector asked.

"Now wait a minute inspector. I don't know what you are trying to insinuate but Tracy and I are old friends. We were at school together. We dated when we were both thirteen. We lost touch about twenty years ago then met by accident a week or so ago and my wife invited her to drop in for a drink sometime. Last night she turned up with a bottle of wine not knowing Sue, my wife, was in London. We talked and drank the wine. When she came to leave she realise she had drunk too much to drive so I offered her my bed and I slept on the couch. No Tracy Longhorn and I are not having an affair. Good God man, I only got married a few weeks ago!"

The inspector kept up this style of aggressive questioning for over fifteen minutes then left, without so much as a thank you.

D.S. Peters apologised for his senior officer's attitude, then followed the inspector out onto the drive, where the scene of crime officers were preparing to get started. Rob left them to it and went to his office at the academy to finish catching up with his paperwork.

After his lunch, Rob rang the hospital to check on Tracy and was told she was sitting up in bed, having just eaten her lunch. There was no long term damage and she could have visitors from 6:00. At 5:30 he set of to drive to the hospital.

"Hello you," she said as he entered her private side room. "I hear you saved my life. You acting quickly is the only reason I'm still here."

"I'm sorry, Tracy. You were in the wrong place at the wrong time. Your D.S. Peters thinks Sue was the real target, but we don't know why. It looks like an attempt at another one of your overdose murders."

"This is different Rob. They found no trace of heroin in my blood. I apparently had an allergic reaction to some other substance which that bastard pumped into me. Samples have been sent to a government lab for analysis."

"What's going on Tracy? Why would anyone want to do this to Sue?"

"We'll know more once we find out what I was injected with. I should be out of here by tomorrow and my things are being taken to London for me, so I won't need your help, but thanks for the offer anyway. This has all suddenly become very personal and believe me I shall be searching for answers, as soon as I get back behind my desk.

Chapter 6

"D.S. Longhorn, this is Stuart Patterson at the biological weapons lab, Aldershot. Good morning, ma'am. Samples of blood were sent to my lab for analysis. I believe a mutual friend of ours called me and asked that I give you a verbal report before I do my official report and state my findings. In the sample we tested we found considerable alcohol and a small amount of a drug called QZ-71. QZ-71 reacts violently in some people, normally resulting in multi organ failure and death. It was developed by Lacon Chemicals as a hypnotic drug to aid people wanting a cure for alcoholism, but was banned after a death occurred in trials. It's a cumulative drug, meaning that after a number of doses, possibly only three or four, the recipient can be primed with a word or phrase, that when heard, puts the recipient into a state where they will do whatever is requested of them. Very dangerous indeed."

****

"Sue had been in bed for almost an hour, bored with no one to talk to. She'd had a long soak in the bath, with candles all around and read her magazines. All that was missing was a nice glass of red wine. She was in bed before 10:00 but hadn't been asleep when she heard someone knocking on her front door. Cautiously, she went downstairs taking a walking stick from the stand by the last step. She held it above her head ready to strike and moved to the door. "Who is it?" she asked.

"It's your loving husband. Hurry up and let me in, it's pissing down out here and I'm getting soaked!"

Sue drew back the bolts at the top and bottom of the door and quickly opened it to let him in.

"What are you doing here and why didn't you ring to let me know you were coming?"

"My phone is dead. Not even enough power in the battery to turn it on and there's no charger in the car. Having spoken with

Tracy about what happened to her last night, I was worried about you down here alone."

"You could have rung me from a public phone at a service station."

"That's the problem with modern phones, we all use contact lists and don't learn numbers any more, so I couldn't dial yours because I don't know what it is."

"Whatever. I'm so glad to see you Rob. You must be tired; can I fix you a drink? It will have to be tea or coffee I'm afraid, there's nothing else in."

"There is now," he said pulling a bottle of red wine from a carrier bag he was holding.

I hope it will taste okay out of china mugs. My best glasses are packed to go to Yorkshire and all the others are out in the garage packed to go to the charity shop. Have you heard how Tracy is doing? Will she recover okay?"

"She's going to be just fine. She's got to stay in overnight for observation but she should go home tomorrow."

"That's a relief. What a good job you found her. I would like to know why she was in our bed and where you were, when this murder attempt took place? Let's take that bottle through to the lounge and you can tell me all about what's been going on."

Next morning they were woken by loud banging on the back door. It sounded like someone was trying to break in. Rob hurriedly pulled his trousers on, then bent over the bed to Sue, kissed her quickly and whispered, "Don't worry my darling I'm here so you're quite safe."

As he left the room Sue slipped out of bed and stepped across the room to the window. She pulled the curtains open just far enough to be able to look out but the bedroom was at the front of the house and the window faced the road. Although it was light outside, she saw nothing out of the ordinary. She climbed back into bed, pulled the covers up around her naked body and sat listening. She heard Rob open the back door and immediately heard voices. It was normal conversation, not the shouting she had expected. The voices were not loud enough for her to hear what was being said, but whoever it was was, now in the house.

The voices stopped and she could hear someone coming up the stairs. Then Rob appeared at the door with a broad smile across his face. "You need to put some clothes on and make yourself decent. The Parfitts are here to finish the cleaning. They've been knocking on the front door for ages and were worried that you were ill or something, so went round the back to see if they could get in. We overslept, it's almost 9:00. I'm putting the kettle on for coffee. Come down as quickly as you can."

"Why didn't they realise you were here when they saw your car was on the drive?"

"Because it wasn't. You had put the bin out in the middle of the drive, so as there was a space, I parked out on the street two doors down. They wouldn't have noticed it."

"I did wake earlier, but my alarm clock is packed and it was too dark to read my watch, so I don't know what time that was. I must have dropped of again pretty quickly. I'll be down in a couple of minutes, just need to put some old clothes on to work in and splash some water on my face," she said as she bent down and picked up a pair of knickers off the floor.

The Parfit's were already hard at work by the time Sue got downstairs. Mr. Parfitt was cleaning the lounge window while Mrs. Parfitt had the brush attachment fitted to the vacuum cleaner and was going along the skirting boards, then wiped them over with a damp cloth. Sue could see where she had been because they shone as if freshly painted.

Mrs. Parfitt saw Sue watching her and said, "Just in here, your bedroom and ensuite to do now Miss. The carpets are as all good , we don't need to clean them."

"Thank you both, so much. This would have taken me all week . I'll finish my coffee then get Rob to help me clear the rest of my stuff out of the bedroom."

Rob pulled his car onto the drive and loaded Sue's bags and boxes. She was right, there wasn't that much and it did all fit.

They all stopped for lunch at noon. Rob had been out to get some food, but as it was Sunday, the options were limited and he ended up bringing back a selection of sandwiches, some crisps, beers and a packet of cakes.

By 3:00 they were satisfied that the whole house was as clean as they were going to get it. Sue gave the Parfitt's a set of keys and Rob drove them back to their flat. There was just enough space for Mrs Parfitt on the back seat squashed up against the bags of Sue's clothes.

When he returned to the house, Sue had packed the last few bits into a box and they drove on to Rosebury House and Rob's flat. Rob went down to see Paul the door security man and check he had recovered from being beaten up by members of the River Gang, who had broken in and trashed Rob's flat a couple of weeks earlier. Sue went straight in the shower and when Rob returned she was sat in the lounge with a bath sheet wrapped around her and was towelling her hair dry with a small hand towel.

"Don't look at me like that Rob. Haven't you ever seen a woman drying her hair?"

"Yes, but usually with a hairdryer."

"Ha, bloody ha. It's packed."

"Your whole life seems to be packed. What do you want to do this evening?"

"Well, you haven't got any food in the flat, so I guess we should go out to eat. Somewhere romantic. I feel in a romantic mood."

"That sounds promising," Rob said as he took the hand towel from her and finished drying her hair. Then he lent forward and kissed her gently on the neck.

"That was nice, you can do that anytime," she said as she turned to face him and her lips met his in a long lovers kiss. Her body rose from the chair to press hard against his and as she did so the bath sheet slipped from her body exposing her nakedness beneath.

"Of course, we've got a couple of hours before we need to eat," she said and took him by the hand and led him to the bedroom.

Rob suggested a couple of restaurants he thought would meet Sue's requirements. He knew that her choice of clothes was extremely limited, basically it was tee shirt and leggings. So he factored that in knowing how she always insisted on wearing the right clothes for the environment she would be in. Sue chose the Java Sunrise, she had been there before and had always promised herself she would return one day. It was also in a quiet part of the city, well away from the hustles and bustle of the city centre. Rob rang to book a table for two then ordered a taxi for 7:00.

They were shown to their table as soon as they arrived. Rob ordered a bottle of red wine while they studied the menu. Neither of them wanted a starter so they had a long wait before their main dishes were served, giving them time to talk, mainly about Sue's job options.

"Rob, a man over there keeps looking at me. It's making me nervous. I've a feeling I know him from somewhere. He came in just after us, do you think he's following us?"

Rob turned to look in the direction Sue was looking and saw a man in his late thirties or perhaps early forties, sitting at a table on his own. He saw Rob looking at him and rose from his seat to walk towards them. As the stranger approached, Sue and Rob turned to face one another, hoping he would walk straight by, but he stopped at their table and they both looked up at him as he spoke.

"Captain Williams. It is you isn't it? You don't remember me do you? Ryman of the forty fifth Commando, or should I say ex of the forty fifth. You found the man who murdered my wife in Colchester in 2015."

"I do remember you now. Two small children. Wife killed by a drug addict for the contents of her handbag, so he could feed his habit."

"That's right Captain Williams, sir," he was standing ridged to attention.

"Relax soldier and less of the sir, Mr Ryman. Neither of us are in the army now and it's Mrs. Blackstock. This is my husband."

"Sorry miss. Old habits and all that. I'd heard you had bought yourself out and were working for a security company. When I saw you come in here, I was out on the street just opposite. I knew it was you and thought I'll try and speak to you on the off chance to ask you if you had any vacancies. See I left the forces eight months ago and can't find work anywhere. With two nippers to fend for, things are getting desperate."

" I'll see what's available then get back to you."

He wrote on the back of the card and handed it back to her. "I can't thank you enough miss. I'll leave you to your meal now. Sorry for the interruption."

"Well, the cheek of some people," Rob said scornfully. "You're not going to do anything about it are you?"

"He's a desperate man, Rob. His children must be about ten or eleven now. Imagine what it's like having to give up a very promising army career and unable to find work. From what I remember, he was a top marksman and all round quality soldier, I'd certainly hire him myself, no question. I'm going to get in touch with the H.R. department at Williams Security and have them get him in for an interview. It's funny you know, when he first stood up and started to walk towards us all I could think of was being attacked, either shot dead or stabbed . I felt helpless, unable to move."

"Hey, easy girl. This is because of what happened to Tracy on Friday night isn't it?"

"This drugs murder thing is dragging us in Rob, whether we like it or not. We are becoming very involved. It's now getting personal and I think we need to talk to Sir Bernard."

Rob took her hand across the table.

"Firstly I don"t agree that what happened to Tracy was a murder attempt, but it was more likely an attempt to drug you for some reason. They mistook Tracy for you and she had an allergic reaction to what ever it was she was injected with. But I agree it was something directed specifically at you, making it very personal. Are you saying we should change our minds about Sir Bernard's offer of places in his task force and go to Miami, like he wants us to?"

"Yes that's exactly what I'm saying."

"Well for once, I totally agree with you," Rob replied." We can't ignore this. It's not going to go away. I'll ring Sir Bernard's office tomorrow first thing."

"Hello. Good morning."

"Can I help you sir?"

"Yes. Is Sir Bernard Howe in the office today please, I'd like a quick word with him if possible."

"I'll just check for you sir. Who may I say is calling?"

"Robert Blackstock." The line clicked and soft classical music began to play.

"Robert, I thought that you would be calling me when I read a report about Tracy Longhorn. Things could have been very different if you hadn't discovered her when you did and reacted so quickly. Of course very unfortunate for Miss Longhorn, she just happened to be in the wrong place as I understand and was mistaken for Mrs. Blackstock. A shock for her no doubt. How is she?"

"She's made of tough stuff but the reality of what might have been has rattled us both and we want to do something about it. We were wondering if your offer was still on the table?"

"Glad you called me. We are about to launch the team and you are both needed if it is to be successful. One of my very best task force leaders is pulling plans together for a team briefing one week from today. We've pulled in resources from all regions, selecting the very best to create this team and you would fill the two places left. The task is not so much a battle, as a reconnaissance mission. There's no need for us to meet again, I'll speak to Michelle this morning, that's Michelle Rivers, the task force team leader, tell her that you both are now on board and she'll arrange to meet you. I know she is especially keen to meet you Rob, she sees you as key to this whole exercise as do I. Good luck to you both."

Phil had arrived while Rob was talking with Sir Bernard. He was sitting in the kitchen with Sue when Rob walked in. "Darling what did he say?" she asked. "Am I still going with Phil today."

"No reason why not. It's as good an opportunity as you're going to get to see what goes on and I can't see anything here needing your input today. So yes, go."

"We've only got one runner there, in the 3:30," Phil said. "So there's no rush, we don't need to be on the course until mid-day. As far as I'm concerned this is the final part of your training, then all you need to do is practice. You have proven more than capable and I'll tell Eric that when he comes back."

"Thanks Phil," Sue responded. "You're very easy to learn from."

"You two had better not leave it too long," Rob said. "You can never be certain of traffic in London. You can easily be delayed or just whizz through. You don't want to be late."

As they left Rob's phone rang. It was not a number he recognised. He pressed the green button. A woman's voice on the other end said, "Mr. Blackstock? Mr. Robert Blackstock? I believe you spoke with Sir Bernard Howe earlier today. My name is Michele Rivers, Sir Bernard instructed me to ring you today and set up a meeting with me.

"Yes, I'm Robert Blackstock, but please call me Rob."

"Could you possibly come in to see me sometime today, perhaps 2:00?"

"Can we make it a little later say 3:00, I have some business that needs my attention."

"3:00 will be fine. I'm looking forward to meeting, you Rob. Until later then, good bye."

Rob hailed a taxi outside his apartment and was soon sitting in the producer's office at the Warners Studio where, he presented his contract papers for signing.

Business done, he took another taxi to Thames House, the building housing MI-5 head quarters. He was early, it was only 2:40 when he signed in at reception. He sat in reception watching people come and go, until a young round faced girl collected him. They took the lift to the third floor and walked through an open plan office. Ahead were three private offices. One had a brass plaque that read, Michele Rivers, Field Task Officer. The young girl knocked on the door. A voice from within responded.

"Come in." The girl pushed the door open and stepped aside so that Rob could enter.

"Mr. Blackstock?" Michele said standing up and walking out from behind the desk.

"Call me Rob, please," he said walking forward to shake her hand.

"Please, take a seat." She pointed to a couple of easy chairs and a low table behind him. Can I get you a drink, tea, coffee or perhaps a water?"

"No thank you, I'm fine."

"Sir Bernard has been singing your praises for the last month or so. It seems you impressed him with the way you conducted yourself in Russia. So with his recommendation, I'm glad to have you join us. In one week's time, next Monday morning in fact, I have to present my plan to the joint heads of MI-5 and MI-6 for approval and budget authorisation. Sir Bernard had been very clear how we are to approach this."

"Yes, he said to me something about building a relationship with the son of a rich Venezuelan and use that relationship to learn about the father."

"Something like that. It's the basis of the plan I'm working on. We know the son has aspirations to win a major car rally event but has not been successful, whereas you are a former champion. We want to use that to build a bond of trust between you. I'd like to discuss with you how we might best go about that."

"I'm happy to do that of course, but what about Sue, my wife, doesn't she need to hear all this as well?"

"I'm afraid that after recent events at your home, we feel your wife is in danger for some as yet unknown reason, and we are concerned it would be too great a risk, to both her and the operation for her to go into the field with you. Besides we have a role in the team that cries out for someone with her skills."

"I'm not sure I agree with you, but let's go through your plan."

"In outline, we have an agent already established close to our target. Being a woman in a male dominated environment limits what she can do. But posing as a relation of yours, she can get you and your target introduced. Then it's up to you to build a relationship. Your target has entered the Dakar rally for each of the last four years, but always crashed out on day one each time. So, we want you to help him improve and at least finish an event and thus gain his trust. We need you to be invited to his house to find out what his father is up to and to study the place, so that if we need to attack, it we'll know the best route in."

Michele and Rob continued to discuss the plan in increasing detail through the afternoon. Michele made many notes from suggestions Rob made to improve the plan and eventually they agreed that they had something that had at least a fifty fifty chance of succeeding and which should be acceptable to the joint heads. The rest of the team would see it after the presentation on Monday.

"You'll need to be at the presentation to the team on Monday, Rob. They all need a chance to meet you and get to know you. You'll be depending on them while in the field. Between now and then, you'll need to prepare your family for you being away for several months. Do you think your wife would be available sometime to come in and speak with me?"

"She's not going to like not going into the field with me, but I'll deal with that and get her to ring you, first thing tomorrow?"

It was 6:10 when Rob called Sue from the taxi taking him back to the flat.

"Hello darling, how did your day at the races go?"

"It was great, Rob," she replied. "I think I've got a handle on it all. Where the hell are you? You said your meeting would be over by 2:00."

"It's a long story, I'll tell you all about it when I get home in about twenty minutes or so. But we won't be going back to Yorkshire tonight, so Phil might as well be on his way home. You can give some thought to where you want to eat this evening, have a shower and get dressed up. I'll jump in the shower as soon as I get back then we'll need to be off out to eat."

"Sue, are you still in the shower?" Rob called as he entered the flat.

"No, I'm in the bedroom getting dressed." Came the response.

"I'll go straight in the shower then. We've got a lot to discuss this evening."

Chapter 7

"Good evening Michele, I've just received a call from my opposite number in the C.I.A. He says they have seen that over the last week. Someone, assumed to be working for Ernst Luggard, has been checking out Sandra Brown. Her driving licence and driving history have been scrutinised, as has her passport. Someone has even downloaded copies of yearbooks from her high school and college. Agents monitoring two clubs in L.A. have also reported a Latin type woman asking questions about Sandra's days as a stripper. It's good to know how thorough the C.I.A. are in creating a backstory for their undercover agents. Of course using real names and history helps. I'm not sure she was a stripper but probably all the rest is true so we are all pretty certain that, whoever was having her checked out has no idea she's an agent."

****

The lift doors opened and Sue stepped out into the reception area of Thames House. Rob was sat waiting for her. He stood and walked towards her.

"She's a nice lady isn't she? Apparently her son is a junior rank in my old M.P. unit."

"What did she say?"

"She wants me to be her number two and also lead the intelligence group. I told her that Sir Bernard had said we would be traveling as husband and wife but she explained, and although I'm not happy, I can understand why. We talked a lot about your role in all of this and we think it would be wise for you to learn to shoot."

"I grew up in the country. I've been shooting most of my life."

"A shotgun or air rifle yes, but not a hand gun, it's very different! She's going to book a range and I'm going to teach you. Hopefully, we can start next Monday. Oh and we need to be ready to relocate next Monday with bags packed for a six week stay minimum. You, of course, need to pack for Miami. There's four of you going out there but she didn't give me the names of the other three. Now let's get on the road back to Yorkshire, we've got a lot to sort out before next Monday."

They were back in the flat just long enough to grab the things they needed for the journey then into the car and away heading north.

"Rob, we need to tell the children. We should get them home for the weekend and tell them face to face what is going on."

" I was thinking the same. I'll ring them both when we get out of the city traffic. I just hope I can get hold of them. If not I'll try again when we get home. It will be around 5:00 and they should have finished their after school activities by then. Mum and dad are not back for another week. I don't want to worry them with any of this while they're away enjoying their holiday, so I'll write it all in a letter for them to read when they get home. If the kids are back for the weekend, perhaps we can ask Madge to prepare something special for supper on Saturday."

Rob was concentrating on the traffic ahead so didn't see Sue's facial rejection to his suggestion. "It's only mid-September and the weather is good and still promises to be good this weekend. We should make the most of it and all walk down to the Dog and Gun for the evening, Ana and Eva will be singing, they're booked to do most Saturdays now. We can have a nice meal together and talk things through when we get home afterwards. We'll need to be heading back to London on Sunday though, so we can get to Michele's meeting Monday afternoon.

They made good progress despite the heavy traffic and were outside the M25 ring within thirty minutes. As they headed north on the A1 and the traffic volume reduced at each junction, Rob rang Justin. *"The number you have dialed is not in service."*

"What has that boy done with his phone this time? He's broken at least one phone a term since he's been at that school. I'll have to ring the school and get a message to him to ring me." He ended the call and selected Luci from his phonebook and dialed.

"Hello dad, can you be quick? I'm between lessons and only got a few minutes before the next one starts."

"Sure sweetheart. I'd really like you home this weekend. We've really got some important news to tell you that we can't talk about on the phone."

"If you've got Sue pregnant, that's great dad but I just can't be home this weekend. Friday night is just so important. I've been seeing this boy, Peter, He's in the year ahead of me. We've been out a couple of times for coffee and he's asked me to go to a party with him on Friday night. Rachael is going with her boyfriend and I'm going back to her parents 'house after the party. It will be late and we'll both be wrecked on Saturday."

"Okay sweetheart, Sue and I will be away for a few weeks but we'll get together again soon. Just be careful. Love you!"

"Love you too, daddy. Bye."

He pressed the button to end the call. "Well that didn't go quite to plan, did it," he said to Sue.

"They're growing up Rob. You have to give them their own space, otherwise they'll hate you."

"If you say so," he replied then turned to Sue and smiled. "At least the two of us can have a nice evening together and you're right we do need to head for London on Sunday. Then Monday we've got the meeting with Michele and who knows what we'll be doing or where we'll be after that."

Sue's phone buzzed to notify her of the arrival of a message. She pressed a sequence of buttons, then spent several minutes studying the screen very closely. "That's what I thought. He'll do very nicely," she said.

"What are you talking about woman? Who'll do very nicely?"

"Do you remember Ryman?"

"The soldier that interrupted our meal the other night?"

"That's him. Well I was certain I should have remembered something about him so, this morning I rang Williams Security and asked Julie to dig out his army records. She's just sent me the key points from his career. At twenty five he dropped out of medical school after three years and joined up as a medic. He transferred to the marines a year later in 2010. In the following years he represented his unit in both pistol and rifle competitions and was unbeaten in four years. He was selected for the S.A.S, but just days before his transfer, his wife was murdered and he was left with two small children. He left the army at the end of his term two years later and now lives with his parents in Richmond. As we know he has been unable to get a job."

"Why did you want to know all that?"

"Well if I'm not going with you to South America, I need someone I can trust to go with you to watch your back. It's a dangerous place and we're dealing with murderers. I want you to offer Ryman a job as your driver and bodyguard."

"I'm not going to get you to accept a no on this am I?"

"No."

"In that case I'll ring him tomorrow and arrange to see him first thing Monday."

"Thank you darling. I'll sleep easier while you're away, if he accepts."

Tracy Longhorn was released from hospital on Sunday morning; her sister had collected her and taken her home. She had taken her sister and family to the Dog and Gun for Sunday lunch as a farewell meal before leaving for London to join her new team. The sister knew no details of Tracy's secondment, but was happy that her big sister was getting on with her life again after her marriage break up.

Tracy spent a couple of hours with her own two children and there were tears all round when she had to leave.

Early next morning an MI-5 car collected her and her luggage and she was driven to her allocated flat in London. When she entered the flat she saw a note on the coffee table addressed to her. It invited her to a meeting at Thames House with Michele Rivers at 2:30, just two hours from now.

She had never met Miss Rivers but knew her by her reputation for getting things done. Now sitting in Michele's office on a Tuesday afternoon, just days after being close to death, she was looking across the desk at a very well dressed middle aged woman with a no nonsense look about her.

"How are you?" Michele asked. "Are there any lasting effects from your poisoning?"

"I'm still a little tired but each day I feel more like my old self. The doctor's say I should be okay, with no lasting effects."

"That's good news," Michele continued. "We need you fit for the role I have planned for you. I need you out in the field. You have a reputation for being a terrier like investigator. Initially we need you to go to Miami. Our chief suspect is an extremely rich owner of a shipping line and a known drugs shipper. You are to get close to him and find evidence so that we can start proceedings against him. You'll get full details of the plan when we all get together next week at the team briefing. Are you up for it?"

"Yes certainly," Tracy replied. "I'd really like to know how these murders link back to your suspect, but I guess that's my job to find out."

"Exactly," Michele smiled. "You'll be called for the formal team meeting on Monday afternoon and afterwards the team will be relocating to our operations house. You'll need to pack for a few weeks away and can I suggest you get your hair cut short and change the colour. We'll give you papers and back story for a new ID, these people may just have been watching you and a new name and appearance should be enough to throw them. From now on you'll be Viv Turner. Nice to have met you, I hope you get your energy back soon."

Saturday came round all too quickly for Rob and Sue. Sue had spent all three days running the stables as manager, with Phil watching on very closely but not interfering. Then on Saturday morning she said she had business in York that would take most of the day and got in the car and drove off.

Rob had heard from Justin, Saturday was final trials for the school rugby team and he couldn't come home and miss that. So Rob spent his time sorting out things with the academy team so that they could run the business while he was away for what might be several months. Of course he had every confidence that they could cope, but he just wanted to be sure. Anyway Phil would be around until the end of October, if they had any problems.

It was coming up to 5:00 and he was beginning to get concerned that he'd heard nothing from Sue. He had no idea where she was or what she was doing and why wasn't she back yet? He'd tried to ring her twice, but got no response. He was about to try again when he heard a car pull onto the drive and come right up to the front door. He went to the door and opened it to see who had arrived. Expecting it to be Sue, he was surprised to see his two children rushing towards him.

"What's this? You both told me you were busy this weekend."

"We were, but I was only at rugby until lunch time and Sue drove up to get me," JB explained.

"And I made sure I wasn't too late last night, so I would be ready for when Sue picked me up," Luci added. "Peter was totally understanding. In fact he even walked us back to Rachael's house. He's really nice dad, you'll like him." She stepped forward and kissed him on the cheek.

"I rang them both Thursday evening when you were working late,   Rob,
Sue explained. I know how disappointed you were when they said they were both busy."

Sue was right about the weather, it was a beautiful late summer evening, perfect for them to walk down to the Dog and Gun. During the evening Rob explained what he and Sue were about to do and stressed that although they would be away for several weeks, there was no danger. Luci became very tearful but Sue took her off to the ladies and they talked for a while. When they returned to the table Luci sat as close as she could to her dad and Sue gave her a reassuring smile.

The landlord appeared at the front of the small stage in the corner of the pub and tapped on the microphone to get everyone's attention.

"Welcome everybody." He started. "Here at the Dog and Gun tonight, we have something really special for your entertainment. When I heard them rehearse in here this morning, I was taken back to my youth and evenings listening to pirate radio under the bedclothes at night. Here with their Sixties Special are Eva and Ana!" He left the stage clapping as Eva appeared from behind a curtain at the back to the opening bars of '*These Boots Were Made For Walking*'. She was dressed in boob tube, the shortest possible mini skirt and knee high boots. As she faded out at the end of the song Ana, dressed the same, joined her on the stage with her own solo of '*Down Town*' And so they continued for the next hour and a half with hit after hit, all receiving enthusiastic applause from the audience. They ended the evening with Frank Sinatra's '*I Did It My Way*', changing the lyrics to '*We Did It Our Way*'. They left the stage to cries of more, whistles and loud applause. The Landlord, still clapping, came back to the stage. "Thank you Eva and Ana, They're back here again next week folks. But for now I hate to say Last Orders Please."

Ana and Eva walked to Rob's table and sat with them.

"That was great, girls," Sue said. "I hope Sid pays you well."

Ana lent forward and whispered in Sue's ear, "Ten percent of the evenings takings. Almost £400."

"Are you two ready to go back to the stables?" Rob asked Ana. "We can all walk back together."

"Yes, Mr. Blackstock," she replied. "We just need to get our coats and bags. We'll meet you out the front in five minutes."

The pavement ended at the edge of the village and they continued up the hill to the stables walking in single file at the edge of the road. As they reached the limit of light shining from the village street lights, JB turned on his torch to show the grass verge for everyone. Rob turned to thank his son and noticed the headlights of a vehicle behind them at the bottom of the hill. It appeared to be moving slowly forward, matching their own walking pace. As he watched the vehicle suddenly accelerated and raced up the hill dazzling Rob with its lights on full beam.

"Everyone off the road NOW!" he shouted. "Quickly on the grass!"

The urgency in his voice thankfully made everyone instantly react and step off the road onto the verge. Seconds later the vehicle raced by at speed only inches away from them. At the front of the line Eva screamed and fell.

"Eva!" Luci called "Are you okay? Did he hit you."

Eva responded, saying something in Russian.

Ana translated, "She said something hit the back of her arm. It's not bad but she hurt her knee when she fell."

"Who the hell was that idiot?" Sue asked. "Someone who's had too much to drink to be driving, no doubt."

"I don't think so dear," Rob said. "I think that was deliberate."

Ana spoke out, "We remember that car or one exactly the same, don't we Eva? We were out late last Friday night and didn't get home until after two o'clock. When the taxi dropped us at the gate, we saw that car a few yards down the road and someone, a man with beard, was getting in the driver's seat and drove away quickly."

"Friday," Rob said, " the night Tracy was poisoned."

"Justin and Rob," Sue said. "Can you two strong men help Eva up and get her home, she'll need to be carried. I want to check her over and I think a drink is called for each of us."

"I like that idea," JB said smiling.

"Cocoa for you, young man," came Rob's instant response.

The two helped Eva to her feet but her knee hurt when she put weight on it. It was obvious she wouldn't be able to walk the final half mile home, so Rob lifted her in his arms and walked on up the hill with Eva's arms tight around his neck. It had been a long time since he had been this close to a twenty five year old brunette. He breathed in the sweet flowery smell from her hair, mixed with the heavier scent coming up from her body, made slightly musty by the exertions of the earlier stage performance. He thought of his first wife, Jayne. She was a brunette, same age as Eva is when they had first met and so tragically killed by a drunk driver just a few years later. Sue of course is also a brunette, but much older she will be forty in the new year.

"Are you alright, Mr. Blackstock? I'm not too heavy?" Eva asked

Rob just shook his head and smiled at her. He wondered why her Russian accent came so strong when she spoke, but there had been no trace at all earlier when she sang.

When they reached the house Luci unlocked the door and Rob carried Eva through to the lounge and set her down on the sofa.

"Let me have a look at you," Luci said. "I did a first aid course after my exams last term." She felt all around Eva's knee and then her upper arm. Eva pulled away in pain as Luci lifted her arm so she stopped immediately.

"I think the knee is just bruised but it needs an x-ray to be certain. And the arm isn't broken, but I think she may have a whiplash injury. She really needs to go to hospital as soon as possible," Luci insisted.

Sue responded, "We can't take her we've been drinking. Rob call an ambulance."

Ana went with Eva in the ambulance and promised to ring them with news just as soon as the doctors had checked her friend.

It was late. Luci and Justin had taken themselves off to bed and Sue and Rob sat back on the sofa, each holding a large whiskey.

"Well that was a nasty end to an otherwise very enjoyable evening. Let's hope Eva is okay," Sue said.

"Nasty end is an understatement," Rob claimed. "I'm certain that car was deliberately trying to run us all down. It was attempted murder, I'm sure of it. You heard what Ana said, they saw the same car here the night Tracy was poisoned."

"It was a dark colour, maybe black, Toyota Auris," Sue said "Registration AO or AD or perhaps AU, 17 and I didn't get the rest."

"You did well to get that much. I couldn't see a thing once he put his lights up full"

"There was a black Toyota outside the pub where we were waiting for the girls and didn't Ana say the man they saw on Friday night had a beard. Well there was a man drinking by himself in the bar. I saw him when I took Luci to the ladies. I remember thinking poor soul, all alone drinking orange juice and looking serious, when all around everyone was in party mood."

"Would you recognise him again?"

"Definitely. I'll talk to Michelle later and let her know what happened. She may be able to trace the car."

"I doubt that. I don't think you got enough of the reg to get a positive ID. But it's worth a try."

"Why, Rob? Why should anyone want us dead?"

"I've got no idea but I'm sure going to try and find out. One thing that Tracy told me that has stuck in my mind ever since. She said that the drug she had been given wasn't a poison as such. She was so ill because she had an allergic reaction to it."

"If that's the case, then they weren't trying to kill me, after all. But why try to drug me? Did Tracy say what the drug was?"

"Some kind of hypnotic thing, giving the one administering it total power over your actions"

"Okay, so they were not trying to kill me but likewise why would anyone want that sort of control over me. What have I possibly got that someone would want?"

"Is there anything at Williams Security that you were dealing with that they may want to sabotage?" Rob enquired.

"Lots," she replied. "We looked after dozens of visiting heads of state, many from countries on the brink of civil war. Then there's the summit meetings, they are always under attack from various political opposition groups. And of course next year we have the seventy fifth anniversary of D-day in June which will see President Trump make his first visit to England."

"We've got a lot of digging to do in the next few weeks, but we'll keep that list in mind, it could be important."

Chapter 8

"Gabriel, we have a slight problem. I've been removed from the task force. I don't know why. I'm certain they're not on to me and no one has been put in to replace me. Once the team moves into the operations building they will be isolated and I won't be able to report their activities to you. However it does mean I'll be free to hook in to the next Williams Security employee just as soon as you identify a target."

****

Ana rang Rob from the hospital just after 9:00, while he was still sitting at the breakfast table talking quietly to his children and Sue was on her phone updating Michele.

"That's great news Ana. Thanks for letting me know, I'll tell everyone and see you soon." Rob pushed his phone back into his pocket. "That was Ana. Eva is going to be okay. Just bad bruising around her knee and upper arm and she's been given a collar to wear for a couple of days to support her neck. I'm going now to pick them up."

"Can I come with you dad?" Luci asked.

"If you are ready to go because I'm leaving this minute."

"I'm ready."

Sue spoke to Phil and he agreed to take Justin back to Edinburgh after lunch. So Sue did her packing and as much of Rob's as she could. Rob returned after about an hour and a half taking the girls straight to their flat above the stables. He left Luci making them coffee and went to complete his packing. They left after lunch, following Phil and Justin out to the main road, then turning in opposite directions and heading back to London.

At exactly 9:00 Monday morning, the flat's doorbell rang and Theo Ryman stood in the corridor, waiting for the door to be opened. Rob answered the door at the same instant as Ryman pressed the doorbell for a second time.

73

"Ryman come on in." Rob said as he stepped aside to let the visitor enter. He closed the door and gestured for Ryman to go through to the lounge where Sue was sitting with a cup of coffee.

"Ryman, good to see. Take a seat. I was deliberately vague on the phone but we'd like to offer you a job. It's nothing to do with Williams Security but we think you'll be interested. I'll let Rob outline what's happening, then we'll explain where we see you fitting in.

Rob outlined his role in the operation, then Sue explained her concern over Rob's safety. "We're putting out a story that Rob has injured his foot and can't drive so needs a driver," she said. "In reality that driver would be Rob's bodyguard and have his back covered at all times.

A smile crossed Ryman's face and he said, "I'm certainly very interested, though I'm surprised you're offering me the job."

"Not at all," Sue replied. "I strongly believe that there is a reason why things happen and you seeing us go into that restaurant the other evening and deciding to follow us in and come to our table, like you did, was fate. At that time we didn't know there was a job. Will your children be a problem? You could be away for several weeks?"

"They will, but nothing that can't be resolved. My parents are excellent and both in good health and I'm certain will be more than happy to have them for me and the kid's will love it, because they see their grandparents as an easy touch. When do you want me to start?"

"Well, immediately really, this afternoon if possible. You'll need to contact my office as soon as possible," Rob told him. "They will sort out your travel to Miami then on to the film location and someone on the crew will know where you can go to get weapons for yourself and for me. They will also arrange for a hire car which you will collect and pick me up from the airport when I arrive later in the week."

"I assume everything I've heard this morning is confidential and I can't tell anyone what I'm doing?"

"Quite so. You can say you have been hired as my driver, but that's all.

Before he left, Rob gave Ryman a list of names and numbers for his contacts, plus numbers for Michele Rivers, Pippa Johnston and Sir Bernard Howe, in case things go wrong.

Rob stood and walked Ryman to the door. "Good luck Ryman, see you at Miami airport."

Rob opened the door and Ryman called goodbye to Sue as he left.

"Michele, this is Pippa Johnston. You requested a car identification search yesterday."

"That's correct. Sue Blackstock rang me, she believes the car is being driven by whoever poisoned Tracy Longhorn. She also said that this car tried to run her down on Saturday evening. She was walking home in a small group when the car drove at them at speed. One of their party was hit, but thankfully, after spending the night in hospital, she is home again with nothing more serious than whiplash."

"Yes, and I've received notice that the search came up with three possible owners, one of whom is our own Doug Green," Pippa announced."

"He is a good investigator. I originally selected him for 'Operation Polecat', but when Sir Bernard told me Sue Williams was joining the team, I had no need to include him. I told him this on Friday and he was due to meet with me this morning to talk about it, but he didn't turn up," Michele replied. "I've left several messages for him to ring me and reschedule, but so far he's not been in touch. I guess I'll have to send an agent to bring him in."

"There's no need to do that. Doug Green was found dead on the kitchen floor by his wife this morning. It looks suspiciously like some of the other murders, made to look like a self administered heroin overdose. We already have assumed the poisoning of Tracy Longhorn was a mistake and that Mrs. Blackstock was the intended target. Now it appears that Green, having failed at the first attempt, had a second go and failed again. At which point his bosses decided to cut him out."

"Either that or the attempt to run her down was aimed at injuring her so that he would be back on the 'Operation Polecat' team. In which case he was a mole feeding our progress back to his bosses, so that they could stay one step ahead of us all the time. Then when he failed, he was of no further use to them, so they disposed of him to safeguard everything he knew about their operation."

"That's a very good point. So if he was their mole in your team, is there another? And what information has he already passed over?"

"Well there's not a lot of information he could have passed on, because I've only spoken about the plan to three people. The Blackstocks and Tracy Longhorn, Green was already off the team when I did that."

"Good, well keep things tight Michele, until you are certain you can trust your people. I've sent a couple of agents to Green's house to see what they can find. I'll let you know if they uncover anything that may be of use to you."

" Hello, Zoe. I almost didn't recognise you. You've had your hair cut, it suits you," Sue said when she saw a friendly face that she knew as they all assembled in Thames House for the team briefing.

Zoe smiled, "Oh Sue, surprised to see you here! Has Sir Bernard roped you in on this one, too?"

They were interrupted by Michele Rivers. "Ladies and gentlemen I'm glad to see you all. I'm not going to bore you all with mission plans here but get you all across to the operations house and we'll begin the briefing at 7:30 this evening. You transport is ready for you in the parking bay. If you'd all like to get your luggage loaded, we can get moving."

Sue turned to Zoe, "How are you Zoe? That was a nasty business in Russia. It's still less than a month ago and you were out of hospital so quickly. I'm very surprised to see you in an operational team again so soon."

"I'm fine. I've been thoroughly checked over physically and mentally and passed fit, so here I am. I hear you and Rob got married. Congratulations."

"Yes, he caught me at a weak moment." They both laughed and walked on dragging their luggage.

Sue and Michele travelled to the operations house in the same vehicle which gave Sue a chance to talk over a theory she'd been working on for a couple of days.

"Michele, when Tracy was attacked, the analysis of her blood performed by Stuart Patterson at Aldershot reported there was no evidence of heroin at all, but showed she had been injected with QZ-71, a hypnotic drug. Has anyone analysed the blood from the other victims? There may be some clue to what's going on. If we can establish those who died from a heroin overdose, we can say that they were certainly murdered and any that died from a reaction to QZ-71 we can be pretty certain that death was not intended."

"That's very clever thinking, Sue. If we can establish any sort of pattern we could start to understand what this is aimed at."

"Yes, Rob and I were discussing what happened to Tracy, which should have happened to me. She was injected with QZ-71. Obviously, someone wants to have some control over my actions in the future. Rob asked me what I would be doing at Williams Security that someone would want to interfere with, but I can't think of anyone. Having failed in their attack on me, they will most likely target someone else to achieve their goal. The same will be true for those that die from a reaction to this drug."

"We need to get on to this immediately. As soon as we get to Brent House, you and I will contact F.B.I. and Interpol and get them started tomorrow morning on testing whatever samples they've got. I'll call round all our forces, that have reported victims, to get blood samples to Aldershot as soon as possible. You say Tracy Longhorn knows the guy who tested her blood. I'll speak with her and get some information on this drug."

"Welcome to Brent House, to your new home and to 'Operation Polecat'," Michele said, standing in front of a small raised platform at one end of the meeting room, with her team sitting on chairs in a semi-circle around her.

"You have all now had a chance to get to know a little bit about one another over dinner. You should also have recognised that this is not the standard format team we have been members of in the past, but rather a unique team, to solve a rather unique series of crimes. Yes, it is in fact a joint MI-5 MI-6 operation. In truth it goes even further, because we are linked with teams from both the F.B.I. and Interpol. Managing the communications and the relationship with these two fine organisations will be Susan Blackstock. Stand up, please Sue, so that we can all see you. Sue is going to be extremely busy as she is also our lead investigatory analyst and my deputy." Michele pressed a button on her laptop on the table next to her. The screen behind her lit up and the words 'OPERATION POLECAT' were spread across it. She pressed the button again and a word was added. OBJECTIVES. "Everything about these drug murders point to one person. A multi billionaire named Ernst Luggard. He owns Luggard shipping and is said to be one of the top ten richest people in the world. His base is in a remote part of Venezuela, accessible only by helicopter. There is just one footpath in that we know of, but that is guarded by his private army."

The man sat next to Rob put up his hand.

"Yes Brian."

"This private army, what are we talking about? A few men armed with ancient rifles or what?"

"We don't actually know. We believe his base camp is a training camp with some fifty to sixty soldiers. We are also aware of a large camp thirty kilometres outside Caracas. We have monitored transport helicopters transporting men between the two, fifty or so at a time, we can only assume for extra training. It is therefore very possible that we are facing a highly trained unit of three hundred plus troops. The Americans have reported at least one shipment of arms from China being unloaded at the base near Caracas. It is therefore assumed they are armed with the latest technology."

"Why is our intel so vague? Haven't we looked closely with satellite imagery or at least sent a drone in to take a look?" Brian added."

"Firstly the Venezuelan government have banned us flying over their territory. You have to remember this is a very new country, very politically unstable, rapidly becoming rich through its oil sales, but still run by rich men who got rich through drug trafficking. People like Ernst Luggard pull the strings. Secondly, both camps operate signal jamming systems which interfere with the drones and prevent us using satellite imagery. The only clear pictures we have are of extensive new vineyards around the base camp, plus what we believe to be an extensive training area, covered by camouflage nets."

She turned back to the screen. "Our objectives are quite clear: To discover what Luggard is hoping to achieve from all these murders and stop him. To do that we need to uncover his plans, find a weakness in his defences and go in and neutralise his organisation."

Michele then handed each member of the team a briefing pack, outlining their role in some detail and a simple statement of what other members of the team would be doing, not enough information to be of any great use if there was another mole in the team.

"Tracy, I didn't recognise you. What have you done to your hair?" said Rob.

"It's my new image. Soon to be a divorced woman and all that" she replied as Sue walked over to join them.

"Get off, he's mine," she joked. "Hi Tracy. Like the hair, suits you. Makes you look quite sexy. So you, Mr. Blackstock keep your hands off. Are you fully recovered Tracy?"

"Thanks Sue. Yes, I'm fully recovered and I like the new look too. I appear to be stepping into your shoes. When this plan was outlined to me last week, you were to be travelling as Rob's wife, now I'm going instead."

"Yes, but you're only going as his P.A., hands off," Sue concluded and they both smiled.

Rob turned to Sue and said, "I see you've got Zoe with you. She was good in Russia wasn't she?"

"She was very good. We could have done with her on the chase down south on those dreadful roads. Pity she was injured so early in the mission."

Michele spoke with her team in small groups.

"Rob and Tracy, you two know one another quite well, but do you know Julie and Roger? The four of you are booked on a scheduled flight to Miami tomorrow morning, leaving Heathrow at 9:30. Rob you will need to arrange transport for you and Tracy from the airport, to wherever your film crew are located."

"Already done boss, just need to confirm day and flight," Rob answered.

"Good man," she said. "Roger and Julie you are booked on a connection to Caracas and then on a domestic flight to Ciudad Bolívar, then finally you will take the local flight to Canaima. I'm afraid this will be via a small twin propeller plane, over some rough terrain and the turbulence is nearly always bad, so I hope neither of you get airsick. At Canaima you will be met by Rev. Clive who will be your host. Your cover story is you are brother and sister missionaries who have volunteered to work with Rev. Clive for a few months and you are keen to do some exploring while you are there. But of course your real purpose is to find routes that troops could use in an assault on Luggard's property. All details and your cover background story are in your briefing pack. We have already dispatched two trail bikes to help you get around, but they might take a couple of weeks to get to you. Canaima is a four hour river boat ride from the falls, so you'll need the bikes. Right, any questions?" No one answered.

Michele added, "That's good. Now don't forget this is very remote country, communications are slow and very public. You all have satellite phones for emergencies, but for normal comms back here, send coded messages to Uncle James at Cardale House etcetera. Good luck."

"I didn't think you would be going as soon as tomorrow," Sue said when they were finally alone together, on their way to their room. "Just remember you are there to get information, so that others can get in and do the job. Don't be a hero. We haven't had time for me to teach you to shoot."

"Didn't you say Ryman was a marksman? He can teach me."

"That should be okay. Just make sure it happens."

"So you won't miss me then?"

"What do you think?" She gave him a quick peck on the cheek.

"Well if I'm leaving for Heathrow at 4:30 in the morning we'll have to set the alarm for 4:00. Will you get up to see me off?"

"No, but I'll give you something now to make you want to come back soon," she said pulling him towards their bedroom.

Chapter 9

"Michele, my agents searched Doug Green's home yesterday. Someone had been there first and taken his laptop's hard drive and made a total mess of the place, searching for something. But my chaps found his secret hiding place and his drug stash, two boxes. I've had them analysed overnight and they prove what your team have been thinking, is on the right track. One batch showed to be a mix of heroin and QZ-71 and the other highly concentrated heroin which would certainly bring about heart failure.

My agents also found a D.V.D. and a couple of lists of names, I'll get them sent over to you this morning.

This QZ-71 is some funny stuff. I've spoken with Stuart Patterson at the lab about it. It doesn't actually hypnotise you but makes you very susceptible to being hypnotised. The slightest attempt could put you under. However the mortality rate is around twelve per cent so it never went into full production. It was believed that all samples had been destroyed, but obviously that is not the case."

****

It was coming to the end of Eric and Rose's cruise. They had left the Mediterranean and were heading north, leaving the west coast of Portugal and Spain just over the horizon off the starboard side, and now getting tossed about in the Bay Of Biscay. Eric said,

"This stretch of water is possibly the roughest place in the world and I can well believe it. I don't remember ever crossing in smooth waters. Just look out the window. We must have at least a five metre swell out there."

"Well, I hope it stops soon," Rose replied. "I don't like it when the boat is moving up and down like this. At the moment, I don't know whether I'll feel like dinner this evening, my stomach is heaving around almost as much as the sea out there."

"You do need to try, dear. Remember we've been invited to sit at the Chief Engineer's table this evening. It's your last chance to wear a posh frock and outshine all the other ladies."

"Maybe in your eyes, you old devil, but I've never outshone anyone in my life."

"Just one day left, where have the last three weeks gone? We've seen so many things and done so much in such a short time, it doesn't seem possible that this time tomorrow, we'll be back home."

"And you and I will need to go on a diet as soon as we get back. You must have put on a stone, eating all day every day," Rose commented.

"Don't worry dear, I'll soon be back to my best fighting weight working around the yard. Phil will be leaving in less than three weeks and I haven't found anyone to replace him yet. So I'll be back doing the manager's job until I can get someone in."

"Isn't there someone already working there, who could be promoted?" Rose asked.

"Not anyone I could completely trust," Eric replied. "What would be really good is if I could get Sue to take it on. I know she wants to move up to Yorkshire. She's wonderful with horses. She raced when she was much younger, so knows that side of the business and will know how a yard runs. She must also have some good management skills to have been a captain in the army. Phil could show her the basics in the time he has left before he leaves, then, until she's fully up to speed, I could oversee her."

"Then why don't you ask her?"

"I intend to, as soon as I get home."

Sandra Brown had been undercover posing as Kurt Luggard's girlfriend for about six weeks. She was enjoying the life of a playboy's woman, expensive clothes and jewels showered on her and in return, all she had to do was to keep her body looking good for him to show off at his side, whenever he was in public view. In private he had no interest in her sexually; he was gay and was in a new relationship with a well-known actor who was certainly very keen to keep their private life out of the media. Over the weeks he had known her Kurt's relationship with Sandra had become more than a business arrangement. He realised that she was a very bright girl and he could trust her opinion on things. He knew that his father would, by now, have had someone check out her history and would have said something if anything suspicious was found.

This was Sandra's first solo undercover operation. She had been recruited into the F.B.I. as an analyst just three years ago and had soon been transferred into operations, where she had performed well, as a team member, in several operations.

"You could have been killed this time, Kurt! The car is in bits and Tony may never walk again," Sandra said standing next to him, lying in a hospital side ward at Miami Central Hospital. "If you're going to continue racing, you need to get some help to improve your driving skills. You are having too many accidents."

"I'm going through a run of bad luck at the moment, that's all. Get through it and I'll start winning," Kurt replied as the door opened and a doctor crossed the room to the bed side.

"Mr Luggard," The doctor said. "You don't appear to have done any serious damage to yourself. You'll need to take it easy for a week or so because I think there is some mild concussion. Your navigator has not been so lucky. We won't know the full extent of his spinal injuries for some days, but it doesn't look good. We can't start tests until he regains conscious and can talk to us."

"You see Kurt. You were very lucky," Sandra said. "If you want to compete at the highest level you need some help."

"I just need a few more races under my belt," he insisted. "You know nothing, woman."

Sandra was quick to see her opening and launched straight in. "I know more than you think. I was taught to drive by my Uncle Robert. He was a British Rally champion at eighteen, after winning nine out of twelve events in the championship. He could show you areas that you could improve in. At least speak to him sometime."

"I'm sorry, I guess it would do no harm to speak to him, I know you mean well. Thank you," Kurt conceded. "Do you know how to get hold of him?"

"I can ring his office and see where he is. He travels all over the world. I know he is quite often here in Miami."

As they walked though arrivals at Miami airport Rob was looking out for Ryman, but could not see him among the crowd waiting to greet their passengers , loved ones, family or friends. His first thought was to curse the man for not getting there on time, but that thought was interrupted by the public address system.

"Will Mr. Robert Blackstock and companion please go to the V.I.P. exit where your onward transport is waiting for you."

Rob looked at Tracy with a questioning expression.

"There," she said pointing over his shoulder.

It was just five metres behind him. So they turned away from the press of the other arrivals and pulled their cases through a slowly revolving door, to be greeted by a smartly dressed Ryman on the outside, standing next to a highly polished black BMW with the boot and rear door open.

"Welcome to Miami, sir, miss," he said in greeting. "I thought this would save you having to haul your heavy luggage across the car park after your long flight, sir."

"Thank you, Ryman," Tracy said as she left her luggage for him to load into the car boot. "And please call me Tracy."

"Sorry, Miss. Can't do that, I know my place. It wouldn't be proper."

Rob smiled to himself as he turned and watched Tracy climb into the back seat of the BMW. *"Wow just look at that arse!* "he thought to himself. *"Just as firm as it was all those years ago."* A little voice in his head replied. *"Don't touch, you are a married man."*

Ryman closed the boot and climbed into the driving seat. "It's about a forty five minute drive to the location camp. You have been allocated a three bed trailer sir. I've not had chance to check it out yet, as I only arrived myself six hours ago and with collecting the car, sorting out the V.I.P. pick-up and collecting those other two items you wanted, there just wasn't enough time to get out there and back."

"I'm sure Mr. Blackstock's staff will not have let us down and the trailer will be fine," Tracy said. "If you only arrived six hours ago, you've done very well to have done all that you have."

"Thank you Miss," he replied. "But it wasn't all down to me. Mr Chuck Tanner ordered and paid for everything. All I had to do was collect things and sort out the VIP pick-up."

"Chuck is my crew boss out here," Rob added. "Been with the company a long time. Very loyal and completely trust worthy. I rang him last evening and told him the whole story."

Tracy gave Rob an uncertain look, then continued. "We can't keep calling you Ryman. What would you like us to call you?"

"Ryman will be fine, Miss."

Roger andJulie had both been brought up in strict catholic families so were well suited to the roles they would be playing. Their cover story was that they were son and daughter of a country parson in North Yorkshire and the MI-5 back room staff had laid out a very reasonable profile for each of them, if ever anyone were to look.

Rev. Clive was a man in his early sixties, with a round face to match his round body, obviously a man who enjoyed his food. When an MI-6 agent posing as the secretary to The Roman Missionary Service approached Rev. Clive with the idea of Roger and Julie spending three months with him in Venezuela, helping him in his mission work, he readily jumped at the opportunity and even offered to meet them at the airstrip.

"That guy over there fits Rev. Clive's description that we were given, Roger." Julie said as they walked across the tarmac dragging their bags, she was pointing a round faced man dressed in a black shirt and black trousers.

"Rev. Clive?" Roger asked as they closed on the man waiting.

"Indeed! Indeed!" The old man responded. "You must be Roger and the lovely lady behind you is Julie, yes? Let me take your bag, my dear girl." Without another word he reached out and took Julie's case from her, as if it were empty. "Do follow me, I have my car, we should be home before dark, if we get away quickly."

In the car park there was just one car and Rev. Clive headed straight towards it. A 1970's Toyota estate, with faded yellow paintwork, dented body panels and large patches of rust. "Can one of you sit in the front, please?" Rev. Clive said as he lifted the boot lid to load the luggage. "There's a spring broken in the seat behind the driver and I'm told it's very uncomfortable to sit on. We've got about thirty minutes of daylight left which should be enough. It's a good three miles to my lodge and only twenty minutes to get there, so hopefully we'll be as quick getting back. The lights on this old thing haven't worked in the last five years."

With all of the luggage loaded the boot was too full for the lid to close so Rev. Clive left it open, climbed into the driver's seat and started the engine. To Roger's surprise it started first time and sounded good, which was more than could be said about the gear box as they moved off and there was a horrible squeaky noise, as the boot lid bounced up and down, when they hit the first bump in the road.

"Perhaps Roger can look at your car lights for you Rev. Clive," Julie said from the back seat. "He's good at fixing things."

"Oh, I know why they don't work, my dear. I took the bulbs out to use in the lodge. Far more important to be able to read the words of our Lord in the evening than to drive a car after dark."

They arrived at the village just twenty minutes later and Rev. Clive stopped outside a rough shack that reminded Roger of the stables at the farm where he grew up. "Welcome to the vicarage and this is my housekeeper, Sun Rise," he said, holding out his hand towards a spindly woman in her fifties, walking towards them.

"I rang my uncle's London office this morning, Kurt. You're in luck. Uncle Robert has got a crew working on a new Tom Cruise movie here in Miami and he's out here to see how it's going. They gave me his personal cell number, so I'll ring him and arrange for us to meet," Sandra was slowly edging Kurt to where they wanted him to be.

"I still can't see what he can do. I just need more experience," Kurt argued.

"Just agree to talk to him. I know we've only been together for a few weeks, but I hope you agree, I've always acted with your best interest in mind."

"You do very well out of our arrangement, so don't push it! I'll speak to this man but that's all I promise to do."

Michele called Sue and Zoe into her office, to talk over Sue's theory about the drug deaths being accidental or intended. They talked to Stuart Patterson at the Aldershot research lab and through Pippa, they were able to agree that any sample received, labelled 'Polecat', would be given highest possible priority and that copies of all results would be sent to Zoe and Sue.

Michele contacted each of the seven forces across the UK that had reported deaths and instructed them to send blood samples to Aldershot, as soon as possible.

Within a few hours, the first results from the London force arrived. Of the eight cases they had reported, one body had already been cremated so no sample was available, five were genuine overdoses, one, a crown court judge, was a reaction to QZ-71. The final sample showed QZ-71 in it, but death was caused by an overdose.

"If my theory is correct, then we can assume that whoever is behind all this, needs a crown court judge, to make whatever they want to do happen," Sue concluded.

Zoe added, "All seven samples contained traces of heroin. I'm not sure what that tells us. What do we now do with our conclusion?"

They took their finding to Michele. "It's not for us to do anything ladies. We hand the facts to Pippa for her to follow up. Almost certainly she'll be monitoring crown court judges; every one of them must be considered a suspect."

"And the five overdoses we can assume were all dealers," Zoe added.

"We don't know why they are doing that, either," said Michele.

Sue piped up with, "I think I do. They are replacing dealers with their own people, where the dealer is supplying someone they want to target. These supply that client with supplies laced with QZ-71. These clients then take the drug unknowingly."

"There you go again, Sue." Michele added. "Another step forward. Sir Bernard was right to insist you were added to the team."

"So any death caused by an overdose, we assume to be a dealer and we should be looking for a client list and seek out anyone on that list who have important roles," Sue said.

"That's not going to be easy, if at all possible," Zoe added.

"We all at least need to try. I've got six members of the team out with the regional forces, trying to put some order into this mess. I'll update them and get them to push for details as quickly as they can. I'll get onto now," Michelle stated. "We need to do everything possible to identify probable targets, it may lead us to identify what these people are up to."

Madge greeted Eric and Rose on their return and the taxi driver was kind enough to carry their cases into the house and set them down in the hallway. Eric paid him and added £5 as a tip.

"Welcome home, I guess you would like a cup of tea?" Madge said. "I'll put the kettle on. Come through to the lounge and relax. I've got a fresh Victoria sponge cake; I'll bring you a couple of slices."

"Where are Rob and Sue?" Eric enquired. "I half expected them to be here when we got back."

"I don't actually know, London I think. Mr Robert left you a letter, it's on the mantle." Madge pointed to an envelope marked Mum and Dad.

Eric opened the letter and read it slowly to Rose.

"Well, they're off again, like James Bond," Eric said as he pushed the paper back into the envelope. "He says it could be several months, but they'll be in touch as often as possible."

Phil had heard a car on the gravel drive and came into the house. "How was your cruise?" he asked. "Did you have a good time?"

"Yes, thanks," Rose answered. "Too much to eat. I've put on at least half a stone, so need to go on a diet now we're home."

"Everything okay at the stables?" Eric asked.

"Couldn't be better," Phil replied "We've had a string of winners and two new clients signed up. Seven new horses. We're at full capacity."

"Well done," Eric smiled. "I'm going to miss you when you go to India. Have you got a leaving date yet? And any thoughts on a replacement.

"Has Rob spoken to you?"

"No, Why?"

"Well, Sue is interested in taking it on. She has spent several days shadowing me and last week I gave her total charge and just watched. She's very good as you might expect. She needs time to gain experience but I'd certainly back her to make a success of it."

"That's very strange. I was only talking to Rose yesterday and saying I wonder if she would be interested. You know about this MI-6 thing they are off on, do you?"

"Yes, they gave me an overview. It will of course mean Sue couldn't take over until maybe as late as Christmas."

"So I'll be two to two and a half months without a manager. I suppose I could do it myself in the short term, it is only ten weeks or so. Might make a nice change."

Sandra rang her uncle and after a few minutes she held out the phone to Kurt. "Kurt, I've got Uncle Robert on the phone, will you talk to him please? He says he needs to ask you a few questions."

"Pass me the phone; let's see what he wants to know. Mr. Blackstock, Sandra tells me you have some questions for me."

"Just a couple of basic questions, Kurt. Call me Rob. Can I call you Kurt?"

"Okay."

"Thank you, Kurt. Firstly who taught you to drive and did they have rally experience?"

"No one, really. I learnt as a youngster, driving around the family estate in various estate vehicles, then a family friend got me into rallying."

"I see," Rob said thoughtfully. "Do you have the same navigator every time?"

"No," Kurt said abruptly.

"Well, rallying is a team sport. It may be the driver's name that goes on the trophy, but it's the team that gets him there. Even more so as the difficulty increases the navigator has the hardest role. They need to become your closest friend, know your limitations and what the car is capable of. They are not there to balance the weight in the car and read a map. They have to learn about the route and tell you what action is needed. When you approach a bend he will tell you how severe the corner, is what gear you need to be in and what speed you should enter the bend at."

"But I'm the driver, I say what gear to be in and what speed we travel at."

"Then you'll never win a big rally," Rob argued. "You can't expect to remember every rise and fall of the road and every corner in a rally stage, but your navigator can read it out to you as you go."

"My reactions are good. I can adjust my speed to what I see at the time and change gear when I need to."

"The first thing we need to improve is your attitude. I suggest we meet and I can see you drive. I've noticed several isolated tracks near where I am with the film crew. If you can bring a car to me, I will guarantee to improve your driving by ten per cent in a matter of hours."

"Let me have your location," Kurt suggested. "I can be there at dawn on Saturday, if you are free?"

"I can be," Rob replied. "I look forward to meeting you. And you had better put some thought to who can be your navigator, ideally someone who knows you well."

As the blood results came in from the lab in Aldershot, Sue and Zoe tried to build a picture from them. It was obvious from the failed attempt on Sue that whoever was behind this, wanted to control someone in Williams Security, presumably to interfere with something or someone the security company was supposed to protect. The attack on Tracy was the only case where the results showed no trace of heroin. All the others contained heroin only in high concentration, sufficient to cause death or a combination of heroin and QZ-71. All the victims appear to have been regular heroin users, so Sue came to the conclusion that QZ-71 was being added to heroin supplies and the users had no idea what was happening.

When Pippa Johnston's agents arrived to search Doug Green's house in Hammersmith, they found it had been ransacked. Drawer contents were strewn everywhere, a laptop's hard drive had been removed and upholstery had been ripped open. Clearly someone was desperate to remove anything that could lead back to them. The agents were both very experienced and began their own search. For a long time they searched, but found nothing, until under a rug in the master bedroom they discovered some loose floorboards. Under the boards they found a large roll of £20 notes, two shoe boxes filled with small bags containing what appeared to be drugs. They also found a D.V.D. labelled 'Birdbath Master', beneath this were two lists of names, twenty plus names on one list and a few less on the other. Each list had numbers next to the names. All of the items were brought back to Pippa Johnston at Thames House. She sent the contents of the two boxes to Aldershot for immediate analysis.

y the next morning, Pippa had received an email with the lab report on the contents of the boxes. She called Michele and told her about the results and also that her agents had found a D.V.D. and two lists of names that Michele should have her team look at.

When Michele told Sue and Zoe about the discovery of the drugs and the results of the analysis, Sue said, "Okay, but if these people are injecting themselves with QZ-71 unknowingly, who is introducing the trigger word and how are they doing it? Maybe that D.V.D. and those lists will help us understand a little bit more."

A short while later the package from Pippa arrived Michele handed it straight to Zoe. "Here girls, take a break from test results, Pippa has just sent this stuff over. It was found in Doug Green's house. Pippa hopes we can make sense of it." Michele said and tipped the contents out onto Zoe's desk. "That's funny I thought Pippa said two lists. I'll give her a call to check."

"While you and Miss Tracy were out for lunch, sir," said Ryman as Rob and Tracy came back to the trailer laughing at something. "Mrs. Blackstock rang."

"I wonder why she didn't call my mobile? Thank you Ryman I'll ring her back straight away."

"No, sir. She rang to speak to me. She wants me to teach you how to use your hand gun. I've taken the liberty of booking a lane at the Miami Gun Club for 9:30 tomorrow, sir."

"A total waste of time. I can shoot perfectly well. I've handled guns all my life. But I guess a little practice will do no harm. Thank you Ryman."

Chapter 10

"Father, I have received a message from Gabriel telling me to warn you that two British agents will be visiting you soon. They will be invited by Kurt. They bring you danger. Their mission is to discover details about our operation here, in London and in Washington and to stop you. They will be trying to find weaknesses in the defence of Angels' Rest and learn about our military strength. Gabriel warns you not to stop them because the British are stupid and will just send more agents. Better for you to welcome them and let them find what they want, but make sure that the information they find is wrong and Gabriel will destroy the evidence at the London end, to confuse the investigation. The agents' names are Tracy Longhorn and Robert Blackstock. Gabriel also says Kurt's new girlfriend is C.I.A."

****

"How are things going with 'Polecat Pippa'?" Sir Bernard was at Thames House for their weekly heads of department meeting. "I was expecting an update from Michele this morning, but nothing has come through yet and I have a meeting later with the defence secretary and the P.M."

"I'm sorry Bernard, but I'm still short staffed here. Michele sent me an update yesterday evening, I just haven't had a chance to get a copy across to you yet." Pippa Johnston protested.

"Well, I'm here now, so talk me through it," he suggested.

"Well Sir Bernard, I'm pleased to say we have made quite a bit of progress. Thanks to Susan Blackstock, Michele's team appear to be gaining an understanding of the overdose murders and now testing and developing their theories. Robert Blackstock is in America and has reported that he will be meeting Kurt Luggard tomorrow. By now my two agents will be in Venezuela, but it's far too soon for anything to be coming from them. Michele has got the rest of her team out in the regions, trying to gather as much info about the victims as they can."

"I'm glad we managed to get the Blackstocks on board for this one. They are both valuable people who make a huge contribution."

"Yes, they are both contributing a great deal. I'm sorry you didn't get a copy of Michele's report, I'll speak to my admin people and ask them to ensure you are copied in every week."

Rob stood and watched Ryman check the two hand guns. He hadn't asked where he had got them, but assumed they were not legal. That was confirmed when Ryman handed him one and he saw the serial number had been filed off. He pulled the ammunition clip out of the handle, checked it had a full complement of eight rounds and slid it back.

"Right Sir, I've set the target at the fifty metre distance. If you'd like to show me what you can do. Fire all eight rounds at the target, in your own time."

Rob stood side on to the target, held the Glock tightly in his right hand and raised his right arm out straight. He squinted along the barrel and squeezed the trigger. He was surprised at the amount of recoil and lowered his arm before raising it again for the second shot. He repeated the process until all eight shots had been fired.

"Let's see how well you've done, sir" Ryman pressed the button to bring the target in for inspection.

The image of a man standing facing the shooter showed one hole in the upper right arm, one in the lower stomach, one in the right thigh, one grazing the right foot and one in the paper but not in the image of the man, there was no sign of the other three shots.

"Well sir, you certainly will have slowed him down a bit and given him a serious limp. But I must say your style is all wrong for a weapon like this. You'd be alright fighting a duel perhaps, or shooting at a fairground, but not in a serious life threatening situation. Let me show you."

Ryman mounted a fresh target and pressed the button to send it out to the fifty metre mark. Then facing the target, the gun in his right hand resting in his left hand, he stretched out both arms and bent his knees slightly. He looked straight along the spine of the Glock and fired off eight rounds in rapid succession. Rob pressed the button to recall the target. There were two neat clusters of holes.

Four in the lower forehead between the eyes and four in the central chest. Both clusters could have been covered by an egg cup.

"Sue said you were good. I can see now how right she was," Rob applauded.

"Reload your clip, sir and have another go standing as I did. The two handed grip prevents most of the recoil and having the gun in front of you gives a better line to aim and stop you straying off to the right. By bending the knees you will make your body steadier, resulting in greater accuracy as well as presenting a smaller target for whoever is shooting at you."

"I'll try it. Set up another target."

When Rob's next target was brought in eight holes were visible, four in the chest two in the groin and two in the edge of the paper.

"Well, this one won't have children," Rob announced and they both chuckled. "Set up another".

Each time a target was brought in and checked they showed an improvement over the previous one. Rob shot at nine targets in total during their session and with the final three he was happy to see all eight hit the figure drawn on the paper target. The groupings were not very tight but in each case the foe would most likely be dead."

"Can I suggest we practice some more another day, sir, but I'll report to Miss Susan that you could at least stand your own in a shoot out."

"Rev. Clive come quick!" Sun Rise said excitedly as she ran into the lounge where Rev. Clive was drinking tea with Roger and Julie. "Come quick! Big package on lorry for you."

Rev. Clive and the two agents followed the excited house keeper through the kitchen and out into the street. Parked right outside the door was an ancient and very battered pickup truck with a very large wooden shipping crate on the back.

"That looks like it's the two motor bikes our uncle was shipping out for us,"Roger suggested. "I expected them to take far longer to get out here."

"Excuse me, I'll go and get a couple of men to come and open the crate and unload it, then we can see exactly what we do have. But I suspect you are correct Roger," Rev.Clive said as he walked off.

As soon as Rev. Clive was out of earshot, Julie asked Roger. "Now that the bikes have arrived, how long do you think we should wait before we go off and do what we came here to do and find a route to the top of the falls."

"We need to be careful. We don't want anyone getting suspicious and word getting back to the wrong people." Roger spoke quietly as he watched Rev. Clive return with three strong looking young men. The men broke open the crate and two trail bikes were lifted down.

"These will help us get around the outlying homesteads," Roger said to Rev. Clive, "and our uncle is leaving them for you when we leave."

"He's very generous. You've seen my car, I think one day soon I will be giving it the last rites."

After dinner, Julie went to help Sun Rise clear away in the kitchen and Roger took the opportunity to talk to Rev. Clive. "Rev, do you have a place you go to when you want to be closer to God?"

"I do, but why do you ask my son?"

"Our uncle told you that our father was killed in a light aircraft crash, but did he also say that Julie's husband was the pilot and was also killed?"

"No, I didn't know that."

"As you can imagine, our faith has been challenged, more so for Julie. I just think if we can get away for a few days somewhere, where we can be closer to God, we can rebuild our faith."

" Of course you must go. I'll show you where on the map. It's about ten kilometres away. When will you go?"

" I was thinking we'll help you with the services over this weekend, do the schools on Monday then go after that. Just three or four days."

"You must go as soon as you see fit and stay as long as you need to. Your faith is important. I'll speak to Sun Rise for her to pack up provisions for you both."

Julie came in from the kitchen and as Rev. Clive turned to see her, Roger gave the thumbs up behind his back.

Rob sat on the bonnet of the car waiting for Kurt to arrive. Ryman was busy wiping the car over to remove road dust, keeping up the pretence he was a proper driver. They could see a good two miles back down the road towards Miami and there was no sign of Kurt, so Rob decided he had time to give Sue a call. Taking his phone from his pocket, he pressed his thumb on the security button, then selected the icon to display his contact list. He had it organised so that Sue was at the top of the list. He listened to the number dial through then heard it ring.

"Hello darling. You've got perfect timing this morning, I'm just having a quick coffee break and girly chat with Zoe and Michele. It must be very early there. Why are you up, couldn't you sleep?"

"Good morning, darling, I've been up for hours. Ryman and I are sitting at the roadside just a few miles north of Miami waiting for Kurt Luggard to arrive for our first meeting." Rob heard a strange noise on the line, rather like a piece of hot metal being dropped into a bath of water. "Sue, Sue are you still there?" he looked questioningly at the screen of his phone. "Must have lost the signal," he said to himself.

A few minutes later a pick-up truck, with a rally car on a trailer behind it, pulled off the highway where they were waiting and Rob walked over to greet them. "Hello Sandra, you look good. It must be two years since I last saw you," Rob said to keep the cover story going.

"Hello, uncle Robert, yes it must be at least two years." Sandra said keeping up the pretence. "May I introduce my boyfriend, Kurt Luggard."

Rob looked past Sandra to the driver of the pick-up. "Good morning Kurt."

"Good morning Mr. Blackstock."

"Rob, please."

Kurt smiled. "Is this track okay? It runs exactly six kilometres down to a deserted cabin."

"It looks fine. Now get the car off and we'll get started," Rob instructed. He wanted to finish his conversation with Sue so he dialed her number again. He could hear it ring, but no one answered.

Kurt lowered the ramps at the back of the trailer and reversed the rally car down and drove it into a position facing down the track. Then he reached for something on the back seat. "Sandra said you were about the same build as me so I hope these fit," he said, handing Rob a set of racing overalls and a helmet.

"Very thoughtful of you," Rob said pulling the overall up over his jeans and tee shirt. "I suggest we drive slowly down the track, seeing what hazards we face. Then we'll come back here and see what you can do."

They climbed into the front seats of the car and were soon slowly driving down the track. Rob writing notes in a small book. When they reached the cabin they turned round and returned to the highway."Right if you're ready, let's see what you can do. Ready, three, two, one, go!"

With wheels spinning as the tyres tried to find a grip on the dirt track, Rob pressed the button to start his stop watch and they raced off to the first corner.

As they slid to a halt in front of the cabin Rob stopped the watch. "Four minutes and eight seconds. How do you think you did?" Rob asked.

"I'm pretty happy with that, I don't think anyone could do it much faster," the driver responded.

"Well, what if I tell you that your next run will be much faster? Now turn us around and take us back to the start. Have you got a navigator yet?"

"I have, but he couldn't make it here this morning. He is very keen to help. He and I have known one another for many years."

"Right, for the next run I'm going to be your navigator and you are going to drive according to my instructions. But first you need to learn the language of rallying." Rob began. "It's all quite simple.

Just think of a clock face, when I call fifty 1:00 loose full in, six out full, I'm telling you that fifty metres ahead there is a slight bend right, the surface of the track is loose, probably gravel but certainly not tarmac you should enter the bend at full throttle and be in sixth gear as you exit and the throttle should be full. Do you understand what I'm saying?"

"I think so," Kurt was looking a bit doubtful. "All I have to do is drive as fast as I can with those instructions.

"Okay. What does this mean, one hundred 10:00 hard, slow in, three out?"

Kurt thought for a few seconds then said. "In one hundred metres the road turns sharp left on Tarmac, I need to brake into the bend and exit in third gear accelerating hard."

"You are right, but you'll have to interpret a lot quicker," Rob told him. "Of course the language can be changed to suit you and your navigator but you need to keep it simple and brief."

"Where does the navigator get the information from and how does he know about speed and gears etcetera," Kurt asked.

"You and he must drive the course slowly and you tell him how each obstacle should be taken. He notes distance, surface and direction and adds from you, how the corner is to be driven. Clear?"

"Perfectly. I understand now why the relationship is so important. There has to be a lot of trust between driver and navigator."

"Now then, when you did that very first slow drive down, I was making navigator notes," Rob lied. He'd actually made his notes the evening before. "So get yourself ready and we'll race again but this time I'll call the moves. Are you ready? 3, 2, 1, go."

They raced down to the cabin again. As they slid to a stop Rob asked, "How was that?"

"To be honest, it felt much the same. I felt I was still driving on the limit."

"Well, your time was three minutes twenty three seconds. Thirty five seconds quicker. Of course you've done the course several times now, so you would be bound to be a little quicker but only two or three seconds." Kurt nodded his acceptance and they returned to the start.

"How did he do, Uncle Rob?" Sandra asked.

"I think we've had a major win today and things can improve if Kurt finds a good navigator and they work hard together. I next need to work on his driving style, there's a lot of improvement that can be made there as well. What do you say Kurt? Do you want to win? I can make you a winner. Come back with me now and we can start work."

Sue was in almost total darkness, her ears were ringing and her head hurt as if she had been kicked by a horse. It took her a while to realise what had happened. She had been in the dining room having a coffee with Zoe and Michele and she had been talking on her phone with Rob. She remembered an explosion then nothing until now. She had no idea how long she had been lying like she was, nor what had happened to Zoe and Michele. She rolled carefully onto her back and touched another person. "Is that you, Sue?" It was Zoe's voice.

"Yes it's me, Zoe. Thank god you're alive. Are you hurt?"

"I don't think so. I seem to be covered in what I think is broken glass and my shoulder is all sticky. I think I may be bleeding but I don't have any pain. What happened? Where are we? Is Michele here?"

"Hang on I'll use the lamp on my phone to see where we are." Sue reached into her pocket. "Bugger! I was on the phone to Rob, there was an explosion and I must have dropped my phone."

"It's okay, I've got mine." In the light of Zoe's phone they could make out that they were boxed into a space about two metres square and one metre high. Their prison walls and ceiling appeared to be a mix of wooden beams, floorboards and broken furniture. Through a small gap between timbers making up one of the walls, Sue thought she could make out a human form. She shone the torch through the gap. Lying about two metres away was one of the security guards with a metal chair leg protruding from his chest. If he wasn't already dead, then he would be very soon. Beyond the guard she could make out what looked like a microwave oven and a food processor. "Zoe, I think we've dropped through the dining room floor into the kitchen."

Sue heard her phone ringing somewhere near. She knew it was hers and that it was Rob trying to call her, because she had set up a special ringtone to identify him by. The phone was close but there was no way of getting to it.

"There's a lot of damage been done to the house, Zoe. We're going to be down here a long time, but these walls and that ceiling look solid enough, we should be safe until someone finds us."

"I wish I had your confidence."

"Bugger!" Sue said. "If the damage is very extensive the press will be down here and it may make the TV news. If Rob's kids see it, they'll be worried sick. Have you got kids, Zoe?"

"Not yet. I've only been with my partner fourteen months. She's a rugby player, just turned professional and recently joined the England training squad, she hopes to be selected for the team for the six nations in February."

"I'd never guess you to be gay."

"I don't make it obvious. I find in the field that being sexually attractive to both men and women can be an advantage."

"I wish I could get my phone and ring Rob, let him know what's happened and that I'm ok"

"You can use my phone."

" Very kind but I don't know his number, I always use speed dial."

"I've got Tracy's number, she could tell Rob."

"Why would you have Tracy's number?"

"She and I had a thing about fifteen months ago."

"Is she gay, too?" Sue asked as she selected and dialed.

"I think she is bi. You know either or."

"Hi Tracy, it's Sue Blackstock, sorry to bother you but I'm trying to get hold of Rob, is he about."

"I'm sorry Sue, he's somewhere out in the Everglades and there's very poor phone service out there. Can I help?"

"No not really, it's a private matter. Can you ask him to ring me on this number as soon as he can, it's very urgent."

"That's 0798323477 yes?"

"I don't know, it's not my phone. Please don't forget it's very urgent."

They turned the lamp off to conserve the power in the phone and just lay listening for sounds of a rescue.

The first sound they heard was a moan coming from somewhere behind the timber at their heads. There it was again, louder this time. "Michele is that you?" Zoe called out.

"Yes. Who's that?" Came the reply in a very weak voice.

"It's Zoe, Sue is here with me. We are unhurt but our exit is blocked. There appears to have been an explosion and we think the dining room floor gave way and we've fallen through down into the kitchen. Are you hurt?"

" My legs are trapped and I think I have a broken ankle. I'm pinned to the floor by a wooden beam lying across my chest, making it hard for me to breath."

"She sounds in a bad way," Sue whispered to Zoe. "We need to do something."

"But we can't get out, so how can we help?"

"Have you got Pippa's number in your phone? We could ring her and she can apply pressure on the rescue team and connect us up with them. Then we can direct them to where we are and they can get   Michele   out   quickly."

Zoe checked her contact list. "Yes I've got it." She dialed and listed to it ringing. "It's ringing but no one is answering."

"What about Sir Bernard? Have you got his number in there? Try him."

Zoe cancelled the call to Pippa and searched her contact list. "No I haven't got his number.

"Have you got an internet signal? " Sue questioned.

"A weak signal but I am connected."

"Right log on to my email account, sue@blackstock.com password is pound sign, lower case l, o, upper case v, lower case e, r, two, nought, one, nine. Now go to my sent emails and scroll down to find a reply I sent to Sir Bernard about three weeks ago. Open it up and you should see the text from him which includes his telephone number."

"Yes, I've found it." She copied the number across and dialed. "It's ringing."

"Put it on speaker so I can talk to him." After several rings, it was finally answered. "Sir Bernard, it's Susan Blackstock."

"Mrs. Blackstock you are alive!"

"You know that there has been an explosion here. We don't know the extent of the damage but myself, Zoe and Michele are trapped in what was the kitchen on the ground floor. Michele is in a bad way and needs help very soon. Can you direct the emergency services towards us?"

"I'll do my best, I understand the emergency services will arrive with you momentarily. Hang on I'm sure you'll be rescued soon. We are almost certain this is terrorism. You won't have heard this, but Thames House has been attacked this morning as well. We know there are several fatalities, but as yet the full extent of the damage has not been surveyed, we expect to find more bodies. I'm so pleased you're not among them."

There was a rumble in the wreckage above their heads an Michele screamed loudly. "Michele are you okay?" Zoe asked.

"For a moment I thought I was going to be crushed." Michele replied. "There's a large wooden beam hanging vertically above my head nothing seems to be holding it up and it just dropped about two feet, it stopped about six feet above me and I got a face full of dust. The next time it may not be only dust."

"Did you hear that Sir Bernard? Also Zoe and I can also detect a slight smell of gas. We need help quickly," Sue stressed. "This battery is almost dead. I repeat we are under where the dining room was, our surroundings are unsafe and I think there is a gas leak."

Zoe looked at her phone. The screen was blank. "I don't think he heard all that before the phone died," Zoe said.

"I hope he did, because I don't think we've got long."

When Rob got back to the trailer, Tracy was eating her breakfast. "Your wife has been trying to contact you Rob. She says it's an urgent private matter and can you ring on this number." Tracy said and handed him a piece of paper with a telephone number written on it.

Rob took his phone out of his pocket and tapped in the number. He listened to it dial through and go straight to voice mail. "This is Rob Blackstock responding to a call from Susan Blackstock on this number. Please ask her to ring me back when she can." Rob turned to Tracy, "Can't be that urgent, the phone is switched off. Time for you to be a real P.A. now Tracy, Kurt Luggard will be here in about twenty minutes."

"How did this morning go?" Tracy enquired.

"Perfect. I think he's hooked. At least he's coming here this morning for his next lesson."

"That's good news. All we need now is to get him to invite us to Angels' Rest. Right I'll get all the fake papers and the diary out to create the right image."

When Kurt arrived, Tracy had papers spread across the table in the trailer's lounge and was copying something into a desk diary. Rob met Kurt at the door and invited him into the trailer. "Is Sandra not with you?" he asked.

"No, she wanted to be dropped off in down town to do some shopping."

"Watch that girl, before you know it she'll have spent all your money on handbags and shoes. Even as a little girl she loved spending money."

Kurt chuckled, "Thanks for telling me, I'll be sure to keep my eye on her."

"Let me introduce you to Viv. Viv is my personal assistant, without her my life would be chaos. I'd never survive, she goes everywhere with me. She is a real treasure, never takes a holiday."

""You're a lucky man Rob, I'm always forgetting meetings. Nice to meet you Viv."

"Good morning, Mr. Luggard."

At that moment Ryman entered the room from the kitchen carrying a tray with a pot of coffee on it and four cups and set it down on a low table in front of two easy chairs. "Thank you Ryman," Rob said. "Ryman was with me earlier Kurt, I expect you saw him in the car. He came to me almost two years ago when I had my driving license taken away. I was lucky to find him. Not only is he a great driver, he's an amazing cook and he does laundry better than any woman I've ever known. We have become a family and always go everywhere together. I have recently married and Sue, my new wife, is finding it difficult to fit in, which is why she is not with us on this trip." Rob was continuing to build an image and Kurt appeared to accept it all.

Tracy interrupted, "Don't forget you have a meeting with the director at 10:30, Rob. You'll need to leave in about thirty five minutes."

"Thanks, Tracy." Rob led Kurt to the easy chairs and they sat as Ryman poured coffee.

"Kurt, as I said earlier. I can see a lot of potential but you need to find a good navigator and practice, practice, practice. If you don't get it right you will end up killing the pair of you."

"I can see that from what we did this morning. I'm sure my partner is up to it."

Rob continued to push. "This morning I suggested I can also improve your driving technique. I'm quite sure that after perhaps fifteen to twenty lessons I could get your time on that track down to under three minute fifteen seconds. That's an average of more than seventy five mph which is what I'd expect the top drivers to do."

"What do I need to do? Can you teach me? I'll pay whatever you ask," Kurt asked enthusiastically.

"I'll be pleased to help you over the next few weeks, before I return to U.K. All I ask is that you treat my niece well. She has always been a favourite of mine and I'd not be happy if she were hurt."

"I understand Rob."

""Well I have to go to a meeting now, so I'll leave you with Viv to fix a time for our first lesson in a day or two. I need to go and have a shower and get ready. I'll see you soon."

Chapter 11

"Rob I'm so pleased to see you. I've been through a real nightmare. At one time I really believed we were all going to die. The bomb took out the end wall of the building so the whole thing collapsed in on itself. It's a miracle only two people died. Zoe and I have only a few scratches but poor Michele will need surgery on her ankle and it will possibly need pinning. She is also going to need plastic surgery on her face. Zoe thought she had cut her shoulder badly, she could feel a sticky mess and a liquid running down her arm and neck. It turned out to be ketchup fallen with her from the dining room. We're still laughing about that. Sir Bernard called in and I've been speaking with him. We both agreed we expect to be up and running again in a couple of days, four at the most."

****

"Rob had continued to try and get hold of Sue all morning, using both the number Tracy had given him and Sue's number, the former going directly to voicemail and the later ringing but not being answered. At long last his phone vibrated in his pocket. He took it out checked the screen and pressed the green button, disappointed that it was neither of the numbers he had been calling. "Good morning Sir Bernard, what a pleasure. Are you checking our progress or sharing new information."

"Robert, I have some bad news for you I'm afraid. The Operations house was bombed this morning and virtually destroyed."

"Is Sue safe?"

"She is alive and in one piece, but was unconscious when the rescuers reached her. She was trapped in a gas contaminated space for some time. Her doctors are concerned that her brain may have been starved of oxygen for some time and may have suffered some damage, but they won't know until she wakes up."

"Christ! I must come back to be with her."

"Of course you must. I would expect nothing less. In fact I've already asked my admin team to get you and Miss Longhorn on the first available flight to London from Miami. They will contact you soon with the details. I won't keep you talking now, I'm sure you have things to do. Should the situation change I'll give you a call."

"Thank you, sir."

"Tracy." Rob called into the trailers lounge. "We're going back to London today. Right now in fact. The operations house has been attacked and destroyed. Sue is in hospital unconscious. You need to go and pack and be ready to leave A.S.A.P."

"Is Sue badly injured?" Tracy enquired.

"She was unconscious when the rescuers got her out, the doctors need her to wake before they can see the full extent of her injuries. Find Ryman for me, please and send him in."

"Will do. I'll also ring Kurt Luggard and tell him we're heading back. I'll keep him on the hook by saying you'll be back as soon as you can and will pick up on his training, as soon as you return."

"Can you also tell him to get as much practice with his navigator as he can? Also to enter as many small rallies as he can."

A few minutes later Ryman appeared. "I'm going back to U.K. unexpectedly today and don't know when I'll get back. I suggest you get my admin team to arrange a flight home for you and you spend some time with your kids and I'll be in touch when we're ready to return."

"Is something wrong at home, sir?"

"My wife has been injured in an explosion. I need to get home to her."

"I'm very sorry, sir. I do hope she'll be okay."

Sue's head was pounding and the light hurt her eyes as she slowly opened them. Her vision was cloudy, but she could make out the unmistakable shape of Sir Bernard Howe sitting in a chair by her side, studying a bundle of papers. She was aware that she had something lying across her face and a mask over her nose. She lifted her head a little and saw a tube connected to her arm and leading back to a bag of liquid hanging on a hook behind her head. She also had something on her finger with wire from it going into a monitor.

"Good to see you awake, my dear." Sir Bernard said and he stood and pressed a button in the panel above her head to call a nurse.

Sue's vision was clearing and she was trying to put her memories into a sensible order. "How long have I been here?"

"You've been unconscious for twenty four hours, we've been very worried about you, dear. Your husband will be here later this afternoon."

"Where are the others? Are Michele and Zoe alright?"

"Zoe is fine. Like you she suffered from breathing in gas, but she was up and about yesterday with no I'll effects. She has been here sitting with you all night. I only arrived a few minutes ago and stayed here while she's gone to the bathroom. Michele has not been so lucky. She has a number of broken ribs, her ankle is badly broken. She's in surgery this morning to have that fixed, it may need pinning. She also will need some surgery to the left side of her face. As the rescuers got to her a beam fell scraping the side of her face, taking quite a slice off her cheek. Six inches to the right and it would have smashed into her face and possibly killed her. She's going to be okay, but it will take a few months."

Roger and Julie were making good progress towards the base of the falls. They had taken the track from the village down to the river then followed the bank northwards and were now resting about ten kilometres from their goal.

"You know these falls are supposedly one of the great tourist attractions in the world, yet they are so remote and difficult to get to," Roger said to his partner. "Here we are in 2018. Almost fifty years since we put a man on the moon, yet just about the only way of getting to see these falls, is via a native long river boat and days of uncomfortable travel."

"Unless you've got a trail bike," Julie joked.

"We're not there yet. Don"t count your chickens."

They set of again, sticking as close as they could to the river bank, but occasional obstacles forced them a few metres inland and they had to fight through dense undergrowth. Progress was painfully slow.

They stopped again for a drink of water. It was mid afternoon and incredibly hot under the overhanging trees. "You know this is increasingly seeming less and less practical. Getting armed troops up here is going to be very difficult," Julie said, "even if we can find a route to the top."

"The only practical way would be via the river. It looks a bit shallow and rocky in places for R.I.B.'s, but a flat bottom marsh boat like they use in the Everglades or a hovercraft would work," Roger suggested.

"Both are incredibly noisy transports. They can be heard for miles," Julie commented.

"Maybe, but the noise of the waterfall will drown that out. Just listen, it sounds like the falls are just around the corner, but in fact we've still got more than five kilometres to go."

"So that's what we report back then. Hovercraft or marsh boat up the river," said Julie

"I can't see any other way, can you?"

"No, I agree. Shall we get going again? I'd like to be in sight of the falls before dark to set up camp. The next couple of days are going to be hard work."

Sir Bernard had sent a car to meet Rob when he landed at Heathrow, it took him directly to the hospital, where he found his wife sitting in a chair in a side ward, drinking tea with Zoe.

Sue burst into tears on seeing him and Zoe politely left them with their privacy and for Sue to fill Rob in with all the details of the last day and a half.

"They want me in overnight tonight, and perhaps tomorrow as well, because they want to do more tests to be sure there are no long term problems. Same for Zoe."

"Better to be checked over fully than rush things."

"Did Tracy fly back with you."

"She did. The car was taking her back to her flat."

"Did you know her and Zoe had an affair a few months back?" Sue told him in a low voice, as not to be overheard." Zoe told me this in confidence, and you're never to tell anyone. Tracy bats for both sides so to speak."

"I'd never of guessed it of Tracy. Yet Zoe, I'm not surprised. I'll have to watch out for Ryman then. He and Tracy were getting very chummy in Miami."

"How is Ryman? Is it working out with him okay?" Sue asked.

"He's invaluable. Not only does he drive but he cooks like a master chef and like you said, he is a remarkable shot. In fact he's working out so well that I'm thinking of asking him to stay on after this little adventure is over."

"I hope he accepts."

A nurse came to the door with a porter pushing a wheel chair closely behind her. "Sorry to interrupt, but we need to take Mrs Blackstock for an M.R.I. and a few more tests."

"Well it's probably best that I go now, love. Now that I've seen you're alright I'll get a taxi back to the flat and ring home to update everyone and I'll be back tomorrow morning. He leant over and kissed her."

"Give my love to everyone. I've got Zoe here for company, so I'll be fine."

Rob was back at the hospital early the next morning and stayed the whole day, talking about everyday things with Zoe and Sue. Each of the girls were occasionally taken for a further test. Towards the end of the afternoon, Sir Bernard turned up with Tracy. "I need to speak with you all quite urgently and with you two still having tests, I thought here would be best. Or rather Michele's room would be best as she is not very mobile. So if you'd all like to follow me, we'll head upstairs. Sue claimed the chair and Zoe perched on the corner of the bed, the others had to stand.

"Our investigation of the recent events has led me to think we may have misjudged Ernst Luggard and he may not be the master criminal behind the drugs murders. There are a number of unexplained items which we need to look at closer, but I now want the team to look at another possibility.

A few months ago we had reports that a Chinese Triad, The Yellow Dragon, were becoming active in London, led by Ti Bri Yan, Brian Tie as he is known to us, started a drugs war against the South American drug Barons fighting for distribution in the UK. A leading member of the triad Lo Pee Tah, Peter Lowe, was caught and charged with possession with intent to distribute, but two days into his trial Judge William Rider and leading witness and arresting officer, D.S. Paul Stevens were both found dead from a heroin overdose. The trial had to be abandoned and Lowe went free. With no firm evidence linking Lowe with either death, no further action was taken."

"Judge Rider and D.S Stevens were two names on the list found in Doug Green's house," Sue said she remembered.

"It begins to all fit together quite well," Sir Bernard declared. "Furthermore Lowe's Barrister was a certain Sir Gabriel Hunt."

"Gabriel was the name at the top of the list that was heavily underlined," Sue added.

"There is more." Sir Bernard smiled and continued "Investigations following the search at Doug Green's house discovered a witness, who claimed to see two people, a man and a woman, leaving the house moments before our agents arrived. The witness claimed they both had Chinese features. Finally to the car bomb at Thames house, which incidentally has now claimed seven lives, the seventh died last night. They were all innocent passers-by. We have three witnesses who saw a Chinese man park a transit van with two wheels on the pavement outside the building and leave the vehicle just seconds before it exploded."

"Looks to be a very strong case against them," Rob concluded.

"But it doesn't make any sense," Sue said. "Why all this messing about with QZ-71, if all they are doing is taking over the distribution from the South American's?

"Good point, Sue," Sir Bernard replied. "Even more need for you and Zoe to complete your analysis of the blood test results. You are now leading the team Sue, until Michele here is back on her feet, so to speak. You'll report directly to me as this is now solely an MI-

6 matter. Rob, if you and Miss Longhorn would be good enough to report to my office tomorrow at 9:00, I have something special for you to undertake. For now we put the Luggard work on hold."

Chapter 12

"Gabriel we have a new problem in Europe and America. The Chinese are making moves on our distribution, you and your team need to be extra vigilant. I have spoken to the triad leaders. They are not interested in long term distribution but more to use the controlling power to attack the western law and government. We discussed common ground and similarities for our plans in Britain. They intend attacking individuals at the Remembrance Day celebrations whereas we will be destroying the Houses of Parliament and hitting the leaders separately. Their targets in America are not the same as ours."

****

The doctor appeared at the open door of Sue's private room where he found Sue in the chair and Zoe on the end of the bed, chatting together over a bowl of breakfast cereal with two cups of coffee waiting on the side table . "Ah I thought I'd find you in here Miss Crump. I'm pleased to say all your tests are clear so you are free to go home this morning. Same for you, Mrs. Blackstock. I would recommend you both rest for two or three days. Your bodies have been put under a lot of strain, they need time to recover."

"Thank you," they said in unison, as the doctor turned and left the room.

Zoe had thought of something and chuckled. "What's so funny?" Sue asked.

"Well," Zoe said, "neither of us have any clothes and I had this vision of us walking bare assed down the road to the bus stop in these hospital gowns."

The thought also made Sue chuckle. "They don't do a lot for your modesty that's true. I've got Rob's number here, now I'll ring him and ask him to bring some clothes in for us both. He's got to see Sir Bernard first thing, so it will be late morning, but I'm sure he'll be happy to drop you off at your place."

A dumpy little nurse put her head through the door. "Excuse me girls. Zoe, there's a Miss Masters on the phone for you in your room."

"Thanks Ruth," she said to the nurse. As she left the room, she said to Sue, "That's my partner, Sarah, I wonder what she wants?"

While Zoe was taking the call from her partner, Sue rang Rob. "Good morning darling. Zoe and I have been discharged this morning. Could you come and fetch us after you've seen Sir Bernard. And can you also go to my wardrobe and pull out some leggings, a tee-shirt and a thick jumper, plus the same for Zoe and bring them in for us to travel home in?"

"It's likely to be after 11:00 before I can get there, is that okay?" Rob said.

"That's okay, we'll probably be in the day room by then. See you later."

Zoe rushed back into the room with a broad smile on her face. "Sarah's been picked for the game on Saturday. She's going to get her first England cap at Twickenham against South Africa. Isn't that great news? She's a bit emotional though, she lost her dad five weeks ago. He had brain cancer. Went to the doctor complaining of a persistent head ache and was dead just nineteen days later. She says he was her biggest fan and he always took her eighty year old grandad to her games. He would have been so proud. She's got two spare tickets allocated to her that her dad and grandad would have been using, would you and Rob like to come?"

"I'm not sure if Rob's into ladies' rugby."

"No, it's not just the ladies game. The tickets are for the whole day. It starts with the under twenties game between England and South Africa at 1:00. Then the men at 3:00 and finally the women at 5:00."

"In that case I'll say yes, please. Rob loves rugby. He's promised to take me to see a six nations game next spring. I take it you'll be going?"

"Of course".

The dumpy nurse appeared at the door again. "It's a busy morning for you girls this morning. A courier just left this for the two of you." She handed Zoe a padded envelope.

Zoe tipped the contents out onto the bed. Two i-phones and a note.

'Ladies, please find replacement phones for those you lost at the operations house. They have been set up as the same number as you had and pre-loaded with a number of useful contacts.

I am told by the doctor that you need a few days rest to fully recover, so on Monday please report to my office at 9:00, where you will be directed to your new operation centre.

Bernard Howe.'

Rob pushed Sue's clothes into a hold-all, grabbed his car keys from the table in the hall and took the lift down to the underground carpark in his apartment building. He was running later than he really wanted to. He had offered to pick up Tracy on his way to the MI-6 building and their meeting with Sir Bernard. He had planned to go by taxi but after Sue's call asking him to collect her and Zoe from hospital, he had decided it was more practical to use his own car. Now he was having second thoughts, traffic was heavy and when he got there he knew it would be difficult to find somewhere to park.

As it happened, after dropping Tracy at the door, he moved off and just a few yards down the road a car pulled out in front of him leaving a metered place free. He fed the meter for a three hour stay, then ran back to the MI-6 building and found Tracy still in the foyer, waiting for someone to escort her up to Sir Bernard's office.

It was only 9:05 when they sat in an interview room near Sir Bernard's office. "Good morning to you both, I'm a little pushed for time this morning, so I'll come straight to the point. If the Chinese are fueling these troubles then Brian Tie, Peter Lowe and Gabriel Hunt are right in the middle of it all. I want you two to find out everything there is to know about these three. Watch their every move and if possible discover what they are planning. You'll need these." He handed a piece of paper to each of them. "These are licenses that authorise you to carry a hand gun. I hope you won't need to use them. My secretary will take you to the armoury for you to draw your weapons. Any questions?"

"Do we report directly to you, sir?" Rob asked.

"That's right. Keep me in touch with everything, you have my number. Take a couple of days to get yourselves organised, then see what you can get. I'm told they are regular visitors to the Chinese restaurant at the northern end of Victoria Street. Now I really have to go. Good luck."

'Well," said Rob, "talk about tough assignments! They don't come much harder. I suggest my flat will be a good place to use as a base. It might be easier while we're doing this, if you move in to one of my spare rooms. I've got to collect the girls from the hospital. So, if I drop you at your place first, so you can get a few things together and I can pick you up on the way back."

"Sounds sensible to me, if you're sure Sue won't mind."

Rob thought back to what Sue had told him about Tracy's sexual leanings. He smiled to himself. "She'll be fine about it. I think Ryman would be of use as well. I'll give him a call, see what he's doing. Now let's find the armoury. You can shoot can you?"

"I passed the police training. I think I'll prove good enough. What about you?" she responded.

"Ryman gave me lessons in Miami. I'll do fine. Let's go!"

"While we're in the armoury, we had better pick up a surveillance kit as well. You know camera, long range microphone, recorder etcetera. The location of this Chinese restaurant is going to give us problems. There's no on street parking anywhere near enough to watch them from."

"You're saying we need some reason why we should be there for hour after hour?" Rob questioned.

"Telephone engineers is probably our best option. We erect one of those red & white tents over a telecoms junction box then sit in the back of the Open Reach van with cameras and microphones at the ready. I'll speak to the quartermaster and see what he can provide. We've also got no idea what these three guys look like; I don't suppose there are any photos of them anywhere?"

"I'll check with Sir Bernard's secretary on the way out," Rob answered.

Rob found the girls in the day room at the end of the corridor, where Sue's room was. He handed them the bag of clothes and they went off to get dressed. Sue's private room had been cleaned ready for the next occupant but was empty so they slipped in there.

Sue tipped the contents of the bag onto the floor. "It looks like we're going commando Zoe. He's not put any knickers in." Sue looked up at Zoe who had already pulled her gown off and was standing naked. "You've had your nipples pierced."

"Yes," Zoe responded. "Sarah did them for me a few months ago. Really heightens the sensitivity in my tits and does great things for Sarah, when she touches them."

"So I've heard. But at thirty nine I'm far too old for that sort of thing."

"Nonsense, give it a try, nothing to lose."

"I might well do that. I know two girls who I'm certain will help me and it would be a wonderful Christmas gift for Rob."

They finished dressing and walked out to the car with Rob telling them about his meeting with Bernard Howe and about his idea that Tracy and Ryman should both move into the flat, to save needless running about. They dropped Zoe off at her flat, having made plans for meeting her at Twickenham on Saturday, then went on to pick up Tracy.

"Are you sure you're okay with this, Sue?" Tracy said as she climbed into the back seat.

"I let the two of you go off to Miami together, didn't I?" She replied. "It makes total sense. Of course you must move in for however long it takes."

They parked the car and Rob helped Tracy carry her things up to the flat. "Honey, will you show Tracy round the place while I ring Ryman? She can have the twin room and Ryman can have the single."

Roger and Julie had spent three days trying to find some sort of path to the top of the falls. The best they could find was a couple of well-trodden animal paths both of which had sections where a man would need to be roped on to pass safely. They didn't try so didn't find out how difficult the paths got further up. "We've only found one possible path in three days and that is only passable by one person at a time and only if they were not in full kit. We're not going to find anything better on this side of the falls, Julie and we've now searched about five miles from the falls. We need to get back to the village tomorrow then find some excuse to come up here in a couple of weeks 'time and try the other side of the falls."

"When we get back to the village we had better use Rev. Clive's short wave to give Uncle James at Cardale House an update, such as it is," suggested Julie.

"It's not looking too good is it?" Roger concluded.

"Ryman only got back in the early hours this morning. His flight was delayed, some sort of mechanical problem. He wants to spend the weekend with his kids then he'll come to the flat early Sunday evening. He's got a licensed handgun which I've asked him to bring with him," Rob told the girls.

"As member of the public, his license will only be valid for him carrying the gun to and from his home to a gun club," Tracy announced from her knowledge of the law. We should let Sir Bernard know about him and get him issued with a special license."

"I'll ring Sir Bernard's secretary and get her to sort out the necessary, " Rob said. "Then I'll ring that Chinese on Victoria St. We've got to eat somewhere and there's as good as anywhere and we can check out their customers at the same time. Then perhaps over the week end we can start following them around."

"Not on Saturday, you can't," Sue interrupted. "You're taking me to the rugby at Twickenham. Zoe's got tickets for us."

"How did she get them? It's England playing South Africa, it will be a total sell-out."

"Long story, I'll tell you later."

Tracy and Sue were the same age and similar build. Both knew how to dress their bodies to turn heads and when Rob walked into the Victoria Street Chinese restaurant with a lady on each arm, heads did turn. His wife wore a skin tight, casual, white cotton dress that clung to every curve like a glove, showing her ass wonderfully and gripping her legs to mid-thigh where it stopped. Tracy, like Sue was wearing a dress. In her case a tight, short pale blue one. Every head in the room was turned and the new arrivals quickly became the subject of several conversations. Not that they looked out of place as the majority of the female customers were also dressed to impress.

They were shown to a table to one side of the restaurant, laid out with four places. A waiter quickly removed one of the place settings and pulled away a chair, whilst two others pulled back chairs to help the ladies sit, then shook out neatly folded napkins across their laps covering long exposed legs. Rob took the seat with his back to the wall, giving him a good view over the whole restaurant. There was no sign of either of their targets, but it was a Thursday evening and the place was not overly busy.

They shared a bottle of wine with their meal and had liqueurs and coffee afterwards, stretching their meal out as long as possible. Although there was a steady stream of customers entering and leaving their targets didn't make an appearance. Perhaps the intelligence was wrong or maybe they just weren't hungry this evening. Either way, Rob and Tracy had failed to make contact but at least they had an excellent meal and Rob had enjoyed the company of his first and his latest lovers, whom he sensed were beginning to relax in one another's company and become friends. They even joked about Rob forgetting to pack any underwear for Sue and Zoe when he took clothes into the hospital.

Naturally Sue was tired by the time they arrived back at the flat and excused herself and went off to bed. Rob and Tracy stayed up discussing their next move. It would look strange them going back to the restaurant next evening, but Tracy thought if she dressed down a lot, did her hair differently and wore her glasses instead of her lenses, she could get away with returning on Saturday evening. She was sure she could talk one of her girlfriends into joining her, even the married ones would be up for a free meal and an evening out. Accepting that Saturday was possibly the most likely day for their targets to be at the restaurant, Rob agreed with the plan. Once they had confirmed that they did use the restaurant, plans could be made to begin surveillance.

"Hi dad, I thought I'd give you a call to see how things are going. Sue is just about fully recovered and has gone out shopping up the West End with Tracy." Rob announced to his father at home in Yorkshire.

"That could be expensive," Eric replied. "You didn't lend her your credit card, I hope."

"Not a chance," said Rob with a chuckle. "I was actually ringing to see how you were coping with the yard. Sorry to dump all the extra work on you for so long and we still can't see an end to it all."

"Don't worry about me son, your mother is making sure I don't overdo things. She has even organised Ana or Eva to travel to race meetings with me, sometimes both. Having one, sometimes two stunning girls at my side, is getting me quite a reputation. You can just imagine the comments. We have quite a laugh over it all. I've been getting some of the staff to do a lot of the work. Two or three have really done well, they'll be a great help to Sue."

"Well, if things are okay I'll let you get on. But before you go, if you watch the big game on Saturday you might see me and Sue. We've been given complimentary tickets for seats, just to the right of the royal box."

"Lucky bugger! Should be a great game. Tell me about it next time you ring."

Rev. Clive was leaving his house as Roger and Julie arrived back at the village. He stood in the road with outstretched arms, greeting them as if they had been away for months rather than four nights. "Welcome back my children," he said.

"It's good to be back," came Roger's response.

"You didn't find the place I told you of?" Rev. Clive questioned. "I had some free time on Thursday, so thought I come and pray with you, but your motor bike tracks went in the wrong direction."

Roger desperately tried to think of a response, but Julie cut in first. "Roger never was any good with maps, neither am I. We only got back here today by following our tracks."

"That's right. We went through to the river and found a quiet spot around two miles upstream. I say quiet but there was the continuous roar coming from the fast flowing river and I guess the falls, but we didn't get that far upstream," Roger lied.

"Was your trip of value?" Rev. Clive asked. "Is your faith strong again?"

"I think we both feel better for our few days of prayer," Roger said. "Do you agree Julie?"

Julie nodded, "Yes I feel so much better."

"I spoke with your uncle yesterday, he called on the radio. He asked me to tell you that Uncle Bernard is getting married again but no one expects you to come back for the wedding." Rev. Clive said as they all walked around to the back of the house where the bikes were kept.

"I really should give him a call back. If I could borrow the radio sometime."

"Any time, just let me know when and I'll show you how it all works. It's a very old set and it has a few peculiarities. Now, how about a nice cup of tea? I'll go and find Sun Rise," Rev. Clive said as he turned through the back door of the house.

As soon as he was out of earshot, Julie whispered "What does the message mean?"

"It means a second suspect is now being investigated, but we are to stay with our original objective."

Tracy entered the flat on the stroke of midnight. When she walked through to the lounge, she found Rob and Sue drinking hot chocolate. "I didn't expect you two still to be up," she said, "I thought you'd be in bed long ago after your day at the rugby."

"We didn't expect you to be quite this late, how did you get on?"

"Well I'm late because it's Jill's birthday on Tuesday, Jenny finally got her promotion to D.S last month and I'd told them about my divorce. We decided we needed to celebrate so we had champagne with our meal and when the meal had finished we moved into a small lounge area they have at the front of the restaurant and had more drinks. We've not had a night out together for a couple of years, with me based in York and the girls both with the Met. It's been difficult to get together, so we had a lot to catch up on and time got away from us."

"Did the targets come in?" Rob pressed.

"They did. We'd moved into the lounge area, when they walked in as if they owned the place. The staff all stood back and allowed them to walk through the restaurant and through the door at the back. A minute or two later we heard noises overhead, like a chair being dragged across a boarded floor. We also heard some muffled shouts, as if a couple were arguing."

"So from what you saw and heard, do you think that they are based at the restaurant?" Rob asked.

"Yes I do. Just looking at the staff you could see something in their eyes."

"Okay, tomorrow we get organised and get surveillance set up for first thing Monday," Rob said. "Do you want a hot chocolate?"

"No thanks, I'm ready for bed. So I'll say goodnight to you both and see you in the morning."

Rob was first one up on Sunday morning. On the kitchen worktop was a coffee machine capable of producing a variety of different drinks and Sue had filled all the various pods and hoppers, so all options were available. But Rob drank Americano, and that was the only option he knew how to get from the machine, so he poured three Americano's. Carefully carrying one of the mugs, he knocked on the door to the twin room and was answered by a muffled, "Come in."

Rob opened the door and walked in to see Tracy sitting up in bed writing in a small notebook. She had the quilt pulled up about her and her painted toes were exposed. "Coffee?" he announced.

"Thank you Rob. I was just making some notes for when I ring my kids later," Tracy said.

"I should try and talk to my two as well. Maybe later."

Tracy reached out a hand to take the coffee and the quilt slipped a little to give Rob a glimpse of bare flesh, enough for Rob to see that Tracy was naked under the covers. "There's no rush to get up. I'm drinking my coffee before I make a move," he said as he left the room. He thought to himself *'She's still a very attractive woman. If I didn't have Sue, I'd be very tempted.'* He picked up the other two mugs of steaming liquid and took them into the master bedroom. Sue was out of bed and softly singing in the shower. The door of the en-suite was open enough for him to stand and watch his wife of just a few weeks, slowly soap her body under the cascade of water.

"Don't just stand there gawking. It's not a peep show. Come here and scrub my back for me!"

Two mugs of Americano sat on the bedside tables and went cold.

Mid-morning Rob rang home to speak to Luci. Rose answered the phone and told him his daughter had gone riding with her new boyfriend, a very nice, polite lad. It's Peter Mills, Duncan Mills's oldest boy. He's about eight months older than Luci and apparently he's extremely bright, he wants to be a vet and has had an offer from Edinburgh University."

"Isn't Duncan Mills Tracy's brother?" Rob asked.

"That's right," Rose answered. "He and his family came back to Yorkshire when his father died back in 2014. Since then he's turned the place into a very profitable livery stable. Luci and Peter have become very close over the last month and go everywhere together holding hands."

"Do I need to worry, mum? You know what boys of that age are like."

"Absolutely not. Eva and Ana are keeping an eye on things, as stand in mums. I would suspect Luci knows more about the birds and bees than I do."

Rose had no time to chat longer because she was on her way to church. Next he tried ringing Justin's dorm at his Scottish boarding school. Rob was surprised to hear a female voice. He was told that she was the cleaner, she didn't know Justin but all the boys were out on a cross country run. Dejected, he left the girls and went out into the street to buy a newspaper. As he walked back to the flat, he glanced at the sport headlines England 12, South Africa 11. Yes it was a very enjoyable game. Sue still hadn't told him where the tickets had come from. He couldn't find any mention of the ladies match, which he had also enjoyed very much.

"It will be nice to get back to actually be doing something again," Sue said to Zoe as they walked out of the lift on the eighth floor of the S.I.S. building. "I don't know about you, but I really want to get the bastard behind all this now. It's become a personal issue. That's twice I've been almost killed, three times if you count the attack on Tracy."

"I agree. He must have a weakness some where and we need to find it. I wish we hadn't lost that list of names in the explosion, it might have helped," Zoe said.

They walked into the new office that they had just been allocated in their meeting with Sir Bernard. "He said it was only a small room." Sue said with a gasp, "but I expected something a bit bigger than a store cupboard."

"At least we've got a window," responded Zoe, heaving on the heavy pane of tinted glass to open it an inch. "Phew, that's better. Now we can get some fresh air in here. The computers aren't on and there's no one working here, yet it's already hot and stuffy. We're in the last week of October for Christ sake, we should be wanting to warm the place up, not opening a window to cool it down."

"I got the impression that Sir Bernard doesn't go along with the Chinese triad theory," Sue suggested. "He's definitely pushing us back to Luggard and co. He's also leaving Roger and Julie out in Venezuela. But he has told the agents that are out in the regions, to be back by the end of the week, to help on the surveillance of those two Chinese."

"I agree. He's a wise old man. I've known him a long time. He personally recruited me while I was at Oxford, just starting my second year. He arranged for me to be sponsored through to my graduation and everything. Told my parents that I'd won a government scholarship and had a job waiting for me at the treasury. He's looked after me ever since, six years now. I've always trusted his instinct and never known it let him down."

126

'All this equipment is high spec. It's all brand new," Sue claimed. "Shame we've got nothing to do on it. I suppose we start work building the analysis of the blood results again."

"You know Sue," Zoe suddenly sparke., "if Pippa's agent, who searched Doug Greens house, followed the correct protocol, they will have taken loads of photos of the evidence before it was removed and a copy of the D.V.D. and photo copied the list of names. I'll nip over to Thames House and see if we can borrow their copies. I'll pull rank if I need to."

"From what Michele was saying, you get more out of them by showing a bit of leg," Sue suggested.

"I might just try that," Zoe chuckled as she grabbed her bag and left the room.

Sue followed her out and went to find a coffee machine. Then she rang Michele to brief her on the meeting she and Zoe had just had with Sir Bernard. After that she rang Rob. "Hi lover, how's things?"

"Not bad," came Rob's response. "Tracy and I got here about forty five minutes ago. The van was already here, and guess what? It comes with an engineer who's opened up the BT box and there are wires everywhere. No one would know it's not real. Tracy and I have been in the van listening to Ken Bruce on the radio and staring at a TV screen showing a view of the Chinese restaurant. For now we're assuming they will come and go through the front door, but they may use the rear in which case we'll not see them. We could do with someone around the back."

"Sir Bernard has recalled the three agents out with the regional police forces to help you," Sue told him. "They should be available by Wednesday."

"I hope something will have happened and we'll have moved on before then. I'm already bored and it's not even an hour yet," Rob moaned. "Oh, Ryman has just joined us with coffees and a bag of bacon rolls."

"Tell him I've had his gun license application signed. He should have the license by the end of the week. My request for a gun to replace the one in my handbag has to wait for the old one to be found and proven to be unusable. It's all because we're not real MI-

127

6. Sir Bernard has promised to get that over ruled. Well, have a good day and let me know if anything happens."

Zoe didn't return until after lunch. "I was about to send out a search party out looking for you," Sue joked. "What took you so long?"

"I know, I'm sorry but they wouldn't let me have their copies, so they had to make me a copy of everything and the D.V.D. took ages to copy," Zoe explained.

"But there is only a short training video on it." Sue said. "I watched it. It could only be about fifty meg at most."

"No. There's almost seven gig on this," Zoe handed the disc to Sue. "There's some real weird stuff on there, looking at it gave me a headache, so I turned it off after just a few minutes. And there are two lists of names, not just the one we've already seen. They are both laid out in the same way and at least three names are on both lists. I would say that they came from two different sources, or at least printed on different printers."

"How do you know that?"

"Look at this one," Zoe said as she passed Sue one of the lists. "Can you see a band about six characters wide running top to bottom, about two inches from the left edge of the paper where the ink is slightly lighter?"

"Yes, I can see that," Sue replied. "I've seen that before somewhere recently."

"You have. Pippa's printer has the same fault. Now, this one doesn't show the same fault." Zoe passed the page to Sue.

Sue looked carefully at the second document and nodded. "That could be important. We'll look at that more later, but for now I'm interested in this D.V.D." She said as she lifted it out of its case and slid it into the slot on the side of her laptop, then turned the laptop on. Instead of the normal picture being displayed as the laptop loaded, followed by the password screen, weird swilling streams of vibrant colour swirled across the screen and the speakers emitted a barely audible hum.

They watched the screen for just a few minutes then Sue heard a crash behind her and turned to see Zoe unconscious in a heap on the floor. "Zoe, are you okay?"

Zoe could hear Sue's voice but for a moment could not reply as if in limbo. She felt she was outside of her body looking in. Slowly she came too and regained her senses. With Sue's help she sat up. Sue gave her some water and after a few minutes she was able to get up onto a chair. "Wow, that was strange! One moment I was looking at those images on the screen and the next I was floating."

"We need to get an expert to look at this," Sue said. "Have you ever seen the James Bond film where the villain hypnotises young girls with something very similar to this?"

"Is that the one where Bond gets married?"

"That's right," Sue confirmed. "I think this may be how our friends are getting the trigger phases to their victims."

"But why didn't we see this on the other D.V.D?" Zoe queried.

"Some sort of mix-up or someone deliberately trying to hide evidence," Sue replied. "My money is on the latter. But let's get the techies to tell us exactly what it is, before we worry about that. Meanwhile we can have another look at the names on that list."

"That must rank as one of the most boring days of my life," Rob said as he, Tracy and Ryman sat in a taxi on their way to Rob's flat.

"Welcome to my world," Tracy sad. "I've had lots of surveillance jobs where we've just sat for day after day and nothing has happened. You had better get used to it. We need to be back on the job again tomorrow."

Sue was paying her taxi when they pulled up at the apartment building. As they all entered the building and travelled in the lift up to the flat, they discussed Sue's meeting with Sir Bernard and Sue's discoveries.

As they entered the flat, Rob went straight into the lounge and threw his jacket across the arm of a chair. "Anyone else in need of a drink?" he asked.

"Yes please, darling," Sue replied. "I don't feel like going out again this evening. Why don't we just relax and order a takeaway."

"I could cook us all a meal," Ryman said.

"If you're sure. Rob says you are quite a cook," Sue said

"It will be a pleasure, miss. I find creating good food very relaxing," said Ryman. "I'll just nip down to the corner shop and pick up a few bits. Give me forty five minutes to an hour and it will be ready."

At his first opportunity, Roger drew a rough map on a page in his bible, showing the path they had discovered. Then he planned his report carefully, needing to include a warning about the depth of water in the river, the fact that they had found a poor path to the top and the fact that they needed to return to complete their search.

" Uncle James, it's Roger. I got your message. We won't be able to attend the wedding we still have much to do here. Julie and I have had a few days away re-building our faith. We found a quiet spot by the river. It runs very fast and shallow, even the native canoes struggle. I guess only hovercraft and air boats are the only craft that could go upstream with any speed. I think we found our beliefs, but it's not strong and we may need to go again."

"Glad to hear you and Julie are getting things together again and it's good to hear you're getting your faith back, although I'm disappointed you think you need to do more work on it. Rev. Clive told me you both have settled in well and the bikes will help you get to some of the more remote spots." The fictitious Uncle James responded in case anyone was eavesdropping. "I'll call you again after the wedding, take care."

"Your uncle seems like a very nice man," Rev. Clive said as Roger turned off the short wave radio.

"He is a real country vicar, lots of time for everyone. A real saint," Roger lied to support his story. "Of course he's not really our uncle. He and our father grew up together, went to the same school and was our father's best man when he married our mother."

"A good family friend," Rev. Clive concluded.

"Rev. Clive, Julie and I were wondering if it's possible for us to see Angel Falls while we're here? It's so close it would be a shame not to see it, if it's at all possible," Roger enquired.

"We do get a few tourists through here and some of the young men in the village earn a little money, taking them upstream in their canoes," Rev. Clive explained. "I'm sure one of them would be happy to take you. I'll ask around for you, if you like."

"That would be wonderful. Thank you," Roger smiled. "Do you know of any path to the top of the falls? I don't recall seeing any photographs taken looking down over the edge of the escarpment."

"I've been told that there was once a path, but it was destroyed by the Germans and the rock face is far too difficult to climb. Several have tried and a few have died trying."

"What, Germans?"

"Way before I came out here. Back in the forties, I'm told a small party of Germans on the run from the Nazi's, crashed their plane near the falls. It took them weeks to find a way down. It is said that the leader of the group returned to the top to build a shrine in memory of the pilot who got them out of Germany, but died in the crash. He may have said he was building a shrine, but he actually laid the foundations for a castle. He never finished it because he became a politician and moved away. Some years later his son came back. He was very rich, something to do with ships, I think. He finished the castle his father had started and now lives there. I've never seen him, he comes and goes by helicopter."

"Does he have a family living with him?" Roger asked.

"I've got no idea, but I know a lot of people live there. I'm told this by village girls who get taken up there every few weeks. They come back next day with money in their pockets."

Roger looked shocked. "Are you saying that village girls are selling themselves up there?"

"Don't judge them badly my son, remember that our dear Mary Magdalene plied the same trade."

There was a knock on the door of Sue and Zoe's new operations room and before either of them could respond, the door opened and in walked a red headed girl in figure hugging sweater and short tight skirt.

"Sue Blackstock?" she queried. Sue nodded. The girl handed over an envelope and left immediately.

Sue ripped the envelope open and read the contents. "Roger and Julie have sent a report. They apparently have found a path to the top of the falls but it's not very good. He also said the river is not very navigable and we'll need specialist transport. It doesn't look possible to launch an assault from that direction, but Roger says they'll be searching more in a few days time."

"Let's hope we don't need to make that assault," Zoe said. "The more I find out about that place, the harder it appears to break in."

Chapter 13

"You were correct Gabriel. Those two agents did go to the falls. I watched them for three days working along the Eastern bank, checking out every animal trail leading up from the base of the falls. They were obviously searching for a path to the top. They did eventually find the Eastern path, but as yet, not searched the western bank. I'm quite sure they haven't reported their findings yet. Roger did use the radio once but that was to return a call his uncle had made earlier this morning. But I listened to every word and nothing was said. I'll deal with them tonight and make it look as if bandits took them."

****

"Who taught you to cook like that, Ryman?" Tracy asked when they were once again sitting in the vehicle. "That meal you dished up last night was out of this world. I don't normally like corned beef but that hash was wonderful and those beans, I never knew baked beans could taste so good. Then to top it all you gave us those grilled bananas with caramel sauce. Can you cook for us again tonight?"

"Thank you miss. I'm glad you liked it. The corner shop was a bit limiting but I think I did alright. I taught myself out of necessity, my wife couldn't boil an egg. Me and the kids would have starved. Once I got started, I found I could produce all kinds of meals and the kids seem to enjoy it."

Rob suddenly sat upright in his seat. "Wake up folks! At last something is happening." Tracy and Ryman quickly donned their headsets and listened to the sounds that the directional microphone, aimed at the floor above the restaurant, was picking up. They all heard a door close then footsteps cross a bare wooden floor. On the monitor they saw the shape of someone standing at the window. Net curtains at the window prevented them from getting a clear view, but they could at least make out that whoever it was, now had their back to the window and was perched on the window sill.

Rob looked down at the surveillance equipment. A quiet hum and a row of green lights satisfied him that everything was being recorded. His eyes went back to the monitor when they all heard a short piece of unrecognisable music. Possibly a call to a mobile phone. Confirmed when the figure in the window raised their hand to their ear and started talking.

"Damn, I knew I should have taken a course in Chinese, while I was at Uni," Tracy said.

"I once spent three months in Hong Kong and picked up a few words," Rob added, "but it's not helping here."

Ryman spoke up. "He's talking to someone called Gabriel about a bomb to be planted underground at the Cenotaph and be detonated remotely during the service on Remembrance Day. They are using QZ-21 obtained from Luggard via this Gabriel, who is here in London. It's to be used on several people involved in security and a couple of legal buffs, involved in something that happened in China. Gabriel is also supplying the C4 for the bomb. The whole thing is some sort of retaliation strike against the British for something we did a couple of years ago to some triad leader. Now they are discussing some dark haired whore."

"Are your talent's without end, Ryman?" Tracy asked. "You can drive, you can shoot, you can cook and now we learn you speak fluent Chinese."

"It's Mandarin, miss. My wife was Chinese. My mother-in-law lived with us after my father-in-law died. She didn't speak a single word of English so I learnt Mandarin so that I could communicate with her."

All eyes were still on the monitor. They watched the figure stand and turn to face the window lifting the net curtain as he did so. They could now clearly recognise Brian Tia. He looked firstly to the far end of the street, then slowly turned, scanning the whole street and finally resting his gaze on the van he was being watched from and smiled broadly. They heard a female voice call out then watched him turn and walk away from the window. Footsteps again crossed the bare floor followed by a door being closed.

"Remembrance Day is only thirteen days away," Rob said. "We'd better call this in to Sue."

They heard nothing more all morning. "Looks like this rain is going to be with us all day. Who's ready for some lunch?" Rob asked.

"I'll go boss," Ryman said. "I need a pee anyway. Who wants what?"

"Skinny Latte with a shot of ginger for me please, Ryman," Tracy requested. "With a toasted muffin. Thanks."

"Americano black and Big Mac for me please," Rob added.

"Right I'll be straight back. Don't let anything happen while I'm gone," Ryman chuckled as he climbed out through the back door of the van into the crowded street.

Moments later the door opened again. Without turning to look at the door Rob said. "That was quick! What did you forget?"

"You two, out of this van now!" Rob and Tracy turned to see two men at the open door. One of them holding a gun and the other standing holding the door, so that passers-by could not see what was happening.

Both Rob and Tracy recognised the two men as their targets; obviously they had left the building by an exit other than the door to the restaurant. "I said, get out. NOW!" The man holding the gun waved the gun in a directional movement.

Tracy slowly moved her hand towards her side arm. "Don't even think of it dearie. Use just your thumb and first finger on the butt and pass that to me," said the gunman and he held out his hand and took the weapon from Tracy.

The gunman put the gun and his hand in his hoodie pocket and stepped back from the door. Rob and Tracy climbed out and the other man closed the door. Then they all crossed the road and the gunman followed his two captives through the front door into the restaurant, while the other man stood watching up and down Victoria Street, looking for anything out of the ordinary, then followed the others into the building.

Ryman came out of McDonald's balancing three coffees in a flimsy cardboard carrier and food in a carrier bag hanging from his elbow. It took him a moment to get into the stream of pedestrians moving towards the van. As he looked ahead, between the heads of the people in front of him, he saw Rob and Tracy climb out of the van and cross the road with two men close behind them. He threw the coffees and bag of food into the gutter and barged through the crowd towards the workman's tent erected over the telephone junction box where he expected to find the engineer working away. He pushed the entry flap to one side and looked in. The engineer was slumped forward over his tool box, his throat cut and blood pooling on the floor beneath him. There was no need to check the engineer's pulse, it was obvious he was dead. So Ryman carefully backed out of the tent and carefully closed the flap. He stood and looked across the street, in time to see the second man disappear into the restaurant.

He retraced his steps back into McDonald's and found a seat at the high bar by the window, so that he could look out, regain his composure and think about what he should do next. From what he saw, Rob and Tracy weren't forced to get out of the van, or were they? He hadn't seen the faces of the two men who had taken them, but assumed it was the two they were meant to be watching. At least one of them was armed with a knife, the dead engineer was testimony to that. Maybe the other one had a gun. Yes, that would explain why Rob and Tracy didn't put up a fight, he thought.

What should he do? Should he rush in and rescue them? That would be stupid, there were at least two of them, both probably armed. He didn't know where in the building they would be, these men had already killed once. They wouldn't hesitate to kill again, him, Rob or Tracy or perhaps all three. No, rushing in was not an option. Should he just keep watch and see what happened. He couldn't use the van because they knew it was a surveillance vehicle and from where he sat, he couldn't see the restaurant door, only the alley that ran down the side of the building. If he stood outside a little further along the street he could see more, but would be easily spotted. He finally decided that there was nothing he do immediately by himself, so he rang Sue.

"Ryman, what have you got for me now?" Sue had picked up her phone and caller id had told her who was calling.

" Miss Susan, Mr. Robert and Miss Tracy have been taken by the Chinese."

"What do you mean taken?"

" The two Chinese guys we were supposed to be watching, must have come out of the back of the building, crossed the street to the van, killed the engineer and taken Mr. Robert and Miss Tracy back into the restaurant with them."

"Where exactly are you now?"

"I'm a little way down the street in McDonald's."

"Stay there. I'll brief Sir Bernard, then I'll meet you there. In the meantime keep watching the place in case they leave. I'll be with you in forty five minutes, an hour tops. Just stay put until I get there."

Rob and Tracy were taken upstairs and into the room at the front where they had seen Brian Tia earlier. Tia had his gun out of his pocket again and was pointing it at them from across the room, while Peter Lowe fastened their hands behind their backs with cable ties and made them sit on the floor, leaning on the wall under the window.

Lowe bent down and lifted Tracy's chin, forcing her into eye contact. "Who do you work for?" he ordered.

"Walt Disney," Tracy replied defiantly.

Lowe pulled back, then slapped her face hard with his hand. "Leave her!" Rob shouted.

Lowe took his knife from the pocket at the front of his hoody and pressed the button, to allow a wicked looking five inch blade to spring out. He held the knife so that the point was pressing at Rob's throat. "What are you going to do about it then?" he said and moved the blade to the top button of Tracy's shirt. With a well-practiced twist of the wrist the button flew across the room.

"I'll ask you again. Who are you working for?"

"Get lost."

Another slap across the face which made Tracy wince. Then another button spun across the floor exposing her bra-less state. Lowe dragged his blade from her throat down between her partially exposed breasts, then across under a barely covered nipple where he stopped. He smiled at Tracy and gave the knife a quick jerk. Tracy pulled away as best she could, but the knife had pierced the skin on the underside of her breast, not a serious cut, but enough to draw blood which quickly spread across the front of her white cotton shirt. "Tell him what he wants to know Tracy before he hurts you more." Rob said reluctantly.

"Mr. Ralph Mills. We are working for Mr. Ralph Mills. We are private investigators watching his wife as part of a divorce case," Tracy thought quickly, using her own father's name, to build what she hoped would be a believable story.

Rob quickly backed her up. "That's right. His wife has gone missing. Mr. Mills thinks she's shacked up with some writer chap, but has no address for him. This restaurant is known to be a favourite lunchtime haunt for Mrs. Mills, so we are just sitting, hoping she would make an appearance."

The two villains had a short conversation in Chinese. Then dragged Rob and Tracy to their feet and marched them out. They were pushed past the open lounge door. Sitting in the room were two young girls, wearing only a bra and G-string. Tia said something to them and they jumped up and went into what appeared to be a bedroom. Tia then prodded Rob in the ribs and indicated he wanted them to go down the stairs. At the bottom, they went through the back door out into a yard. In the corner were three broken chairs and a damaged table all from the restaurant and against the far wall were three large wheelie bins, one of which was over flowing with cardboard boxes. They passed between the bins to a solid gate which gave them access to a narrow passageway beyond, where a paneled van was parked.

Lowe opened the sliding side door, Tracy and Rob were bundled into the back of the vehicle where there was a strong chemical smell. Brian Tia climbed into the driver's seat and Peter Lowe filled the passenger seat. Tia carefully manoeuvred the van along the passageway into the side street, then waited to pull into the traffic on Victoria Street.

From his window seat in McDonald's Ryman saw the van pull out onto Victoria Street, Lowe and Tia were clearly recognisable in the front seats as the van passed him. He glanced at his watch. It had been just twenty minutes since he had seen Rob and Tracy marched off. Sue had told him to stay in McDonalds until she could join him, so he would just sit tight and wait.

Sue had not been able to speak with Sir Bernard. He was meeting the Home Secretary, discussing her previous report containing Rymans translation of the telephone conversation between Brian Tia and someone called Gabriel.

"We have to take this threat seriously," Sir Bernard explained. "Both the P.M. and Prince Charles will be laying wreaths. Other members of the Royal family, politicians and other V.I.P.s will all be at risk."

"To be totally safe, we should cancel the event or at the very least postpone until a thorough search has been carried out," the Home Secretary suggested.

"Neither option is acceptable sir. The whole world will be watching the ceremony. We can't be seen to let terrorists alter any part of the day. The message must be clear. Britain does not deal with terrorists," Sir Bernard said.

"Are they still in there Ryman?"

"The two Chinese men have certainly left. They drove off in a black, possibly dark blue or dark brown panel van. Mr. Robert and Miss Tracy could easily have been in the back," Ryman stated.

"There's only one way to find out," Sue said.

"You mean we're going in there," Ryman asked.

"I wish I had a gun," Sue said. "I'm still waiting for the paperwork to hit the right desk for my replacement gun to be issued. Have you got your gun with you?"

"No. Miss Tracy has submitted the application for a special license. Until that arrives I thought it best to leave it in the flat. Mr. Robert's gun may still be in the van. It was laying beside the monitor, when I last saw it."

"If it's there, we'll take it, but we're going into that restaurant."

Ryman found the gun and crossed the road with Sue. The restaurant was quite full with late lunch diners. One of the staff approached them. Sue flashed her travel card in front of the waiter not long enough for it to be recognised for what it was and said,

"Police, where are the stairs?" The waiter pointed to a door in the corner at the back of the restaurant.

As Sue and Ryman moved towards the door it opened and two young women came through. Ryman had Rob's gun in his hand and when the two women saw it they both gave a muffled cry out and stepped to one side, to let Sue and Ryman pass. At the top of the stairs they were confronted by an elderly Chinese man.

"A man and a woman were brought in here. Where are they now?" Sue demanded.

The elderly man obviously, very angry about the intrusion, responded with something in Chinese. Ryman repeated Sue's question in his best Mandarin. The old man was calming down and he responded to Ryman.

"He said that they were here briefly but the Triad warriors took them when they left. He doesn't know where they were going. I think he's telling the truth, he's absolutely terrified of the triad."

"Fuck. We have to find that van quickly. Did you note the registration of the van. Give it to Zoe and she'll get it on to all the lists it need to be on, then every copper in London will be looking for it. We'll pull out the recording from the van and get that back to the S.A.S. building for analysis. The clean-up team should be here soon. We'll wait for them to arrive then we'll get back."

Kurt had convinced his actor friend to be his regular navigator. Between them they had developed a short hand language in just a couple of days. They had spent their first day together, just driving around the Miami area, each defining every obstacle, corner, hill crest, dip and road surface in their new language. By the end of the day they were confident that they were consistently describing obstacles identically and that Kurt was able to visualise any obstacle his navigator called.

On day two, they drove out beyond the everglades to find deserted back roads and tracks to practice on. At each new track they first drove along it, with the navigator making notes about every bend, and hill etcetera. They then did the same driving back to the start. Then they drove the route at full rally speed in both directions. To begin with they had a couple of errors, which almost put an end to their day. Once they entered a corner too quickly for the road conditions and spun the car and at another they actually left the road and were fortunate to miss all the trees that lined that part of the track. They did much better on the second day and agreed that their next step was to try things out in a rally. At this time of year there was always a rally, they just had to choose one.

"Chuck, do you think we are ready to try a big event?" Kurt asked his navigator. "I know we haven't tested ourselves in any competition yet, but everything feels good. I feel I'm driving better and safer than I've ever done. Today is the last day for entries for the Costa Run, Vail to Las Vegas. We could enter in the unmodified works cars class. I've got a contact that could get a Lamborghini ready in time. It would be a different type of challenge for us. There would be no slow drive first we would have to prepare using maps, but I think we could do well."

"When is it?" the navigator asked.

"It's the first week of November."

"That's only just a week away. Do you really thing we could be ready?"

"I do. We just need to do some map work which we can start this evening. Come on, let's give it a go," Kurt urged his friend.

"It's your money. I'm happy if you are."

"Good morning girls, are you both coming racing with me today?" Eric greeted Ana and Eva as they crossed the stable yard.

"We are," Ana answered. "We both enjoy the atmosphere at Doncaster. We've both been working hard on plans for the catering business, so we think we have earned a day at the races."

"How is the catering business shaping up?" Eric asked.

Ana was quick to answer. "We weren't doing very well. But since we've now had a few days out with the crew, we've seen first-hand where the problems lie. It's been very difficult. For weeks there have been no crews working in this country, but now Blackstock Stunts are at three locations, one here in Yorkshire. On the days when there is no racing, we go on location and study the problems they have with food and drink supplies."

"We believe we have a workable solution to present to Mr. Robert," Eva added. "We're now looking at the equipment and prices. We're also trying to construct an operating costs model."

"Gosh you two are more than pretty faces. You sound like you know what you are doing," Eric said.

"We haven't always been x-rated Mr. Blackstock, we were forced into that trade to stay alive. The people that brought us to Britain were not nice but before we left Moscow, we were both students just graduating from Moscow University. We both have degrees in Business Management."

"Does my son know this?"

"He is a very careful business man. He told us that before he offered us this job, he'd had our backgrounds checked. Yes, he knows."

Rob and Tracy lay on the floor in the back of the panel van. It was empty apart from a metal toolbox. The bare metal floor of the van was cold and the ridges that gave it it's strength, made it very uncomfortable to lie on. Thankfully they were only travelling for fifteen minutes. Brian Tia pulled the sliding door open and dragged them both out. Rob recognised that they were in dockland, he could smell the river. Only a few years ago this would have been a bustling area, but today they were the only people around.

Peter Lowe was unlocking the side door to a warehouse, then he struggled to pull it open. The hinges looked rusty and the door would only open half way. Tia pushed the two captives towards the door.

The inside of the warehouse was just one large open space, smelling of fish. The air inside actually felt colder than the air outside, particularly to Tracy who was still only wearing her blood stained white cotton shirt with half the buttons missing and with her hands tied behind her back, the neckline of the shirt was being pulled open, exposing a lot of bare flesh to the cold air.

Lowe led them to mid-way along the wall. On the floor, next to a tall pile of thick woollen blankets, were about a dozen concrete or stone cubes, all with an iron ring and a short length of heavy chain attached. Across more than half the floor was a jumble of broken furniture, old dining suites, lounge furniture, a large iron bedstead, a pile of mattresses, even a couple of old wardrobes. To Rob it was as he imagined the pile of bones lay at the place where elephants go to die, perhaps this was the place where old furniture came to die. It didn't really make sense why all this furniture had been piled in this old warehouse. When he looked around he saw a small office or maybe a toilet tucked in the corner between the door and the front wall. The only windows in the place were at the top of the two side walls, about ten feet off the floor, no good for looking outside or providing fresh air, but they did allow a considerable amount of daylight into the space. More daylight came from two very large glazed roof panels. Tracy and Rob were pushed to the floor and Lowe used a cable tie to fix one of the concrete blocks to the ankle on each of them, he then cut the ties at their wrists. "I hope that will be more comfortable," he said and he tossed one of the blankets towards the captives. "You are now free to move where ever you like, but those blocks weigh over forty kilos so you won't be able to drag them very far," Lowe gloated.

Rob got to his feet and helped Tracy to her feet, together they then slowly dragged their blocks to the nearest sofa, where they sat wrapped in their blankets.

The two Chinese men pulled a table and two dining chairs out of the heap and sat talking in their native language. Rob could understand the odd word but not enough to follow what they were talking about.

"He hasn't recognised me at all, has he?" Lowe said. "I'm not really surprised. It was twelve years ago and my face was all cut up when he pulled me out of the car after the accident. He saved my life that day, the car exploded just seconds after he pulled me out. That's why I'm letting him live and by letting the girl live, he'll be less likely to do anything rash that might endanger her."

As darkness fell Tia left the warehouse and they heard the van drive off. After about fifteen minutes, it came back and Tia came in carrying a large plastic bag. He pulled out a four pack of beer and two packs of sandwiches and set them on the table. The remaining contents he tipped out on the sofa between Rob and Tracy. Two packs of sandwiches and four small bottles of water. "Eat," he said and went back to the table.

With only the hazy moon and starlight to illuminate the warehouse it quickly became intensely dark and it was not long before the captives could hear two rhythmic snores coming from the table.

"See that?" Tracy said. She pointed out of the window above them.

"See what?" said Rob.

"That star." She pointed again. "The red, green and white one. Can you see it?"

Rob followed the line of her finger and saw a bright point of light. It was twinkling madly through the slight evening mist which gave it a multi coloured hue. "That really bright twinkling star?" he asked.

"Yes. That's Sirus. The brightest star in the heavens," She said lowering her hand. It's the star that shows winter is on its way."

"Where did you learn about the stars?"

"From as far back as I can remember, me and dad used to sit outside some nights, when mum was at a Tupperware or Avon or make-up party and he'd teach me. He'd told me that our ancestors didn't have calendars, but used the position of the constellations to tell when the seasons changed. That plus changes in the weather. He was a wise old man and I miss him. Rob, are we going to get out of this?"

"I honestly don't know but I would have thought if they were going to kill us they would have done so, not buy sandwiches. I've got a strange feeling I've met Lowe somewhere before."

Sue and Ryman sat late into the night talking about nothing in particular. Sue was obviously worried about Rob.

"I'm sure he'll be okay miss." Ryman said. "They'd be dead by now if they were going to kill them."

"I know you mean well, Ryman, but can we talk about something else please. I've only known Rob for a few weeks but he means everything to me and I don't want to think of what might be happening to him."

144

Ryman pulled out his phone and showed Sue pictures of his children and they talked about how things had been for them, since his wife had been murdered and how he felt about them no longer talking about their mum. Sue told him about her own little girl, who had been abducted and killed and she showed him a rather dog eared photo of a little girl with pig tails on a swing. At around 2:30 they both agreed they should try and get some sleep.

"Good morning, Sue," Zoe said as her friend arrived late at the office. "Have you heard from Rob?"

"No. Have you?" came Sue's reply.

"No, I'm sorry. How come you're late this morning?" Zoe enquired.

"I called in to see Sir Bernard to let him know about Rob and Tracy but he already knew. The clear-up team sent in their report last night."

"Well I've got some good news," Zoe said. "The IT experts have looked at that DVD and confirm it is hypno-suggestive, to insert the trigger phrase 'Begin Operation Birdbath', into the subconscious of the victim."

"So if someone says that praise to one of these victims they will take control of that person and can make then do anything they want them to do?" Sue said.

"That's about it. Worrying isn't it?"

"Have you seen Ryman this morning?" Sue asked.

"Yes, he was in before me. He's gone up to the language department with that surveillance recording, to confirm his translation," Zoe replied.

"Then we had better get back to that list, or rather those lists," Sue said. "But before we do that I'm going to call traffic to see if they have done anything with that vehicle reg that Ryman noted."

As the morning got brighter, more and more light came though the high windows. Rob was quite impressed with the architect who designed this warehouse, the windows were set in exactly the right place for spreading light across the warehouse floor. He could now see that the two end walls consisted of four panels in each wall. Each panel was suspended from wheels running in an overhead track and rested on more wheels running in a track, cut into the concrete. This construction meant the four panels could be pushed aside to open the whole wall. Rob was now able to deduce they were in an old fish processing factory and cannery.

Tia went off and came back with bacon rolls and bottles of milk shake. Nature running its course meant that a toilet was necessary. It needed all the strength Tracy could muster to drag the block she was tethered to across the floor to the office structure in the corner. Inside was a structure that might have been a coat cupboard but for the letters W.C. on the door. Inside was nothing more than an oil drum partly full of something Tracy didn't want to think about. Her need was pressing, she had no choice, but got out as quickly as possible, barely managing not to throw up.

Ryman returned to the office late morning with three coffees. "Would you believe it. This is MI-6 and they only have one person fluent in mandarin and she's off for the day for a midwife appointment. At least the techies are extracting all the bits of conversation, so that when she comes back tomorrow, she will only have to do the translation. But I'm confident I'm right."

"I'm sure you are Ryman, but we have to be certain," Sue said. "We're not getting very far with tracking down that panel van. Traffic treated me like an idiot when I rang them."

"Oh, what did they say?" Ryman asked.

"They said that there were twenty three vehicles with plates that matched the partial we gave them. None of them are a panel van or a van at all. They now have to check out all twenty three to see if they can be accounted for, but our Chinese friends may just have had a random plate made up. Traffic said there are two thousand five hundred plus vans registered in the Greater London area alone that fit the description you gave. It's not possible to check them all."

"That's not good," Ryman said.

Zoe swivelled her chair round so the she faced the others. "This is very interesting," she said.

"What is?"

"There are six names that are on both lists. One of them is yours Sue. But apart from that I can see no connection. I've traced everyone on the longer list and there are a few things that concern me. Have you got time to discuss them now or shall I just continue."

"No, I've got some time now, we can at least make a start. What have you found?"

"Let's start with you then. Your name has got a cross in front of it, possibly to show that the attempt to drug you failed. At the bottom of the list there are five hand written entries; one of those is Russel Billman."

" I know a Russel Billman," Sue interrupted. "He works for Williams Security. We've worked together several times. He specialises in security for visiting heads of states. I know him very well, I'm certain he's not a drug user."

"Neither are you, but that didn't stop them. Any idea what he would be working on?"

"He'll most likely be starting work on next year's big event, the D-Day 75th anniversary. If I hadn't left the company, we would have been working on it together."

"How many heads of state are we talking about?" Zoe pressed.

"It's too soon for exact numbers, not all are likely to be at any one event. There are a week of events planned, Theresa May will be scheduled to be at all the events as hosting P.M. Donald Trump is almost certain to be at some of the events. The US president will also have an audience with the Queen at the palace while he's here. But I've been away since August, so things might have changed, they do, with annoying regularity."

"That gives us some options to look closer at, but as a matter of urgency Russel Billman needs to be checked for QZ-21, so that we know whether he is already hooked or not."

"Leave that to me," Sue said. "I'll ring my brother-in-law, it's his company now. He needs to be warned about what's happening."

"Russel Billman is another one of the names on both lists. If, as I suspect, these lists are from two groups, possibly the Chinese and Luggard, then we could be looking at multiple targets."

"Good work Zoe. That is very significant. Have you found any other connections?"

"A few," Zoe responded. "This one is worrying. Its husband and wife soldiers, based in Aldershot. He's a sergeant, assigned to the armoury. His wife is a S.A.W expert; sorry S.A.W is Sight Aimed Weapons, things like a rocket launcher to ground to air missiles. There is a third name which I think ties in with the husband and wife. It's a redcap at Aldershot."

"A member of the military police. Okay, I'll follow that one up as well and talk to the station commander and suggest an audit on the armoury and blood tests for all three. Anymore?"

"Just one at the moment. Lucy Reed. She's the teenager who broke into Buckingham Palace and got into Her Majesty's private apartments and Lucas Durrell, a palace footman. The bit I don't understand is that Lucy is in prison, so what use could she be?"

Sue shrugged her shoulders.

"Finally, the handwritten name at the top of the list, Gabriel. The number next to the name is for a burner phone. The number is in a range of numbers used by MI-5."

" Are you saying the phone came from MI-5?"

"It certainly looks possible."

Sue's phone vibrated on her desk. "It's Sir Bernard, what does he want this time?" She pressed the green button. "Sir Bernard, how can I help you?"

"I've just been re-reading your report Sue, and putting one and one together, I'm convinced Luggard is at the centre of all of this. Your team members Roger and Julie have found a route to the top of the falls so I'm sending a small military force out there to watch and report comings and goings. I've given the team leader, Captain Mike Phillips, orders that he is to report to you daily at noon our time that's 08:00 in Venezuela. They will be parachuting in at first light tomorrow so please make sure you are ready, at noon, to receive his report. His call sign will be 'Blackbird 'and yours will be 'Nightingale'. I've arranged for the satellite radio equipment to be installed, set-up and tested in your office overnight tonight. You do know how to operate a satellite radio don't you?"

"Yes sir," she answered. "We had them in the army for several years, I've used one many times."

"Of course, of course, I was forgetting you were formerly a Redcap. However the techies have built an APP to load on a phone that can link to your satellite phone. They'll come in tomorrow and install it on your phone and show you how to use it. Any news of your husband?"

"No, sir. It's been twenty four hours and we still don't have any leads."

"Shame, we really need him back and building that relationship with the Luggard boy. We must get eyes and ears on that mountain. I hope you get him back soon."

"Yes sir. So do I."

Chapter 14

"Nightingale this is Blackbird. We landed at first light and made our way to the village by approximately 06:00. As we arrived, we witnessed an angry mob led by an elderly lady dragging an old man in torn clothes, off into the forest. We didn't interfere; instead we went to seek out the priest and the two agents. They were not at home. The mob returned about twenty minutes ago and their leader, a lady called Sun Rise, came across to greet us. She told us that at first light this morning her twelve year old grandson had come to her and told her that last night, he saw Rev. Clive march the two young church people into the forest. Her grandson followed them down to the river, where he witnessed the two young people being tied to a tree and left for the animals. On hearing this she roused her son and went to the river but was too late. The noises from the forest and the river would have drowned their screams, but it must have been a terrible death. What we saw when we arrived, was the priest being taken away for execution, after his trial by the village elders. He was stoned to death. I have sent men to retrieve the remains of all three bodies for burial."

****

The day went very slowly in the warehouse. More sandwiches and water were fetched for lunch and again late afternoon. Tracy and Rob reminisced about their early lives together and of their children. Rob talked of his first wife Jayne who was killed in a car crash, along with his eldest son, Luci's twin brother. Tracy avoided returning to the toilet for as long as she could, but eventually bowel and bladder pressure won over and she had to go. When she returned it was obvious to Rob that she had thrown up. "Are you okay Tracy?"

"No. Why are we here Rob? What are they going to do with us? I don't think I can take too much more. Have you notice those two disappear for a few minutes at a time. I've not seen them go into that toilet, even once. I bet they go outside when they need to pee. It's alright for you men. I remember when I was young and out with

150

my little brother, he was always taking it out and peeing against a wall when he needed to go"

"Hang on in there, Tracy. The longer we are here the greater the chance of someone finding us. Look there's your star. What did you call it?" Rob asked as he looked out of one of the high windows."

"Sirus," Tracy replied. "But that's not Sirus. It's not dark enough to see Sirus yet. That's the planet Venus."

"But you said yesterday that Sirus is the brightest star in the sky."

"It is, Venus is not a star. You will also see it move across the sky like the moon does."

"I suppose your dad told you that as well?"

"He did," she said. "It's been a nice sunny autumn day today and the sky is still clear so we should see loads of stars tonight. I'll point out a few constellations to you and improve your education."

"I hate this time of year when the nights are drawing in," Sue said to Ryman as they left the S.I.S building at the end of the day. "The week after the clocks go back, I feel is always the worst. I can't face going back to the flat just yet. Can I buy you a drink."

"That sounds like a good idea. The Black Dog or The Riverside?"

"Not The Riverside, it's been a sunny day and it was probably very nice there at lunchtime but that place never appeals on dark winter evenings."

They quickly walked the short distance along Albert Embankment in silence, then turned onto Glasshouse Walk, under the mainline railway toward the pub. At the bar, whilst waiting to be served, Sue read the menu. "They've got a few dishes on here that sound a bit different. Can I buy you a meal?"

"Yes, that would be very kind. Thank you."

They ordered their drinks and took two copies of the menu to a vacant table. A few minutes later, a slim waitress appeared to take their order. Once she had gone Sue asked. "Has Rob spoken to you about you staying on as his driver, once this nonsense is all over."

"No, he hasn't, miss."

"Well Ryman, whatever happens in the next few days, I'd like you to consider a permanent position as driver. Take your time to think about it."

"I don't need time miss. I gladly accept."

"Good man. Of course it will mean you'll need to move to Yorkshire."

"That's no problem miss. My dad retires in January and they are planning to sell up and move to the country. I'm sure Yorkshire will suit them as well as anywhere."

"Excellent. We'll sort out contracts etcetera some other time, but this calls for a celebration."

Their food arrived and the waitress asked if she could get them anything else.

" Yes please," Sue answered. "I'd like a bottle of your very best champagne and two glasses, please."

"Chuck, I've had confirmation." Kurt said to his navigator while they were eating their evening meal. "Our late entry into the Vail to Las Vegas rally next week has been accepted. We're allowed a support team of five and two vehicles. I called them in yesterday; they are going to meet us in Vail on Tuesday evening. There will be little or no time for me to get familiar with the car. We'll need to do what we can on Wednesday and early Thursday morning, we've been given a 10:55 start time."

"I've started work on the maps; I'll be ready for Thursday," Chuck said.

"So now we need to focus on this weekend's local event. Tomorrow and Friday we are allowed access to drive the course. We're the sixth vehicle on the start on Saturday, so we'll be away at about 10:30. The first stage is a road stage of fifty kilometres. Saturday afternoon, we have a woodland track. Then there's a night drive and finally on Sunday morning we have forty kilometres run on a combination of track and road."

Kurt turned and looked towards Sandra. "The Vail to Las Vegas rally will be your type of event, my dear. All the wives and girlfriends will be dressed up and strutting around. The TV cameras will be there, so you had best be prepared to play your part. Go into town tomorrow and get everything you need. I also expect you to be at the rally this weekend, but jeans and a sweater will do there."

"Don't worry Kurt, I'll make you proud," Sandra said. "I'll book at the salon for Monday to get my hair done, plus manicure and pedicure." Her C.I.A. contact was the hairdresser so this would be the ideal opportunity to send in an update, not that she had discovered anything about what was being planned by Kurt's father.

Sue and Ryman shared a taxi to their office; both had a lot to do and wanted to make an early start.

"Good morning you two," Zoe greeted them.

"My God girl it's only 7:30. Have you been here all night?"

"No, but Sarah gets up at 5:30 to go for a run before she goes for squad training. So if I'm awake I may as well be working."

Ryman had a puzzled expression on his face.

Zoe looked straight at him and said, "Sarah lives with me. We're gay."

Ryman's embarrassment showed, "I'll get the coffee's," he said and left.

"I've been able to pair up all the handwritten names on the lists with the printed names and cross checked it with the murders we know about. If my theory is right, we've got three categories. We have people clearing a path to make things possible. For instance a security guard not checking something, or ignoring something that shouldn't be there. Then there are ones that are doing things like firing rockets or setting off bombs. The final group are the ones that cover up things, the ones that erase C.C.T.V. footage and change records."

"So what do we do next? Do we get blood tests done on all of them and try to work out the target?" Sue suggested.

"We could do but we don't have all the pieces. We know there must be at least one other list, because your jockey and your neighbours are not on these."

"Very true. But I think it's worth a try. We've said before that some of these deaths are about taking over drug distribution. Didn't the blood test on the jockey and the twins all come up negative for ZQ-21."

Ryman returned with the coffee. "If anyone wants me, I'll be upstairs in Languages."

Gabriel arrived at the warehouse late morning as planned. Tia went out to help Gabriel carry the C4 into the warehouse. When Rob saw them enter he said, "So you are Gabriel. Now everything makes more sense."

Gabriel turned to Peter Lowe, looking very angry. "What the hell is he doing here? I told you to kill him, not take him hostage. Let him live and you might as well forget your plan and possibly Luggard's too. Get rid of him today, her too! They both know who I am, they could ruin everything."

"I'll see to it this afternoon. Peter is the bomb maker. I'll do it while he connects the C4 to the detonation mechanism."

"Make sure there is nothing to tie it back to any of us. No finger prints, no bullets and be certain there's no D.N.A," Gabriel instructed.

"I'll dump them in the river, there's enough crap in there to destroy any D.N.A.," Tia said.

Sue took her noon call from the task force in Venezuela. When she had finished Zoe could see something was wrong, all the colour had drained from her face.

"Sue, what's wrong?" Zoe enquired.

"Those two young agents we sent out to find a route up Angel Falls, are dead. Murdered, tied up and left to be eaten alive by wild animals."

"My God, That's awful! I just can't contemplate something like that. Do they know who did it?" Zoe asked.

"It was the priest, Rev. Clive. The task force found his radio log book with a lot of references to Gabriel and to Luggard. Apparently he was on Luggard's payroll and we assume he was in the village to prevent strangers getting too close to the falls. Anyway he's dead as well now. Tried by the village elders then executed by the village men."

"I can't imagine what it must have been like for those two at the end. Horrible," Zoe added.

Ryman burst through the door, "I've got a lead on where Mr. Robert is being held."

"That's great, where is he? How did you find him?" Sue said.

"Actually the Chinese themselves told us. The surveillance recorder was running all afternoon. They took Miss Tracy and Mr. Robert into that front room. The microphone picks them up trying to get Miss Tracy to say who she is working for. They didn't try very hard, almost as if they already knew. Then they had a conversation in Chinese discussing what they should do with their captives. One of them said Mr. Robert had saved his life, so he wanted to keep them alive. They were due to meet Gabriel at the canning factory today so they would go there and wait it out."

"Canning Factory. There must be a dozen of those at least," Zoe said.

"But only two or three are empty and deserted and they are all in the dockland. Come on Ryman, we're going on a hunt for a panel van. Zoe, look after things here for me."

Sue signed out a pool car and with Ryman at the wheel, they were quickly out of the underground car park at the S.I.S. Building and into the heavy traffic crossing the Vauxhall Bridge.

"Have you got any idea where we're going?" Sue asked.

"East," Ryman answered bluntly as he switched lanes once, twice, three times.

"Is there a copy of the A to Z in the glove box?" he asked.

Sue reach forward and opened the small compartment in front of her knee to pull out a small dog eared map book. "Yes, got it."

"Right, now find Vauxhall Bridge, then follow the river eastwards until you reach the North Docks."

She turned several pages and eventually found it. "Now What?"

"Type one of the street names from that area into the satnav."

She did as instructed and after the machine had calculated a route she pressed GO. "It's saying twenty minutes to our destination."

"No way," Ryman replied, "not in this traffic."

Brian Tia fixed Rob and Tracy's hands behind their backs again before freeing them from their chains. Then at gun point, marched them out to the van and forced them into the back of the van, climbed into the driver's seat and started the engine.

It took Ryman and Sue almost an hour to get to the North dock district and daylight was beginning to show the end of the day was coming.

"It's a bit of a guess but I know there are a lot of empty buildings in this area. One of them might be what we're looking for, if not we'll try South Docks," Ryman said.

They drove up and down between buildings for more than twenty minutes.

"There it is!" Sue pointed to a dark blue Peugeot Boxer van parked next to a large empty looking building, bearing the name St Peter's Fish. "It's got to be the right place."

As Ryman slowed the car they saw the van move off. "What do we do now, Miss Susan?"

"We would be crazy trying to enter the building without back up and if anyone is in there, they won't be going very far, because their transport has just driven off. So we follow the van but keep well back, we don't want to get spotted.

Tia drove the van about three miles downstream and pulled off the road onto a slip way. The tide was out and it was a long way down to the water's edge. Waving his gun he ordered his captives out of the van and down to the water. The slipway was part of a long since abandoned river ferry crossing and there were metal posts either side, where the water was now gently lapping. These were probably once supporting an overhead sign. Using a heavy duty cable tie he secured Rob and Tracy each to a post. "On a good day the tide rises about four feet but the bad news for you two is that a tide of six feet is expected tonight." Tia returned to his van satisfied that he'd done a fine job. Now all he had to do was wait for the tide.

Ryman pulled the car into the side of the road well away from the van, too far away from the slipway to see clearly what was happening.

"Look there's Rob and Tracy getting out of the van." Sue said excitedly. "I can only see one of the Chinese."

"The other may still be in the van," Ryman suggested. "Why are they standing there like that?"

"He's tying them to those metal posts," Sue said. "When the tide comes in they are going to drown. We've got to cut them free."

"Wait a while, miss," Ryman grabbed her arm to stop her leaving the car. "If we go rushing in the Chinese may just shoot their prisoners. The tide will take a couple of hours to get high enough to be a threat. By then it will be totally dark and we stand a chance of getting close enough to take them quickly."

"Tracy, you're shaking," Rob said.

"Of course I'm bloody shaking. I'm fucking freezing. Its late afternoon on first November and we're stood in freezing cold water. To top all that my tits are exposed to the wind."

"We're still alive and while that's true, there must still be hope. We've got quite a wait until the water gets too deep," Rob said.

"We're going to be dead from hypothermia, long before we drown," Tracy protested.

"They must be getting really cold. We should get an ambulance here. The water is up to their waist, they'll be getting bloody cold," Sue said.

As Ryman called for an ambulance, the van pulled away and they watched it drive off round a corner and out of sight. "Ryman, we've got to save them. Get something to cut them free with, Sue called over her shoulder as she got out of the car and ran towards the slipway.

"Sue. It's really great to see you. We're both tied at the ankle to these stakes; we'll need to be cut free. Do Tracy first, she's really suffering from the cold," Rob said.

Sue was now stood by the rising water's edge, about ten feet away from her husband. She turned to check where Ryman was. As

157

she turned she heard a gunshot quite close, an instant later a bullet hit the ground by her feet. She turned a little further to see Brian Tia, with a gun in his hand, walking towards her.

"If I'm not mistaken, it's Mrs. Blackstock. I don't know how you found us but that doesn't really matter. You've arrived in time to die with your husband." Tia gloated and raised his gun towards her."

Sue closed her eyes, a million thoughts going through her head, she heard a gunshot and waited to feel the pain, but it didn't come. She opened her eyes and there in front of her lay Brian Tia, the front of his skull in pieces where the bullet had exited. Looking up from the body, she saw Ryman standing some fifty metres away. "Ryman that was some lucky shot. If you had missed, you could have hit any one of us."

"Pardon me, miss Susan but, I always hit what I aim at."

There was a splash and they all turned towards Tracy. She had passed out, her knees had buckled and she had fallen face down in the water. Without a second thought, Ryman ran to the water, throwing his gun and jacket down on the slipway. He waded out to Tracy and lifted her head out of the water. In a semiconscious state she groaned and coughed.

"Miss Susan, can you come and hold her head out of the water and I'll cut her free."

Sue waded in and round behind Tracy, so that she could hug her to hold her up. Ryman pulled a small pen knife from his pocket took a deep breath and ducked under the water. He could see nothing in the dirty river water so had to feel his way down the metal stake, until he felt the cable tie which he cut. He came to the surface to take another breath and went back down and freed Rob. The two men carried Tracy out of the water and laid her on the slipway. Ryman covered her with his discarded jacket, then ran back to the car. He drove the car right up to the slipway and got out leaving the engine running.

"Get Miss Tracy into the front seat and you two climb in the back. We've been driving for an hour and a half, so the engine is good and hot. If we run the heater on maximum we may just start to thaw her out."

Chapter 15

"Father, Gabriel has been arrested. We've lost a vital member of the team just a month out from the first phase of 'Operation Birdbath'. I know the plan inside out so I can continue making things happen at the right times but we have lost our eyes and ears on what the British are doing. Thankfully Gabriel doesn't know I'm in London, otherwise I might have been given up for interrogation."

****

"......and the winner of the 2018 Miami Freestate Rally by a huge margin is the Luggard Shipping sponsored team of Luggard and Morris. Kurt and Chuck, if you'd like to come up to receive the cup and a cheque for $23000 presented by, on behalf of Freestate Tyres Inc., we have the lovely Miss Miami 2018, Miss Linda Betts. Incidentally ladies and gentlemen, Kurt is the first driver in the twenty seven year history of this event to win all four stages. Ladies and gentlemen please put your hands together for Kurt Luggard and Chuck Morris.

Kurt and Chuck bounced up the five steps and onto the platform to generous applause from the small but knowledgeable crowd, made up mainly of mechanics and competitors' relatives. The pair climbed onto the podium between second and third place winners, to be given their prize. Kurt held the cup high and the volume of the applause momentarily increased, then died away as the three crews left the stage.

"Well done, honey, I knew you could do it." Sandra said as she threw her arms around Kurt's neck and gave him a kiss. "I've got someone who would like a word."

Sandra passed Kurt her phone and he looked at the image on the screen, "Rob."

"Well done Kurt, Sandra has just told me about your weekend. I'm glad to see your hard work has paid off so soon. A few more events like that this winter and you'll be ready for the big league next year."

"Actually Rob, we're entered in the Costa Run Vail to Las Vegas starting on Wednesday."

"That's either very brave or very foolish. Let me know how it goes." Rob said.

"Will do. What's that behind you? Are you in hospital?" asked Kurt.

"It's nothing, just in for a few tests. I'll be out in a couple of days. I have to go now; the nurse wants me to take a shower. Good luck for Wednesday. Bye."

"I think the only good thing about working seven days a week, is you don't get the Monday morning blues," Zoe said to Sue. "But you don't get the high from Friday. In fact every day is the same. Pretty boring really."

"It's not all bad," Sue responded. "You do get time off. You had time last week to go to the rugby. Now let's go over what we've found out in the last couple of days. Sir Bernard has asked to see me at 11:00 and I want to take him something positive."

"Sue, before you go, do you know a Les Rudd at Williams Security?" Zoe asked.

"Les Rudd, or Sewer Rat Rudd as he's better known," Sue answered. "Everyone at Williams Security knows Sewer Rat. Whenever there's a pre-event search being planned, he always volunteers for the dirty jobs. That normally means checking the sewers."

"Well his name's on the second list," Zoe explained. "The last of the hand written ones, but it's been written with a different pen, like it's a later addition."

"My bet is that whoever is running this attack, wants Sewer Rat to ignore the bomb under the Cenotaph, when he carries out the inspections both the day before and a couple of hours before the ceremony begins," Sue surmised. "It's next Sunday when the ceremony takes place isn't it? So they could plant a bomb anytime in the next six days and the one person who should find it, will be programmed to ignore it. I'll give my brother-in-law another ring and see what he comes up with. We don't want to take Les off the job because that would give away that we know their plans and they could change them."

"Gosh, you're late this morning, Ryman," Zoe said as the driver entered the room and hung up his jacket.

"I had to go to internal affairs, to take in my gun license. They only had a copy of my old license, which doesn't allow me to carry the weapon around with me. Fortunately the new license arrived in the post on Saturday, with a start date of last Wednesday. Otherwise they were going to charge me with unlawfully carrying a firearm and unlawful homicide. They are only open 9:00 to 16:30 Monday to Friday, so I've been sitting around waiting for them to open this morning."

"That's all total crap," Zoe said. "Sue, can't something be done about this. You would most certainly be dead if it wasn't for Ryman carrying his gun."

"Until you shot that guy the other day I didn't know you had your gun with you," Sue said.

"Since Mr. Rob was taken, miss," he replied

"I for one am glad you did. This is a ridiculous waste of money and resources. I'll mention it to Sir Bernard."

"Have you heard from the hospital today Miss Susan?" Ryman asked.

"Rob rang while I was on my way in this morning. He's doing great, they just want him in another night for observation. Tracy is finally doing much better. Apparently, she was up walking unaided yesterday and the tests have shown no serious problems. She could be out in a couple of days."

"That's good news. Now what have you got for me today?" Ryman asked.

"For these terrorists to set off their bomb at the optimum moment they will need a clear view of the site. I'd like you to spend a couple of days around the Cenotaph area looking for likely places. We can stop the bomb but it would be good to get the bomber as well."

Sandra was really enjoying her assignment, perhaps too much. No longer was it the lifestyle, the clothes, the jewels and the parties, but it was beginning to be the man as well. She had been excited when he had led the rally after the first stage, that excitement grew with each following stage. Finally, when he climbed out of the car, after the final stage, she was the first person to congratulate him, she threw her arms around his neck and kissed him full on. She may have been imagining more than reality, but for the first time she thought she felt a response. They never kissed in private and never passionately. Her presence was merely for public show and she knew that so long as she played her part well and looked good, her reward would be this lifestyle, but even so she should ignore her emotions.

There was no time to party after the rally. Kurt gave his support crew ten thousand dollars from his prize money to share between the three of them, then left them to clear up all their equipment, load his car into the transporter and get everything back to his garage the other side of Miami. He knew that a large part of that bonus money would be spent on booze, girls and parties, but they had worked hard preparing his car and keeping it at its best throughout the two days of competition. But for himself, Sandra and Chuck it was home, something to eat then an early night, because tomorrow morning they were booked on a flight to Vail, leaving Miami at 5:30.

As they drove back home Kurt was thinking back to that kiss from Sandra at the finish line. Why had he responded to her? Was it emotion from winning just overflowing? That had to be the case, because he was gay. He had always known he was gay. He'd never given any girl a second thought. Even when his last girlfriend was murdered, he felt nothing. Yet Sandra seemed to care, after all she had introduced him to Robert Blackstock. He sat in the car and looked at Sandra and then at Chuck, he could feel emotional attachments to both but in different way. His mind was spinning. He was totally confused.

"Come in Susan, take a seat. How is your husband?" Sir Bernard asked as Sue arrived for their meeting.

162

"Doing well now, thank you sir. The hospital are saying they may let him go home tomorrow, I'm taking his clothes in when I see him this evening."

"Very good to hear. What about Miss Longhorn, we almost lost her I understand?"

"Yes sir, apparently her heart stopped twice in the ambulance. Luckily she survived. The doctors say it was being so cold that kept her alive. She's a very tough woman and is now recovering well. She could be out in two or three days."

"That is good news. I don't want to be too hard but I really do need them back the other side of the Atlantic as soon as possible to pick up the threads and get on down to Venezuela so that we can sort out what this Luggard chap is up to. My latest reports from those monitoring his ships say that he is using the threat from Somali Pirates. to install guns and troops on all his ships and the Chinese have just sold him a dozen helicopter gunships, which can land on the helipads of his larger vessels. It looks like he's preparing for war with someone."

"And what about the Ryman chap?" Sir Bernard asked. "I've registered him as a civilian secondment to MI-6 on your husband's request, but now Internal Affairs tell me that he's gun happy."

"That's total crap. Pardon me, sir," Sue apologised for her outburst. "I mean they are absolutely wrong about him. If Ryman hadn't shot Brian Tia when he did, I'm certain I wouldn't be here today. That Chinaman had his gun pointed at my head from less than a yard away and I saw him start to squeeze the trigger. I was certain I was dead and if I died, I knew the other two would die as well. Yet Ryman, some fifty yards away, was brave enough to take his shot, even knowing that if he missed he would have hit either me or one of the others. The kill shot was the only one fired, sir."

"I know you've got a lot to thank him for, but I.S. claim he was carrying a firearm illegally."

"Again they are wrong, sir. If you remember, sir I brought you his gun and the application for a license extension last Monday. You authorised the application and gave me the gun back, telling me to keep it safe. So technically Ryman was licensed to carry the gun from then. It just so happened that the paperwork got all caught up."

"Now that you mention it, I do recall it. Leave this with me, consider the matter closed. But I haven't yet seen his signature on an O.S.A form and we need that in case, walking freely in this building, he comes across anything top secret. Now tell me about these Chinese characters."

"Well sir. As far as we know there were two of them, Brian Tia and Peter Lowe, members of an ancient Triad based in Paris. Tia was the one shot by Ryman and Lowe is a known bomb maker. As far as we can tell, they are in London to seek revenge for something the British government did that resulted in the death of their Triad elders. Somehow they got hooked up with Luggard. Possibly through Gabriel."

"Yes we know all about Gabriel," Sir Bernard interrupted. "Thank you for your papers on that one. Some very clear circumstantial evidence and then the clear visual identification from your husband and Miss Longhorn, we have a watertight case. Gabriel is going down for a long time. The arrest was made yesterday but Gabriel's true identity must remain secret for now, to protect the agents on operations. Please continue."

"It would appear that Luggard or Gabriel encouraged the Chinese to use a similar tactic to what we think Luggard is doing. Perhaps Luggard sees it as a practical test of his plan, a sort of dummy run. Anyway the Chinese have used the drug QZ-21 on several targets. They used Doug Green to do their dirty work; we found a list of targets when we searched his house. Their objective is to plant an explosive device in the sewer beneath the Cenotaph and set it off next Sunday during the wreath laying ceremony."

" Both the P.M. and Prince Charles will be victims," Sir Bernard interrupted again. "But I thought the sewers and any other likely place got searched in the morning. The armed officers watch all around for any potential dangers."

"You are right, sir and Williams Security will do that. However the person crawling through the sewer will be Les Judd whose name is on the list of targets for QZ-21. We assume Judd will be programmed to ignore the package. The bomb will be set of by telephone. I've spoken with my brother-in-law. He is totally up to speed. Unfortunately we can't watch all the entrances to the tunnel and prevent someone going down there, because there are literally hundreds of entrances. So we'll let them plant their device and we'll check that part of the sewer, using two men the evening before and two different men on the morning of the ceremony. When we locate the device it will either be disarmed or removed to a containment container. In case the site is being watched, Les Rudd will still do his search and the additional searches will start from a point further down the line."

"All sounds very thorough, but what about the man pressing the button?" Sir Bernard asked.

"As well as the normal rooftop observers and marksmen, I've sent Ryman down there to scout around for any spot that has a clear view of the proceedings and we'll watch those carefully on Sunday."

"OK. Now where are we with the other matter?"

"If we start with the random murders. The evidence indicates QZ-21 is being used to aid a takeover of the drug distribution network in Britain. The pattern is consistent across the whole country and the timing is probably deliberate to cloud our investigation into these attacks."

"So why feed them QZ-21 and then murder them?" Sir Bernard asked.

"Client lists, sir." Sue replied. "They put their victim under to obtain a list of the victim's clients, so that they hit the road running, so to speak. Then simply give the victim a fatal dose and step into his space."

"Very clever, very simple. You've done well to uncover this. How do we stop it?"

"Easy to say, but difficult to do, sir. We stop the supply of QZ-21 and that stops further takeovers. Like everything else we just need to stop their supplies to close down the dealers."

"As you say, if it were that easy, drug dealers would go bankrupt over-night."

"Exactly, sir," Sue continued. "That leaves what I think we should focus on. What is Luggard up to? Zoe and I have gone over and over the list of names. We have grouped names together and analysed why they could possibly been targeted. For instance, there are two soldiers at Aldershot, one is in charge of the armoury the other is an expert in firing weapons. So it is our reasoning that one will steal a weapon and the other will fire it at a target yet unknown. Our problem is that we can't link these groups. We desperately need to know what Luggard's objectives are. It pains me to do so, sir but I must agree with you we need to get Rob out there, as soon as possible."

"And what about the village near Angel Falls?"

"The loss of Roger and Julie is terrible. Their deaths must have been horrific."

"Quite. The official line is that they were killed, when the light aircraft they were traveling in, crashed in a remote part of Venezuela. There is a memorial service being planned for next week."

"Captain Phillips has reported in at noon each day. After a long search they did find Roger's Bible and eventually the map he had drawn showing a narrow path to the top on the eastern side of the river, approximately a quarter of a mile from the falls. He dispatched three of his men to go to the top. They reported the track was very treacherous in places, where it gets a lot closer to the falls and the bare rock face is permanently wet from spray. In other places it became so steep that they had to remove their kit, climb up, then haul the kit up after them. At the top, the path comes out in undergrowth, under a cluster of trees, right on the edge of the cliff, giving them plenty of cover and the river just fifty yards to their left will drown any noise they make. From there, they have a clear view across a nine hole golf course, beyond that was a large lawn running up to the front of a very large house. Phillips is planning on sending out his roaming drones to see if he can get a better view of the house. The rest of his men, sorry one of them is a woman, the rest of his team have searched the western bank for another path, but found nothing."

"Well thank you Susan and thank your team for me. You've all done some excellent work. Now let's pray that all goes well on Sunday and we can move on."

Kurt spent the morning they arrived in Vail getting used to the Lamborghini Huracan, 5.2 litres of raw power, capable of two hundred miles an hour. This was not a normal rally, it was more like a road race and this car would be perfect. Across the bonnet was displayed the logo and name of his sponsor, Luggard Shipping, the rest of the car was gleaming white. At $248,000 this was not a cheap car but his father was one of the richest men in the world so why shouldn't he have a car capable of competing with the very best. The support team had arrived three days ago and had tuned the car to Kurt's requirements as best they could, now he was there they could finish their work.

In the afternoon he had to go and register for the race. Unusually Sandra asked if she could go with him. As a couple they fitted in the environment extremely well him in his racing gear and her showing herself off in white trousers emphasising her long legs, a pastel blue strapless top under a white blazer style jacket, the outfit was completed with white open sandals with four inch heels. She was five feet eight inches tall and the heels brought her nearly up to Kurt's height of six feet one.

Kurt was entered in the class for cars of four litres or more and from what he could see of the list, there appeared to be fifteen to twenty other drivers in that class. As they walked around the holding area where mechanics were busy doing last minute tweaks, to vehicles Kurt put his arm around Sandra's shoulders and she put hers around his waist, to the world they looked like a loving couple.

"Dad, how's things?"

"Hello Rob, we're all fine. What about you two, what have you been up to?" Eric asked.

"Sue is okay, working hard as usual, but appears to be really enjoying herself, stretching the old grey matter. I on the other hand am not busy at all. In fact I've been in hospital for the best part of a week," Rob confessed.

"Oh yeah, what have you been doing then?" the concerned father asked.

"I fell in the Thames. Not only was it bloody cold but I also swallowed quite a bit of water, you can just imagine how ill that made me. But I'm better now and Sue's bringing some clothes in this afternoon, so that I can go home. How's mum and the kids?"

167

"Luci is spending all her time with Peter. Where you see one, you see the other. It's not affecting her school work, in fact her marks are getting better week on week. Justin rang on Sunday to say he'd scored his first try for the school on Saturday, when they beat another school thirty seven - thirty five. Your mum has been making Christmas puds with Madge, so she's been busy as well. We had seven winners from fourteen entries last week, which puts us about fifth on the trainers' list. The girls have helped a lot, so I've been able to enjoy the racing. The more I get to know those two, the more impressed I am. I think you'll be impressed with what they are planning for that job you've given them."

"I can't wait to see it then. We still have no idea when our work here will be finished. I just wish I could tell you more about what we are doing, but that's not possible. Well, I'd better let you get back to whatever I interrupted you doing and go and eat my last hospital meal."

"Kurt, what are you getting your dad for his birthday?" It's only three weeks away, he'll be seventy so it's an important one. You need to get something memorable," Sandra said.

"I'm going to get him a trophy from this rally," he replied. "It is going to be my first trophy from an international event. Nothing could be more memorable for him."

"You're so damn sure of yourself, aren't you?" she said angrily. "You'll end up killing yourself or Chuck or both. Concentrate on the day not the prize."

"That sounds like good advice," Chuck said as he joined them by the car. "Twenty minutes until we're off. Time for last minute checks and to roll on down to the start."

Sandra threw her arms around Kurt's neck and kissed him. "That's for luck. There are a lot more coming if you come back in one piece."

Chuck gave them both a quizzical look and Sandra, wanting to avoid a situation, walked over to Chuck and put her arms about his neck. He quickly turned his head and Sandra kissed his cheek. As they separated Sandra said, "Look after him, Chuck." She turned and walked away to join other wives and girlfriends at the start gate.

Even in boots, with just two inch heels, she was the tallest in the group. Tall enough to see over their heads and see the starter's flag raise and lower to send off each car. She wasn't able to see the drivers, but Kurt's Lamborghini was distinctive by its lack of sponsors along its sides. So as soon as he had passed, she left the crowd to watch the on course monitors, spaced several miles apart along the two hundred miles scheduled for the first day, across the acrid Utah dessert.

Sandra watched as cars passed the first camera. With all the dust the cars were kicking up, it was difficult to recognise any of the cars, so she concentrated on colours. At the start Kurt was preceded by two red cars and followed by a green one. Every time she saw a red one, she waited for the next one to be red. She watched a red car pass with a white one close behind; as it passed the camera she saw the side had no advertising. It had to be Kurt, he'd already passed one car at least and was close to a second. He was driving well and a glance up at the leader board confirmed his time to the first of six markers placing him in thirty first place out of nearly fifty entries.

Watching cars pass the next camera she didn't spot the white Lamborghini at all. Then at the second marker, he had slipped back to thirty fifth. She gave a sigh of relief; he was still running at least. She stayed with the leader board and watched him climb, only to fall again, but each time he climbed, he got higher. At the final marker he had risen to sixteenth, but as they crossed the finish line for day one he was eighteenth and almost four minutes behind the leader. After the last car had come in, Kurt was confirmed in eighteenth place overall and eighth in his class with forty one cars left running.

Day two and three followed a similar pattern. At the end of day three, Kurt was up to ninth overall and third in his class. Another twelve cars had dropped out and he almost joined them. For the last ten miles, the car was slipping out of gear and he had to nurse it home to get his back up team to work through the night to fix it.

Brian Lowe was concealed in his chosen spot before sunrise. He watched Les Rudd descend into the sewer and ten minutes later emerge again empty handed. He didn't see two members of the army bomb disposal unit fifteen minutes later carry away a suitcase from a manhole in a street two hundred yards away. Sue and Zoe were there watching the army experts place the bomb in a containment box and take it away. Sue turned to Zoe, breathed a sigh of relief and said, "Well done girl. Let's go and get warm with a coffee."

"I'm just glad we were right," Zoe said.

As the two walked towards a mobile café, brought in to supply an expected large crowd, Sue's phone rang. "Yes, Ryman. Have you found something?"

"I have miss. An Asian looking chap lay under an overhang about seventy five yards from the target area. He's high enough to have a clear view and is armed with what looks like a Chinese QBZ-95 Automatic rifle. Where he is, it will be impossible to approach unseen," Ryman reported.

"Does he know you've seen him?"

"No miss. When you sent me down here to scout around the other day, I brought a few cameras with me. He hasn't noticed the pigeon sitting looking at him from twelve feet away, hasn't moved."

"Let's hope he doesn't notice. I'll call in the A.R.U. that's on standby. Stay where you are and I'll get them to ring you when they get here. They'll need you to direct them. When he tries to detonate that bomb and nothing happens he is likely to open up with that rifle. He has to be neutralised as quickly as possible."

Five minutes later, a fire engine arrived in the square. Two firemen climbed out of the cab and squatted behind their vehicle. Sue and Zoe watch as the water cannon mounted on the roof of the red truck, turned towards a building on the west side of the square. Suddenly a pressurised jet of water shot into the air striking the side of a building, with considerable force. Something fell from the side of the building, followed by a scream and something large fell from the building hitting the ground thirty feet below. The water stopped and two armed police rushed forward. One picked up the first object which Sue could now make out as a weapon of some sort. The second police man checked over the second object, then dragged into the square, what was now clearly a man. A cough behind them made Sue and Zoe turn around. "I thought it best not to wait for the A.R.U. to arrive, so called in a favour from an ex-squaddie mate of mine. You saw the result," Ryman said. "I did say that it would be impossible to approach without being spotted and I just knew if the

A.R.U. went in there would be gunfire and that would cause panic. This way there was no one in danger."

"I forgot you were recruited by the S.A.S. That is the sort of stunt they would pull off," Sue claimed.

"Yes, miss."

"HENRI!" Ernst Luggard shouted for his manservant.

"Yes, sir". The servant stood in the open doorway to the billionaire's oversized study.

"Henri, have you seen any news from London this morning. Anything about a terrorist attack or a bombing of any sort?"

"Sorry, sir. No. Nothing at all," Henri sheepishly replied.

Ernst Luggard was a man bent on reviving Nazi glory, strength and power and was not prepared to suffer anyone who stood in the way of his destiny, to the slightest degree, whether they were misguided rich business men or ineffective servants. "Get my son Josef on the phone!"

"Yes, sir."

"Well get a move on man, I want to speak with my son."

"Mr. Josef, I have your father on the line for you. Please hold," Henri passed the phone to Ernst then left the room."

"Josef, what news of the Chinese?"

"Nothing father, and I've not been able to contact them. There's been no report of any attack on any of the news programmes. I watched the ceremony on TV, it all ran very smoothly."

"See what you can find out and get back to me as soon as you find anything."

"There was an incident very early this morning. Apparently an ambulance was called because someone tried to commit suicide by jumping out of a window. The fire brigade and police were there, too."

"Find those Chinese quickly," Ernst slammed the phone down on his desk.

Chapter 16

"Father, I have at last been able to get Angel Michael in place and he's proving to be extremely good value. I'm well aware of what Josef has been able to get from his Angel Gabriel and I'm expecting to get similar from Michael. On a more personal note, I've received three or four personal threats from some of the big distributors and suppliers. So I have been making deals with some distributers to supply our product at far lower price and they appear to be happy."

****

Sandra was up early for the last day of the rally. Her plan was to see Kurt off at the start, then catch a ride on one of the helicopters to Vegas to be at the finish, when he crossed the line. The hotel they had been allocate was small and there were no suites. Normally they would have had two bedrooms, she would have slept alone, while Kurt and Chuck shared the other, but last night she had shared a standard twin room with Kurt. He still lay snoring when she went to shower and wash her hair. He was beginning to stir when she returned to the bedroom naked with her in a towel turban. She flicked the switch on the kettle and turned towards Kurt, who was now awake and staring at her strangely. "Do you want a coffee, Kurt?"

"No thanks, I'm going for a shower," he said as he looked down and slid out of bed and padded towards the bathroom.

Sandra smiled to herself on seeing the effect seeing her naked had had on his body. She made her coffee and decided to sit and drink it and read the messages on her phone before getting dressed. Kurt returned to the bedroom the towel around his waist failing to hide the effect of seeing her body was having on him. "Do you need any help with that?" she said nodding towards his tented towel.

"You are forgetting your part in our relationship, my lady, Get some clothes on! he scowled.

She dressed plainly in floating white trousers, a simple white shirt and a pale blue scarf at her neck. Living out of a suitcase all week had been a challenge and a way of life she would never get used to, each day having to get bags packed and ready for collection by a set time for transfer to the next hotel. This was the last time, Kurt had booked them in at the five star Wynn Las Vegas for a week of pampered luxury days and casino evenings.

Kurt had watched her dress without thinking what he was doing. When he realised he had been staring at her, he felt confused again. But shook off those feelings quickly, in order to begin to focus on the drive ahead. He had double checked the route on the map with Chuck the evening before and if the Lamborghini held together for the final one hundred and eighty miles, he was confident he could make up at least two more places, maybe even more. The leader was now over nine minutes ahead of him and the car currently in second place was over eight minutes ahead. These two would battle for the first two podium places but the other five cars ahead of him had, only seconds between them.

When Kurt and Chuck arrived at the holding paddock to collect the Lamborghini, the mechanics were still working on the gearbox and uncertain if the car would be ready for their allotted start time. If they missed their slot they would have to start at the back. It wouldn't affect their race time, but they would be running behind slower cars that he would need to pass and would ultimately cost him precious seconds, but it would give the mechanics an extra twenty minutes to keep him in the race.

Those twenty minutes were needed, but the mechanics weren't overly confident that their repair would hold under the strain it was going to be under. Sandra kissed them both and they climbed into the car and rolled up to the start line. The starter raised and lowered his flag and the Lamborghini was lost in a cloud of dust.

When Sandra arrived at the finish line, she found a spot to sit where she could watch the times ticking on the leader board. The board display was confusing to follow, because it was showing the cars in the order they were running, which wasn't necessary the same as their position, according to their race time. One thing she was sure of was that the two cars that had been leading now had the word OUT next to them and as her eyes scanned down the board, she could only find four cars faster than Kurt but that was only at the fourth check point. There were still sixty five miles to go, she knew better than starting to plan any celebrations.

Less than an hour later, the cars began to cross the line. Then she saw the white Lamborghini, the eighth car to cross the line. But their final finishing position would not be known until the last car crossed the line in about twenty minutes time. Sandra went into the holding paddock to be with Kurt and Chuck. The three of them sat on the bonnet of their car and waited for the officials to climb onto the stage and announce the winner.

At last the results appeared on the leader board. Luggard and Morris were shown fourth in the overall competition. "Damn fourth place, just eight seconds off the third place podium." Kurt's voice showed his disappointment.

The winners were presented with their prizes and the official began to read out the class results. "Class A Unmodified Factory Vehicles Three Litre and More, second place Swartz and Swift. First place and winner of the Randolf Trophy, Luggard and Morris."

"Kurt you won! You've won the trophy," Sandra excitedly announced. "Isn't that great? Well done honey."

All Kurt could manage was to puff out his cheeks and breathe out hard.

The post rally celebrations in Las Vegas went through the night. They started as soon as the results had all been announced, with a parade of all the cars. Only twenty seven cars finished and of those two were in no fit state to join the parade. The race marshals organised the cars into their finishing position and one by one they were driven out of the holding paddock and out through the cheering crowd. Kurt's head mechanic was driving the Lamborghini, Kurt and Chuck were sitting on the bonnet and Sandra was perched on the roof with her legs dangling down the windscreen. Several of the other cars had drivers sitting on the bodywork to give their fans a good look at them. The procession was fronted by a marching band, so moved very slowly, with the crews all waving at the crowd gathering to watch. The race drivers of the first four cars, each had a trophy in one hand. First came the overall race winner, his co-driver held a second trophy awarded for winning Class 'C'. The next two cars had race runners up trophies, next came the white Lamborghini with Kurt holding the Class 'A 'winner's trophy above his head. The parade went the length of the strip, turned and came back down on the other side ending up back at the holding paddock.

Kurt went off and spoke with his support crew, using a lot of arm waving and gesturing, then returned to Chuck and Sandra. "They're all happy again now. I've told them that tonight's party is on me, their entry and bar bills, all to be charged to my account and $2,000 of casino chips waiting for each of them at the casino under the Wynn hotel."

"Were you that confident of winning?" Sandra asked.

"Far from it. But I was up at around 3:00 this morning and went for a walk and there they all were working on the car. If we lost, it certainly wasn't going to be because they didn't put in the effort."

"But we won Kurt, you should be happy," Chuck said.

"We were fourth and it's my fault," Kurt claimed. "With you navigating we can compete with the rest but if we want to win, I need to become a better driver. After six hundred and fifty miles of dessert road we were just eighty four seconds behind the winner, that's only just over a mile and that comes down to just two metres in every mile. Less than a fraction of a second. That's how close we were Chuck. I've got to improve."

Sandra went up to him and kissed him full on. Disappointed that he didn't respond this time, she stepped back. "Do you want me to call Uncle Robert tomorrow and see if he can suggest anything?"

"That would be good. I must thank him anyway. Today's result is as much credit to him as anyone. Why did he retire so young, when he was at the very top?" Kurt asked.

"No one in the family ever talks about it, but I have heard it's because he had a big accident doing over one hundred miles per hour." Sandra had found this out when she had done some background research on members of the team. "He was thrown clear and walked away with just a few scratches, but his navigator was killed, decapitated by a wire fence."

They both watched the blood drain from Chuck's face, but he managed to speak. "So now, someone else drives him around."

"Sir Bernard, what can we do for you so early on a Monday morning?" Sue said as the head of MI-6 walked into the team's office and sat himself at an empty desk.

"I've come to congratulate the team on a magnificent result yesterday," he said. "We couldn't have hoped it would go that well. Not only did you prevent an attack on the P.M. and H.R.H. Prince Charles, you also captured the terrorist behind the attempt."

"Thank you, but we've got a lot more work to do, sir. What the Chinese were doing just happened to be running at the same time and if it hadn't have had connections to whatever Luggard is up to, we may not have solved the crime. We were extremely lucky, sir."

"I prefer to think of it as the result of hard work by a talented group of people. And as for you young man," he said as he looked at Ryman, "you can come and work for me anytime you want. Bringing in the fire brigade, like you did, was a pure stroke of genius. The Blackstocks are lucky to have found you. Now what about Mr. Blackstock and Miss Longhorn, when will they be fit to return to work?"

"Not for another week, I'm afraid sir. The doctor has told both of them they must have complete rest for a week while they are on medication. Apparently, it wasn't the cold that caused them problems, but the river water. Their long term exposure to the water has allowed toxins to get into their blood stream which could seriously damage internal organs, if not dealt with quickly. Rob says that the medication is knocking him out and all he wants to do is sleep."

"Sounds nasty. I was aware that the water was not healthy, but I had no idea it was that bad. Whatever must it have been like before we started to clean it up?" Sir Bernard queried. "Well I've taken a lot of your time up and I know you've got a lot to do, so I'll let you get on."

"One thing that still bothers me, Sue," Zoe said after Sir Bernard had left, "why was your name on that second list? We've fitted everyone else into the plot but not you?"

" Hello darling, are you very busy?" Rob called Sue, hoping she could spare a few minutes to hear what he had been planning, with input from Tracy.

"You just wouldn't believe the amount of work we are getting through and we had Bernard Howe in here for half an hour this morning."

"What did he want?" Rob asked.

"Well, he said he'd come to thank us for preventing a disaster at yesterday's ceremony. But I got the feeling he was pushing us on to start getting some answers."

"That's pretty much why I'm ringing. I've just got off the phone talking to Sandra Brown in Miami. Kurt has taken the bait. He's had a couple of successes but wants to do better. He's asking when I'll next be in Miami and can we meet up."

"So what did you tell him?" Sue asked.

"I said I thought I would be back in the next couple of weeks but needed to check with my P.A. to confirm my schedule and when I can confirm things I'll get back to him," Rob said.

"So what are you thinking Rob?"

"I'm thinking he's asking for my help, he wants me close. It may lead to me being invited to Angels' Rest, if we can find a good reason. I'm thinking if we don't strike now we may not get another opportunity. He's keen. He's eager. If I delay he's likely to find someone else," Rob explained.

"Although I hate to agree, you're probably right," Sue conceded. "But the doctor said you must rest for a week at least. What about Tracy? Will she be fit enough?"

"I thought of that and told Kurt she was with her sick father. I said I'd sort something out with her tomorrow, then speak to him again later tomorrow or on Wednesday. If Tracy isn't fit when I'm ready to travel, then we can use the sick father again, as a reason for her late return and she can follow when she's stronger."

"We need to discuss this in more detail. We'll talk this evening when Ryman and I get home. What is Tracy doing now?" Sue asked.

"She's sleeping," Rob replied. "These drugs are really wicked. As soon as you take one, you just can't keep your eyes open, I've only just woken myself."

"Okay darling, we won't be late," Sue said and ended the call. "Ryman that was Rob on the phone. He's planning to go back to Miami and will need you to back him up. There's little for you to do here at the moment, so it might be the right time for you to have a couple of days with your children and talk over a move to Yorkshire with your parents. Rob wants to talk us through his plan this evening, but I think you'll be free until at least the week-end."

"Thank you miss. I'll make some calls and see what the family is doing," Ryman said. "What would you like to eat this evening miss?"

"Something spicy, I think," Sue replied.

"I'll go now and pick up a few bits. Does Thai Green curry sound okay?" Ryman smiled as Sue licked her lips.

Rob stood and collected the four plates and put them with the rest of the dirty dishes for loading into the dishwasher later. "Once again you've fed us well Ryman. Now while I'm up, does anyone want a coffee?"

"Can I have a black Americano decafe please, love?" Sue asked.

"Same for me, please," said Tracy.

Rob looked to Ryman for his response. Ryman declined the offer with a simple shake of the head.

The doorbell sounded and Rob pressed a button on a small video screen mounted on the wall. "It's Mrs. Parfitt," he announced. "I wonder what she wants at this time of night?"

"Well if you let her in, we might find out," Sue said.

"Mrs. Parfitt, what brings you here at this time of night? Come in and take a seat. Can I get you a coffee or a tea?" said Rob.

"No thank you, Mr. Robert," Rob's cleaner answered with a worried expression on her face. "I can't stop. I just came over to give Miss Susan this."

Sue took a very crumpled piece of paper from Emily Parfitt's outstretched hand. "What's this Emily?"

"It was delivered, wrapped around a brick, thrown though the lounge window of your house about an hour and a half ago. I came as quick as I could. I left Paul boarding up the broken window to make us secure, until he can fix it tomorrow. I should really get back as quickly as I can. We just thought Miss Susan needed to see that. It worried Paul and me."

"What does it say?" Tracy asked and they all looked to Susan as she smoothed out the paper and read what was written on it.

Sue read the letter out aloud. "It says, Captain Williams I've missed you twice but only cats have nine lives. You won't be that lucky again, your husband wasn't. I got him and I'll get you for what you did to me. Watch your back, lady!"

"I must go miss. I hope it's not as bad as it sounds," Mrs Parfitt said as she moved to the door.

"Thank you Mrs. P.," Rob said and pressed some money into her hand. "Here, take this for your taxi and a piece of glass. Let me know if you need more. Thank you, good night."

"What's this all about, Sue," he asked.

"I honestly don't know. Tony was killed by a landmine, not some revenge seeking mad man. This note makes it sound like someone is trying to get revenge for something Tony and I did to him, or her. But Tony and I only ever worked on two cases together that I can recall. One of those was the murder of Ryman's wife. The other was a major, who we caught pushing cannabis to the troops. But he's dead, committed suicide while waiting for his court martial, leaving behind a young foreign wife, Spanish I seem to recall."

"We have to take a threat like this seriously, Sue," Rob said. "You need to get a look at your old army cases and draw up a full list of any of your cases, where Tony added anything and all Tony's cases, where you added anything. You have to get this person before they get you."

"Zoe should have some time over the next couple of days," Sue said. "She can help. We'll get onto it first thing tomorrow."

Ryman was just finishing his breakfast when Rob came through from the bedroom. "I'm off in five minutes, sir. Back Sunday afternoon."

"Are you okay, going back to Miami next week?" Rob asked.

"I signed up to be your body guard for the duration of this operation, sir, so yes, I am okay."

"Have you thought about after this operation, because we'd very much like you to stay on working for us?"

"Yes sir. Miss Susan asked me last week, when you were missing and I accepted. I really must go now, sir. See you on Sunday."

Next morning before leaving for the office, Sue rang her former commander. She explained the situation to him and asked to have access to the archive case notes. He apologised but said he couldn't give her access without ministry authorisation. She tried ringing Sir Bernard, but was told he was in conference with the P.M. So she made an appointment to see him at 1:30.

When she got to the office, Zoe had been copying the names from the two lists onto the white board that covered most of one wall. She had written the names from one list on the right hand side and from the second list on the left hand side and was now sitting back in her seat just staring at the board.

"What on Earth are you doing, Zoe?"

"I was looking at those numbers next to the names on the lists," Zoe said and held up the lists for Sue.

"Have you discovered what they mean?" Sue asked enthusiastically.

"I think I have," Zoe grinned. "I was playing with the lists and thinking about when these people would be activated. I was going to build a spreadsheet so that I could sort them. I started with Les Rudd. We know he was activated for the poppy day ceremony, so I entered the date 11th November 2018 into my spreadsheet, but the spreadsheet was set up for numbers, not dates. When I entered the date it was converted to a number of days since 1st January 1900, 43415."

"43415, that's the number next to his name on this list," said an excited Sue. "Let's get all these numbers converted to dates and see what it gives us."

Zoe went back to the spreadsheet on her computer and added a column containing the numbers from the paper lists. She then sorted the data into date order. "That's interesting, Sue. Look how they group, 43410 to 43415 that's the days leading up to 11th November 2018 and all of the names are on the shorter list. The second group starts in a week's time and ends on 7th December. The final group are in the last week of May or the first week of June next year. All of group two and group three are from the longer of the two lists. There are six names, including yours that don't have a number next to them. I don't know what that means."

"That's great work, Zoe, but I need you to take a break from the lists to do some research for me," Sue explained about the note from whoever was stalking her, not being able to check her records and of the two cases that came to mind.

"Well, I think we can rule out Ryman. So I'll start digging around the other case," Zoe said.

"Thanks, Zoe. You're looking for Major Timothy Lawson. It was Germany January, 2012," Sue added.

"What can I do for you today, Mrs. Blackstock?" Sir Bernard said as Sue entered his office and sat down. Sue explained about the letter, their theory about it being someone seeking revenge for something Tony and her had done and her former commander blocking her access to case notes.

"I agree with your theory, it seems to be the most logical answer," Sir Bernard said. "I can also understand why your former commander refused you access to the case notes. He'd be hung out to dry, if he let anyone access that material without authorisation. As you are now a civilian that authorisation has to come from the ministry. Don't worry, leave it with me. I'll speak to the minister as soon as I can. Meanwhile how's the operation going?"

"Rob and Tracy have just about recovered and plan to fly back to Miami next week to try and pick up where they left off with Kurt Luggard. Zoe and I are working on those lists of names again, trying to work out what those numbers against the names mean."

"Thank you, Susan. Please keep me updated. You need to talk to the police about this stalker Susan, it's for them to sort this out, not us."

" You're right of course, sir. I'll go this afternoon."

Chapter 17

"Sue, glad you called in. Come and see what I've found. Your Major's wife, Joanna Lawson is not Spanish but Venezuelan. She is the sister-in-law of Josef Luggard and the live in girlfriend of Doug Green. I don't think we need to look any further through your cases. We've found your stalker, it's now down to the police to apprehend her."

****

"Hi Pops, have you heard the news?" Kurt asked his father over the telephone.

"I'm your father, not some breakfast cereal, so please address me as father," Ernst responded. "You've waited until Thursday to tell me about something you did on Sunday. What kind of a caring son keeps his father waiting like that?"

"I'm sorry father, but we've been incredibly busy and I've not had the opportunity." Kurt grovelled.

"So you won your class I hear and nearly earned a podium place. I'm pleased for you, son. What's made the difference? I've always known you had the ability but you've never delivered in an event. Now you've won outright at a local event in Miami last week and now this. So what's changed?" Ernst enquired.

"Sandra's Uncle Robert was a world class rally driver in his youth and he's been giving me lessons and with some of his training ideas Chuck and I have completely changed our approach and well, you've seen the result. He's coming back to Miami next week and has promised to spend more time with me."

"What's his name? I may well have heard of him,," Ernst said, knowing already that it was Rob and that he was currently working with MI-6.

"His name is Robert Blackstock, he was racing about twenty years ago. Now he owns a horse racing stable in Yorkshire, England. He also runs training academies for film stunt men, supplying stunt men for loads of films in England and America and just about every horse you see in movies or on TV, is owned and trained by a

Blackstock company somewhere. He's a very rich man. I count myself very lucky to have met him and that he is willing to help me."

"I don't recall the name, but it was a long time ago. I'd very much like to meet him, why don't you invite him down to Angels' Rest? Your brothers and their wives are coming down for a couple of weeks to be here for my birthday. We could have a party to celebrate your victories, as a whole family. We don't get the family all together very often. Your friend would be very welcome. Is he married?"

"He is married and he's got children, but they won't be coming to Miami. He does have a secretary that goes everywhere with him," Kurt said.

"Is she his bed warmer?" Ernst queried.

"I don't think so, but she is a good looker," Kurt smiled at the thought. "He also travels with a man he refers to as his driver, but he does far more than drive him around."

"Well you had better invite them all. Bring them down for the 24th. I'll get Hilda to sort out a family party so we can properly celebrate your new standing as a competitive driver and at last a winner."

"I'll ask him and get back to you with his answer."

Zoe focussed her attention back onto the short list. There were three names on the list without dates next to them. One was Susan Williams of Williams Securities, an out of date reference. Sue had been Susan Blackstock for three months and she had left Williams Security around the same time. Zoe took this as an indication that the list had been compiled some time before September. The attack on Tracy, when she was mistaken for Sue, was on 23rd September. The second name was an ex-army officer. Zoe discovered he had been killed in a car accident on 25th September. The third was a private investigator, reported to have hung himself, with no history of depression or anything else that may have pushed him to take his own life. There was no obvious connection between the three so,, Zoe called it a day and left for home.

184

In the taxi home Zoe had a dozen or more questions going round in her head. At least she had been able to help Sue identify her stalker. She continued thinking over the lists then something struck her. "That's it!" she said to herself. "Now all I have to do tomorrow is prove it."

When Zoe arrived at the office on Friday morning, Sue was already working hard, reviewing her notes and preparing her status report for Sir Bernard. "It's not very often you beat me into work Sue, couldn't you sleep?"

"I want to get away early, so I'm just getting in the hours," Sue explained. "It's Rob's mum's birthday tomorrow so we're off up to Yorkshire this afternoon and back again Sunday, for Rob's flight to Miami first thing Monday. We're taking Tracy with us, so she can see her kids for a few hours tomorrow."

"Go as soon as you like. I can keep things ticking over here," Zoe said.

"Thanks Zoe. I'll just finish my weekly report for Sir Bernard, get it emailed to him, then I'll be off."

"I think I'm on to something with those lists," Zoe announced. "I may have some news for you by Monday."

Once Sue had left, Zoe got to work and it didn't take long to prove her theory. She started by searching newspaper online archives for January 2012 looking for a court martial. There was so much data to look through that she was beginning to wish she hadn't started. Eventually there it was, just a small piece in The Telegraph, reporting the death of Major Timothy Lawson, while awaiting court martial. The article said that although the major was dead,, the court martial would still go ahead, as there was more to this case than just deciding whether a man was guilty or innocent. The arresting officer was reported as Captain Susan Williams. The leading Judge was Brigadier Brian Trent and the prosecution team was led by Captain Peter James. Trent and James were the other two names on the list.

Zoe circled the three names on the white board and drew lines tying them together with the name Joanna Lawson. The other six names, which included Les Rudd she circled in red and tied them together with the word Cenotaph. It was clear now that the three odd ones were targets, added by Joanna Lawson and her revenge, for driving her husband to commit suicide and totally separate from the other names. They were just three people that were to be eliminated. The other six were to be hooked in with QZ-21 for the Chinese to aid their attack at the Cenotaph. There was also one hand written name with a date next to it. Zoe assumed that this meant that one of the six had died and the hand written entry was a replacement. She made a note to check the current state of the six. At that point she decided to call it a day. The other list needed a fresh brain, not a tired one. She was planning to work a half day on both Saturday and Sunday. With luck she would solve the second list by Monday as well.

"I wish I could fly like this every time I fly," Tracy said as she lay back in her first class seat, sipping from a glass of Prosecco. Rob had paid out of his own pocket for the upgrade for the three of them to travel first class. He knew he still felt the effects of the time he'd spent in the Thames. Tracy had suffered more than he had, so he assumed she was still struggling a little as well and being cramped up in what he called 'Peasant Class', would not be comfortable for either of them.

"Don't get too comfortable,," Rob said. "I paid six hundred dollars each for these upgrades. I doubt you could afford to do it yourself on what you must be earning."

"You are so right," Tracy said. I could have a holiday for that sort of money. In fact, I've got a cruise booked for next February which isn't costing very much more."

"I didn't take you as the cruise type, I took you for more of a pool and sun lounger. I can just see you stretched out in your bikini, cocktail in one hand and Mills and Boon in the other. Where are you going, anywhere interesting?" Rob enquired.

"I love cruising ever since my first cruise about five years ago. I'd love to do more, I just wish it were a little cheaper. In February I've got a short cruise booked. Just four nights sailing from Southampton for one day in Rouen, then back to Southampton. Four days of absolute luxury. Can't wait."

"Back to the job we're on," Rob instructed. "Whatever we do, we need to get into this Angels' Rest place and find out what Luggard senior is really up to. Last week's episode at the Cenotaph was serious enough, but I have a feeling that this will be far bigger. Zoe and Sue have been working on those two lists of names. They know the shorter list relates to the Cenotaph attack. It only had about a dozen names on it. The larger list has about thirty names. That in itself indicates whatever Luggard is planning is much much bigger. The girls also believe we're looking at more than one attack, at least one next month and one next spring or early summer."

"Mr. Robert," Ryman spoke up from the seat behind Rob and Tracy. "When we land, can you collect my luggage please? I left the hire car in the long stay car park. It will take me about twenty minutes to collect it and get back to the pick-up bay."

"Well done, Ryman. I assumed we would need to hire another."

"We left in such a hurry last week there was no time to return the car or deal with the weapons. You said we would be back within a few days so I concealed the weapons in the car and left the car in the car park."

"Good man. As soon as we land I'll give Chuck Tanner a call to make sure he's expecting us."

"It's been four days now Kurt since your father suggested you invite Uncle Robert to Angels' Rest and you still haven't invited him," Sandra asked Kurt as they sat on their terrace having breakfast.

"I'm not sure I am going to," Kurt replied. "Father never celebrates anything, so why is he so keen to do so now? He's gathering the whole family together to celebrate his birthday and now he wants a family party the week before to celebrate my win. I just don't understand, this sudden change in him."

Sandra was thinking this would be the only opportunity to get Rob into Angels; Rest so reacted quickly. "I think you are reading far too much into this. Ernst will be seventy at the end of next week. That's three score years and ten as written in the Bible. He obviously is thinking he is no longer invincible and wants to do something so that he goes to heaven and not the other place."

Kurt laughed. "My father going soft and thinking of the afterlife."

"I didn't actually say he was going soft but perhaps he is thinking that at seventy his best years are behind him and it's time to change. I don't think it a very good move for you to go against his wishes. If he is behaving oddly he could react unpredictably."

"You're right, as usual. Don't look a gift horse etcetera. I'll ring your Uncle Robert this morning."

Two other planes had landed at Miami just minutes before the London flight, so there was a long delay at passport and immigration control. While waiting, Rob took his phone off flight mode and immediately it started buzzing as it received dozens of e-mails and messages, sent to him during the nine hour flight. A quick scroll though the screens told him that mostly it was stuff that could just be read and deleted, with no follow up, but there was a message from Kurt Luggard which he opened and read. Then turning to Tracy and Ryman in the queue behind him, he whispere,d "We've done it. I've got a message from Kurt Luggard. We're invited to Angels' Rest. Kurt wants me to ring him at first opportunity."

"That's wonderful," Tracy said. "Now we can actually do what we've been sent out here to do. I was getting bored sitting around playing the sexy secretary."

"We still need you to play the role, but you're right, we can now get the job done. I'll know more once I've spoken to Luggard. I'll do that as soon as we get to camp."

Once through the arrivals gate, Ryman went off to collect the car, whilst Tracy and Rob went to the baggage hall and stood by the carousel. Considering how long it had been since they landed, they still had a long wait for their luggage. With three bags loaded on a trolley,, they walked out into the warm Miami sunshine, where Ryman was just pulling up in the only vacant space in the pick-up bay. As they left the airport, Rob rang Chuck Tanner, his crew manager, to confirm their imminent arrival.

"Hi boss." Chuck said, "I got your message yesterday and we're ready for you but we're only going to be here for another couple of days. The backers for the movie have pulled out, so the location is being mothballed until new backers can be signed up and we're heading back to L.A. on Wednesday."

"Okay Chuck. We'll be with you in about an hour so, we'll talk about things then."

"We're being evicted folks," Rob announced. "The crew are going home on Wednesday,, so we'll need to move to a hotel. I'm not too worried about it. The movie being filmed here was good cover to justify us being in Miami in the first place and for us returning today. Being invited to Angels' Rest will support our moving into a hotel, when our home gets taken away."

"Do we know which hotel Kurt Luggard is in, Rob? It might be an advantage to be close to him." Tracy suggested.

"I agree, if possible we should start getting closer to Kurt and earn his trust," said Rob.

An hour later, Ryman pulled the car up alongside their assigned trailer. Chuck Tanner saw them pull in and walked across to greet them. "Welcome back boss. How was your flight?" He turned his head towards Tracy and Ryman and raised a finger to the front brim of his cowboy hat, as a greeting to them.

"Good thank you, Chuck, Rob said as he looked across the camp site in chaos. Specialist equipment was being carefully packed into crates, crates then packed into shipping containers and containers being winched onto lorries. "I see the packing has started, he said and nodded his head towards the chaos.

"That's right. The local authorities have told us that nothing is to be left, not even a sweet wrapper. Some stuff will be going by rail tomorrow, but all the big stuff has to be at the docks for Friday, to be loaded on Friday and Saturday. The ship is due to sail mid-night Saturday."

"At what cost?" Rob asked.

"No cost to Blackstock Stunts Inc," Chuck smiled. " All covered in the contract and we get paid our agreed daily rate plus thirty percent. All thanks to our contract lawyer's boss."

"We do moan about them, but they do save us a shed load of money at times like this," Rob agreed.

Chuck turned to walk away then stopped and turned back, his hand pulling something out of the breast pocket of his shirt, which he handed it to Rob. "I almost forgot, a guy came by this morning looking for you. Driving a flash Mustang with a tasty piece in the passenger seat. When I told him you would be back this evening he left this."

"Thanks Chuck." Rob looked down at the business card he had been handed. It read; *Kurt E Luggard Promotions Manager, Luggard Shipping* plus the standard contact details. On the back of the card had been written a telephone number and the words *my personal line.* Rob went for his wallet in his pocket to keep the card safe. He found nothing. He tried other pockets but came up empty.

"Something wrong Rob?" Tracy asked.

"Yeh, my wallet is missing." He searched the car and still found nothing. "Somewhere between home and here some sneak has pinched my wallet. They've done well, credit cards and almost two thousand US dollars. I'd better call Sue and get her to cancel the cards. SHIT….!"

"Hi Rob, do you realise it's almost one a.m. here, I've been in bed two hours and fast asleep, said a drowsy Sue.

"Sorry darling,, but I've had my wallet stolen and I need you to cancel my credit cards urgently."

"Don't panic, love. I found your wallet on the bedroom floor when I got home this evening. You must have dropped it in your rush to leave this morning. I did send you a message to say that I'd found it."

"Wow, that's a relief. I had so many messages when I took my phone off flight mode, I haven't read many yet. No wallet still means I'm without money or credit cards over here. I guess I'll have to sell my body to some rich widow."

"You won't get much for that," Sue laughed. "Now can I get back to sleep? I was in the middle of a lovely dream."

"Of course. I'll speak to you tomorrow. Bye."

Rob followed Tracy and Ryman into the trailer. "Panic over, Sue found my wallet at home. However it does give us a problem paying for a hotel."

"Would this help?" Tracy said, taking a platinum American Express card from her purse. "I've had it three months and not used it yet."

"That would be great. Are you sure you don't mind, Tracy?"

"And I've got a little over a hundred dollars cash, sir," Ryman added.

"Thanks both of you. Now let's try ringing Kurt Luggard."

Ernst Luggard had spoken with his son, Josef early in the morning when he was in a London restaurant waiting for his lunch order to be served. Ernst was calling on his satellite phone as Angels' Rest was so isolated, satellite or radio were the only options. Josef had a receiver in his pocket that received a signal from the satellite and decoded it, so that the signal could be read by a standard mobile. They had discussed the impact the loss of Gabriel was having on their plans. Josef was able to reassure his father that everything was under control. The first attack would be a trial run for communications and was far enough in advance of the main attack that there would be plenty of time to make changes. Josef also confirmed that he had begun to stockpile food, water and other essentials in a London warehouse, ready for when one thousand fully armed Luggard troops are landed from the three Luggard ships, that every week for the last fifteen months had delivered Venezuelan oil to the Thames storage tanks. Over the last couple of month three new ships had taken over the route. The new ships had been modified to house up to three hundred and fifty soldiers in full kit. They also had mounted across the hold, a helipad large enough for a gunship.

Confident that Josef was on top of everything, he told him about inviting Rob to Angels' Rest.

"But he's a British spy who has been ordered to get into Angels' Rest and identify our weaknesses, ready for an attack," Josef claimed.

"Yes, Gabriel told me. If this spy is any good he would get in somehow and we wouldn't know what he was doing. At least by inviting him in, we can watch him carefully, even feed him false information," Ernst explained. "It's all a game and we have the upper hand and I intend keeping it that way."

Having checked with Josef his travel arrangements to Angels' Rest, Ernst rang Ralph in New York. Ralph reported that he had been having regular reports from Michael, the mole they had in the CIA. The plan was a simple one. Just one hit and the country would be in total chaos. Although there was still a lot of detailed planning needed, there was still over six months until the strike, so Ernst was happy with the update he got and Ralph also confirmed his travel plans.

Ernst then tried to call Kurt to check that Rob had accepted the invitation to enter the trap he had set,, but he couldn't get connected, so instead he decided to go ahead on the assumption that the invitation would be accepted. After all the British spy needed to get inside Angels Rest. He pressed a button on his desk to summon his manservant. "Ah Henri, would you be so good as to locate Hilda for me and tell her I'd like her to come and see me as soon as she can?"

"Yes sir, right away ."

"You wanted to see me," said a tall leggy female, standing on the threshold of his office.

"Yes I've got a couple of jobs I'd like you to at least think about." Ernst paused expecting a comment, but none came. "I would like you to organise two small parties for me. The first to be next Saturday, a celebration for Kurt to mark his break through into the top ranks of rally drivers. You'll need to get in touch with Kurt to see who he wants to invite and liaise with him to sort out transport.

"Sounds like a barbecue would be best," Hilda said.

"The second is to be held on the following Saturday, the day after my birthday. It is to be a proper party with music, a buffet, sparkling wine even a birthday cake if you like. I've made a list of people I'd like you to invite and arrange transport for. The one's I've underlined, you can offer a room for the night, then return transport on Sunday after breakfast. The others will need transport back to Canaima and onwards to Ciudad Bolívar on the Saturday evening."

Hilda looked at the list. "Seems to be straight forward enough. I'll start work on it right away," she said.

"Finally, all three boys will be home on Friday. They and their partners will need transport from Canaima. Kurt has three special guests who will be arriving with him on Friday, a woman and two men, all of them staying the whole week. They will need transport and rooms in the main house. These three are to be given VIP treatment, I want someone watching them twenty four-seven. That means someone outside their rooms at night as well."

"Very well, all noted," she said tapping her head with her finger.

"Is that Kurt??" said Rob speaking into his phone.

"Rob, thanks for calling me back so soon. I hope your journey was not too stressful," Kurt enquired.

"The flight was quite comfortable thanks. Your message said you wanted to speak with me quite urgently."

"Yes, but not over the phone. Can I come and see you tomorrow morning?"

"Sorry, I can meet you but not here. We're packing up the camp and shipping everything back to L.A. on Wednesday. I could come to you."

"If you wouldn't mind. I'm at the Novotel Miami Brickell."

"I've driven by it. About 10:00 suit you?"

"That would be great. See you tomorrow."

For the second time in less than a week, Sue was already grafting away when Zoe arrived. "In early again, Sue. With Rob away, I can't imagine it's because you want to get away early. So I can only think you've found something."

"Sort of, but this time it is because I couldn't sleep. Rob rang me in the early hours when I was deeply asleep, having a lovely dream. Since then I've had these darn lists on my mind. I'm your glad you're in early as well, I can talk you through my latest thoughts."

"Okay. What have you come up with?"

"Well, I'm only looking at the longer list. Firstly the list has thirty one names in all, six of those we know are dead. Three of the six died from QZ-71 allergic reaction, which ties in with there being three handwritten names at the bottom of the list.two of the others died from a heroin overdose, the sixth one we don't have blood results for, but as there is not a forth name been added, I am going to assume he died of an overdose. So that's three wanted for recruitment and three for elimination."

Zoe nodded, "I agree with you so far."

Sue continued "So the thirty one is down to twenty five. Your work on spotting that the numbers next to the names are actually dates and assuming that those dates are the dates when the victim needs to be triggered into action similar to the first list, then these twenty five names can be clustered into two. One group of eleven names, targeting the first week end in December. The other fourteen targeting the first week of June next year."

"Keep going, I'm still following you," Zoe encouraged Sue.

"The first group contains an army officer in charge of weapons store at Aldershot barracks and his wife who is an expert with Sight Aimed Weapons. The Major responsible for the weapons at Aldershot and a junior officer under him. The final two are security, a Red Cap at Aldershot and me, or more correctly my replacement at Williams Security. I'm thinking that with that mix we are looking at weapons being taken from Aldershot in the first week of December and being used against somewhere or someone at the end of that week. I can't make a connection for the other five."

"I agree totally. The pieces all fit in. But that is only a couple of weeks away and we've got no idea where or who the target is," Zoe said, "We need to get this to Bernard Howe."

" I will but first I've got more to say," Sue continued, of the nineteen names on that list that have a date within the first week of June, five have a connection with Buckingham Palace. We've got that girl who broke into the palace and was found in the Queen's private apartments, the judge that sentenced her, the police officer who arrested her, a senior member on the palace staff and an officer in the palace guard. All this leads me to believe that sometime in the first week of June next year there will be an attack made on members of the royal family."

"Jesus Christ this is serious, Sue! We've got to tell Bernard Howe now."

"You agree with me, then?"

"It's a solution that fits and there's nothing to say we're wrong and we've only a few days ago seen a planned attack that could have killed Prince Charles."

"I'll try Sir Bernard now, but we still have another fourteen names on the list. We must see whether there are any similar connections amongst them."

"Sir Bernard, it's Susan Blackstock. I need to see you urgently."

"Certainly Sue. I'll get my secretary to call you and fix something up for tomorrow."

"No sir, it has to be today, this morning if possible," Sue stressed. "We believe that there is an attack on the royal family, being planned by Luggard."

"Stay there I'll be with you in twenty minutes." The phone went dead before Sue had chance to say another word.

As the head of MI-6 left his office, he stopped at his secretary's desk. "Gillian, I'm just going down to the new operations room to see Mrs. Blackstock. Please clear my diary for the rest of the day and arrange for me to speak with the Minister and the P.M. sometime this afternoon. Stress to them that this is about a possible threat against the royal family and is extremely important." He then rushed out towards the lift.

Just ten minutes after receiving Sue's call, he was sitting in the operations room with Sue and Zoe. "Right ladies, you've said all the right things to get my attention. Now fill in the details and convince me I should be worried."

Sue walked him through the conclusions they had drawn from researching the first list and how that led her to look at the second, larger list. She then repeated everything she had told Zoe earlier.

"I can't fault your reasoning," Sir Bernard said and then took a death breath before blowing out hard. "So what should we do about this?"

"Well sir, as Zoe pointed out to me earlier, the first week in December is only a couple of weeks away, so I believe that has to be our priority."

"I agree." Sir Bernard was getting red in the face and Sue could see the concern in his eyes and she knew he was one hundred percent focused on every word she said.

"First of all we must get the five tested for QZ-71 again. Three of them were tested last week but wouldn't hurt to test them all. Then we need to keep them all under close observation. We can't replace them, because whoever is running this will just find someone else. We've seen them do that before. When we first identified these people with Aldershot, I spoke with the base commander."

Sir Bernard interrupted, "Let me guess he said he would follow-up on it but didn't sound enthusiastic."

"That's right, sir. I got the impression that he thought I was just some woman making things up."

"That's Tommy Lawson. He still thinks that women should stay at home. He's a good officer but getting too old for the job, so to see him to his retirement, he's been given Aldershot. The place practically runs itself, so he can't get much wrong. He is actually a cousin of mine. I'll ring him and kick him into life."

"Thank you, sir."

"So you're saying we let the terrorists' plan go ahead and we just sit back and let it all play out."

"Yes, sir. At least until the point where the weapons get handed over. Then we swoop in and nab the lot red handed. There is just one risk I need to point out sir. That's the possibility that one of these people may have a reaction to QZ-71 and that can be lethal."

"That's a risk we'll have to take, I'm afraid. What do you suggest we do about the threat on the palace?"

"Nothing yet, sir. Zoe and I will continue working on it, we've still got several months to crack that."

"Alright, but can I remind you that the first week of June next year will herald the seventy fifth anniversary of the D-Day landings and many of the world leaders will be in Britain for the celebrations, including Donald Trump who, incidentally, will be meeting the Queen at Buckingham Palace during his visit. Mr Trump, on the final day of his state visit, will be joined in Portsmouth by German Chancellor Angela Merkel, French President Emmanuel Macron, Canadian Prime Minister Justin Trudeau and Australian Prime Minister Scott Morrison. The leaders of the Czech Republic, Belgium, Greece, Luxembourg, the Netherlands, Norway and Poland, as well as representatives from Slovakia, Denmark and New

Zealand, will also attend the commemorations on Southsea Common."

"A security nightmare, sir. All those high profile people in an open space. All of them or any one of them could be the target and the weapon to be used could be anything from a knife to a chemical weapon."

"Quite! So we need a lot more pieces of this jigsaw to give the picture more clarity. But you are both doing a grand job ladies." Sir Bernard rang his secretary to check if she had managed to arrange the meetings with the minister and the PM.

"I'm meeting the minister at 1:30 today to update him with all this, then speaking with the P.M. at 7:30 this evening. In the meantime, I was speaking with my American counterpart yesterday evening and I need to brief you all on the latest discoveries made by the C.I.A. Susan, can you contact your husband and prepare him for a conference call at 2:00 pm and can you and Zoe please, be in the conference room next to my office at that time?" The girls both nodded and Sir Bernard left.

Chapter 18

"Good evening Prime Minister, there have been some major developments in our Venezuela operation which I must make you aware of. Following the identification of a mole in MI-5, I have declared this an MI-6 operation with the team leader reporting back to me. In the last few days the C.I.A. have informed me of a rapid build up of arms in Venezuela and of possible nuclear capability in the near future. The Americans will be taking the lead in neutralising this threat and will keep me informed on progress. I will, of course, keep you up to speed. Closer to home, my team have uncovered plots that threaten you, the royal family, Trump and several other heads of state next spring. However, more urgent than any of these, my team have identified a planned terrorist attack during the first week of December. We don't know yet where or who the target is, but we know that this is the first of several planned attacks."

****

Rob's phone ringing woke him from a deep sleep and it took him a moment or two to realise that he wasn't still in a dream and that his phone was telling him someone was calling him. A quick glance at the screen told him that the caller was his wife and the time was 6:41 am.

"Good morning, darling. Thanks for the alarm call. Are you trying to get your own back for me waking you last night?" he said.

"I'm not that spiteful," Sue replied. "I'm ringing on business. Zoe and I have made some discoveries. We believe that Luggard is planning some sort of strike during the first week in December, but we don't know who or what the target is. We also think a much larger attack is planned for the first week in June, next year, against multiple targets, at more than one location. We think the Queen and other members of the royal family are one target and another target is a gathering of world leaders including Trump, Merkel, Macron, Trudeau and Morrison at a seventy fifth anniversary of D-Day event, on Southsea Common."

"Shit, how did you discover all that?" Rob asked.

"Long story, I'll tell you later but this does increase the importance of you learning more about the plan and getting into Luggard's house."

"Well I'm meeting Kurt this morning, so that may well be happening very soon."

"Good. Sir Bernard was in the office this morning and I briefed him on all this and he has asked me to prepare you for a conference call at 2:00 today, our time. He's had an update from the C.I.A. that we all need to be aware of."

"Okay, I'll be here. It sound like Ryman is up and making some coffee, so I'll have a quick shower, some breakfast and speak to you later this morning."

While Rob was eating his breakfast Tracy staggered out of her bedroom in a vest top and brief sleep shorts. "What's wrong with you two? If you have to get up this early, just don't make so much noise. Is there any coffee left, Ryman?"

Ryman smiled and poured her a coffee. She took it from him and sat at the table next to Rob.

"It's my nephew Peter's birthday, today. Can't believe he's seventeen, almost a man. I sent him a birthday message and he sent me a lengthy reply. He seems to be totally besotted with your Luci. They are going everywhere and doing everything together."

"I was worried, but now I've had chance to think things through, I'm not worried at all," Rob said. "I have every confidence in my daughter. She won't let anything get out of hand. Ana and Eva have educated her beyond her years."

"That's good to hear. I'm off for a shower, so please no one touch the water."

"Don't be too long, Sir Bernard wants us available for a conference call shortly. Something the C.I.A. have discovered which we need to hear about."

Sue and Zoe walked into Bernard Howe's meeting room at a few minutes to 2:00. "Michele," Sue said in surprise. "What a surprise! How are you? Are you coming back to work?"

"Sir Bernard has asked me to come in for some sort of meeting this afternoon, so here I am," Michele said.

"How is your ankle?" Zoe asked.

"Some good days, some bad. The doctors say it could be painful for as long as six months or as little as two weeks, I just hope it's the latter."

"Ah ladies, good of you all to be here on time," Bernard Howe said as he entered the room, closing the door behind him then taking a seat at one end of the table and indicating to the others to join him. "Susan, can you please set up the conference call with your husband?"

Rob answered his phone on the first ring. "Good afternoon London, " Rob said.

"We can hear you, Robert," Sir Bernard said. "Can you hear me okay?"

"Loud and clear, sir," Rob replied.

"Good. I've gathered you here this afternoon because we've all been making progress in this investigation and there is some important news coming from the C.I.A. which has had a considerable impact on what we do next.

I think you are all aware that Venezuela is a relatively new country, only established mid nineteenth century and is currently in political meltdown. Hyperinflation, escalating starvation, disease, crime and rising mortality rates has resulted in massive migration. It is estimated that twenty five percent of the population have left the country in the last five years. Venezuelan financial stability is dependent on oil production. In the sixties and seventies the high demand for oil saw the rich owners get richer and the poor get poorer. Venezuela's oil production quickly declined, largely due to poor equipment maintenance, but the rich still got richer. In 2016 inflation was running at eight hundred percent, this year it's currently one million percent.

The government is totally corrupt. There is clear evidence that presidential elections have been rigged for decades. The current president, Nicolas Maduro is quite simply a bully. Last year alone, saw more than five thousand people who showed opposition to his policies, murdered. Madura is protected by the armed forces. He pays them well, equips them with the very best arms and kit, he even feeds them well. So has no issues recruiting young men. New military camps are springing up almost daily. Any questions?" Sir Bernard looked at Sue and Zoe who both shook their heads.

"We're okay so far, sir, Rob said.

Sir Bernard continued, "The C.I.A. have been watching the situation in Venezuela very closely. They tell me that the purchase of arms and equipment from Russia and China has increased over the last few months. Venezuela's population is only thirty one million, yet it has the largest army of any South American country. Our man, Luggard, has been throwing money at the government and is largely funding the build-up almost single handed, but in the last few months, further donations have been received from a source in Argentina. The C.I.A. claim the money comes from Raymond Nell, head of a German family in Argentina, suspected as being the offspring of a former Nazi SS officer."

"Sounds like a similar background to the Luggard family," Sue said.

"Wasn't the Nell family reported to have been the finance behind Juan Peron's political success and the rise of Eva Peron's popularity in Argentina?" Zoe asked.

"Yes, it has always been believed that the Nazi treasure was divided into three and all three parts ended up in South America," Sir Bernard added. "Anyway all this money has enabled Madura to buy two inter-continental rockets from the Chinese. They have also been secretly building a stockpile of nuclear waste from various suppliers and Luggard is funding some sort of research project, which the CIA believe to be a project to develop a nuclear weapon, as payload for the two Chinese rockets. The C.I.A. is convinced that in six months Venezuela with have nuclear weapons within range of all major cities in USA and Madura is reckless enough to press the button at the slightest provocation. The C.I.A. and I spent a long time talking last night. The evidence is that Luggard's strike, planned for next June, will cause enough uncertainty and chaos for Madura to sweep in behind and take control of major western powers."

Rob interrupted, "We can't see your face, sir ,but by the tone in your voice you're not convinced it's that simple."

"I'm not. My gut tells me there is more to this than an aggressive military manoeuvre," Sir Bernard explained. "Madura may appear to be in charge, but Luggard is a big influence on him. We can assume Luggard is not just the bank manager but is pulling the strings and Madura is simply his puppet. Luggard and Nell obviously know one another and if the third part of Hitler's gold did end up somewhere in South America, you can bet Luggard knows where it is. My gut tells me that this is Luggard's show. I just don't know why."

"Well, I'm seeing Kurt Luggard this morning. I'm expecting him to invite us to Angels' Rest so we can start the job we came out here to do," Rob said.

"And Zoe and I will keep trying to make sense out of these lists. I agree with you, Sir Bernard, Luggard is more than just the financial backer in this," Sue added and Zoe nodded her agreement also.

"Where do I fit in all of this? What do you want me to do, sir?" Michele asked.

"We need to watch closely what the yanks are up to," he replied. "I agreed with them that they would deal with Madura diplomatically and we would sort out Luggard. I'd like you to watch them like a hawk. As soon as they shift from that plan, I need to know. I don't care how you do it. Whether you need to go to the States or you can do it from here. I just want them watched. I think that's all. Unless there are any question, its back to work everyone. Thank you for coming."

Kurt, Chuck and Sandra were still eating breakfast when Rob and Tracy arrived. They had left Ryman arguing with the doorman, Ryman had parked the car in a reserved slot, but there was nothing to say it was reserved. The argument looked set to last.

"Robert, thank you for coming over," Kurt said as he stood to shake Rob's hand. "Please take a seat. Would either of you like a coffee?" They both shook their heads.

"Congratulations on your recent successes," Rob said as he took a seat on the sofa and Tracy settled beside him, like a well-trained employee. "You said you wanted to speak with me. My time in Miami is very short, we ship out tomorrow and head back to Los Angeles."

"Is it important that you leave when your workers do?" Kurt asked

"No, I don't have to, but there is nothing to keep me here when they go."

"That's part of what I wanted to talk about. Chuck and I were just eight seconds off a podium place in the Costa Run. Our position in that race is all down to your work. When we were last together,, you said you could improve my driving skills. Is that still the case?"

"It is. There are many little things that will shave seconds off your times."

"I really would value your help, Robert. My father is throwing me a celebratory party at our family home. He is asking me to invite my support crew. He specifically asked me to invite you and suggested you stay with the family for the whole week and attend his own seventieth birthday celebration on 1st December."

"That's very kind of him, but I don't think I can accept."

"I insist, the house is more like a hotel. There's a pool, a gym, tennis courts, a nine hole golf course and the most spectacular views in South America."

Tracy spoke out. "You deserve a break, Rob. You've been working too hard recently, I know because I keep your diary. It would do you good to slow down for a few days, maybe learn how to play golf."

"And at the same time, show me a few of those driving tips," Kurt added.

"If you are all against me, I'd better agree. But we don't know where your family home is."

"Don't worry about anything. I've got someone who will make all the arrangements. I'd like you to move to this hotel as my guests until Friday when we'll fly out. I'm afraid it's an eleven hour journey, but you will of course travel first class."

"That's very good of you Kurt."

"It's the very least I can do for the man I owe so much to. There is just one thing to warn you about, my family home has no internet or telephone signal. We rely on shortwave radio and satellite phones."

"That doesn't worry me, but Tracy may struggle. Without the internet she won't survive," Rob made it sound more genuine.

Tracy continued the pretence,, "Nonsense Rob. I'll be happy with the pool."

Sandra joined in, "If you like,, you can join me poolside on the sun loungers. The sun can be wonderful there, I've been told. It would be nice to have some company. The men will be off playing with their cars."

"Sounds wonderful," Tracy replied.

"That's set, then," Kurt said. "I'll ring down and arrange for three single rooms and get someone sorting out travel arrangements."

There were nineteen names on the list that Sue and Zoe were struggling to fit into any pattern. Neither did they appear to have anything in common or have any known special skill. "We must be missing something, Zoe." Sue said.

"Just a minute, Sue, I may have found something," Zoe said. "I was looking at how we might contact them. I was thinking that if we just talk to them, something may emerge and maybe we'd want to test them for QZ-71. But look what I found." Zoe passed Sue the note pad she had been writing on. Zoe had listed the nineteen names. Against each name she had written an address and the highlighted a few of them.

"Six of them live in Portsmouth," Sue said. "It's not conclusive, but it does make me think that the gathering of leaders on Southsea Common on 6th June is one of the targets. We've got a little over six months to follow up on that, so why don't we park that, remove the six from the list and see what we can get from the remaining thirteen."

"Are you thinking there are still more targets, Sue?"

"Let's put it this way. If you wanted to remove the British government, where would you target?"

Zoe thought for a few minutes then said, "Westminster, the Houses of Parliament would be top of my list."

"Exactly," Sue said, "and how would you go about it?"

"Well a bomb is the most obvious, a car bomb would be easier but more random in the damage it causes. Then there are rockets, probably a number of different weapons could be used."

"What about chemical weapons?" Sue added. "Most MP's will be present on the 6th of June. If there's something big being planned,, Williams Security will almost certainly be involved. Let's look at those last thirteen, looking for anything that could relate to anything that could be used to attack the House of Parliament."

"Well guys, we're in," Rob said to Tracy and Ryman once they were safely back in their car and heading back to the camp. "Now we have to be extra vigilant. From here on in, I think we're in considerable danger."

"What do you mean,, Rob?" Tracy asked.

"Why would Luggard specifically ask for us to attend, not just for Kurt's celebration, I can justify that, but to stay the whole week to attend his birthday party? He doesn't know us, nor are we best friends with Kurt. He knows who we really are. It's the only explanation. He can't kill us because that would draw too much attention to himself at a critical time in his preparation to strike. If he leaves us free, we are able to report anything we discover. But if we're inside Angels' Rest, there are no phones and no internet, so if we discover anything it would take several days to get a message home. Plus, it gives him time to lay several pieces of bogus information, so that when we can get communication out, we'll mislead our bosses."

"So why won't he kill us when we get to Angels' Rest?" Tracy asked.

"Because if we don't return when we say we will, he'll be in the spotlight again,," Rob suggested. "As soon as we get back to the trailer, I'll ring Sue and see if anyone has come up with a clever way to get messages out."

As Ryman pulled the car into the camp, it was amazing how it all looked. What had been chaotic mess, was now an organised area, with transport containers stood in two rows, some with their doors wide open, with men carrying cardboard cartons and stacking them carefully into the transport containers. Other men were moving larger pieces into other containers. The whole site had been virtually cleared and now their trailer stood alone in a wide open space. Ryman went off to prepare lunch and Rob sat in the lounge and rang Sue.

"Hi honey," Sue said, "how is your day going?"

"Not too bad," he replied. "We've got our invite to Angels' Rest."

"That's wonderful, darling. So Kurt came through?"

"Not Kurt. The invitation came from Ernst himself and it's not just for the weekend but it's for about ten days. So whatever we discover, it's going to be old news by the time we get it back to you and I can't think of any way round it, unless we put a message in a bottle and send it over the falls," Rob jested.

"There is a way, Rob," Sue responded. "We got a small force in the area, the leader, Captain Philips, contacts me via a scrambled satellite link at noon each day. It's totally secure. He and his team have made their way to the top of the falls and are hidden in a thick band of trees and under growth, approximately three quarters of a mile from the house. There is a golf course between them and the house and in the week that they've been there, all they have seen is someone mowing the greens, no one playing at all."

Rob interrupted her, "Tracy and I both have the same model mobile phone. We could take pictures and record messages on one phone and drop it on the perimeter of the golf course, near your Captain's men and they can get stuff to London and put the phone back to be picked up next day."

"That sounds feasible but I don't know how we'd get the pictures."

"It's only a computer, there must be a way, get the techies working on it. Kurt is moving us to his hotel for tomorrow and

Thursday night as his guests. We're booked on a 6:45 flight from Miami to Caracas Friday morning, then a connection to take us down to Ciudad Bolívar, where a helicopter will meet us and take us on to Angels' Rest."

"Hardly worth going to bed Thursday night then, you need to be up at about 3:00 to get that early flight."

"I'm not all together happy about that or the fact that the invite came from Ernst. There's no reason for him to do that, unless he knows our true identities and wants us near him, where he can control us and keep us from communicating with yo. Maybe he'll also feed us false information to lead us away from what he's really up to."

"That's a logical conclusion, just take care; I don't want to lose you."

"Don't worry, I won't do anything to put any of us in danger."

Sue ended the call with her husband and immediately rang Sir Bernard and made him aware of the conversation she'd had with Rob.

On Wednesday morning the three agents packed and moved to the Novotel Miami Brickell hotel. They had been given rooms on the sixth floor, Kurt was on the ninth. After unpacking, Rob went up to the ninth floor and knocked on the door of the suite he'd been in just twenty seven hours earlier.

"Good morning Sandra, is Kurt about?" Rob asked as the C.I.A. agent opened the door.

"No, he's gone to the gym with his boyfriend. He'll be gone a couple of hours. Come in."

Rob closed the door behind him and followed her to two chairs out on the balcony.

"I thought I'd better try and speak with you before we go to Angels' Rest. Is there anything you can tell me about the place?"

"Not really. I've only been there twice myself and both were very brief visits. No real chance to look around. Kurt did give me the tour of course, but I wasn't taken anywhere that wasn't accessible by everyone."

"Well, that's why we're out here."

"I've drawn a crude map of what I've seen. It may be of some use. It's on page ninety nine of this." She handed Rob a Dan Brown paperback.

Rob flicked though the pages and was looking at the map, when Kurt burst through the door into the suite. Rob closed the book quickly before Kurt saw the map.

"You're back quickly, lover," Sandra stood and walked to meet Kurt but he threw down his kit bag and slumped down onto the sofa.

"We had only just started our workout when Chuck slipped on the treadmill and injured his ankle. So I had to get him to the hospital. I left him waiting for an x-ray. The doc thinks it may be broken. If it is he won't be coming with us this weekend. I've come back to put some clothes on."

"Oh lover, what rotten luck," She bent down and kissed his forehead. "Kurt, Rob's come to see you."

"It appears your girlfriend and I share a common liking of the author Dan Brown." Rob said, who was now stood behind Sandra's shoulder. "I haven't read this one, so she said I could have it."

"So you finally finish that book, doll. You've been reading that for weeks," Kurt said.

Rob stepped forward. "I came to see you, Kurt, to say thank you again for the rooms, they are great, very comfortable."

"No problem, Rob. I'm afraid you're going to have to excuse me. I need a shower then I want to ring the hospital to see how Chuck is. Glad your rooms are okay. Sandra will see you out and I'll see you Friday morning, the cabs are booked for 5:15."

At dinner, Rob gave Tracy and Ryman the bad news about the early taxi on Friday. He suggested they had Thursday off, see the sights of Miami and all meet up for dinner at 7:00

Rob woke a little after 7:00 the next morning, used his fingers to work out what time it was in London and deciding it was midday and Sue would be at lunch, he rang her. "Hi sexy. If you were here in this bed right now I'd…….."

Sue quickly interrupted him, "Hi Rob, can I call you back later?? I'm in a meeting with Sir Bernard and the minister. We're at number ten waiting to go in to see the P.M. to brief her on the operation. Just hold those thoughts and I'll ring you back in a couple of hours. Bye."

He put his phone down on the bed, picked up the house phone and ordered breakfast from room service. He then had a shower, shaved and got dressed. He was sitting at the desk, making a copy of Sandra's map onto hotel note paper, when there was a knock on the door and a female voice announced, "Room service."

Rob called out, "Come in!"

The door opened and a Native American featured woman wheeled in his breakfast. "Will that be all sir?"

"Yes,, thank you," he replied and handed her a few dollars as a tip.

She nodded her thanks, turned and left, but before she closed the door,, Rob heard her talking to someone. She pushed the door open again,, "Two gentlemen here to see you, sir. Shall I let them in?"

Before he could respond, two men, both in their late fifties, one tall and one very short, pushed by her. "Robert Blackstock? I'm Cruise, Executive Producer of 'Black Dawn', this is Christopher McQuarrie director?" The shorter man said as they approached Rob.

"Black Dawn?" Rob said, questioning what it was.

The short man answered, "Yes, 'Black Dawn', the movie we're making that your team are walking away from. I want you to get them back on set, today."

"My team have walked away because of failure to be paid and there being no likelihood of being paid, because the backers have pulled out."

"Yes I'm aware of the money issue, but that's all been resolved."

"How can you be sure?"

"Because I'm putting up the money and I give you my word. To show I'm genuine, here is a cheque to cover what you are owed plus an advance of two hundred thousand dollars towards completing filming. Please also let me know your expenses for the last few days and I'll reimburse you immediately."

"If you two gents go down to reception and wait for me, I'll contact Chuck Tanner and see about getting the team turned round and back to Miami.

As they left Rob's room, Tracy came out of hers and had to step back to let them pass. She knocked on Rob's door and walked straight in.

"Hi Tracy. You're up early, can I help you?"

"I didn't know you knew Tom Cruise."

"I thought he looked familiar. So that was the famous actor was it? He just given me a cheque for almost a million dollars, I guess it won't bounce," Rob grinned and Tracy left.

Chuck Tanner listened to what Rob had told him, then said. "I can probably stop most of the kit leaving, but we'll lose an awful lot of good will with the shippers, as well as a couple of deposits we've paid."

"Just do what you can please Chuck and get the team back on the job. Let me know any costs you incur and I'll put the bill in."

Rob went and found the two film men, gave them the good news and told them that he expected to be reimbursed for costs which may also include replacement of any equipment lost or damaged.

He was in the lift returning to his room when his phone rang. "Do you know how embarrassed you made me in front of the minister?" Sue began. "But I am interested in what you were about to say. You were saying that if I were there in bed beside you you would what?"

"If you had been in the bed next to me, I would have given you the ride of your life."

"Oh, I really missed out big time. We'll have to remedy that when you get home. I'm sure I can come up with something to make your waiting worthwhile. In fact Zoe gave me an idea when we were in hospital which I'm thinking of following up on."

"Now you've got me thinking."

"Just make sure you do comeback and in one piece."

Back in his room Rob finally got to eat his breakfast. He was okay with the cold bacon and sausage, the hash brown was acceptable too, but the mushrooms, beans and scrambled egg he couldn't face. He finished copying Sandra's map then using the hand held scanner plugged into his laptop, he uploaded an image of it onto the laptop then e-mailed it to Sue with a row of kiss emojis on the bottom.

Chapter 19

"President Mandur, my operation plan is on track. My small army continues to grow in number and in strength. We now also have over five hundred people in Britain, eleven hundred in United States and more than eight hundred across Europe all prepared with the drug QZ-71. By the time we need them, there will be ten times that number, just waiting for the command to attack. With their commanders in chief removed, our enemies will be slow to respond and victory will be ours within days, if not hours of the first strike. Long live Venezuela!"

****

Zoe was talking on the phone when Sue arrived at the office on Friday morning. Sue could see she was upset about something and the conversation ended quite abruptly. "Are you alright Zoe? Has something happened? Do you want to talk about it?" Sue asked.

"That was Sarah. The ladies' leagues have a mid-season break this weekend, so Sarah wasn't going to be playing, and I was taking her away for the weekend, it's her twenty fifth birthday on Sunday. Nowhere too grand, my parents live in Hythe in Hampshire, they've got a two bedroom fourth floor apartment that looks out over the Solent."

"Sounds lovely." Sue said.

"It can be if the weather is good. Anyway I had it all planned out. I was going to take her for a walk on the beach tomorrow morning and give her this," she held out her hand and rolled back her fingers to reveal a diamond solitaire ring.

"That what I think it is?"

"Yes. I was going to ask her to marry me, but she rang to say she has been called up for the England training squad, as replacement for an injured girl. She's booked on a flight to Spain this morning."

"Oh Zoe, you must be gutted."

"I'm certainly not very happy. Not because she's been called up, I'm pleased for her. It's her greatest dream, to become an

212

England regular. But I really wanted this week-end to be special for both of us. Now here I am week end bag packed with sexy nightwear and going home alone."

"I really sorry for you. What you need is something to lift your spirits. Why don't you come up to Yorkshire with me for the week end? Meet Rob's daughter Luci and the girls. We could have a girly night out tomorrow. Let our hair down, forget all our troubles."

"Who are these girls? I've heard you and Rob talk about them before."

"Ana and Eva, a couple of Russian sex workers."

Zoe raised an eyebrow. "Do you mean prostitutes?"

"No. They are two very nice, extremely attractive young women who have been through some bad times, but now work for Rob. It's a long story, I'll tell it to you sometime. What about it, then? Are you interested? Do us good to get away from these lists for a couple of days and come back to them fresh again on Monday."

"I'm not sure Sue. I wouldn't be good company."

" I'm sure it would do you good. The girls will lift your spirits, they have that effect on everyone."

"Oh go on, then. I'll come with you."

"Good girl, be ready to leave just as soon as I've spoken with Captain Phillips, at 12:00."

Rob had set his alarm for 4:30 but was awake long before it went off. He just lay on his bed looking at the ceiling and trying to imagine how the next week was going to work out. Did Luggard really know who they are? Are they walking into trap or was he reading more into this than he should? His thoughts were interrupted by the alarm. He had packed his bags the evening before, so he was able to take a long hot shower, dress and was still down in reception handing over his key by 5:10.

Tracy, or Viv, as he now had to be careful to call her, came out of the lift with Ryman just behind her. He was carrying his own luggage and dragging Viv's oversized bag behind him. She handed two keys to the girl on reception and the two of them walk across to join Rob. He greeted them with a cheery, "Good morning."

"It's not yet morning and it's not good either. So what's making you look and sound so cheerful today?" she asked.

"I'm always happy, hadn't you noticed. Today especially so, I love flying. Careful now, Kurt has just got out of the lift."

"Good morning Kurt, how is your friend?" Rob asked.

"Chuck's ankle was worse than we thought. Such a silly little accident with such serious consequences. His ankle is broken in two places. They have not been able to do much because of the swelling but he is scheduled for surgery this morning, to insert a screw."

"Sorry to hear that. And Sandra, is she not coming either?"

"Oh yes she's coming, she just wasn't quite ready. You know what women are like. She'll be down in a minute."

They drove to the airport in two taxis. It was already 6:30 when they arrived at the airport terminal main door. Rob was rushing to get the luggage onto a trolley. "Don't panic Rob, the plane won't go until I say it can, Father owns the airline, he bought it outright last year."

Kurt lead them all through the airport, out onto the tarmac and up the steps onto the plane. No tickets or passports were asked for. A flight attendant showed them to a block of seats in first class, reserved for them. There were seven other seats all empty and stayed that way.

At 11:55, an alarm on Sue's phone sounded. It was her reminder to be ready for Captain Phillips's satellite phone call from Venezuela. Five minutes gave Sue time to fire up the app on her phone to link with the satellite phone which now sat under her desk. At 12:00 exactly she heard "Blackbird calling Nightingale."

She responded with, "Nightingale receiving you loud and clear. Go ahead Blackbird."

Captain Phillips gave his report. Then Sue explained how Rob would drop his phone on the golf course near the marines 'position and she read out the instructions that the techies had given her on how to send pictures and video via the satellite phone. "Rob is due to arrive mid-afternoon your time, expect first drop tomorrow."

The call ended and Sue put her phone in her bag. "Are you ready to leave Zoe?" Sue asked.

"Just got to log off and shut down my laptop and pick up my bag, then I'm ready. Are we driving up to Yorkshire?"

"No we're going by helicopter. We must get a move on, we need to be at City airport by 12:45."

A" helicopter ride must cost you a pretty packet?"

"Actually it's costing me nothing. I was out with my brother-in-law on Tuesday evening and we bumped into Alasdair Rose. He was my first husband Tony's best man at our wedding. I haven't seen him since the day of Tony's funeral. He was still in the Marines then. A helicopter gunship pilot. He was saying he's been out almost a year and landed a job almost straight away. He delivers new helicopters to customers all over Europe and today he's flying one to a customer in Scotland. To cut a long story short, he offered to take me with him and drop me off at home, as it was only a short way off his route. I rang him this morning to confirm and see if he was okay to take you along and he said it would be fine."

"Sounds great, I love helicopters."

It was lunchtime when Kurt and his guests arrived at Ciudad Bolívar. "Wow guys have you seen the countryside we've been flying over since we left Caracas?" Tracy said. "From about ten minutes out I've hardly seen a house. It's mostly jungle. There were a few patches that looked like they might be vineyards. I understand it's a fast growing industry down here."

"You'll see far more on the next part of our journey," Sandra said. "We'll be in a helicopter just two hundred feet up. You'll probably see some wild game, especially as we fly over the rivers."

"We'll be here for a little over an hour, so I suggest we get a drink and have a light lunch," Kurt suggested. "Don't overdo it though, the helicopter journey can be a little rough sometimes as we go through the mountain, we don't want anyone being ill. Also there will be a large dinner for us all this evening, when we get to Angels' Rest. My father is always very generous when he has house guests. There are a couple of vending machines in the helicopter waiting area with fresh baguettes, sandwiches and that sort of thing, they are generally very good. The coffee out of a machine is not too bad either, but it does come in a plastic cup."

"Kurt is right to warn you about the helicopter ride being rough," Sandra told the others. "The sun heats the land during the morning. That warm air rising from the valleys mixes with the cooler air coming off the mountain tops causing vast swirling turbulence, like giant holes in the air. You won't see many birds flying in the afternoons. It can be very dangerous if you're not familiar with the area. Our pilots are very experienced; they know where not to go at certain times. The return trip is always smoother because it's a morning journey and the sun hasn't had chance to heat the land. If you do get the slightest travel sick, I advise you to take your medication before we take off."

Kurt showed his guests to the waiting room. Out of the window they could see a large Russian built transport helicopter with the Luggard Shipping logo on its flanks "Looks like they've started loading, we should be able to board in half an hour, maybe a little longer."

"It's a Russian MI-26 isn't it? I saw a lot of them when I was in Afghanistan," Ryman said.

"You know your aircraft, sir." Kurt said. "You're quite right, it's the MI-26T2 improved version of the Mi-26, equipped with a new electronic system, allowing it to fly any time, day or night, under good and bad weather conditions. Luggard Shipping bought six at the beginning of the year. One is used to keep Angels' Rest supplied. Monday to Saturday it flies up here in the morning bringing our rubbish and up to eight passengers, then returns with eight passengers and supplies in the afternoon. Sundays are different; the cargo bay is fitted out with seating for fifty six passengers, giving total capacity for sixty four passengers."

"That's a lot of people being moved around," Rob said.

"Adjacent to Angels' Rest is a military training camp for new recruits and re-training seasoned soldiers for new weapons and tactics. The place is so remote that it prevents desertion of new conscripts. There is troop movement in and out of that camp every week."

Rob excused himself from the party on the pretext that he was going to call his wife, as this would be his last chance for over a week. He went back outside, saying he was trying for a better signal, but actually wanting some privacy. Sue answered her phone on its third or fourth ring. 'Hello darling, this is a pleasant surprise."

"Just thought I'd ring as it's the last chance to speak to you for a week. We're at Ciudad Bolívar waiting to board the helicopter for the last leg of the journey but I've got some information for you." He told her all about the Russian helicopters and suggested that if an attack was to be made, it should be planned to happen on a Sunday after 9:00 when sixty four soldiers will have left on the helicopter. After ending his call with Sue, he placed his phone in the breast pocket of his shirt so that the camera was just showing over the top of the pocket, then he went back inside for something to eat and drink.

Everyone else had, by now, got something to eat and drink. Kurt got himself a coffee and a baguette and went and sat next to Rob.

"Do you play golf Rob?" he asked.

"I'm a whiz at crazy golf, but proper golf, I have to say I've never tried. I've been on a few golf courses over the years,, but only to shoot rabbits. Do you play?"

"When your family home has a golf course in the back garden, you do tend to learn at an early age. I do play, but I don't particularly like the sport. I prefer something faster moving, something to get the adrenalin levels rise and the heart pump harder. But if you like, I'll take you out on the course, let you try your hand, see if you've got a natural ability. You never know, I may be able to give you a few tips to help, like you helped me with the driving."

"I'd certainly like to give it a try. I'm told it takes four hours to play eighteen holes and you walk over four miles. I'm not sure that I even know the rules. I have watched a little on TV but it's never really gripped me. Like you, I prefer my sport to be fast and furious or at least have competition between two teams or two individuals."

A man wearing a flying officer's suit with gold braid on the sleeves, appeared at the door out onto tarmac. "Mr Luggard, we are ready for you and your guests to board, we can leave as soon as you are all seated." He turned and walked back to the helicopter.

Kurt stood and took his empty cup and food wrapper to the bin. "Right folks, you heard our Captain, we can now board."

The first few miles of the flight were smooth, but as they left the broad river valley and began to climb to higher ground, things changed quite rapidly and Tracy had to stop looking out of the window and concentrate, so as not to throw-up. Sandra appeared to be suffering exactly the same, but the three men looked to be having no problems at all. Like all helicopters, it was extremely noisy and there was no possibility of having a conversation, but the men seemed to be communicating though hand signals and gestures.

Eventually the violent movements eased and stopped altogether. Kurt turned and faced the others. He tapped his watch and held up ten fingers to indicate ten minutes to go. Tracy tried looking out the window again, she no longer felt sick. The landscape was now totally different. As far as she could see was rain forest with very few breaks or clearings. Then ahead she saw Angel Falls looking like liquid gold in the bright sunlight. They slowly approached flying at about two hundred feet above the rain forest canopy. Where the water of the waterfall hit the water of the river below, it sent up a large cloud of misty spray, reaching almost as high as the helicopter.

When they were about four hundred metres from the falls, the helicopter started to rise. Slowly at first, then slightly quicker they continued upwards. The ground could no longer be seen through the mist. Looking upwards, the head of the falls came into view. As they rose above it, they were disappointed. They had expected to see a raging river like at the head of Niagara or Victoria falls. Instead there was an insignificant river, almost totally obscured by rain forest. The Angels' Rest estate was sitting on the horizon and the helicopter made a rapid approach, landing on a large fenced off heliport.

Once the engines were cut, they were able to hear one another once again. As they stepped out and walked away from the helicopter, following Kurt towards the main house, he turned and said. "I hope you enjoyed your first view of Angel Falls. I always like to arrange to approach the estate from the south like that, when I bring new people down here."

"Most spectacular," Rob said.

"But the river at the top was a big disappointment," Tracy added.

"That's what everyone says," Kurt replied. "I'm sure the main house will not be a disappointment."

It was quite a walk from the helicopter to the house, along an avenue of mixed European trees, which offered them shade against the hot afternoon sun. On route, they passed an apple orchard and two small fields planted with grapes that looked like they were beginning to ripen. The avenue came to an end and opened out to a large lawn, spread out in front of a large house, built in the style of a grand European palace. The group followed Kurt along a wide gravel path to the front door, up four stone steps, though an oversized wooden door and into an entrance hall that rose to the roof, four stories up. There were doors leading off the hallway on either side and in front of them was an impressive staircase that spiraled all the way up to the top floor.

Stood at the bottom of the steps was a tall thin man, dressed in smart black trousers, a plain white shirt and highly polished black shoes. "This is Henri. Henri runs this house. If you need anything at all, just ask Henri and he'll get it for you." Kurt said. "We've had a long journey, I expect you are a little tired. May I suggest you take a shower and rest a while and come down at 6:30 for a drink before dinner and meet my family? Dress code is smart casual, no denim please. Henri, would you please be so kind as to show these people to their rooms?"

"Certainly, sir. Miss Hilda has allocated them to Bach, Beethoven and Mozart, sir."

Kurt answered their unasked question. "You are all on the music floor, that's the second floor, each room named after a German composer, Sandra is in Haydn. Rooms on the third floor, the literature floor are named after German authors, the fourth floor is the sports floor, rooms named after German sportsmen. The family all have rooms on the first floor, named after German leaders, I am in Erhard. Please follow Henri, your luggage will be left outside your rooms shortly. Oh Henri, have my brothers arrived yet?"

"Mr Josef arrived yesterday, sir and Mr Ralph is due at six pm today, sir."

"Thank you Henri. My father is in his study, is he Henri?"

"Indeed he is, sir."

"Come on Sandra, we'd better go and say hello to the old man."

As soon as he was in his room with the door closed, Rob took his phone from his pocket and stopped the video recording he had started when they had been at the falls. He quickly scanned the recording and thought there was some very useful material for anyone needing to know about, the layout of the estate. The battery was down to just five percent, so he put the phone on charge. He would need it again tomorrow.

Kurt knocked on the door of his father's study and walked straight in without waiting to be invited. Josef and his father were standing by the desk, studying a map. From the doorway Kurt could see it was a city map, he could also see that a number of Xs had been drawn on it, but he could not make out which city it was a map of. Before he could get closer to see, Josef rushed towards him with his arms out stretched and Ernst folded the map and put it into a desk drawer.

"Well, hello little brother," Josef said. "Congratulations on your break through into the big boys. Is this your latest bed warmer then? Oh, I forgot you prefer boys."

Kurt just stood and stared at his sibling for a moment before replying. "Sandra meet my oldest brother. This is Josef, thirty seven with three failed marriages under his belt. It could have been four, but one left him standing at the alter. These days, if the society pages are to be believed, he prefers his women in pairs."

"That's enough, you two. If you must squabble take it outside. Josef, Sandra is a guest in this house and while I'm still head of this family you will respect all guests. Do you understand."

"But father she's a........."

"Do you understand Josef?"

"Yes, sir." Josef hung his head like a naughty boy who's just been told off by his teacher. He thought to himself. *"It will be my house soon enough and things will change."*

Sue and Zoe sat next to Alasdair in the front seats, very uncertain of the windows down by their feet, as they hovered high above London's rooftops. They all wore headsets, so they could talk to one another. Alasdair explained that he used points of reference on the ground, as much as his instruments, to navigate. He talked to them about how flying has changed in the last five years and how technology had made helicopters almost capable of flying themselves. He explained that the biggest danger had always been mid-air crashes but this helicopter was fitted with the very latest electronics. In particular, a system that when it detects objects moving on a direct collision course with the helicopter from up to five miles away it switches to auto pilot and takes avoidance action. "It was developed by the marines for combat about four years ago and recently the commercial version became available."

"I remember you talking to Tony about an idea you were working on that sounds very similar. Is this your invention Al?" Sue asked.

A smile spread across the pilot's face. "It is and it's made me a rich man."

"That must be the M25," Zoe said pointing down at a motorway crossing their path, "and that must be South Mimms Services."

"Well spotted. From here we can follow the A1 north," Al said. "Is there anywhere close to your house that we can land? A small field or football pitch would be perfect?"

Sue thought for a moment, then said. "Yes there is and it's right next to the house. It's the paddock we use for schooling horses, getting them used to wearing blinkers and things like that. It's only ever used in the mornings."

They were soon hovering over the house and Sue pointed out the schooling paddock for Al to land in. As soon as they touched down, Sue lent over and gave the pilot a big kiss on the cheek. "Thank you so much for this Al. You don't know how much I hate the train journey from London to York." The girls stood at the edge of the paddock and watched the helicopter rise from the long grass. They waved at the pilot and he waved back, before turning the helicopter north once more and accelerating away and at the same time climbing higher."

"Hello Sue, this is a very unexpected but pleasant surprise. Are you back for good or only the week end?" Eric said as he met the two arrivals. "Have you heard from Rob, is he keeping safe?"

"Slow down Eric. Too many questions all at once. Rob's fine, I spoke to him yesterday evening," Sue said. "This is Zoe, she's working with me at the moment. She's had a big let-down, so I thought the girls could work their magic on her. We've got to be back in London for Monday morning, so I was thinking perhaps we'd catch the early evening train on Sunday, it leaves at 6:30. Zoe, this jaded old man with all the questions, is my father-in-law, Eric Blackstock."

"Please to meet you, sir," she said holding out her hand to shake with Eric.

"The name is Eric, Zoe, not sir."

"Are you sure you don't mind me tagging along with Sue? I can easily go to a hotel or a B and B?"

"Nonsense, Sue is a member of the family, so she can invite whomever she wants to. You're very welcome. Now Sue, tell me how you managed to arrive by helicopter."

"It's a story I'll tell you over supper. Are the girls about?"

"Due back soon. They've been to see a solicitor about the money they owe. Apparently the gang they were mixed up with, is claiming that they haven't paid enough and there is interest, so I booked them in with Bridges & Sons in York. They should be back around 5:30."

They went into the house and Zoe was introduced to Rose and Madge. Rose told Sue to make up the bed in the front box room for Zoe and she and Zoe climbed the stairs. Sue pointed out hers and Rob's room, grabbed bed linen from the airing cupboard and opened the last door on the landing. It was a cosy warm room about ten feet square containing a single bed with bedside cupboard, a dressing table and a small wardrobe. "This is very nice," Zoe said.

"Give me a hand with the sheets," Sue said. "Zoe, can I ask you a personal question?"

"Depends how personal."

"Nothing too deep I promise. I just want to know what Sarah thinks of your pierced nipples?"

Zoe laughed, "She likes playing with them, but more importantly I like her playing with them. They are really sensitive and Sarah loves what it does to me when she plays. Why are you thinking of getting yours done?"

"Thinking about it, but also thinking I'll be forty next birthday. I'm too old."

"My mum is five years older than you, Sue. She actually looks fifteen years older than you and she had hers done at the same time as me. She says it's improved her sex life ten fold. Dad died when I was seven and since then she's had boyfriends but they never stayed long. Now she's more confident and enjoying life."

"You've convinced me. Where did you go to have yours done?"

"A friend did it. It's quite safe so long as you make sure everything is sterile."

"I'll speak to the girls. I think I heard Luci a few minutes ago. Come down and meet Rob's daughter."

They found Luci in the kitchen, just about to exit through the back door.

"Luci, I'd like you to meet Zoe. She's working with your dad and me and we decided to have a weekend off, recharge the batteries and all that."

"Hi Sue, pleased to meet you Zoe. I'm just going across to see Eva. I'll be back for supper. Madge says I've got half an hour before it's ready."

"Are they back, then?" Sue asked.

"I guess so, their lights are on," the young girl replied.

"We need to see them both, so we'll come across with you."

Eva answered Luci's knock on the door to the flat above the racing stables that Ana and Eva called home, "Hello Sue."

"Eva, this is Zoe, she works with Rob and me down in London."

"Hello, Zoe. Ana is in the lounge, go straight through."

"Can I have a word before we go in please, Eva." Luci asked.

"Hello Sue and I think I heard you introduce your friend as Zoe. Welcome Zoe." Ana stood and gestured for them to sit on the sofa.

"Ana, I've got a question for you and it's probably best if I just come out with it. Have you ever performed nipple piercing?"

"Yes. Eva was my first, she did mine at the same time. We've done several since. Do you want me to do yours? I'm sure Rob would like it. What about you Zoe?"

"Mine are already done, thanks," Zoe said hastily.

"You two never fail to surprise me. You're both so uncomplicated, Sue said. "Yes, I'm thinking about it."

"Do you want me to do it now? It will only take about ten minutes. We've got everything we need here.

"Do it now, before she changes her mind," Zoe said.

"Yes. Do it now."

Sue was sitting topless when Eva and Luci came into the room.

"What are you doing, Sue?" Luci asked.

"She's getting her nipples pierce," Zoe said.

"Magic. Can I have mine done as well?"

"NO!" All four women said in chorus.

Rob collected Tracy and Ryman and together they went down to the bottom of the stairs, where Henri was waiting for them. "Good evening. I trust your rooms are satisfactory? Please follow me."

"Ah, Robert let me introduce you to my family. My father, Ernst Luggard." Kurt beckoned Rob forward and he shook hands with the ageing man.

"Robert Blackstock, pleased to meet you," Rob said then stepped aside to allow Tracy to reach forward.

"Viv Turner, Rob's personal assistant."

"Welcome to Angels' Rest miss we don't often have the company of such attractive ladies in this remote place," Luggard said in a lusty tone as they shook hands.

"Theobald Ryman, Mr. Blackstock's man." Ryman eased past Tracy with his hand out and shook with Luggard.

Josef was sitting with a drink in one hand and a book in the other. "This is my oldest brother, Josef," Kurt said to the three guests. Josef didn't lift his gaze from his book just said one word, "Welcome."

Kurt gave his brother a criticising look and moved to another man who turned and put an arm around Kurt and gently slapped him on the back. "Well done, little brother, a champion at last minute, I hear. Congratulations!" he said.

Kurt raised his hand towards his guests. "Robert Blackstock, Viv Turner and Theobald Ryman, this is my second brother Ralph. Second by only a few minutes, they are twins."

"Pleased to meet you, hope you enjoy your stay at Angels' Rest." Ralph said smiling.

"And finally, we have over here, talking with Sandra, my beautiful, brainy twin sister Hilda." Kurt was walking towards a tall slim but curvy woman with golden blonde hair that hung down her back as far as her waist. She was stood with her back to them but when she heard her name mentioned, turned towards them and revealed a horrendously scarred face. The left side of her face was stunning but the right hand side was all scar tissue from her hair line down at least to her neck and possibly further, if her dress wasn't obscuring the facts. The flesh of her ear was gone and her right eye socket was deformed.

Tracy's reaction on seeing Hilda's face, was to noisily draw in a deep breath. But realising how bad that must sound tried to apologise "Oh I am sorry Hilda but I ………."

Hilda interrupted, "Don't worry, miss I'm used to it. I can even shock myself sometimes when I look in the mirror. Now you're thinking how did she get those scars? We'll I was three years old, getting ready for bed, wearing a new nightie and pretending to be a fairy dancing around the room. I tripped and fell into the open fire and ended up like this. You must be Kurt's new driving instructor,"

She said looking straight at Rob. And who is this gorgeous woman with you?

"That's Viv Turner, Rob's P.A."

"We must talk sometime, Viv. Do you swim?"

"Yes"

"Right, then join me tomorrow morning at the pool. You'll join us won't you Sandra?"

Sandra smiled and nodded her acceptance.

"Henri, get our guests a drink, please," Kurt said. "I hope you all like whisky. This is something new produced by Hilda. Hilda has been playing around developing new grape varieties that will produce better wine in our climate, but she has also learnt the art of whisky making. If you like single malt, then I'm sure you'll like this. We're trying to convince Hilda to increase production to commercial volumes."

At 7:00 they all moved into the dining room. The seating placed Rob next to Josef, with Ryman and Sandra opposite, Tracy opposite Hilda, Ernst was at the head of the table and the two brothers, Ralph and Kurt took the last seats on either side of the table.

Rob having failed to get conversation started with Josef, started talking with Ernst about the construction of the house, asking where the quality materials had been sourced and what influenced the design. Ryman joined in the conversation with surprising knowledge and revealed his father had been a master stone mason, who had done restoration on many of Britain's historic buildings.

Tracy was deep in conversation with Hilda, trying to create a relationship. She showed an interest in what Hilda was trying to do with grapes. Hilda was interested in the films that Rob was involved in. She was shocked when Tracy told her about meeting Tom Cruise only a few days ago. Throughout the evening, Hilda was making eye contact and Tracy was getting a warm feeling that she was actually getting close to this young lady. She learnt that Hilda's room on the first floor was named after Chancellor Willy Brant but wasn't sure why Hilda had told her that.

Coffee and brandy followed the meal and they all sat around the table until it was time to retire.

Once Tracy was convinced that the house had settled down for the night and gone totally quiet, she left her room and went down to the first floor in search of the room with the name Brant. She found the room, even in the dim light coming through the landing window. She put an ear to the door and her hand on the round door knob. She could hear soft voices talking, then footsteps getting closer and her hand on the doorknob felt it move. She reacted instantly and stepped backwards across the hallway into the shadows of an alcove. The door opened slowly and silently. In the light from the room, Tracy could clearly see that it was Sandra leaving. The door was closed as quietly as it had been opened and Sandra turned to walk back to her own room.

As she walked past Tracy, she turned to the agent in the alcove and raised a finger to her lips, telling Tracy not to make any noise. Then she repeatedly curled the finger into her palm, to tell Tracy to follow her. On the stairs she stopped and whispered, "Don't speak, all the rooms are bugged." Tracy followed Sandra to her room. Sandra opened the door as slowly as she had opened Hilda's and closed it again when they were both inside. Sandra picked up a notebook from the bedside table, wrote on it and showed it to Tracy for her to read. *H not allowed certain things by dad. I smuggle in 4 her. Chocs, romantic movie DVDs.* She pulled the notebook back and wrote another message *Kurt knows 0, H lives here, must know more. U must get close,, suggest talk about romance by pool.* Tracy took the pen from Sandra and wrote *? U DO.* Sandra took the pen back again and wrote *I go on tour distract Kurt so Rob can search Now U go.* Sandra opened the door, Tracy smiled and left.

Rob was the first of the three to go down to breakfast. Kurt and Sandra had used plates in front of them and were drinking coffee. "Rob, come and join us so I can tell you what we have planned for you today."

"Rob took a banana from the fruit bowl and a glass of fruit juice from a tray on the sideboard and carried them to the table. Then went back to the sideboard for a coffee, before taking his seat next to

Kurt. "Tell Henri what you would like for your breakfast and he'll get it for you,," Kurt said.

"I'll be fine with this banana thanks. Your family not coming down for breakfast?" Rob asked.

"Good God man its 8:30, they came down ages ago. Father and my brothers are out riding, checking the perimeter fences. We get a lot of animal damage even though its high voltage and Hilda will be out in her grape fields."

Ryman appeared and was intercepted by Henri who asked what he'd like for breakfast. He ordered toast, poured himself a coffee and went and sat at the table next to Rob.

"My guests are due at 11:45, so I will have time this morning to give you a quick tour of the estate. I expect you'd like to see around a bit?" Kurt asked.

As soon as Ryman had finished his toast and they had all finished their coffee the three men stood ready to leave. Sandra said, "I'll stay here and wait for Viv to come down then, I'll come and find you."

The three men set off through the front door. Rob had his phone in his shirt pocket with the camera just showing again. In a moment when Kurt's attention was elsewhere, Rob turned the phone on, pressed the icon to select the camera, then changed the settings to video and placed the phone back in his pocket.

A knock on her bedroom door woke Sue from a deep sleep. She called out, "Come in," and a quick look at the clock on the bedside table said 8:45.

The door opened and Luci's smiling face appeared round it. "Coffee Sue?"

Sue nodded and Luci walked in with a steaming cup in her hand. "Gosh are they as sore as they look?" she said looking down at Sue's exposed breasts.

"Not really, Ana told me to bathe them in surgical spirit three times a day and within a week I won't know I had it done. Is Zoe up yet?"

"Ages ago, she's down in the kitchen talking with Gran and Marge."

"Thanks for the coffee Luci. Tell everybody I'll be down in a minute."

"Are you going to the Dog and Gun this evening?" Luci asked.

"I was thinking I might take Zoe down for an hour or two, why?"

"Eva and Ana want me to be part of their New Year event. I've been rehearsing with them for weeks and tonight I've got an onstage trial to see how I get on in front of an audience. There should be around thirty people in the pub this evening, so it shouldn't be too nerve racking."

"In that case, we will be there."

"Now I am getting nervous."

Kurt had walked Rob and Ryman out of the front door and around the building. The house faced east to catch the morning sun. From the corner of the house, the building line was extended by an eight foot high wall, approximately fifty metres long, enclosing the recreation area. They continued past the wall and as they turned the corner to walk along the Northern side of the property, they could see laid out in front of them, was a mass of solar panels. We used to run on generators and have oil lamps throughout the house, but father had these installed about fifteen years ago with a battery system to store the electric. Two hundred and fifty of them generating enough electricity in one day, to run the whole estate, including the training camp for three days. We've kept one of the generators for emergencies,, but in fifteen years, the only time it runs is once a month when we test it. That building over there is the battery house where the electricity is stored."

Behind them was the recreation area with grass tennis courts and, a swimming pool. On the other side of the wall they had passed was a row of buildings. Kurt listed them as changing room, sauna and pump room. There were no walls on the north or west sides, so from mid-morning the area would be a sun trap. In fact,, the sun was already crossing the tennis court in a diagonal sweep.

Rob was careful to turn and face all directions so that the camera in his pocket collected as much of what they were being shown as possible.

Moments later they were joined by Sandra and she and Kurt linked arms as they all moved on. "Hilda came back and she has taken Viv off for a swim, so I've come to join you for the tour," Sandra said. "Henri says to tell you that your guests have just left Ciudad Bolívar."

Kurt glanced at his watch. "They are a little ahead of schedule. We had better move a little quicker if we're to finish before they arrive. The building you see here is our vehicle hanger. We have a dozen or so vehicles in there, mostly quad bikes for working around the estate, plus a service bay. We have two mechanics on site that also do the property maintenance. Behind the hanger are our fuel tanks, two thousand gallons of diesel."

" What's the building back there,, next to the Battery House?" Rob asked.

"That's not in use, father uses it to store some of his stuff in." Kurt moved on. "These are the stables, twelve horses. If you want to go for a ride at any time, just ask Henri. The last building is our communications house. It contains the equipment for the radio and the satellite communications boxes. It also houses the controls for the electrified perimeter fence and something that isn't radar but works like radar, which we use to monitor our helicopters, as they fly in and out of here."

From the corner as they turned to the final side of the house, they could see a road some way off. To the left, it came from the helicopter landing area and to the right, it cut through the rainforest in a straight line for as far as they could see. "That leads to the military training area. It's a restricted area, so no go for us, live ammunition and explosives in daily use, apparently. But we're safe so long as we stay this side of the fence. Well that completes the tour what do you think?"

"Most impressive." Ryman said.

"It is, isn't it? I really love it here. I'll miss it when I can't come here anymore," Kurt said.

"What's going to stop you coming here?" Rob asked.

"Dad's seventy next week. He can't live for ever and when he goes, Josef as oldest son, will inherit and you may have noticed we don't exactly get on with one another. We are completely different and just not compatible. He was almost eleven when I was born. By the time I was five, he had been sent to Europe to finish his education, so we never had the chance to grow up together. Why don't you three go back round to the pool and see what the girls are up to and I'll go and get Henri to organise some coffee.

Tracy had jumped in straight away with the romantic theme and Hilda lapped it up. They talked about movies that Hilda had seen trailers for on DVDs she had. It came easy for Tracy because from a young age she and her mum had always watched weepy movies together every Thursday, when her dad had been paid and gone to the dog track for the evening. Talking about the movie 'Ghost' almost had Hilda in tears. She quickly pulled herself together when she saw the others come round the corner of the house.

"Have you finished your tour already?" Hilda called as they approached.

Sandra called back, "Sorry if we're disturbing you two. Kurt's organising coffee, his guests will be here in an hour or so."

As they sat down, Rob saw that Tracy's phone was in the top of her bag and knowing that the battery on his must be low after recording video for more than an hour, while Sandra kept Hilda talking, he switched phones.

Kurt came out of the house with his father and Ralph close behind him. "Hi Pops, did you have a nice ride?" Hilda asked.

Ernst's face showed he disliked being called Pops. "Nice enough." Seeing Rob's phone was in his breast pocket and the camera was clearly visible he was suspicious that the spy was filming everything he saw. "Is that a Galaxy S10 phone you have there, Robert? I'm thinking of upgrading. Would you mind if I had a look at it, see how it feels in the hand?"

"No problem. I broke my watch the other day, so I carry it everywhere as a time piece. I have this thing about needing to know what the time is all the time," Rob said and handed Luggard his phone.

Ernst looked it over pretended to judge its weight. He pressed a few buttons still pretending, but actually checking the file history. No files had been added either today or yesterday and the battery was ninety eight percent charged, so he knew he was wrong. The phone hadn't be secretly videoing the estate. "Nice phone, I might just get on," he said handing it back to Rob.

Henri appeared with two jugs of coffee and set them down on a table by the pool. A servant girl followed him carrying a tray of cups. "Leave it Henri, I'll pour the coffee you've got work to do to get this place ready for a party."

"Thank you, Mr. Kurt." Henri went back inside and almost immediately returned with a work force of six young workers. By the time the coffee had been consumed, the area around the pool had been transformed with barbecue, mobile bar, banners and balloons and in the middle of it all on a small round table was Kurt's trophy. Now all that was needed was the eighteen guests Kurt had invited. Six were bringing their partners, so twenty four in all, on a helicopter about to arrive. Henri appeared again and announced that the guest were fifteen minutes out. Ernst stood and said. "It's time we all got our party clothes on."

When the guests arrived, they all had the same look on their faces. A look of amazement at the scale of the estate. They were shown to the two ground floor cloak rooms to freshen up and then outside to the pool area where Kurt stood to greet them.

When everyone had assembled and had a drink in their hand, Ernst stood and gave a speech congratulating his son and thanking his support team. He ended his short speech with a toast to Kurt and Chuck.

Hilda and Tracy had taken a bottle of Champagne and sat getting drunk together at a quiet table on the edge of the area. Tracy was careful that she only looked drunk, but stayed sober enough to protect her cover.

"Do you run, Hilda? I'm going to be running in next year's London Marathon, so I try and run a few miles every day and was thinking I might run the perimeter of the golf course, a couple of laps tomorrow morning."

"Yes I run. I find it the best way of keeping my shape. I'd love to join you tomorrow. This bottle is empty I'll get another."

Chapter 20

"Sir Bernard, at last we're getting good intel out of Angels' Rest. Rob's plan is really working. We're getting good video images and commentary. Rob says that he is convinced Luggard has made him and is attempting to feed false intel. As you know we have been continually testing the three people at Aldershot armoury. They failed the test two days ago and an audit today confirmed a missing Stinger rocket and portable launcher."

****

Luci spent Saturday afternoon with the girls, going through their programme just one last time. What started in the morning as light drizzle, slowly worsened as the day went on and by 5:30 the rain was absolutely pouring down.

"Granddad can I ask you for a favour?" Luci pleaded.

"I know, you'd like me to drive you down to the Dog and Gun."

"If you wouldn't mind. You are my favourite granddad."

Sue and Zoe entered the room, having changed for the evening.

"Sue, granddad has offered to drive us down to the pub. Sid wants the girls there early, to do their sound check before the pub gets busy. If you don't mind going at 6:20, he can take you two as well. The Range Rover holds up to six passengers. It would save you getting wet walking down later. Have you seen how hard it's raining?"

"Sounds like my step-daughter knows how to pull her granddad's strings," Sue said looking at Eric.

"Okay, I'll go and tell the girls the good news." She was back only moments later. "Second thoughts I'll ring them. That rain is getting worse."

There was only one customer in the pub when they arrived.

"I thought we might share a bottle of red wine, if you're okay with that?" Sue asked Zoe.

"Red wine will be fine thanks. Where do you want to sit? I'll claim a couple of seats for us."

"We like table seven over there by the wall. It's got a lovely view of the whole of the stage," Sue said and pointed towards an empty table and Zoe hooked her coat over the back of one of the chairs and sat.

"A bottle of your Australian Merlot and two glasses please, Sid," Sue said.

"No Rob tonight, Sue?" the landlord asked.

"He's in South America. I've brought my work colleague for a night out. She's had a bad couple of days and needs cheering up."

"Will you be eating this evening? Do you want me to set up tab or I can put this on Rob's tab?" Sid offered.

"Rob owes me a drink or two, so let tonight be on him. Everything on Rob's tab please, Sid."

"How are your piercings?" Zoe asked.

"I'm trying to forget about them. I just hope Rob likes them."

"He will."

They continued chatting together and slowly the level of wine in the bottle dropped. The pub had filled and by 8:30 when the entertainment was due to start there were about fifty customers eating and drinking. Sid stepped up onto the stage and tapped a microphone to get everyone's attention. "Ladies and gentlemen, our regular entertainers are once again here with some of your favourite songs and tonight they are introducing a newcomer with loads of talent. Please put your hands together and welcome Ana, Eva and Luci."

The three girls stepped out from behind the curtain at the back of the stage singing 'Penny Lane'. Ana then soloed with 'Alfie' and instantly received loud applause. Eva then sang lead vocals on a couple of tracks before it was time for Luci's solo 'My Heart Will Go On'. At first the audience were totally silent, which just made her more nervous, but slowly she saw signs of appreciation in the faces in front of her. People were swaying to the music and miming out the words and as she finished the song, she was given the loudest applause of the evening so far. Ana took the lead vocals for the next song. Part way through the track, Zoe suddenly sat upright in her seat.

Sue noticed that for no apparent reason, Zoe was smiling then suddenly she said, "That's it. Of course, why haven't we seen that sooner?"

"Seen what sooner?" Sue asked.

"The connection between those last names on the list. That song that Ana was singing '*More Questions Than Answers*' the original was by Johnny Nash in the early seventies. He was one of my mums favourites, she played his albums, all the time. This song is the last track from an album called 'I Can See Clearly Now' and that's what's given me the clue. We know that five people neither work or live in London. All the rest live or work in central London. I think that if we go to all these homes or offices, we'll see that each has a clear line of site to one or more potential targets. The target that is common to all of them will be Luggard's target."

"That's brilliant Zoe. You may well have solved it."

"Yes, but we have a dozen or so locations and the attack may come from any one of them and we don't know what form the attack will be made in. It could be a remote detonated bomb, remote chemical release, a rocket or any one of a dozen other options."

"But we have the date and we'll have the target."

Hilda knocked gently on Tracy's door and without waiting for a response walked in to the room. She crossed the room to the bed and touched Tracy's bare shoulder. The sleeping agent stirred and slowly opened her eyes. "It's 06:45 and if you want to go for a run, we should get going soon before the sun gets too warm." Hilda said and pulled the bed covers back revealing Tracy's naked body beneath.

"Enough Hilda! I get the message just give me five minutes to get dressed."

Hilda didn't leave, instead she sat on the end of the bed and watched as Tracy pulled on her clothes and off they set. They crossed the lawn in front of the house at a steady pace. The white picket fence on the far side of the lawn had a gate that lead out onto the golf course. The sun was pulling itself off the horizon and the two women were glad they had brought water bottles with them. At the tee to the sixth hole, Tracy spotted a tap tucked away at the edge of the undergrowth, presumably used for watering the greens. That must be the spot where she was to drop Rob's phone *"I'll do it on the next lap,"* she thought to herself.

"I love the sound of the waterfall. It's a noise that goes right through your body. We must be quite close," Tracy said.

"We're still a good three hundred metres away. Not close enough yet to feel the cold water spray," Hilda replied.

"Can we get nearer?"

"A little, but not close enough to see the falls. There is a lot of bare rock around the head of the falls which is covered in moss and algae, with the spray keeping it wet all the time, it is incredibly slippery and dangerous. All too easy to slip and go over the edge and it's a kilometres to the bottom."

"That's a shame."

"There is a path that takes you to a small clearing under the spray. You are still a hundred metres from the falls but the spray is very refreshing. On a hot summer's day, I love to go in there, take off all my clothes and just let the spray softly fall on my naked skin. Terribly refreshing."

"Sounds wonderful, I'd like to try it sometime."

As they approached the sixth tee on the next lap, Tracy who had been just behind Hilda's shoulder for some time, allowed the water to leak from her bottle, so when they got to the there she said, "Keep going Hilda I need to refill my water bottle."

"Okay, I'll go a little slower so you can catch me again," Hilda said.

As Hilda moved on, Tracy filled her bottle and left the phone she had hidden in her waistband tucked out of sight behind the post supporting the tap. She quickly caught up with Hilda and they were soon running again at the slightly faster pace.

"One more lap will make it five K. Can you manage another?" Hilda asked.

"I've got no problems doing another lap. It's nice to have someone to run with. I normally run alone. That's so boring. Most people I see are wearing headphones and listening to music to help them to keep going. But where I live that can be dangerous because you can't hear the traffic coming."

Tracy looked but couldn't see her phone as the passed the tap so it must have been retrieved successfully and the first message would soon be on its way to London.

As they crossed the lawn, heading back to the house Tracy said, "I need a shower. I think my skin is leaking, it must be all that water I've drunk."

"You're probably affected by the altitude up here. We're ten thousand five hundred feet above sea level, it makes a difference. I need to shower as well, why don't I join you?"

Tracy took a step back. "That's okay I can manage, thank you. I'll perhaps see you at breakfast or by the pool later."

As they entered the house, Rob was just coming out. "Can I help you Mr. Blackstock?" Hilda said.

"No, I'm just out to fill my lungs with fresh air before breakfast." He stepped past them through the door and was outside. The phone was again in his shirt pocket on record. He walked in the direction of the heliport and as he passed the end of the house, he could hear the rumble of heavy vehicles coming towards him, along the track from the training area. He stood and watched six open wagons loaded with troops in camouflage uniforms, heading for the helicopter. *"This is obviously the exchange of troops that happens on Sundays,"* he thought to himself before returning to the house for breakfast.

Zoe thought that Sue was looking worried. She had seemed strange ever since her call with Captain Phillips. "Are you alright Sue? You look worried about something."

"Not really worried, more like concerned. This is Rob's third day at Angels' Rest and Captain Phillips has had nothing from him," Sue said.

"I think you're worrying needlessly, girl," Zoe said. "They only got there late Friday afternoon, They'll only just be having their Sunday breakfast now, so there hasn't really been time for them to gather any information and get a message to the Captain's men and for them to climb ten thousand feet down the rock face to get it to Phillips."

"You're right of course, but I can't help worrying about his safety. After all he's had no front line training."

"From what I saw in Russia this summer, he is well able to look after himself, so stop worrying."

"Rob, there you are," Kurt said. "I've been looking all over for you. I thought perhaps you could show me some of those driving skills. We can make good use of the week we have here. I was thinking you could teach me in the mornings and I'll try and turn you into a golfer in the afternoons."

"Sounds good, except I haven't seen any suitable cars for you to work with."

"Follow me," Kurt beckoned Rob to follow and moved swiftly out of the house. They walked round to the back of the stables where there was a large wooden lean to shed. Kurt unlocked the big double doors and Rob could see that inside was what appeared to be a sports car covered by a tarpaulin. Kurt smiled at his new friend, as he pulled of the cover, to reveal an E-Type Jaguar in British Racing Green livery,, with a bold black number six on a white circle on the bonnet and both sides.

"Wow!" Rob was shocked.

"Grandfather bought it from Graham Hill the day after he clinched the British Saloon Car Championship with a second place at Brands Hatch in 1964. Father gave it to me on my eighteenth birthday. I haven't driven it since that day. Our mechanics have kept it serviced and have it running regularly so it's in perfect order. Will it do? And is the track up to the base good enough for what we'll be doing."

It's bloody beautiful, you're a very lucky young man, I am so so envious. It was a car way ahead of its time, a classic never to be repeated. There are not many still running. Yes this will do very nicely for the work we have to do and the track is good as well."

"Right, I'll get her out into the open and we can get started."

Tracy didn't see Hilda all morning, so in the late afternoon, she went looking for her.

Hilda's jacket was hanging on the post at the end of a row of grapes at one end of the vineyard. Tracy knew she wouldn't be too far away, so decided to sit and wait on the wooden bench outside what looked like a storage shed, in the corner of the field.

It was several minutes before Hilda arrived, surprised to see Tracy waiting for her. "Miss Turner is there anything I can do for you? Are you looking for someone?"

"Actually I was looking for you. You appeared somewhat distracted at dinner last night. Not altogether with it, if you know what I mean. Do you want to talk about anything, woman to woman? The men have gone off again playing with their racing cars so we won't be interrupted."

"It's nothing really,," she said as she opened the shed door and entered indicating Tracy to follow and closing the door behind them. "It's just that whenever we have outsiders staying here, it makes me unsettled. You see I've never been anywhere, never left this mountain. Everything has been brought here to me and hearing people talk of places they've been to, things they have seen and so on, kind of makes me realise I'm actually a prisoner in my own home." Tracy moved closer and put a hand on the girl's shoulder to console her. Hilda reacted by resting her head on Tracy's shoulder, put her arms around her and held her tight. As they parted they looked one another straight in the eye. Then Hilda kissed Tracy full on the mouth. It was only a quick kiss but it was immediately followed by another more passionate kiss. Tracy parted her lips to accept Hilda's probing tongue.

Tracy had kissed girls before and had been in a few relationships with couples since her college days, but if she were to be asked, she did prefer boys. However, she found herself becoming excited and her body was reacting. Her heart rate increased, her temperature rose, her small breasts were tingling and her nipples hardened. Because her breasts were small and firm they didn't need support so she never wore a bra. As her nipples grew hard they pushed the fabric of her shirt. When fully erect they were the size of her little finger from the last joint and Hilda couldn't help but notice. She raised her left hand and pinched Tracy's right nipple between finger and thumb, causing a low moan in response.

Tracy moaned again showing her acceptance of what Hilda was doing. Hilda lowered her head and took the nipple in her teeth through the shirt and bit it gently. With her hands,, she slowly unbutton Tracy's shirt and slipped it back off her shoulders. Hilda took Tracy's nipple back into her mouth, running her tongue along the underside then flicking it across the tip. Then moving to the other nipple and doing the same. Tracy threw her head back and felt the cool evening air on her wet nipples as Hilda stood and began to remove her clothes. "Take your clothes off," she instructed Tracy, who readily followed instructions and removed her shirt from her wrists and pushed her leggings down her legs to her ankles then off her feet,, leaving her in just the smallest of thongs.

A now totally naked Hilda grabbed Tracy around the waist, pulled her close, kissed her passionately running her hands down her back to her ass and paused to caress her cheeks before parting them and moving her fingers to Tracy's most private parts.

Tracy was finding it more and more difficult to remember her purpose for being here as Hilda continued to tease her. Hilda seemed to read her thoughts "You like that, don't you?"

"Guurrhh,," was the only sound Tracy could make. She was feeling a mixture of pleasure and apprehension. Where would this lead? But at the moment she was enjoying what Hilda was doing to her and didn't want it to stop.

Hilda led her to a sofa strewn with rugs as big as a bed.

Tracy woke at 6:30. Hilda was still asleep, naked beside her. She lay trying to recall everything that had happened the previous evening. She felt she should feel guilty but she didn't, Hilda had proven to be an exceptional lover. She gently slid out of bed as Hilda began to stir. She walked across the room and stood in front of an old mirror. "Not bad for someone in her forties," she thought

Tracy went back to the bed, leant over to Hilda and kissed her full on the mouth. "Good morning you." She lifted her head, rubbed her eyes and said, "we need to get over to the house. My skin feels terrible, I need a shower. I feel like one of those whores father brings in for his soldiers every month."

"Soldiers? Has he got an army then?" Tracy asked as she followed Hilda to the house.

"Not here," Hilda explained. "He trains them here then they move on to one of his camps. There are only ever ninety to one hundred recruits here. He brings them in, young men and young women, from all over South America. They spend eight or nine weeks being turned into soldiers, then he ships them off and brings in the next lot, about fifty at a time. I know the training is very hard. Sometimes the recruits die.

Tracy knew that if she continued to push gently Hilda was in the right mind to give up lots of useful information, she just needed to ask the right questions. "So how many camps does he have?"

"Six at the moment, I think. But he said last week that he needed to have three more built. He's also putting more soldiers on his ships and big guns."

"That's quite an army."

"The last time I heard, it totaled more than two and a half thousand soldiers, but that was last Christmas time. All are armed with weapons he buys from China. Only last week he received a shipment of gunship helicopters from them. It worries me to think sometimes why he is so set in building his army."

"Have you any idea why he is building it?"

"He says it's his insurance for when Angels Gabriel and Michael have beheaded the corrupt nations in Operation Birdbath next Dooms Day and he is proclaimed founder and first Chancellor of the new republic of West World. Now I really do need that shower. Join me?"

Tracy was tempted, but said she needed to get ready for when Rob came down for breakfast "He will need to be reminded to take his medication." In reality she needed to speak with Rob and share her news with him.

Chapter 21

"Tragic news, we've just learned of a helicopter crashing in the mountains of central Venezuela. Witnesses traveling in a second helicopter report that something happened to the main rotor, causing it to break away and the aircraft fell like a stone and burst into flames as it hit the ground. Because of the remoteness of the crash site and the density of the rain forest in this area, it could take days for anyone to get to the scene. On board were the pilot, plus three passengers who are believed to be all British and have been named as Robert Blackstock, owner of Blackstock Stunt Action, who train and supply stunt men and women to the movie industry. Travelling with were his personal assistant Miss Viv Turner and his driver Theodore Ryman. However it has not been confirmed that these three were actually on board when the helicopter crashed. The second helicopter stayed in the area as long as fuel allowed but no survivors were seen and due to the total destruction of the cabin, none are expected."

****

Rob was not a novice at golf. He had been an Oxford Blue. He had been good enough to play professionally, but life had taken him in another direction and now he hardly played. After playing the first few holes he felt his old skills were returning and he was more or less able to put the ball where he wanted it to go, not to win the hole but to make it look like he was a novice, unable to hit the ball straight. On the fifth hole he deliberately hit the ball over the green and towards the undergrowth by the sixth tee, so that he could retrieve one phone and place the other behind the post supporting the tap.

Rob visited the tap on the tee for hole six to swap phones on each of the next four afternoons, each day using a different excuse. On Monday he needed a pee so walked across to the undergrowth, on Tuesday he dropped a glove somewhere so he ran back to the sixth tee where he had last seen it. On Wednesday he hit his drive off the tee into the rough. When they found the ball, it was the wrong side of the boundary fence. Kurt told him he would have to go back and play the shot again, so Rob was able to switch phones unobserved. Thursday started warm and sunny and got hotter as the day went on, so Rob made sure that he needed to refill his water bottle at the sixth tee.

There was something to report each day. Ryman had spent the week getting to know the staff. Most of them had come from local villages, so conversation was difficult, the staff not knowing much English and Ryman only knowing a little Spanish that he had picked up on holiday. Every year, as far back as he could remember until the time he signed up for the army, his parents had taken him on holiday to a Spanish island. Despite the language difficulties, he had discovered that the building they had been told was empty and only Ernst went into, was in fact a weapon store for the staff and they had regular training days with hostile and friendly targets suddenly appearing in the house and the grounds. He had also discovered that, mounted on the roof, were two anti-aircraft cannons, but no one has ever seen an aircraft other than the helicopters in Luggard's fleet.

All of what Ryman was discovering, the snippets that Tracy was getting from Hilda and bits that Rob was finding out, were all being sent back to London. A copy of everything was sent to an S.A.S. unit being readied to enter Angels' Rest, should force be needed. They had been flown out to the destroyer H.M.S. Dragon, currently patrolling twenty miles off the north coast of Venezuela. Rob was just hoping that someone was making sense of it all.

Thursday night was unbearably hot and morning couldn't come soon enough for most people. Tracy was one of the first down for breakfast, closely followed by Kurt and Sandra. "Kurt says that every few years, they get these extremely high temperatures at this time of year. It should break this evening and we'll get heavy rains for a few days," Sandra said to Tracy.

"And that's bad for father's birthday, Kurt added.

"Good morning, everyone," Rob said as he came into the room. "Anyone else want a coffee?"

"Sandra was just saying it's going to be hot today and then we'll have heavy rain," Tracy told him.

"Too hot to be doing any training today and not very comfortable for another round of golf, I think Robert," Kurt said.

"I think I've shown you all you need for now Kurt. If you take all that on, you'll certainly improve your times. You just need to practice and remember, driving is no different from any other sport, you must be fit and you must practice your skills. Your past performances mean nothing; you are only as good as your next drive."

"Thank you for all you've done for me. In five days, you have taught me so much. I feel so much more comfortable behind the wheel now, thanks to what you've taught me."

"So what are we all doing today to stay cool?" Rob asked.

"Well, my brothers have lumbered me with giving a speech at the party tomorrow, so I guess I'll be in my room trying to be a little creative," Kurt said.

"Hilda said she would meet me by the pool at around 11:00. So we'll be in and out of the water to cool down," Tracy said.

Sandra spoke up and said. "That sounds a good way to spend a hot day. I'll join you, if I may. 11:00 did you say?"

"What's the time now?" Rob said lifting his phone from his breast pocket. "Ah, 9:45. I think I'll pour another coffee, find somewhere in the shade and settle down with a good book," he said and laid his phone down on the table. He picked up his cup and carried it across the room, refilled it, then left the room heading for the library.

"He's left his phone," Sandra said.

Tracy picked it up. "He's always putting it down and walking off without it and I have to go catch him up to give it back to him. Sometimes I think that's the only reason he employs me. If ever he buys himself a wrist watch, I'll be out of a job. He only ever uses the clock on the phone, he never looks at his diary, instead he asks me and he rarely uses the internet." She had quickly covered for Rob's apparent laps in concentration, knowing that what he had done was telling her he wanted her to do the phone switch.

As she stood, she looked out of the door across the hall way to Ernst's study. The door was being opened and Josef and Ralph appeared. Henri was in the hallway and as Josef passed him, he said something to Henri and the servant went scurrying off. Ralph crossed the hallway to the dining room and from the doorway called,

"Kurt, Father wishes to see you and Hilda in his study now! Henri has gone to fetch Hilda, but you had better get across there smartish."

Sandra and Tracy looked at one another, puzzled as to what was going on as Kurt obeyed his brother and went across to his father's study, knocked and went in. About thirty seconds later Hilda did the same.

"Perhaps see you by the pool later then, Sandra," Tracy said as she left the dining room.

"Maybe," Sandra replied.

Ernst had been discussing with Josef and Ralph what they should do with the three British agents that Gabriel had warned them about,, who were now at Angels' Rest, snooping around and the pretty young American girl who they had discovered was worked for the C.I.A. "Leave the girl, she's harmless enough at the moment and a useful distraction for Kurt. Keeping him away from interfering with what we're doing. Just shoot the other three," Josef suggested.

"Why shoot them? Why not dose them with QZ-71, tell them to forget everything they have discovered about our operation and then send them home. I'm sure it would be a big advantage to have three agents that we can control inside British intelligence next May and June," Ralph said.

Ernst nodded his agreement. "Very clever idea. They have not had an opportunity to contact their masters since they arrived and this will totally stop them getting intel back to their bosses. If we put out a story saying they have been killed in an accident, then their bosses won't get restless when they don't return on Sunday. I'll need some QZ-71, we don't have any here."

"I can bring that from London when I come back on the come back on the eighth," Josef said.

"What do we tell Hilda and Kurt?" Ralph asked.

"I'll deal with that. I think we've finished for now, so go and find them and tell them I want a word, now!" Ernst ordered.

"Come in Kurt and take a seat. Is your sister coming?" Ernst asked.

"I haven't seen her this morning; Josef has sent Henri to find her," Kurt answered.

At that moment Hilda knocked on the door and walked in.

"Right I have spoken with your brothers and we have agreed that there is something you need to know about our visitors. They are not who they tell us they are." Ernst paused and Hilda looked at Kurt. "They are here to spy on me and to find out about my plans, to stop the rising of the New Republic."

Hilda gave her father a shocked look of horror. "You're planning something very serious. So serious that whoever you are rising against feels they need to send spies to stop you! Why are you doing this? You are one of the richest men in the world, what more do you want?"

"Power. He wants power, Kurt said.

"No," Ernst insisted. "I want to save the world, put right the wrongs of past generations. For two hundred years the human race has messed about with nature. Germany in the first half of last century had leanings towards doing the same, but both of the great statesmen, Bismark and Hitler went about it in the wrong way. They set out to get rid of those that didn't fit into their objectives. Hitler tried to create a superior race by getting rid of those he classified as inferior races. His thugs took things too far, millions died and the world retaliated."

"So how does what you are planning differ?" Hilda enquired.

"The New Republic simply wants every race to have its own superiors. Your grandfather started the movement over half a century ago, his goal, which he wasn't given time to achieve, was to re-establish genetic boundaries. An African doesn't have black skin to make him stand out, no nature gave him a black skin to protect him in the African climate. Asians people have narrow eyes to protect their eyes in the Asian climate and so on. These differences have come from evolution over thousands of years. The human race is killing itself by moving people to climates that don't suit, in turn this leads to unrest, mis-trust and for the want of a better description, civil disorder."

Hilda interrupted, "So you're saying that the U.S.A. should be populated by only First Nation people and all others should go back to where they came from?"

"Not a good example to use Hilda," Ernst explained. "North America, Australia etcetera have only been populated for a few hundred years, not long enough for natural selection and evolution to provide the features best suited to the climate. Unlike South America which was populated long before and evolution has created the right mix. However, mankind can't wait for thousands of years for these new worlds, so the plan is to seek out the weakest in all races and put them back in the pool where they belong."

"What makes you think this will help mankind?" Kurt asked. "Surely millions of people would be uprooted. How can that be good?"

"And what if they don't want to go?" Hilda added.

"They will not be given an option," Ernst answered.

"So what makes this any different from the Nazis?" Hilda asked in disgust.

"It's quite simple really, child. The New Republic is aiming to get the most out of every part of the human race,, by creating not just one superior race,, like the Nazis tried to do in the forties, we want to get the best from every gene pool. A black African in Europe does not add any value, but put him back in his own gene pool he may be one of the strongest and be a valued leader," Ernst explained.

"Didn't Hitler and his Nazi's try to do something similar and try to take over the world?" Kurt said.

"Hitler wanted a world with just one race of people, the Superior Race and tried to get there by bullying the weak and eliminating those who opposed him. When he came up against a powerful foe, like the Romans and many others across history, his resources were stretched so thinly protecting and policing his expanded empire that he would ultimately be defeated." Ernst continued to explain. "The New Republic will defeat the strongest opposition first while it is fresh and at maximum strength and we have surprise on our side. Once they see this, the weaker ones will not offer much resistance."

"By stronger opposition do you mean the NATO countries?" Kurt asked. "U.S.A., Britain and most of Europe."

They have hundreds of thousands of well-trained troops and endless resources. You have only a few thousand men. How can you hope to be successful?" Hilda added.

"Not just my troops but also my shipping line, all armed and by far the largest navy in the world. I also have the entire Venezuelan armed forces to call on, but the real strength comes from millions of heroin addicts who we have been giving QZ-71 and by next spring we will have total control over," replied Ernst.

"What is QZ-71?" Hilda quickly asked.

"QZ-71 is a mind drug which when I activate it will allow me to get that person to do anything I want them to do. These people are spread across the whole population, in every walk of life. Military and law enforcement, high ranking officers as well as lower ranks. Politicians, priests, doctors, lorry drivers, every possible skill set, race and religion will be included. Then when I tell them they will not oppose us and just turn away, it will cause such confusion across the nations that opposition will crumble and allow our forces to take over. Our first strike will shock the world soon, when we sever the head off the eagle in London on Pearl Harbour day."

"You are mad! TOTALLY FUCKING MAD!" Hilda screeched at her father. "Who's funding all this? Is it you?"

Kurt put his arm around his sister to try and calm her a little.

Ernst, shocked by Hilda's language, responded, "Everything you see around you is not ours. Our wealth has been built on a legacy from the German Third Reich so therefore is legally the property of the Fourth Reich, the New Republic."

"Do you mean the 'so called' Hitler's gold?" Kurt interrupted.

"Yes, if you must call it that. Your grandfather brought it out of Germany during the last days of the war, to be used for exactly this purpose."

"But surely father, if the weak are allowed to live amongst the strong, they will learn from the strong and become stronger themselves," Hilda continued to argue.

"That is not what has happened. Everywhere where gene pools are mixed, there is civil unrest and the strong have been dragged down by the weak. Now that is the end of it, we all have our work to get on with. I just wanted to tell you about the spies we have amongst us and the threat they bring. They are trying to kill the New Republic before it is even born. They must not be allowed to do that and I will do whatever we need to do to stop them."

Hilda and Kurt left the room and as they crossed the hall back to the dining room Hilda said, "This is total madness. It is certain to end badly for all of us."

"I can't believe Rob is a spy. I'll ask Sandra about him," Kurt said. "He's her uncle, she'll know the truth."

"And I'll quiz Viv, she's an honest girl. She'll tell me, if he's not what he says he is." Hilda said. "She told me that she and Blackstock were at school together and became lovers. She's never quizzed me about anything that goes on around here and if they were spies, they'd be asking questions wouldn't they?"

"I would think they would be asking loads of questions and poking their noses in to everything," Kurt said. "Rob's not asked me a single question about the family, this place or anything at all,, other than things to do with my driving."

Hilda found Tracy by the pool and sat down on the sun lounger next to her new friend.

"You look dreadful Hilda. What's wrong?" Tracy asked.

"It's my dad. I think he is getting delusional. He's talking about building an empire. He thinks he's going to be the first president of the world," Hilda was holding back her tears.

"Well, that's never going to happen is it??" Tracy argued. "So why are you so upset?"

"You don't know my father, Viv. But there again, I'm not so sure I do anymore, I thought I did. I've never seen him like this before, so focused and so certain it will happen. The trouble is that he is rich and powerful enough to try. I tell you I think he's going mad and I feel helpless to do anything about it."

"I'm sure you've got this all wrong, Hilda."

"No, it's going to happen. He's even talked about the first strike being at a target in London on Pearl Harbour Day, when the head of the eagle will be taken from its body. Whatever that means. Do you know when Pearl Harbour Day is?"

"No idea at all. Wasn't Pearl Harbour some sort of battle in a recent war somewhere? I vaguely remember a movie with a lot of soldiers running around with no shirts on, so it must have been somewhere hot. Korea or Vietnam maybe, but when the actual day was I've got no idea at all."

"From the way he talked it must be soon, perhaps in the spring. He was saying that by the spring, he will have control of the minds of every heroin addict in the world. Something to do with a drug they have been given. I was too upset by then to follow what he was saying. Honestly Viv, I'm very worried. He's even convinced that you and Rob are British spies sent to discover his plans."

"Now that really is a crazy thought. Rob a spy! If he is he's a very good one I've known him for more than twenty five years, we were at school together. He was my first real boyfriend. We used to have sex in the bike shelter during our lunch break. No, Rob's not a spy. He is a very rich and successful business man with two teenage kids and a very new bride. Does that sound like the profile of a spy?"

"I guess not."

"What you need is something to take your mind off all this nonsense. How about we do one another's nails, ready for the party tomorrow? I've got just the right colour for you in my bag upstairs, I'll just nip and get it. It looks like you need a good manicure. We can sit at the table out of this sun. It really is getting too hot for me now, I could do with moving into the shade."

She grabbed her bag, stood and walked towards the house, not giving Hilda a chance to object. Once out of Hilda's sight, she quickened her pace and went straight to Rob's room, knocked and walked in.

"Oops!" she said. Rob had just taken a shower and was just coming out of the bathroom naked.

"Don't you wait for someone to invite you to come in, after you knock on their door?"

"Sorry Rob, but I've just found out Ernst plans from Hilda," Tracy explained and told him everything that Hilda had just told her.

"Give me back my phone and I'll get a message onto it and get it back to you somehow. This must be sent today. Pearl Harbour Day is the seventh of December."

"That's next week."

"Yes, it doesn't give Sue much time to sort out what the target actually is."

"I must rush and get back to Hilda before she comes looking for me. I'll be in the pool area when you're ready to pass back the phone."

As Tracy returned to the pool area, Hilda looked up and said something.

"Sorry love, I couldn't hear what you said because of that helicopter taking off."

"I said, you took a long time."

"Yes I know, sorry. I had to search for it. It wasn't in my makeup bag. I eventually found it in my handbag. So it had been down here all the time. If I had remembered that, I could have saved myself the walk back upstairs."

For the next twenty minutes Tracy filed, buffed and painted Hilda's nails then Hilda did the same for her. They had just finished when Rob arrived. "Viv, can you look at this for me? It keeps on beeping and I don't know why," he said as he passed Tracy his phone.

"Leave it with me. I'll sort it for you," she said.

"Good girl," he said as he turned and went back into the house. Tracy dropped the phone in her bag and went back to chatting with Hilda.

They were soon interrupted by the helicopter coming in to land.

"They didn't go far," Tracy commented.

"Just down to the local village to fetch the girls," Hilda explained.

"Girls. What girls?"

"At the end of each month my father pays one hundred US dollars to each girl from the village between fifteen and thirty years old, who will come up here and be with the troops for two nights. Sometimes there are twenty, sometimes as few as twelve. It depends on how many are giving birth. Not that that stops them for long several have given birth while here. A hundred dollars is a lot of money for these people and they appear to enjoy their work anyway. We can have as many as a hundred troops up here at any time. You should see these girls take on four or five of these sex starved men at any one time."

"I'd like to." Tracy interrupted.

"I do quite regularly," Hilda smiled. "I sneak over to the compound and just sit and watch. I can get really hot just watching. The staff here know to keep well clear of me when I've been up there. I can be quite rough getting what I want."

"Stop it! You're getting me going now. I think I need a cold shower. Perhaps we could go to that clearing near the falls you were telling me about the other day and cool off a little," Tracy said with a grin spreading across her face.

They rose from their seats together and set out across the golf course towards the wooded area. As they passed the tap, Tracy deliberately stumbled and dropped her bag so that its contents split out towards the tap. She quickly gathered everything up, except the phone which she made sure was hidden behind the post that supported the tap. *"Sue won't get that until tomorrow. That only gives her six days to prevent the attack."* Tracy thought as they walked on.

When they reached Hilda's clearing, Tracy found a plant with a large leaf, like rhubarb, she thought. She placed her bag under the leaves to keep it dry. As she turned, Hilda was right behind her and she fell into her arms and they kissed. Their tongues played games together and Tracy felt her bikini top suddenly loosen, freeing her breasts. Next she felt the strings of her bikini bottoms being pulled. She moved a little to allow the garment to fall to the ground, leaving her naked. Hilda took a step back and began to remove her own two piece while Tracy watched and enjoyed the fresh cool spray on her hot body. "Now tell me more about the girls," she said as she moved towards Hilda and began a long passionate kiss.

Ernst's special guests arrived mid-afternoon. Two politicians, four high ranking military officers and wives. They were all staying the whole weekend in rooms on the fourth floor. In the early evening the main guest arrived. The Venezuelan President, his wife and a body guard were taken directly to their rooms on the second floor. The weekend guests ate their evening meal with Ernst, Josef and Ralph, away from everyone else. After the meal the wives moved into the lounge and the men stayed in the dining room with all doors closed.

"Father is presenting his plans to his generals," Hilda whispered to Tracy.

"You're reading more into this than there actually is. I'm sure it's all very innocent. They are probably discussing some political stuff that they don't want to be overheard and made public until they are ready," Tracy tried to comfort the younger woman.

During Saturday morning the staff, under Hilda's guidance, transformed the pool area to a party venue. The prediction of bad weather was wrong. It was quite a bit cooler but still pleasantly warm and no sign of the expected strong winds. A helicopter arrived mid-morning with boxes of prepared party food and four musicians, who were directed to a small raised platform erected on the tennis court. Hilda had organised a golf tournament for the weekend guests to entertain them whilst the transformation was taking place.

The remaining guests arrived by helicopter at noon and champagne was served. Josef gave a welcoming speech, wishing his father a happy birthday and toasting him many more years. Then Ernst stood and thanked his guests for coming and told them all to enjoy their afternoon, at which point the musicians started to play and a party atmosphere started to develop.

The day guests were flown out at 8:00, leaving the remaining guests and family drinking and talking for several hours. Hilda and Tracy slipped away un-noticed at around 10:00. Hilda taking Tracy by the hand and leading her back to her room on the second floor.

"Viv, I don't care whether you are a British spy or not. I need your help. If I can't stop my father, he's going to get himself killed and possibly the rest of us too. How can we stop him?"

"Firstly, I'm not a spy. I'm simply Rob's personal assistant and I'm not sure I can help you. I think you need to speak with Kurt, see if he thinks the same and see what you can do together. Obviously Josef and Ralph are supporting your father." Tracy kissed her friend gently and left the room.

Chapter 22

"Good evening Prime Minister it's Bernard Howe here, you asked me to keep you up to speed with the Venezuela situation. I'm pleased to report significant progress. I have three agents under cover at the heart of the enemy's forces. Yesterday their report filled in the gaps in research findings and we have been able to piece together their plan and that has allowed us to take steps to counter it."

****

"Sue, have you heard anything from Rob? I've just been reading about the accident in the papers. You must be terribly worried about him?" Zoe was ringing Sue at home because she had a bad cold and paperwork could be done just as easily at home, as in the office.

"Don't believe everything you read in the papers, especially the Sunday papers. I've just had my noon update from the team in Venezuela. Rob was certainly alive yesterday because he's sent a report that needs our urgent attention. I'll be there in twenty minutes and will explain everything then," Sue replied.

In the taxi on the way to the office, Sue rang Sir Bernard Howe and updated him with the latest news from Rob and to assure him that the reports on Rob's death were false and that all three of them were still fit and well. He asked her to ring him again, as soon as they had any idea of what the target is.

During the previous four days, Zoe had visited all five of the London homes and offices that she had previously associated with names on the list. From each location she noted all possible targets that could be clearly seen from any window, balcony or rooftop. Back in the office she took a large scale map and drew all of the lines of sight from location to potential target. She was able to quickly eliminate most of the potential targets because they could only be seen from one or two of the five locations. So she erased the lines to leave a clearer picture. In fact only five possible targets remained two seen from four locations and three from all five locations; 10 Downing Street, the American Embassy and the Palace of Westminster. She showed her work to Sue when she arrived at the office.

"That's it. Well done Zoe, you've cracked it. Bit by bit you've solved the mystery," Sue said excitedly.

"Sorry Sue, I'm not following you. What do you mean?"

Sue explained. "Rob sent a message yesterday, that's how I knew the report of him being killed was wrong. The message said Luggard was to make his first strike on Pearl Harbour Day, when the head of the eagle will be removed. Well Pearl Harbour Day is 7th December and......."

"And the Eagle is the American Embassy, so the head of the eagle must be the ambassador," Zoe interrupted.

"That's right and he will be going to the Pearl Harbour Remembrance Service at St Paul's," Sue added. "I think we now have enough information to piece together what their plan is. Let's get to work."

Once they were happy, Sue rang Bernard Howe who said that, due to the urgency, he would call the minister and arrange to meet as soon as possible and they could present to the minister and himself. So they sat waiting. Finally, after four hours the phone rang. "Good evening, Sir Bernard."

"My office, thirty minutes," was all he said.

"Quickly Zoe, Sir Bernard wants us in his office in thirty minutes."

The minister was already in with Sir Bernard when they arrived. "Minister, may I introduce the two ladies who have been doing all the hard work on this case. Mrs. Susan Blackstock and Miss Zoe Crump. Come in girls and show us what you've discovered."

Sue opened her notebook and began to explain how they had begun analysing the data. Sir Bernard interrupted, "No, no, we trust your analytical skills. We want to know what the end result is."

"Okay. Well to understand that this plan will only work because of a drug called QZ-71. A drug that leaves a person in a state that allows them to be controlled and made to do things they wouldn't normally do"

"I've already explained QZ-71 to the minister," Sir Bernard said.

Sue continued, "The American Ambassador will be attacked as he leaves the Embassy on Friday at 11:30, to go to St Paul's for the Pearl Harbour Remembrance Service. The attack will come as he passes through the embassy gate. We have ruled out a bomb because of high level of security surrounding the embassy and the ambassador. The route will be chosen at the last minute from six possible routes, which also suggests it's not a bomb. So we conclude the attack will be made using a rocket from a hand held launcher, probably a Stinger fired from one of five identified sights."

"So how can we stop this?" the Minister asked.

"Let me walk you through this as it will unfold then, I think how we stop it will be quite clear. But we must let these people think their plan is working right up to the last minute, we don't want them switching to an alternative," Zoe explained. "Sometime before Friday, Sergeant Mark Moss will steal a Stinger missile and launcher from Aldershot armoury and cover his tracks by altering computer records. The weapon will be driven off camp by Military Police Captain Tony Sparks. Then on Friday 7th December, Sergeant Jane Moss will take the weapon to one of five locations and at 11:30, she will fire at and destroy the ambassador's car, as it exits through the embassy gate. This is how we stop them. Firstly, there are eight Stingers at Aldershot, they must be modified so that they will fire, but not detonate. All launchers to be fitted with a tracking device, so that we will know where it will be launched from. On Friday morning, we remove Jane Moss. Lock her up if we have to. Jane is a weapons expert. She would check the weapon over before using it and we can't risk her finding the modification and reversing it. At this point it will be too late to change to an alternative plan so their only option is to get someone else to make the shot. We will follow the tracker to the location and make the arrest. If he does get the missile away, it will do no damage."

The minister stood. "Sounds good to me," he said. "Make it happen, Bernard. Don't tell the Yanks!" He walked out of the office without another word.

Rob's Sunday report message included the fact that Josef was returning with great haste to London. Ryman made the phone exchange while out on a run. It was getting harder to find reasons for one of the three of them to make the phone switch and there was an increasing fear that they would be discovered and if Luggard became aware, not only would their three lives be at risk, but also the lives of the soldiers who had been relaying his reports back to Sue, in London. Because of the high risk, his report ended saying it was his last report. But he needed to know what MI-6 was planning to do with Luggard and he would collect the response and any orders at 6:00 on Saturday morning.

The weekly blood test of the three soldiers at Aldershot showed the presence of QZ-71. Their base commander had arranged for the Stinger missiles to be neutralised and trackers fitted to the launchers without the knowledge of the three soldiers.

"Zoe, there is one thing about this attack that we don't know," Sue said.

"Oh, I thought we were on top of everything," Zoe queried.

"We don't know the strength of the enemy force in London. There could be hundreds, they could be running more than one plan," Sue said anxiously.

"You might be right, but we've not seen anything to suggest a large force. No, I strongly feel this is a very small team, possibly only one, maybe two people. We've been monitoring Venezuelan visitors through all ports since we started this operation and not seen anything suspicious. Apparently, we don't get many Venezuelans visit us. It's basically embassy staff, a handful of business men and a few tourists in the summer."

"That's reassuring. So you think we really need only worry about Josef Luggard?"

"Yes, I do and Sir Bernard has a team watching him twenty four seven. He can't even pee without someone watching him. Since he flew in yesterday, they picked him up waiting for his luggage at Heathrow and have followed every step since. He has met with two known drug distributers. It's probably through them and their networks that the heroin laced with QZ-71 is being pushed out. Apart from that, he's made dozens of phone calls, spent a few hours in his office and sent out for takeaways for both his evening meals."

"His behaviour has changed quite a bit since we identified Gabriel and made the arrest. I'm guessing he's stepped into the Gabriel role and is now running the operation. He doesn't need a large team, he just needs to have someone distributing the drugs, the rest he can get done by activating one of the addicts who has the skills he needs," she was interrupted by her phone ringing.

Sue answered it and after a few yeses, a couple of nos and a thank you, she ended the call. "That was Colonel Reeve at Aldershot. He says that Sergeant Mark Moss received a phone call whilst he was on duty yesterday and a Stinger missile has gone missing overnight. He also said that Captain Sparks was signed off camp at 3:00 this morning. He was driving a military van."

"I'll ring the agent who's watching the trackers and see where the Stinger is. Can you check the duty roster and tell me who's currently on watch?" Sue was about to enter a number, when she noticed she had an unread message. "Hang on Zoe I've had a message from Paul Youngman, sent at 4:09 this morning."

"He's on the duty roster, should have been on duty from midnight until 8:00," said Zoe.

"He says the tracker was triggered at 3:00 this morning, moving slowly to start with, but then suddenly moving quicker. He tracked it to an end terrace in Carmen Street, Poplar. Can you check out who lives there?"

"I'll get right on it," Zoe said and immediately started working on her laptop.

Within minutes she had an answer. "The house is owned by a property developer and is currently on a six month rental agreement with a Chinese National named Lo Pee Tah."

"Peter Lowe, one of the guys that kidnapped Rob," Sue said.

"He can't be involved in this. The French police have him locked up, awaiting trial for a bombing in Paris."

"But it does confirm that there is a connection between the triad and Luggard. We'll need to keep an eye on that. Meantime we need to get Jane Moss secured somewhere. Colonel Reeve was supposed to be taking care of that. What else do we need to do to be ready for tomorrow?" Sue asked.

Since the week-end, Rob had noticed that extra staff were on duty and the only place he could be alone, was in his room. Even then there was always someone outside his door when he opened it. It was obvious that Tracy and Ryman were being given the same attention and they had very little opportunity to talk together, without being overheard. Rob and Kurt were again working on things to improve Kurt's driving skills. Plans were made for them all to return to Miami Sunday afternoon, on a specially arranged flight, but Rob was concerned that they might be going back in body bags and saw no escape. If they could escape, where would they go? No, their best hope is to stand up and fight when the time comes. If MI-6 does send in a task force, they could be best used sabotaging the defenses, so he needed to get the other two thinking about what could be done.

"Good morning Sir Bernard, how can I help?" Sue had been in the office for couple of hours, double checking every last detail.

"Just checking that nothing has changed and there is no risk to the ambassador."

"Yes sir. Josef Luggard spent the night at the house in Carmen Street and Colonel Reeve says that Jane Moss's phone has been ringing every thirty minutes since 5:30 this morning; presumably it was Luggard trying to trigger her. About thirty minutes ago, he left the house carrying an oversized kit bag. We know the Stinger is in that bag because of the tracker. We have agents stationed at all five possible locations as a safeguard, but we're monitoring the tracker to see which of the locations he will be using. Then we'll send the armed unit in."

"You think Luggard will fire the Stinger?" Sir Bernard asked.

"There's no doubt he will have had some weapons training at Angels' Rest. Plus these things are very simple to operate; it's just a case of aim and pull the trigger. Jane Moss is not available for him to use and there is no time to get anyone else, so he has no choice."

"Well, let's hope all goes well. Call me as soon as it's over."

While she had been talking to Sir Bernard, she had received an email from her C.I.A. contact. It said that the F.B.I. had arrested Ralph Luggard for the murder of Emily Strange and Pip Swan (Kurt Luggard's girlfriend and her lover) back in July. The gun found at the scene had been wiped clean of prints and D.N.A. but Ralph's D.N.A. had been found on one of the bullets in the clip. The C.I.A. were now trying to follow up new leads to continue their investigation.

She was too busy today to respond, that would have to wait, as would telling Sir Bernard.

Sue went down stairs to the armoury and was fitted with body armour, a jacket that identified her as Metropolitan police and a Glock 17 pistol. She then proceeded to the underground garage, where she joined three armed officers in a Range Rover.

"You must be Corporal Hull?" she said to the driver.

"Yes ma'am," he replied. Then pointing at a street map marked with five circles. "I've been ordered to park here ma'am, midway between these two target locations."

"Very well, let's go."

At 10:25 Sue had a call from the agent tracking Luggard. "He's still moving on foot, struggling a bit with the oversized kit bag. He's well passed the first target location and will be at the second one soon."

"Let me know as soon as you know which location he finally ends up at," Sue instructed.

They waited in the Range Rover for what Sue thought to be several hours, but was only twenty minutes. Sue's phone eventually rang and she answered it quickly. The voice on the phone said, "The target has entered location four ."

"It's location four Corporal. Get us there as quickly as you can please."

"Yes ma'am."

Sue studied the papers Zoe had prepared about each location. Location four was a rooftop. The QZ-71 victim was the maintenance man who held the only key to the rooftop. The position was overlooked from the roof of another building a little over a hundred yards away, but that didn't have a view of the Embassy. It was an office block, home to several small businesses. Just inside the front door was a small reception desk where a man in uniform sat. What Sue was wearing was enough for the attendant to know that he had four police officers stood before him.

"We need to get on the roof quickly," Sue stressed urgency.

"Lift to the top. Through fire door on the right, then up the fire escape ladder," he instantly replied.

When they reached the roof, they had a clear view of Luggard on the other rooftop. He was using a rifle site as a telescope, looking Sue assumed, at the embassy.

"What's that on the floor behind him?" Sue asked no one in particular.

"Looks like a sniper rifle ma'am," one of the officers said. "Looks Russian or Chinese and looks capable of firing armour piercing ammo. Unassembled, it could easily have been in that kit bag with the stinger."

"Christ, he's got that as back-up in case the missile doesn't do the job. So as soon as the Stinger fails, he will open up with the rifle. I really would like to take him in for questioning but we need to prevent any harm coming to the ambassador. You two," Sue said looking at the two constables, "watch him carefully. As soon as he realises the missile has failed, he'll use the rifle. When he raises the rifle to shoot. You shoot to kill. Understood?"

"Yes, ma'am."

"Corporal, you come with me," Sue said, as she looked at her wristwatch. "We've got twelve minutes to get onto that roof and talk him down."

Josef prepared the missile and launcher following the instructions on the side of the launcher and at 11:28 had it resting on his shoulder. The embassy gates drew back and, as the ambassador's car came into his sights, he squeezed the trigger. The small missile travelled true, leaving a fine trail of exhaust. In a matter of a few seconds it struck the bonnet of the car but did not explode. Instead it bounced over the car,, onto the driveway behind. Seeing what had happened, Josef reached for the rifle. At the same time Sue and

Corporal Hull reached the locked door out onto the roof. Charging the door with his shoulder, the Corporal broke through and tumbled through the opening. Sue stepped over the fallen officer and shouted, "ARMED POLICE!" Luggard hearing the noise behind him spun round and lifted the rifle and fired wildly at her from his hip. In the second Sue had, while Luggard drew back the bolt on the rifle to eject the spent cartridge and load the next bullet into the firing chamber, she stood and fired two quick shots as she had been trained to do. Luggard fell like a stone, clutching his rifle and with a look of surprise across his face. Corporal Hull was back on his feet and with Sue pointing her pistol at Luggard he cautiously approached the crumpled body, kicked the rifle out of reach then bent down to check for signs of life. He looked up at Sue and shook his head then turned the body over onto its back. Just as Sue had been taught, a disabling shot to the chest, then a kill shot to the head. She'd done it once before in a war zone but that didn't stop her stomach churning and her head spinning now. It had been so automatic, so final.

"Bugger! I didn't want him killed," she said

"You had no choice ma'am, It was him or us."

She looked down as the embassy the car had gone, armed troops were running around and two official looking men were stood by the dead missile, looking up at the buildings around them.

"The British government will have a lot of questions to answer from the Americans, she thought. *"I'd better contact Sir Bernard and let him know about all this."*

"Well done, Susan," Sir Bernard said. "An excellent day's work, your country owes you a great deal. I must now speak to the P.M. before the Yanks get to her. Get back here as quick as you can for a full debriefing. I'll organise a clean-up team."

Zoe took the noon call from Captain Phillip. He had nothing to report, so Zoe triggered the transfer of the plan for Sunday's attack on Angels' Rest. It would need to be downloaded onto Rob's phone, then taken back to the head of the falls and be left back by the tap, before 6:00 tomorrow. There was seven and a half hours of daylight left so he would have to ask his men to do the last stretch of the climb in the dark. He had done the climb twice, so was well aware of the dangers and how much more dangerous it would be in the dark.

There was a knock on the door and Sir Bernard appeared carrying a bottle of Champagne and a handful of vending machine plastic cups. "Good afternoon Miss Crump, have you heard from Susan?"

"I have sir and isn't it great news?" Zoe said, surprised to see him in their office. "She rang me to say she was on her way back. I think she had just left, so she should be here any moment." While they waited, Sir Bernard discussed with Zoe how she had arrived at some of her conclusions.

"Here she is," Zoe said.

"Well done, Susan." Sir Bernard stood and held out the bottle of Champagne towards her. "Shall we toast success? This comes from the P.M. who is very grateful to you. To you both. She has issued orders that nothing of today's events gets reported. You have done this country a great service. Now it's time for your country to do you a great service in return and get your husband back in one piece. A news blackout will at least delay the news reaching Luggard that he has lost his sons. If he were to find out, it might be serious for your husband and the others."

"Sons?" Sue queried. "You said sons, Sir Bernard, what do you mean?"

"You heard that the F.B.I. had arrested Ralph?"

"Yes, I heard just before I left this morning."

"Well he was discovered early this morning dead in his cell, stabbed by a fellow prisoner. The F.B.I. say he'd crossed too many drug dealers in a short period and they put a contract on him."

As Sue relaxed with a plastic beaker of champagne, the realisation of what had happened horrified her. She had killed Josef Luggard. An act that could result in her losing her husband, in some act of revenge by Luggard. But she had no choice; she would surely be dead if she had not shot.

For the last few days, Rob and Ryman had gone out for an early run, twice around the golf course followed by a swim and always were joined by two members of staff running slightly behind them. Saturday was no exception. On their second lap, Ryman stopped at the tap to retie a shoe lace. Rob continued without slowing and the two staff slowed a little, but passed Ryman, allowing him to retrieve the phone unseen and concealed it in his pocket. Then he sprinted to regain his position by Rob's side.

After their swim, they returned to their rooms. Rob went into his bathroom and ran the shower, filling the room with steam and creating a noise so that he could listen to the message on his phone and study the plan, without being spied on or overheard by those who were watching his every move. Once he was happy, he deleted everything from the phone.

The plan was simple; the only action required of Rob was to cut off all electrical power as soon as the attack began.

British Special Forces were landed at Ciudad Bolívar at noon. They watched the helicopter from Angels' Rest arrive and the troops disembark looking for their onward transport. The British troops moved in and hijacked the helicopter and two pilots, forcing them to return to Angels' Rest. They had taken off about an hour ahead of the scheduled time, so the pilot was ordered to travel slowly, so that their arrival would be at the normal time."

They landed without the alarm being raised, but as they disembarked, the pilot shouted a warning. A rifle butt prevented a second shout, but too late, alarm bells were soon ringing across the complex. Staff raced to their defensive positions, whilst others rushed to the building holding the weapons, taking several and rushing back to distribute them. The first shots were fired from the house and the troops returned fire, injuring two of the staff. Half of the invading troops climbed into one of the trucks lined up, they had been waiting to transport arriving recruits down the track to the training camp. Now it would carry the invaders to capture the remaining twenty or so recruits.

Hearing shots being fired, Rob opened his door to the corridor. It was empty. He knocked on Ryman's door. "Ryman, quickly man, we have a job to do urgently! Rob moved on and knocked on Tracy's door. There was no answer. He knocked again and walked in. There was no sign of her; he checked the bathroom, still no sign. "We'll look for her later, right now we've got to get the power cut before the helicopters get in range of those cannons on the roof."

Ryman followed Rob, running down the stairs and out through the back door to the building they had been told was the power station. The heavy reinforced door was locked. There was no way they were going to get in very quickly.

"We need to get this power off now. Any ideas?"

"We could cut the line from the solar panels,, but we know that the system automatically switches to the batteries when there is no feed from the panels. If the batteries fail then the generator cuts in within seconds."

Gunfire was now continuous, but from where he stood, Rob could see that the troops were pinned down in the helicopter landing area and taking casualties. He looked around, then suddenly ran off behind some of the other buildings. Ryman heard an engine roar and Rob appeared driving Kurt's E-Type. Engine noise increased as Rob accelerated hard and moved through the gears as he raced across the grass towards the power station. Ryman ran to the side and at the last moment Rob knocked the gears into neutral and rolled out of the door. Before Rob had stopped rolling, the car hit the structure at speed, demolishing the building and turning the car into a heap of twisted metal.

Rob sat up and looked across at what was left of the building.

"I think that might have done the trick, sir," Ryman said as he offered Rob a hand and pulled him too his feet.

Rob looked around, he could not see any lights or anything at all to suggest that power was still flowing. The sound of incoming helicopters was getting louder and they both looked up.

"I hope it did work. I don't fancy being up there if those automatic cannons start shooting at them." Two gunships came in low over their heads and sprayed the rooftops with gunfire, forcing the defenders to run for cover. Then they came down low over the lawn, between the house and the golf course, allowing six well-armed soldiers to jump out of each. The gunships then rose together back to rooftop height, again firing at the house, keeping the defenders heads down as the soldiers sought cover. Suddenly from a window, an anti-aircraft rocket was fired. At such short range, the gunship pilots had no time to react and the tail section of one of the aircraft was obliterated. The remaining section fell to the ground instantly, the sixty feet that it fell was not enough to destroy the cockpit and the two pilots escaped.

The staff had obviously been well trained and for a long time were a match for anything the attacking force threw at them and weren't appearing to take many casualties, whereas the British had four men down. From where they stood, Rob and Ryman could watch most of the action, but could be very exposed if the action moved their way. "I think we should take cover, sir," Ryman said grabbing Rob's arm and pulling him towards the house.

"Yes, of course and we must find Tracy. She may well be with Hilda. They seem to have become good friends."

"We also need to find some weapons. I don't feel comfortable being shot at and not able to shoot back," Ryman said.

They re-entered the house, unchallenged by any defenders. Staff were still running everywhere, carrying ammunition boxes to where they were needed. Two young women were taking care of an injured defender at the bottom of the main stair case. Rob heard Henri barking out orders, sounding like a sergeant major on the parade ground, shouting at new recruits. They also heard Ernst's unmistakable accent. He was arguing with somebody and his voice was steadily getting louder, to the point where he was almost shouting. It was coming from the landing on the floor where all the Luggard bedrooms were. Rob could see the shadows on the wall of two men standing facing one another. The shadow images came together and merged into one as the two men fought. A gunshot echoed in the stairwell and one of the shadows crumpled. A female scream came from somewhere on the same landing,, out of sight from Rob and Ryman.

Ryman stepped back to the injured man being treated and picked up his rifle then re-joined Rob. Together they cautiously climbed the stairs, all the time their eyes focused upwards, searching for someone they knew had a gun. Above them a step creaked, someone was slowly coming down. Ryman raised his rifle to protect his boss, but Rob waved a hand and pointed back down the stairs. They knew someone was coming down the stairs, but that someone had no idea they were there. If it came to a fight they had the element of surprise on their side. They went into the dining room and stood where they had a good view of the bottom of the stairs and Ryman once again raised his rifle.

It was of no surprise to Rob when the person on the stairs turned out to be Ernst Luggard, but Rob was surprised to see Sandra with him. She obviously wasn't coming down the stairs of her own choice because Luggard had his left hand twisted in her hair and was dragging her along. As they reached the bottom of the stairs, Rob moved out to challenge him and Ryman peered along the rifle barrel to place Luggard squarely in his sights.

"Give it up Luggard you know you've got no chance," Rob said. He then pointed down at the man who had been treated and the two young women who had been taking care of him. These people have shown you their loyalty, now save them anymore pain. Tell them to lay down their weapons."

Ernst was dressed in a German army officer's uniform of 1940's style. On seeing Rob, he pulled Sandra round to shield him and brought the gun, held in his right hand, up to her head. "You've got no idea what you are standing in the way of. Mankind is walking a path to its own destruction. The New Republic will change that. We will gather the best minds in every race to work on solutions for their own people and 'Operation Birdbath' will open the door to make this happen. Now move aside!"

"You know I can't do that, Ernst. Your 'Operation Birdbath' is already falling apart. By now Josef will be sitting down to eat his evening meal in one of Her Majesty's prisons, his attack in London having failed," Rob was guessing that Sue had been able to thwart the Pearl Harbour Day attack.

"Move aside, Blackstock! You may think you are a very clever British spy but you know nothing about our plans and I don't know about any attack in London," Ernst lied. He actually hadn't heard from his son and was eager to know how successful it had been. "Now, let me pass or your little C.I.A. friend here will get her head blown off her shoulders."

"Be careful Rob! He's just shot Kurt upstairs. He's capable of anything," Sandra shouted as she twisted to try and get free of his grip.

Ryman leveled the rifle, ready to pull the trigger, as the struggling Sandra exposed a small part of Ernst's chest for him to target. But in the second it took to aim and prepare to shoot, a gunshot came from somewhere behind where he and Rob were standing. Still looking along the sights of the rifle, Ryman watched Luggard's expression change, as a thin trail of blood ran down either side of his nose from a small hole in the centre of his forehead.

Rob watched, as the uniformed body start to lose its shape as it began to fall. He looked over his shoulder to see Hilda, a smoking gun in her hands, held in a firing pose like Ryman had taught him to shoot with. But before he had chance to take in what he was seeing, another shot was heard from the bottom of the stairs and he spun back and saw Sandra collapse in a heap next to Luggard.

For a moment Rob was stunned, he couldn't think or move. Tracy rushing past his shoulder, kicked him back to life and he watched her run up to the fallen young woman.

"She's dead Rob!" Tracy called out. "A bullet in the top of her spine."

"I actually saw it happen but don't believe it! Ryman said. "I was watching Luggard fall, his hand was wrapped in Sandra's hair and she was struggling and pulling away which turned him as he fell, so that his right side hit the floor and as his hand hit the ground the gun went off."

"And poor Sandra caught the bullet in the back of the neck," Tracy added.

They heard a groan from the stairs and all looked up to see Kurt, struggling to stay upright, as he descended the final flight,, his right hand gripping the rail tightly and his left pressed against his stomach with blood seeping between his fingers. Rob rushed up the stairs and caught him just before he collapsed. Ryman helped Rob carry Kurt down the last few steps and lay him on the floor. The ex-soldier ripped open Kurt's shirt and looked at the wound. "Not as serious as it looks, the bullet went straight through and I don't think it hit anything important. Certainly I've seen worse on the battlefield and they've got up and continued to fight. We just need to stem the blood loss and he should be okay. But I'm not a doctor."

"He had gone completely mad, Kurt. He was no longer our father. Just look what he did to you? I had to shoot. Forgive me," Hilda said kneeling by her brother holding his hand tightly between hers.

An explosion at the main door sent a cloud of gritty dust over them. As they watched the door collapse inward and three soldiers appeared through the cloud. Rob quickly put his hands high in the air and cried out, "Don't shoot! We're friendly.

The lead soldier lowered his gun and the other two others came up on his flanks.

Chapter 23

"Well dad, for a while things got a bit rough and I did wonder whether I'd see another day. We did lose one, a very pretty young American girl, very brave young lady, shot by a gun going off accidentally. At least it was quick, she would not have known anything about it. So, we're on the flight home tomorrow afternoon. It'll be good to see Sue again. Then first thing the day after, we've got a team de-briefing so with any luck, hopefully, we can get away early enough to get up to Yorkshire by early evening."

****

"Anyone in here want a coffee?"

Sue screamed, "Rob What the hell are you doing here? she stood and rushed into his arms.

"What a thing to say to your husband."

"We were not expecting you until early tomorrow morning," Sue said.

"We came back on a military flight with the S.A.S. boys. Regular troops came in to relieve them at 10:00 last night. The long range helicopters that brought them in, ferried us back to the base in Bermuda through the night. We got straight on the plane and into the air and landed at R.A.F. Northolt about an hour ago. A R.A.F. car brought me straight here."

"You must be exhausted," Sue said and then kissed him.

"I'll go and get the coffee shall I?" Zoe said tactfully and left them to be alone together for a few minutes

"So Sue, you've joined all of the pieces together. Can you explain Luggard's plan to me?" Rob asked.

"I believe I can. I had a long talk with Captain Phillips, who observed the action from the golf course and said he'd spoken to you afterwards and had heard what had gone on inside. That, and a few other bits which we've gathered from various sources, we think we know most of the plan. Captain Phillips said he saw you fall out of a car. What was that about?"

273

"I didn't fall, I jumped," Rob said. "We had to get the electricity cut off quickly; it was a calculated risk that paid off. Now, what have you discovered about Luggard's plan?"

" It was a very well thought out plan; you certainly have to admire the genius of the man to come up with a plan that used his enemy's resources to achieve his own goal. We all now know that he planned to destroy the leadership of both Britain and America and while those countries were in chaos,, to step in and take control himself. This dream was to become the President of the new country, combining Britain and USA. Of course this started out as Hitler's dream and 'Operation Birdbath', as he named it, was funded originally by Nazi gold."

"Yes, 1 know all that and I know he was drugging people all over the place. Do we know how he planned to use them and when?" Rob queried.

"I think we've got an answer for everyone on his list and can link each one to one of the five targets."

"Five targets? I thought there were only four," Rob interrupted.

"Four in London yes, but also the Capitol Building in Washington was to be hit. All. Five hits were to be made on the seventy fifth anniversary of D-day, June 6th. A sort of sick revenge on the Second World World War allies, for launching their attack against the German army on that day in 1944. The date was why we were so convinced that the gathering of so many government leaders on the south coast was their main target. The attack on the U.S. embassy on December 7th was to be just a practice for the main event. That date being the anniversary of Pearl Harbour and America entering the war, as you know."

"Luggard certainly sounds like he was a fanatical Nazi supporter."

"Not really surprising, as his father was a big supporter of Hitler and his mother an S.S. officer. So if I start first with the Queen, Luggard's plan to assassinate her involved Lucy Reed," Sue began.

"I know that name," Rob said, "Wasn't she the teenager who broke into the Queen's private apartments carrying a weapon of some sort,, but was caught before she located Her Majesty? There was a big thing made of it and she was sent to prison."

"That's the one. Luggard obviously assumed that having got in once, she could get in a second time."

"But if she was in prison, how was she to get out?"

"That was why a High Court Judge was needed. Their first attempt failed when Judge Potts died from a reaction to QZ-71. The second attempt brought the Honourable William Blyth under their power. At the end of April, he was to get Lucy Reed released, by ruling that evidence used at her trial had been illegally obtained. Inevitably there would be a retrial but that would not be for several weeks. This is where a Williams Security gets involved and why I was targeted, which as you remember, almost resulted in Tracy's death. We don't think they got around to selecting my replacement. Anyway Williams Security plays a big part in the security at the palace, so we think my role would have been to cause some sort of diversion near the Queen's private apartments, perhaps call the guard away on a bogus alert. We also have Lucas Durrell, one of the palace footmen, who looks to be there as a lookout and to make sure palace staff are out of the way."

"Why use Lucy and not you or Lucas?" Rob questioner.

"Because either Williams Security or palace staff could have prevented them passing through. Their role was simply stopping their own people getting in the way and to give Lucy Reed a clear passage through, just around noon, having got into the palace the previous evening and hidden up."

"I presume these people would be doing all this in a hypnotised, state totally unaware of what they were doing, or why. Once they had done their bit, they were expendable and would get their overdose to silence them, just in case any memory broke through their subconscious."

"You're probably right in that. This was the point where we initially followed the wrong trail, by thinking the hit was going to be on the world leaders gathered on Southsea Common and if Josef Luggard hadn't left notes on his phone, they would now be preparing to assassinate our P.M. and the U.S. President."

"The actual plan was quite simple. The P.M., Teresa May, would be shot as she unveils a plaque at Westminster Abbey, in memory to those who died on D-day. The assassin was to be police sergeant, Tony Billings. He is a tactical force leader in the armed police unit. The armed police are sited all around events like this, in theory to protect the VIP. But as team leader Tony would be free to go anywhere and would be able to select the perfect spot from which to fire.

You have to realise that although we said these individuals were heroin addicts, so it was relatively easy to get the QZ-71 into them. Some of them were not addicts, so would have had the drug injected into them like they tried to do to Tracy."

"That in its self must have been difficult. It's not easy to give someone three injections, without them knowing," Rob added.

"Actually, it's not that difficult. With the right equipment it can be done as simply as bumping into them in the street. Think about it, how many times do you get bumped on the subway,, just going from one station to another and think nothing of it."

"You're absolutely right. Easy!"

"We have also discovered that the Luggard organisation has been carrying out a slow takeover of the heroin trade both here and in the U.S. Not for profit but so that they can mix QZ-71 with the stuff and have an army ready to be switched on with just a single command."

"And the dealers not willing to change get eliminated," Rob added.

Sue nodded and continued, "President Trump is to lay flowers at the American cemetery in Cambridge before he goes to Stansted to fly home. A young American airman from nearby Lakenheath had been selected to perform that one."

"And that leaves the parliament buildings in London," Rob said.

"That's right and again this required a number of people. It was to be an exact repeat of last week's attack on the American Embassy. Firstly, the stinger missile had to be obtained. That required someone in military ordinance to actually take the weapon and probably a second person to cover the tracks and alter the inventory. If the missiles have already been taken, they have covered their tracks extremely well, because this is one part of the plan where we've not had any leads. We don't know which branch of the forces the stinger is being taken from, or even if it has already gone or is still to be taken. The investigation has been handed over to the Military Police and, if I know my former bosses, they will see this as their number one priority, breaches in security are not accepted, no matter what."

"I'm sure Sir Bernard won't let it be forgotten either," Rob added.

"I'm sure he won't. We had seen the names of two marines on lists. Either may have been selected to pull the trigger on the stinger launcher. When we tested them, both came up negative for QZ-71, so obviously they had not yet been targeted or our assumptions were wrong. Then of course, as we began to close in, we discovered their plan for a practice run and the attack on the U.S. embassy.the best they could hope to achieve would be to inflict any sort of damage on the US and British government's cooperation. At the time we thought Josef Luggard had knowledge of how to fire a stinger missile. In any case these things have instruction plaques on the launcher. When his whereabouts was traced a surveillance team watched him twenty four seven, he had already narrowed down five possible locations he could launch his attack from and using a tracker we had hidden in the launcher, we followed him and foiled the operation."

"And that's where you shot him," Rob interrupted her.

Sue was quick to respond. "It was him or me. He had failed in his quest and was desperate to get away. He had already fired at us, the public, as well as us, were in danger."

"I'm not judging you Sue, you did exactly the right thing, shoot to kill. You should get a medal and not have to listen or read the rubbish coming from the press. After all, he did fire a missile at the American Ambassador . Had he known that we had made the missile safe, he may have done serious damage with his rifle and many people would have died."

"That's what I keep telling myself."

"What I don't understand is how you identified Pippa Johnston as being Gabriel. She's been at MI-5 for years."

"It was something she said when I first met her that made me think she had something to hide. But it was Zoe who found the connection to Emit and Ernst and her chemistry background. I put things together and went to Sir Bernard, who was concerned enough by our suspicions, that he obtained a warrant to test a sample of blood from James Bull."

"James Bull who Pippa Johnston replaced as head of MI-5?"

"That's right, Rob. Anyway, having spoken with several people who had worked with James, no one understood why he should suddenly resign like he did. Sir Bernard thought, as I did, it was very suspicious. The blood test confirmed the presence of QZ-71 in James's blood, suggesting it was used to get James to resign and allow Pippa to step in. That was enough for Sir Bernard and Pippa was arrested. I don't know how, but Sir Bernard got her to confess and she now faces several counts of murder and attempted murder, espionage and because of the threat to her Majesty, she may also face charges of treason."

"She's going to be in prison a long time, Rob concluded.

"As for the attack on the American target being investigated by the C.I.A., we don't know any of the details. However, I'm assured Luggard's son Ralph was the head man, but he got killed by the mob."

"So if that's true, I assume Kurt and Hilda will inherit their father's empire, a massive challenge for them both. It's a real pity Sandra was killed, she and Kurt were really beginning to connect, despite his sexual preferences. They made a good couple. She was good for him and I think had quickly become very fond of him and I would not have been too surprised to see her resign from the C.I.A. and stay. She was obviously very comfortable in the environment and lifestyle at Angels' Rest. Very much at home with the horses and the dogs. A sad loss.

"Yes, a tragic end. Such a brave, young lady," Sue commented. "Is Kurt going to be okay? I heard he had been shot."

"He had a fight with Ernst and a gun was fired and Kurt was hit. The bullet went through but didn't do any serious damage. He lost a lot of blood, but he'll be alright, physically at least."

"This is certainly going to impact him mentally," Sue added.

"And then there is Hilda. Her life will change rapidly. Once problems get sorted and someone can get her a passport," Rob explained. "She doesn't have a birth certificate so to the world she doesn't exist. But her face, when we left her at Angels' Rest, was a remarkable picture of delight. At long last she is free to lead a normal life and all the dreams that she had will maybe come true."

"Is she so disfigured?" Sue asked.

"Well, she's not very pretty. Her face is very messed up, I'm not sure if the medics can do anything or even if she wants them to try. But I've seen much worse on the streets in London. No doubt people will stare and whisper behind her back, she'll have to get used to that. She is a truly nice person, very intelligent and a very accomplished wine maker. Tracy and her got on very well, they spent a lot of time together and not just because Tracy was gathering Intel for the mission, it is a genuine friendship. They often sat together and chatted away like two lifelong friends."

"And Tracy? Is she okay? Do I need to worry about you and her?"

"Don't you trust me, darling? Anyway I think Ryman might have something to say if she and I got together. He's certainly keen. No dear, Tracy and I were history many years ago."

She kissed his cheek. "Glad to hear it. Now can we get back to the day job and get on with our lives?"

"I do hope so," he said "It's Friday and we need to be at Thames House at nine o'clock for a de-briefing with Sir Bernard. I hope we can get away by lunch time and be on the road for Yorkshire. There's still a couple of weeks before the kid's break for the Christmas holidays. So I think we should get away for a few days, have some time together, do our Christmas shopping, because Christmas Eve will be on us before we know it. Have you spoken to dad at all?"

"Only very briefly yesterday, to say you were safe and on your way home. Why?"

"Well, he rang me last night when I was in Bermuda. It must have been just after you spoke with him. He was very pleased we would be home for Christmas and said he was going to book a table for New Year's Eve at the Dog and Gun, for the whole family."

"That will make a nice end to the holiday. I hope you thanked him," Sue said.

"Of course. But there was something strange in the way he talked. He said he had something important to do and wanted us all together."

"I wonder what he means. Now it's time for me to show you how much I missed you." She stood, grabbed Rob's hand to pull him to his feet then pulled him closer to her.

Chapter 24

"The whole nation, if not the entire world, owes Robert Blackstock and his adorable wife a huge debt of gratitude. Without their contribution over the last few weeks, I don't doubt we would have not even known of this massive threat that hung over Britain and America's governments and I just don't want to think of what this mad man had planned to unleash on the world on 6th June. It's a great pity these two selfless people cannot be publicly recognised for what they have done. It is very good of you, your Majesty, to make time to reward them with a private afternoon tea. I'm sure they will greatly appreciate the gesture."

****

Sue had never had a proper traditional family Christmas and discovered what she had been missing all these years. She and Rob had gone to the races on Boxing Day to help Eric out, he had five horses running. Nothing was mentioned about Sue taking on the stable manager's job, so she kept quiet too.

Luci got very excited as New Year's Eve drew near. Eva and Ana had invited her to join them on stage for their whole set at the Dog and Gun New Year's party, so she had spent the whole week rehearsing with them. They roped Sue and Rose in to help with costume making.

Justin was at a loose end because his best mate, Jake, had flown out to India to spend the holidays with his dad. On Boxing Day the girls had seen him walking around looking lost, so asked him for some help. A couple of songs they were including would benefit from some special effects and asked if he would create something. With something to do, he was far happier. He had his father drive into York with a shopping list of things he needed and he spent a couple of days playing with dry-ice and artificial snow. Then on Saturday morning Rob and he were in the Dog and Gun before 9:00 testing out all the effects. Ana went with them to check that what Justin was doing was what they wanted and would improve their act.

Eric and Rose drove down to the village for the New Year's party with the three girls squeezed into the back seat. All three wore baggy trousers and sweaters covering their stage costumes. Rob had no intention of not drinking so that he could drive home, nor was he prepared to leave his car at the pub until the next morning. So he, Sue and Justin walked down. All the bits Justin needed had been loaded into Eric's boot. They were all deliberately early so that Justin had an opportunity to set things up before the pub got too busy. In fact there were only two others in the pub, not including the staff and no one took any notice of what was happening on the stage.

Eric's table was laid out in a small alcove away from the bar but they had a good view of the stage. As soon as they had arrived, the girls had gone behind the curtains hung at the back of the stage, into a small back room that served as a changing room for the stage acts. Tonight it would also serve as Justin's control centre. The girls applied their stage makeup and arranged their hair in preparation for the first of two sessions this evening. The first, a 45 minute session, was scheduled for 9:30, the second would span midnight and start at 11:30. For the moment they just sat on stools at the end of the bar chatting with a few of the locals. They still wore their baggy trousers and sweaters covering their stage costumes, which were certain to be a talking point for weeks to come in this small village community. Similarly dressed, Luci had taken her place at the family table and once he had finished setting up his special effects Justin did likewise.

"What's this then? A Blackstock family party?" came a voice from behind Rob and Sue, who were sat with their backs to most of the growing crowd in the bar.

Rob instantly recognised the voice and turned in his seat. "Hello Tracy. Are you here alone?"

"No, my sister and her husband are just over there." Rob followed her finger pointing to a couple sat at a low small round table.

"Dad, you remember Tracy?" Rob asked.

"Indeed I do. The young girl you used to hang around with that hot summer. Didn't you come and work for me at the yard at some time?"

"That's right Mr. Blackstock. Tracy Mills I was in those days. It was a long time ago now."

"Tracy was out in Miami with me dad. She's a Sergeant in the Yorkshire police," Rob explained.

"Not any more, Rob. I've joined MI-5 on a permanent basis as of January 6th. I'm moving to London permanently. A fresh start after my divorce. I'm up here for a few days sorting things out and getting things packed and moved down to my new flat. I must get back to my sister. I only came over to wish you a Happy New Year."

"Same to you,," Rob said.

"And good luck with the new job," Sue added.

"What is it you've got us all here to tell us then, dad?" Rob asked.

"Oh that will keep a while. The buffet is out we'd better go and get some before these vultures scoff the lot," Eric said as he rose to his feet.

As they queued for their food, Rob noticed that Eva and Ana were being bothered by two of the village young men, who were insisting that the girls have a drink with them. He left the queue and crossed the room to the bar. "Come on girls, grab some food. We've kept two places at the table for you." Rob lied but his comment had the desired effect and the two young men retreated back to the other end of the bar. "I thought you two needed a little help there, but please do come and join us."

"But you are all family together we can't intrude," Ana said and Eva nodded in agreement."

"If it wasn't for you two, I wouldn't have a family. For tonight you are part of the family. Now let's join the queue for food and sit until you have to start work. What time is your first set?"

"Not until 9:30. We need to go at 9:15 to get ready."

Rob checked his watch. Ten past eight. "Oh you've got over an hour, plenty of time for some food. Sue tells me your costumes are a little daring and you'll raise a few eyebrows when you come out onto the stage."

"We hope they are not too sexy, we don't want to offend anyone," Ana said.

"You'll be alright. Susan and my mother wouldn't have helped if they thought you were going to do that and they certainly wouldn't allow Luci to. Thank you for including her, she is very nervous but also very excited."

"We are very pleased for her to join us, she is very good. You'll see."

"She's growing up so fast," he thought as he watched his daughter carry her plate of food back to the table. "Her mother would be so proud."

"Are you okay, darling?" Sue asked as she passed him on her way back to the table.

"I'm fine love, just having a silly moment, but I'm fine now."

The girls went off to get ready for their first set and Justine followed a few minutes later, to prepare the special effects. He had built a frame around the stage holding a number of lengths of hose pipe through which he could pump dry ice and instantly flood the stage with mist. By increasing the flow, he could raise the level to change the mood.

At 9:30 the background music stopped for the landlord to speak. "Good evening everyone. I hope you've all had plenty to eat and have your glasses full as we introduce a new act to the Dog and Gun. Please put your hands together and welcome 'The Three Fillies'."

A layer of mist spread across the stage, spilling out across the floor as music began to play. The audience instantly recognised the overture to 'Phantom of the Opera and responded with welcoming applause. Gently, the music changed and was joined by Ana's voice singing 'The Music of the Night' with Eva and Luci providing backing vocals. The curtain at the rear of the stage was simply rigged by Justin to drop to the floor. He had blown dry ice into the space behind the curtain where the girls stood waiting to make their entrance. So at the appropriate moment he dropped the curtain and the girls stepped out of the falling mist over the curtain and onto the stage, Ana in front and the other two either side and slightly behind. Enthusiastic applause from the audience greeted their appearance. They were simply dressed in a bright coloured basques, Ana in a ruby colour, Eva in emerald and Luci in sapphire. They wore black seamed stockings and as the mist fell away the audience could see they wore four inch heeled shoes.

Together they performed a short medley from the show. Then Ana stepped back, to leave Luci in the centre of the three. The tempo changed as the three girls raise hands above their heads and clapped in a slow rhythm, gradually increasing. Luci stepped forward to sing as if she'd been performing for years. She sang Lulu's 'Shout' followed by 'The Boat That I Row'.

As she stepped back to a position beside Ana and Eva, Luci noticed Pete at a table with his sister and his parents.

At the end of the set, they stepped off the rear of the stage through the door into the changing room and Rob went forward to help Justin replace the curtain. A short while later the girls returned to the table wearing their baggy trousers and sweaters again.

Sue greeted them. "That was fantastic girls. And well done Luci."

Luci smiled and walked off across to where Pete sat. She sat on his knee, put her arms around his neck and kissed him. Neither of them said anything. Luci just stood up and went back to join her family .

"I can see this becoming a regular thing. Well done all three of you. Now girls," Rob said turning towards Eva and Ana. "I know this has been a long time coming, but I have these for you, if you want them." He handed each a package.

The girls gave one another a quizzical look, then tore open their packages. A large brown envelop fell out of Ana's package and she laid it on the table. Then pulled something else from the wrapping. It appeared to be some sort of clothing. When she spread it out she could see it was an apron in a black and white vertical stripe material resembling a bar code. On the bib was printed the rearing horse Blackstock logo and beneath that the words 'BLACKSTOCK CATERING. Ana slipped it over her head and stuffed her hands in the pocket. She pulled something out of the pocket, looked at it and a great beaming smile crossed her face. The object she had found was a badge with the words 'Oxsana Kolanski Manager 'printed on it. Eva's package contained the same with her badge printed with 'Eva Andelova Manager'. Both girls leapt to their feet, threw their arms around Rob, kissing him on the cheeks they said, "Thank you!" in unison.

"I promised you both this a long time ago, I'm sorry it's taken so long but I've been tied up with other things. Your contracts are in the envelopes. You need to sign them and get them back to me as soon as you can and this week I need to discuss with you how you plan to make this work and what you'll have to do to get started. Luci tells me you've been doing a lot of research. The girls sat down again gave each other a hug and kissed, then quietly talked together in Russian.

11:15 soon came and the three girls disappeared behind the curtain again to get ready for their second set. Justine had gone behind the curtain some minutes earlier.

"Ladies and gentlemen please give a warm welcome back to the stage our very own Ana, Eva and Luci, 'The 3 Fillies'." Warm applause welcomed the opening bars of Abba's 'Fernando'. The curtain dropped onto a mist covered stage with snow gently falling and the girls again stepped over the curtain in a line, dressed this time identically, in pastel pink baby doll pyjamas which brought on a few whistles from the audience and more applause.

As midnight neared the girls began a count down . "Ten, nine, eight," the audience were quick to pick it up. Four, three, two, one, Happy New Year everybody!" The girls then lead the singing of Old Lang-sine ending it with "Happy 2019". They then began again with 'Get This Party Started'. Most of the audience had stood to welcome in the New Year and a lot of them now started to dance. Sue was snuggled into Rob's arms and Eric stepped forward close to them and handed Rob an envelope.

"What's this?" Rob asked.

"It's for you both. A late wedding present".

Rob opened the envelope and pulled out an official looking paper headed.

'BLACKSTOCK RACE HORSE STABLES TRANSFER OF OWNERSHIP TO MR. R. BLACKSTOCK AND MRS. S. BLACKSTOCK.'

Eric smiled at them. "While your mother and I were on that cruise back in September, we decided it was time we retired and had more time for one another. Phil told me that Sue is interested in managing the place, so this is a perfect solution. Don't worry we've not going to emigrate or anything like that, so we'll be around to help out now and again."

"Thank you so much, Eric. This is wonderful, isn't it darlin?" Sue got up and gave Eric a hug.

Eric and Rose left before the girls finished their session but almost everyone else stayed to the very end. At 12:15 the girls sang their final track but the audience demanded more. Fortunately the girls had rehearsed three other tracks that they knew the karaoke machine had in its library. They finally left the stage at 12:30 and people began to drift away. The landlord came across to thank them "Leave everything for tonight girls. We're leaving the clearing up until morning."

Rob and Sue sat talking about the shock of Eric's gift while they waited for the girls to get dressed. With a quick goodbye to the landlord they set out to walk home. There were still several people in the pub car park mostly the worse for drink. Justin showed the way with his torch and they quickly left the revellers behind. As they reached the crest of the hill they heard a vehicle coming up the hill behind them. Eva feared being hit again and quickly stepped up onto the verge as the car raced by. Rob shouted after it. "Slow down you idiot! Are you okay Sue?" He turned to look behind.

"SUE…….."

Printed in Great Britain
by Amazon